THOR'S FIST

THOR'S FIST

BY

Frank O. Dodge

You can believe the
characters in
this story
are real
if
you want to.

Nobody can
prove they
aren't.

To Carrol Mills Morrow.
One of the Little People, and my closest friend
in High School.

CHAPTER ONE

Jar Haz the Viking extended one hand and parted the screen of leaves to look back along his trail at the line of men and dogs slowly questing across the hayfield in the meadow below. The horn-helmeted men-at-arms were thorough in their search, probing each hayrick with sword or spear to make certain that none concealed their quarry.

An expression, half snarl-half grin, twisted one corner of his mouth as he watched the puzzlement on the faces of the dog handlers at the way their charges behaved. Instead of casting about to pick up the fugitive's scent, they were drawing back, and some were shaking their heads and pawing at their noses.

Jar Haz's lips curled. He had no worry that the dogs would take up his trail. He had smeared Bryn's paws and the soles of his sandals with a mixture of deer fat and the red powder from far off Iberia, called pepper, that had been given to him by the spey-woman of his village. No, the dogs wanted no part of *his* trail.

The red-bearded Viking's displeasure deepened as he watched his pursuers. By Schleipnir the eight legged horse of Odin! Would the whoresons never leave off? They'd hounded his tracks for two days, and Jar Haz was running out of patience.

The red-beard's temper, never long, was growing shorter with each passing minute. It wasn't his nature to shy away from a battle, and he had tired of the game.

At first it had been something of a lark, leading the Thane's men on a merry chase, but their dogged tenacity was beginning to irk. The whole affair had been stupid from the beginning.

Three nights agone he had accepted the hospitality of the local thane, a coarse, unpleasant fellow. As the evening progressed and the ale flowed more freely, the roistering and horseplay became rougher and more unrestrained. Several heads were broken, and a pint or two of blood spilled. Nothing more than was to be expected among a company of rough mercenaries.

The red-beard noted that strong drink had an unpleasant effect on his host, turning the lout surly and belligerent. Jar Haz ignored several provocative remarks, restraining his temper out of respect for the laws of hospitality that dictated his behavior as a guest.

The bounds were overstepped, however, when one of the serving girls seemed to prefer Jar Haz's embrace to that of her master, and the surly dog attempted to disembowel his guest with a treacherous thrust beneath the trestle table. All he accomplished was to stab the amorous wench in one plump buttock.

The girl leaped, screaming, from the Viking's lap, blood running down her leg. Jar Haz, fully aware of his host's intent, seized his axe, split the churl's skull to the chin, and departed hastily, leaving behind a perfectly good helmet and various articles of body armor.

In the beginning, the chase had been a game, but now he tired of it. The stubborn persistence of the Thane's men frayed his never gentle temper. He was a Sea Rover. One of those who had, with fire and sword and axe, carved for themselves a place in the land of the Celts and the Britons.

A breed so feared that the islanders prayed to their God, 'A furore Norsemanorum libera nos.' 'From the fury of the Northman deliver us.' The Viking was not a man to shun a fight.

The crystal air of the High Meadows carried the faint shouts of the men-at-arms as they worked their way to the hither side of the field, and the anger that had been building in him over the past hours burst forth. Odin's curse on the bastards! His right hand clenched on the haft of the half-moon axe dangling from its thong about his wrist, and anger rumbled in his throat.

The great brindled mastiff bitch at his side echoed her master's growl, and pressed her shoulder against his thigh. Bracelets of gold and copper clattered on his arm as the Viking again parted the leafy screen and glared down into the meadow. Anger flared in his belly. The Sea Rover fed it, and let it grow. The veins in his neck bulged. Pressure built in his chest. He groped for the round target shield hanging down his back.

The anger flamed into rage and rose from his belly into his chest. The game was over. The sport had ceased to amuse him. If the land-locked fools had not the good sense to break off the chase, then they would have to be reminded that the far-roving Viking warriors were justly feared from one end of the Nine Worlds to the other.

A tremor ran along his limbs and he began to shake with fury. He allowed the rage to build, to take possession of him, deliberately arousing himself toward that stage of battle-frenzy known to the Northmen as 'beserk,' a state of mindless ferocity. He felt a pressure behind his eyes as blood gorged his eyeballs, and he saw the advancing thanesmen through a veil of red fury. His ears roared with the pounding of blood, and the sun seemed to darken as the wild berserker rage mounted. Higher and higher the tension built in him, bringing him nearer and nearer to the brink of madness. Jar Haz opened himself to the rising fury, letting it grow, grow. . . . His lips peeled back from his teeth, and foam flecked the corners of his mouth.

Insanity raced through his veins. His chest felt as though it would explode. A scream welled up from his lungs, gathered in his throat, and burst from his lips in a blood-freezing cry of defiance, a high-pitched ululation of battle madness.

The brindled war-dog looked at her master and lifted her muzzle in a long-drawn howl of challenge.

From a nearby oak, a flock of ravens rocketed skyward amid a mighty beating of wings and startled cawings. One, larger than its fellows, continued to mount, punishing the crystal air with its wings, and disappeared into the distance.

The racketing of the birds of battle cut through the pounding of blood in the Viking's ears.

Ravens! Ravens by hammer of Thor! A good omen! Odin's own messengers had given him a sign!

Voicing another scream, he brushed aside the leafy screen with a sweep of his shield, and charged down the rocky slope at the startled men-at-arms shouting, **"Odin! Odin!"**

The rush of cold air as he ran, leaping over small boulders and sliding on the loose shale, did nothing to cool the fire of madness in his blood. He held his shield before him, and shouted his defiance. The thongs securing his braids came loose and his flame-colored hair streamed out behind him like a fiery gonfalon.

Jar Haz whirled the heavy half-moon axe in flashing circles above his head and in sweeping figure-eights to right and left. Sunlight ran along the razor edge of the axe-bitt like liquid silver.

Below him, the thanesmen raised a shout and surged up the slope. The dog-handlers loosed their charges, and four dogs of war raced ahead of the men, who were making heavy going of the loose-graveled scarp.

The dogs, though obviously well trained, were no match for the berserker, especially when he was backed by Bryn, who outweighed the smaller animals by half a hundredweight.

Jar Haz barely noticed as he dispatched two of the beasts with almost negligent swings of the half-moon, scarcely breaking stride to do so. Bryn threw herself, snarling, on the remaining two. . . bowling them over with her superior weight, and before they could regain their feet, she had disposed of them with wrenching snaps of her powerful jaws.

The dog scrambled down the slope to catch up with her master.

The advancing enemy were strung out in an inverted vee, the apex of which was almost directly before Jar Haz.

The heels of the viking's sandals dug footholds as he braced to meet the first foe. He parried a spear-thrust, and the half-moon rose and fell, cleaving iron helmet and skull bone. He wrenched his weapon free as a snarling, snapping hundred ninety-odd pounds of death hurtled past his shoulder.

Bryn had entered the fray.

The war-dog struck full upon the shield of a tall warrior with hawks' wings decorating his helmet. Stiffened forelegs knocked the man off balance. Slavering jaws opened and closed, and inch-and-a-half long fangs met somewhere in the tangle of yellow beard. Shaking bright drops of blood from her muzzle, Bryn rebounded from the falling corpse, and leaped again.

The men-at-arms surged forward, each eager to deliver the blow that would avenge their liege-lord. Their very eagerness defeated them. Their elbowing and crowding hampered swing and thrust, and the berserker took full advantage of their jostling. The whistling axe rose and fell, swung from side to side, and in its wake skulls were crushed, limbs lopped off, entrails spilled on the ground.

Jar Haz advanced slowly, steadily. He utilized his position on higher ground, and hewed a passage through the disorganized mob before him. The thanesmen began to fall back, giving ground in the face of the seemingly indestructible red-beard.

It was common knowledge among fighting men, that in the grip of the madness, the berserk warrior ignored wounds. It was understandable that such mindless ferocity should strike terror. Jar Haz could see that his attackers were beginning to feel the clutch of dread in their vitals, a cold horror that sapped at their strength, and at their will to face him.

And ever. . . now at his side, now leaping to attack, now falling back to leap again. . . Bryn guarded her master's flanks. The half-moon axe swung right and left, and back again, a grisly metronome of death.

Inevitably, fatigue began to take its toll. The axe swings began to falter. The warding shield was a fraction slower in fending off spear and sword and axe.

Bryn, too, was tiring. Her speed diminished, and the big dog was limping from a sword-cut to the shoulder.

More and more the Viking's guard was being penetrated. He was bleeding from more than a dozen wounds. Still he fought on, the madness of the berserker sustaining him.

From the corner of his eye, he saw Bryn go down under an axe-stroke, her proud head a welter of blood. A great grief welled up inside him and he screamed. A flood of hate-renewed energy flowed along his limbs and he hewed down the man in front of him without conscious thought, all his attention on the churl who had struck down Bryn.

That one raised both axe and shield in a futile effort to ward off the super-human downstroke that sheared through iron, wood, and bone, cleaving him to the girdle.

Yanking free his blade, Jar Haz turned to face only the backs of two men-at-arms fleeing in terror down the scarp.

Nothing else moved on the slope. The hillside was strewn with mangled corpses, and rivulets of blood trickled down to gather in bright pools.

The Viking stood, his chest heaving, and surveyed the field of battle.

The red veil of madness lifted from his eyes, and he slumped to his knees, saved from falling on his face by grounding his axe, and clinging to the haft. Slowly it came to him. *He had won!* By all the gods of Asgard, *he had won!*

Odin be praised! For long minutes he crouched there, gasping for breath, until his heart rate slowed and his
limbs stopped their trembling. He was bleeding from a score of wounds and consumed with an overpowering grief at the loss of Bryn.

At last, Jar Haz shook himself and staggered to his feet. He heard a rattle of gravel behind him and spun, lifting his axe. The Viking gave a shout of joy as he heard a low whine, and saw the great mastiff crawling painfully toward him. Odin be thanked, Bryn was alive!

He dropped axe and shield, and stumbled to the war-dog's side. Jar Haz knelt and took the bloody head into his arms, crooning soothingly while Bryn snuffled and tried to lick his face.

So great was his joy, he failed to hear as one of the fallen enemy rose stealthily to his feet, picked up a four-foot, two handed sword, and crept toward him.

Bryn growled a warning, and struggled in his arms. At the scrape of sandal on rock close behind him, Jar Haz whirled, raising his left arm to ward off the descending blade.

The foeman loosed a scream of triumph as his sword sheared through the upraised arm between wrist and elbow. The Viking's left hand flew through the air and bounced down the scarp, shedding bracelets of gold and copper, and bright drops of blood.

The sacrifice bought Jar Haz a second chance. Deflected, the blade struck sparks from a boulder at his side. Jar Haz surged to his feet, invoking an old berserkers' ploy. He thrust the spurting stump of his arm into his attacker's face. Blinded by the gouting blood, the thanesman fell back. Howling his hate, the Viking sank the fingers of his remaining hand into the throat of his enemy. The treacherous shale shifted underfoot and he fell headlong, maintaining his death-grip on the foeman's throat.

The two catapulted to the bottom of the slope amid a shower of stones and several large boulders, one of which came to rest on the red-beard's arm, grinding the stump into the earth, and halting the jetting arterial blood. He loosed the fingers of his other hand from the throat of his dead enemy.

Stunned, Jar Haz lay staring blankly at the sky.

He was dimly aware that Bryn had dragged herself to him and lay limply across his legs. Slowly his mind began to function again, and he took note of his surroundings. All around him lay the debris of battle. Shattered shields, broken weapons, hacked bodies.

A battleaxe, by its very nature, is incapable of inflicting small wounds, and the amount of blood spilled was incredible. Streams and trickles of scarlet ran among the rocks.

The flock of ravens that had circled the battlefield descended and began to feed on the dead. The battle had begun at midday, and the sun showed that it was only a little past that. Unbelievably, the wave of death that had swept the hill had lasted less than half an hour!

The red-beard's eyes fastened on a tiny dot high in the sky. The dot expanded, grew wings, and developed into a big raven which sailed to a graceful landing on the boulder that pinned his left arm to the earth.

Jar Haz grinned at the bird of death. "So you've come for me, Odin's Messenger? Are you, then, t' lead me down t' th' Misty Realm where Weird reigns with Hel, dark daughter of Loki?"

The glossy black bird cocked its head to one side and regarded the fallen warrior with a bright, intelligent golden eye, then it looked upward and cawed loudly. Jar Haz followed the bird's gaze and perceived a line of figures descending the flank of a towering snowy cloud. A flight of swans? The figures grew and became more plain.

Not swans.

A rainbow arched from the cloud and grounded at his feet. Down the glowing bridge rode a group of smiling maidens. Sunlight flashed dazzlingly from silver helmets and breastplates. Each was mounted on a snow white steed that pranced gracefully down the Bifrost Bridge, the rainbow arch between Middle Earth and Asgard, City of the Gods.

Jar Haz felt the breath catch in his throat. The Valkyries, the Shining Maids of Battle, were coming for *him*. They came *only* for the bravest, *The Heroes*!

Was he, then, one such?

The leading horse halted at the red-beard's feet and reared, golden hooves slashing the air.

The Shining Maid leaned from her saddle and took up the fallen warrior in her arms, cradling him against her silver breastplate. A high, sweet, *triumphant* singing filled the air, an anthem of victory and praise. The Maids of Battle turned their mounts, and ascended the rainbow swiftly, *joyously*.

Jar Haz the Viking glanced downward. He saw his battered corpse lying pinned beneath the boulder, with the limp form of Bryn lying across his legs, then he looked up.

Before him, gates of sacred oak bound with iron were slowly swinging open. . . .

CHAPTER TWO

The blazing car gouged a hole in the night.

The pouring rain did nothing to diminish the flames. Cradled in Janet's arms beneath the partial shelter to which she had dragged him, Jerry Haskins watched the inferno. There it goes, he thought, forty thousand dollars worth of status symbol. He couldn't work up much of a sweat about it though, since he was otherwise occupied.

He was dying.

In a state of drifting euphoria, he was accepting the fact calmly, intrigued at how detached he felt about the whole thing. Surprised to find that dying wasn't all that big a deal. Just one thing disturbed his serene acceptance of the inevitable. . . Janet. He didn't want to leave her, and he hated seeing her so unhappy. He wanted desperately to tell her that everything was all right, but he could see and hear, and that was all.

It had been a cat. A kitten, really. That, and a downpour the likes of which Jerry had never seen. He was concentrating on making the almost one hundred eighty degree switchback from the highway into Maple Lane. It was a tricky enough maneuver in the best of circumstances, and real murder under the present conditions. He had almost completed the turn when the half drowned kitten took that moment to dart from the side of the road into the headlights.

His involuntary twitch of the wheel threw the heavy car into a sideslip that sent it careening through the guardrail and down the steep, rock-strewn slope. Half way down, the front wheels hit a hole, and the car went end over end. Janet who was thrown clear on the first flip, landed unhurt on the thick carpet of pine needles that covered the ground. The car continued to the bottom, struck a large boulder, and burst into flames.

Pinned to the back of the seat by the steering wheel, Jerry could neither move nor feel the flames licking at his body. He realized that his neck must be broken, paralyzing him.

Janet, screaming his name, came slipping and sliding down the slope. Somehow the one hundred five pound girl *ripped off* the jammed door, *bent* the steering column away from his body, and dragged him from the car.

Jerry never knew how long Janet sat there holding his head in her lap while the rain soaked them, before he became aware of movement at the edge of his vision. He cut his eyes to the right and discovered a pair of pointed yellow shoes. The shoes were connected to narrow black trouser legs. Following the pant-legs upward, he beheld a white tunic that reached below the knees and buttoned high around the neck. Above this was a thin brown face with a sparse black beard, a hooked nose, and the largest, most compassionate eyes Jerry had ever seen. The apparition was topped off by a rain-soaked white turban.

Janet looked up at the newcomer, and in the calm tones of hysteria, said, "He's been hurt. If we can get him to a hospital, he'll be all right."

Compassion glowed in the little man's eyes. "No, little Memsahib, it is useless."

Janet's face reflected her rejection of the words. "The hospital," she repeated, "If we can get him to the hospital, he'll be all right."

The little swami knelt on the saturated pine needles and looked into the girl's blankly staring eyes. "Memsahib," he said softly, "it is useless. Nothing can be done for him."

The melodic voice trailed off as a rush of pain flooded into Janet's face. The little brown man's eyes mirrored the girl's agony. Janet felt the intensity of the mystic's gaze and looked at him. She saw something in his eyes. . . something that, impossible as it seemed, gave her hope.

It didn't seem at all strange to her that a little brown man in a turban was kneeling beside her in the rain.

Nothing had seemed real to her since the moment she saw Jerry sitting behind the steering wheel among the flames. It did not seem strange to her that in her hysteria she had found the strength to rip the door off an automobile, bend the steering column, and drag her husband a hundred yards.

Why then, should it seem strange that a little brown man in a turban was kneeling beside her in the rain?

What *did* seem strange was that she disbelieved the finality of his words. That disbelief sprang from the something she'd seen in his eyes. A flash of something he'd immediately concealed. Looking at Jerry objectively for the first time since the car had left the road, she had to admit that the little brown man was right about one thing, no hospital was ever going to put her Jerry back together again. At last she accepted that. *Why, then this irrational belief that everything was to be all right?*

"You know something," she accused.

"About what, Memsahib?"

"About how to save him."

Mukkergee stalled. "Memsahib, what I have in mind is dangerous in the extreme. There are a dozen random factors involved, any one of which could cause disaster. I've seen it done only once, and then by an adept. I'm not entirely sure that attempting it won't leave your husband worse off than he is now."

Janet grasped the little mystic by the front of his tunic. "Please," she implored, "Help him."

"Memsahib, I have seen it done and I know the means, but I have never done it, and it is dangerous to attempt, even by a Ninth Level adept."

"But you can save him!"

Mukkergee said reluctantly, "Perhaps, little one, only perhaps. It is very dangerous."

"But there is a way?"

"There is a way."

"Please, please, oh please. . . ."

The little mystic sighed. "Memsahib, you must understand. I cannot save his body. I cannot give him back to you as he was, which is what you are asking."

"I don't understand what you're saying."

"I am saying, Memsahib, that his body will die. Nothing can be done about that. But if you wish, I can, *maybe*, save his life."

Janet looked bewildered. "What do you mean, you can save his life but not his body?"

The mahatma returned the distraught girl's gaze. "Little Memsahib, life is not at all what it is believed to be. Your life does not begin with your birth and end with your death. What you are experiencing now is merely the present phase of an existence that began eons ago. The human mind has not reached the level of understanding capable of grasping the fullness of that, so one's existence consists of a series of planes and phases acceptable to the finite mind. All of us have lived before and will live again."

Janet looked disappointed. "You're talking about reincarnation."

Mukkergee smiled. "That is one of the words, little Memsahib."

"You're saying that Jerry will live in the future, but I'll never see him again. . . ."

"No Memsahib. *There is no future*, only the past.

"Think of time as a spear thrusting into the void. Our lives, our *present* lives, are merely the tip of the spear point moving into the nothingness. Nothing exists until we have passed through it, then it becomes the past, and the past extends, like the shaft of the spear, all the way back to the hand of the Creator."

Mukkergee hesitated. "It is possible, little Memsahib," he said slowly, "to travel back along that shaft to a previous existence."

"Oh!" Janet's voice broke on a sob. "Either way, I'll never see him again." She bent and kissed Jerry's lips. "But he will live?"

"Yes."

"Where? When?"

"That is what I must determine. A philosopher once said, '*I think, therefore I am*.' He was not entirely accurate.

"He should have said, I *remember*, therefore I am. The essence of a man is his *memories*, and these memories are the *man*. And this essence must enter the body of an ancestor who is at the point of death. There will be many such moments, but if we are to benefit him, the body he enters must be hale and healthy. It would not avail him much to emerge in one who is imprisoned in a dungeon for life. Or one broken on the rack, or diseased or infirm. I must be sure that when all is accomplished, your husband will, in fact, be better off than he is now. Do you understand?"

Janet looked at him. "No. But I don't have to understand, as long as I know Jerry will live. Even if I never see him again, that will make it easier to bear."

"Then you wish me to try?"

"Yes, oh, yes. . . ."

"As you wish, Memsahib."

The little mystic lifted his face into the falling rain, and his bearded lips moved briefly. He looked down, and for the first time, spoke directly to the man on the ground. "You may close your eyes now."

With a sigh of gratitude, Jerry did so.

There was more conversation after that, but drifting in and out of consciousness, Jerry made little effort to follow it.

CHAPTER THREE

Singing.

That was Jerry's first awareness. His ears were filled with the fading sound of joyous, *exultant* singing.

He opened his eyes.

He was lying on his back looking up at the sky. He could make out a line of figures moving against the flank of a towering thunder head. He goggled. Horses? Horses in the sky? Jerry boy, you're losing it! Horses? In the sky? He blinked. A flight of swans. That was it. That had to be it. A flight of swans.

The eerie singing faded.

He turned his head, and looked at the big raven perched on the boulder a couple of feet away. The black bird cocked its head and stared insolently back.

Jerry was immediately aware of a number of things. He knew, for instance, that this new body of his was considerably battered and missing some parts. On the whole, however, it did seem to be a step up. A sort of upgrading from a total 'no-go' to a 'maybe.'

He returned his attention to the raven who sat muttering to itself, and eyeing him with interest. *Why* was it eyeing him with such interest? All around him relatives of the big black bird were dining on the battle casualties.

Jerry shivered

The raven gave a jeering squawk. Jerry looked at it sourly. "Go ahead, laugh."

The black bird turned its head, and stared at something out of Jerry's line of vision. It raised its wings, and glided to another boulder from which it could apparently get a better view of whatever had attracted its attention.

Jerry became aware of a low murmur somewhere behind him, that sounded, he thought, like voices. At one point he could have sworn that one of the voices was Janet's, but the fever rising in his new body blurred and distorted his thinking.

Then the murmur, whatever it was, ceased.

The raven returned its saturnine gaze to Jerry. It hopped from one foot to the other, gave a startled squawk, and leaped into the air as the boulder on which it sat began to rotate.

Jerry stared in amazement as the big rock completed a quarter turn, and lifted to reveal the mouth of a tunnel. The stumpy figure that emerged was even more startling.

The burly little man examined Jerry with a scowl.

"Humph," he grunted. He glanced about the hillside. "Not a bad job o' work, fer a mortal," he commented. The words were spoken in a guttural Norse dialect that Jerry was surprised to discover he understood perfectly.

The little man speaking them stood perhaps four and a half feet high, and was at least half that across the shoulders. The blocky torso was supported by thick stubby legs only half the length of those of an ordinary man, and his arms, though equally short, bulged with knotted muscle, revealing more than ordinary strength.

Despite his height, the little man gave the impression of a transmogrified giant, a hammered down Colossus. He wore a helmet and breastplate of unadorned steel, both of which were dented and scarred from obvious use. He had a short, grayish beard, a lumpy nose, and a pair of intelligent eyes in which the twinkle of humor was not disguised by his scowling expression.

Under the breastplate he wore a tunic of red wool that matched the red wool trousers bound from ankle to knee with a crisscross of leather thongs.

A broad girdle at his waist supported a short, broad-bladed sword, a leather wallet, and two sheathed throwing knives. From his right hand dangled a mace of the sort known as a Morning Star. A stubby handle of brass-bound oak attached to a foot of chain, which in turn was connected to a four inch diameter iron ball studded with inch-long spikes.

Jerry recognized the Morning Star from a course in Medieval History, and knew that in the hands of an expert, the spiked ball could achieve unbelievable velocity. It could smash through shield and plate armor like a hammer through cheese. A formidable weapon that told much about the little man holding it.

The dwarf regarded the wounded man. "It appears ye gave quite an account o' yerself, lad," he grunted.

He took a step in Jerry's direction, and Bryn raised her bloody head, growling a warning. The dwarf crooned soothingly. "Steady, girl. 'Tis a friend I am. I see ye've taken quite a knock yerself. . . ."

He laid aside his Morning Star, knelt, murmuring reassurances, and

Bryn allowed him to examine the ragged gash in her scalp. Apparently having satisfied himself that the dog's wound was more spectacular than fatal, he turned his attention to Jerry.

The callused hands were gentle as he assessed the damage. "Humph," he grunted again, "By all rights ye should be dead, but since ye aren't, I do believe there's a chance ye'll recover. Let's see about gettin' that rock off yer arm. . . .'"

Jerry raised himself to protest, and the movement sent waves of agony crashing through him. The ground seemed to surge beneath him, and the trees danced on the distant hills. He uttered a low cry of pain, and fell back, half-swooning. A look of compassion flooded the dwarf's face. He turned, scrambled quickly across the loose shale to a small brook trickling down the rocks, fishing a small brass vial and a drinking horn from his wallet as he went. He filled the horn with clear cold water and added several drops of something from the vial. Returning to Jerry's side, the little man stirred the mixture with a forefinger. He lifted Jerry's head and pressed the rim of the horn to his lips.

The draft was bitter tasting, but at the dwarf's urging, Jerry drained the cup. Its action was almost instantaneous. A soothing warmth spread out, wiping away pain as it went.

Jerry sighed and grinned at the little man. "Wow," he said, "That's better! Look, we've got sort of a problem about that rock. I mean there's no hand under there. Move the rock and there goes the rest of my blood, I think. . . ."

The dwarf nodded. "Aye, that could be unfortunate."

"That's one way of putting it," Jerry grunted.

The little man grinned and busied himself. He tugged the wolfskin tunic from a nearby corpse, drew one of the knives at his belt, and cut a wide strip. He cast about until he found a small smooth pebble, and lastly, broke a branch from a bush and trimmed it to a billet about a foot long.

The big raven, hopping from foot to foot on a nearby boulder, watched these preparations with keen interest and jeering comments.

The dwarf carefully positioned the pebble against the great artery on the inside of Jerry's biceps, held it in place while he looped the strip of wolfskin around the arm, and used the stick to tighten the tourniquet. He checked the result and grunted. "That should keep th' blood in ye until I can get ye home."

Jerry looked up into the lumpy, but not unpleasant face. "Just in case this doesn't work out, I'd like to know who it was that tried so hard."

The dwarf smiled. "My name is Brokk, an' ye're not likely t' be seein' th' last o' me fer some time, lad. I've had a bit o' practice wi' wounded men afore this. Just ye relax."

The name struck a note in Jerry's mind. "Wasn't it Brokk the Dwarf King who made Thor's hammer?"

The dwarf bristled. "Now by all th' gods, will I never hear th' end o' that piece o' nonsense?" The dwarf snorted. "A few horns o' ale an'. . . . Pah!"

Jerry let it drop.

Brokk braced his feet, spat on his palms, and grasped the heavy stone. "Now, lad," he grunted, and heaved. The rock rolled away.

Jerry got a look at the mangled stump of his left arm and his stomach lurched. Raw purple flesh, shredded and crushed, with dirt and stones ground in, oozed dark blood. But there was none of the bright arterial spurting that would have spelled death.

Brokk eyed the mess and grinned. "Why, 'tis none so bad, laddie. A trifle messy, mayhap,
but still enough left t' strap a shield to. Buck up son, we'll ha' ye up an' hackin' wi' yer cleaver in no time."

Jerry wasn't all that happy at the looks of his arm, but the knowledge that he wasn't about to die immediately, caused him to grin back. "That's nice," he grunted. Brokk laughed, and gently crossing Jerry's wounded arm over his chest, bound it securely.

The dwarf glanced at the sinking sun, and began to gather up a variety of items from the battlefield. He returned with several long spears, and an armful of cloaks and wolfskins taken from the fallen thanesmen. He set briskly about forming the spear shafts into a rectangle which he lashed together with strips cut from the skins. He secured a stout cloak to the frame, forming a stretcher with projecting handles at each end. Upon this he piled more cloaks and furs to make a comfortable bed.

All the while, the big raven hopped about from one perch to another, keeping an interested eye on the activity. Brokk retrieved his mace, and thrust the handle through a loop on his girdle. The viciously spiked ball fit into a thick leather pouch beside it. The burly dwarf hitched up his harness, and taking up the handles of the travois, dragged it down into the tunnel under the rock. He returned, and in spite of the larger man's bulk, gathered Jerry up in his abbreviated arms, and carried him down to place him on the litter. He made a final trip to bring down the wounded Bryn.

Brokk laid the dog across her master's legs, and strapped her into place. The little man turned to a system of levers and pulleys that Jerry hadn't been able to see from outside, and rotated and lowered the boulder that concealed the tunnel's mouth.

Just before the exit closed, there was a strident squawk, and Odin's Messenger swooped through to land amid a frantic beating of wings on the crossbar above Jerry's head. The big raven eyed Jerry, then ducked and rubbed its beak against the man's bearded cheek.

Jerry was oddly touched by the gesture, and stroked the glossy head. Odin's Messenger gave a satisfied cluck and began to preen his feathers.

Instead of the pitch black Jerry expected when the tunnel closed, he was surprised to find that it was well lighted by a phosphorescent glow from the walls. The floor was dry white sand.

Brokk checked his passengers. Apparently satisfied, he took up the handles of the travois and trudged off down the tunnel.

For a while Jerry watched the tracks left in the sand, and listened to the mutterings of the raven perched above his head. His one hand caressed the flank of the wounded dog. Bryn responded by twitching her stump of a tail.

Utter fatigue, weakness from his wounds, and reaction to the drug Brokk had given him, at last overpowered him, and Jerry slept. The last sound he remembered was Odin's Messenger's solicitous clucking.

CHAPTER FOUR

Jerry's return to consciousness was a long journey through rolling gray mists. From time to time the veil parted.

Once Jerry found himself looking down on a man and a boy in the backyard of a comfortable suburban home. The man, in shirt sleeves, brushed back a thatch of carroty hair, and going into an elaborate wind-up, tossed the softball. The redheaded boy swung the bat and connected, driving the ball over his father's head and through the dining room window. Jerry saw himself and his father take to their heels as his mother emerged from the back door waving a broom. All three were laughing.

The mists parted again.

Sixteen year old Janet Hughes cast her eyes down shyly as she answered yes to Jerry's suggestion that they go steady. She lifted her lips to Jerry's kiss.

Again Janet. Spraying diamond-bright drops of water as her skis sliced the surface of the lake. Janet, her face soft in the firelight as they made love before the hearth in their first home. Janet waving from the station wagon as he descended from the commuter train, briefcase in hand.

Janet by sunlight. Janet by firelight. Janet by moonlight, by the light of her own special beauty.

Janet. Janet. Janet. . . . The gray mists closed again, blotting out everything. Jerry wandered blindly, calling, "Janet! Janet!"

Only muffled echoes came back, but he was almost sure he could hear her answering, "I'm here, Jerry, I'm here."

Then her voice blended with a blur of clashing metal, war-cries, grunts, the creak of leather battle-harness. Screams of pain. Jerry recognized the sounds of the battle on the hillside.

The noise of fighting faded to be replaced by triumphant, exultant singing. He thought of swans, that were not swans but shining maidens in silver armor, astride snow-white steeds riding up the side of a towering thunder head.

The visions dissolved and receded, taking the gray mists with them. He was left feeling calm, and for no reason he could explain, *hopeful.*

One annoying fly remained buzzing at the back of his mind, however. It had something to do with Janet and the little brown mystic.

A conversation.

Something damned important had been discussed, but for the life of him he couldn't recall it. What had it been? What had they talked about? It was right on the tip of his mind. . . . Then he became aware of the tinkling of light, rapid taps of a hammer on metal.

From nearer at hand a feminine voice was humming a little tune. He opened his eyes and met the mocking gaze of one golden orb as Odin's Messenger, perched on a shelf across the room, cocked his head and uttered a satisfied "Quar-r-r-k."

"Quark, yourself," Jerry grinned.

There was a scrambling of claws on stone beside the bed, and Bryn raised her head. Eager little whines poured from her as she proceeded to wash Jerry's face with a sloppy tongue.

Laughing, the man tried to defend himself, warding off the excited dog with the shiny pink stump of his left arm. "Down!" he commanded. "Down! Dammit, girl, you're drowning me!"

Bryn obeyed, though her eager whines continued, and her hindquarters wriggled ecstatically as she attempted to wag her nonexistent tail.

Jerry gave a start and stared at his arm.

The stump *was* pink and shiny. Not at all like the ragged, oozing horror he remembered. *How long had he been out?* That stump hadn't healed overnight!

His eyes traveled down the length of his body. No red-soaked bandages. No bandages at all, just a crisscross of neatly healed scars. He looked like a roadmap!

He heard a soft footstep, and the bearskin that hung in the doorway was drawn aside by a small hand.

Jerry gasped. The tiny elf-woman who entered was the loveliest female held ever seen.

Just over four feet tall, she was exquisitely proportioned. Tresses that seemed to be a mixture of silver and gold fell in braids to her waist. The elfin face held a beauty not describable in human terms.

The deep blue calf-length dress was of wool so finely spun as to resemble silk. It was open at the throat to reveal a quartz pendant on a gold chain, and was cinched at the waist by a girdle of interwoven gold links. Her feet were encased in ankle boots of soft doeskin. The sleeves were rolled to the elbow, and she held a wooden spoon in one hand.

Jerry goggled, and grabbed for the woolen blanket to cover his nakedness. The tiny beauty's laugh was a tinkle of elfin bells.

"Ah," she smiled, "you're awake at last."

Jerry cleared his throat. "Yes, ma'am," he mumbled.

Sandals clashed harshly in the passage, and the bearskin was swept aside. Brokk stumped into the room, grinning.

"So ye're wi' us again, are ye, lad! Gods, I'm glad t' see it. 'Tis much worry ye've given us, son Jerry. Fer a while we feared ye'd not return."

Jerry was surprised by the depth of his pleasure at the sight of the dwarf. "It's entirely due to your help that I'm here at all. I don't begin to know how to thank you."

The dwarf grimaced. "Nonsense. Ye owe me nothing."

He grinned and hooked a thumb toward the elf-woman. "'Twas she who sewed ye back together an' clucked over ye like a mother hen."

Bryn snuffled and put her forepaws on the bed. Brokk's grin widened. "Oh, aye. I'd not ferget ye, old girl. Ye've minded him like a sick puppy."

He smiled at Jerry. "She's lain at yer side ever since she recovered enough t' crawl in here."

Jerry saw that Bryn's wound, too, had healed, leaving a ragged scar that ran from behind her left ear, down across her muzzle, and ended at her jawline.

The elf-woman looked at the disfiguring scar. "I tried to sew it up more neatly, but the stubborn lout kept scratching out the stitches."

Brokk laughed. "It gives her a fiercer look. In battle she'll strike terror in th' hearts o' yer enemies."

Jerry looked at the elf-woman. "Ma'am, I've no words to thank you."

She smiled. "Hush, there's no need."

Brokk put an arm around the lovely sprite. "'Tis time ye met th' finest seamstress in Svartheim. An' th' luckiest woman in all Skandia t' be married t' a paragon such as myself. Jerry lad, this is my wife, Freya."

The name fit her, Jerry thought. Freya was the Norse goddess of flowers and spring.

It occurred to Jerry that he had never told the little man his name. He looked at the dwarf. "How do you know my name?"

Brokk chuckled. "We know much about ye, lad," he said, "Ye

wandered long in th' Land o' Weird afore returnin' t' us."

Jerry looked at the little man. "*How* long?"

"Why, over three fortn'ts."

Three fortnights? Jerry gasped. He'd been delirious for over six weeks! No wonder his wounds were healed!

"Durin' all that time ye maundered sick'nly about some yellow-haired wench ye called Janet. Fair turned my stomach wi' yer moonstruck gabble. . . ."

"Brokk, don't tease him."

The dwarf grinned. "Sore fond o' this Janet, ye seem t' be. . . ."

"She is, I mean, was, my wife."

"So we gathered, lad. Ye also babbled considerable o' magic an' marvels, an' chancy voyagin' on th' misty river o' time. Ye spoke o' yer mother an' father an' somethin' ye called baseball. Ye went on at some length about a little brown man, a magician o' some sort I gathered, an' ye fretted sorely that he an' yer wife talked o' things ye can't remember."

The dwarf grinned. "Oh, ye blithered right muchly, but most of all ye went on and on, and on, about yer Janet, until this one pestered me t' do somethin' about it. An', lad, when this one gets somethin' set in her pretty head, 'tis best t' just do what she wants or ye'll get no peace."

"Do something about it? Do something about Janet? What? How?"

The elf-woman smiled. "Sh-h-h. Hush now."

Freya pushed him gently back against the pillow. Jerry was surprised at the ease with which she did so, and realized for the first time just how weak he was.

"Hush Jerry. Not now. There's plenty of time when you get your strength back. And speaking of your strength, you must be ravenous." She hurried from the room.

Freya was back in a moment with a bowl of steaming broth. The delicious odor hit Jerry's nostrils and his stomach growled. He *was* ravenous.

He tried to struggle to a sitting position but, was kitten weak. Brokk raised his shoulders and propped the pillows behind him. The elf woman sat on the edge of the bed, and Jerry reached eagerly for the bowl. Freya hesitated a moment then handed it to him, a little smile quirking one corner of her lips.

Jerry made a manful try at feeding himself, but was too weak and shaky to get a full spoon to his mouth. Freya laughed softly, wiped the spilled broth from his chest, and retrieved the spoon. "Perhaps you'd better let me do it," she said.

Jerry resented having to be fed like an infant, but eagerly gulped down every spoonful. When the bowl was empty Freya motioned for Brokk to remove the pillows and lay Jerry back down.

"But I'm still hungry," Jerry whined.

Freya smiled. "Sleep now," she said soothingly, "I promise I won't let you starve. Sleep."

Jerry started to protest, but before he could get the words out, he was asleep. He woke often, and always the elf-woman was there with a bowl of the strengthening broth. She began adding chunks of soft black bread to his diet. He started feeling stronger.

It was difficult to judge time in the underground dwelling, but Jerry knew that several days must have passed in the world outside by the time he was able to sit up unassisted, and take the bowl himself.

He would tuck it into the crook of his handless left arm and wolf down the contents. He was delighted when hunks of meat were added to the broth and bread.

As strength grew apace, Jerry began to fret, to be anxious to be up and doing, but Freya was adamant. "You'll get up when I say you can get up," she said with finality.

Jerry obeyed, albeit sulkily. The tiny elf-woman smiled.

Always there was the sound of hammer on metal. Brokk explained that he was working in his forge.

"We dwarfs are miners and workers in metal," he informed. "We fashion th' finest o' tools an' weapons. 'Tis our trade. Th' folk come from everywhere in th' Nine Worlds t' barter fer our weapons an' armor.

"Giants, elves, humans, an' even certain o' th' goblins, though not many o' their kind will we deal with."

"Why not?"

"Th' goblin kind," Brokk explained, "be deformed. Hunchbacked an' spidery, they're called th' Twisted Ones. Their hideousness has set them apart from other folk, an' o'er th' centuries this rejection burned into them a hatred for all others. They war mercilessly against all not o' their kind. Only th' giants, an' th' trolls, who be even more hideous than th' goblins, ha' no fear o' them."

"Then why do you trade with them at all?"

"When ye were telling' me some'at o' th' world from which ye came, ye mentioned th' Indians o' yer country. Ye told that, though hostile in th' main, there were certain tribes that were friendly t' yer folk. Well, 'tis that way wi' th' goblin kind.

"There be a few rovin' loners, outcasts from their clans because they've not th' goblin hatred fer all not their sort. 'Tis with them we'll trade, an' them only. 'Tis a sort o' unspoken treaty that's held fer centuries. Not allies, no. But not enemies."

As Jerry's strength returned, the dwarf spent more time with him, describing the world into which he had been propelled by the little Hindu.

"Thousands o' years agone, we dwarfs discovered that here in the south th' mountains were honeycombed wi' caves an' caverns. 'Twas a place built by nature t' be easily defended by folk who were small in stature. As our numbers increased, th' dwarf kind began t' expand th' underground dwellin's, joinin' them wi' tunnels.

"As we tunneled, we discovered th' metals o' th' earth an' began t' learn th' art o' th' forge. We traded our metalwork fer th' things needed from th' outside. Generations upon generations o' miners enlarged, extended, and connected an entire underground world, th' dwarfholm we call Svartheim."

"But couldn't enemies just bottle you up by cutting off the exits?" Brokk chuckled. "'Twas tried 'way back in th' beginnin'. We dwarfs had provided fer that. D'ye mind th' tunnel I brought ye through from th' battlefield? Well, there be hundreds o' secret exits, known only t' us o' th' dwarf kind, that allowed th' defenders t' emerge behind th' besiegers an' catch 'em between deadly pincers. Such attempts were soon abandoned."

Brokk explained that the only entrance known to the outside world was a heavily guarded cavern above a bowl-like depression known as the Trading Glen. This was reached from the land below by an arduous climb up a narrow fissure in the face of a cliff thousands of feet high. To this Trading Glen came those of the Nine Worlds who would bargain with the Little People.

"Th' cavern entrance," Brokk explained, "is guarded by th' Warrior Clan, whose sole purpose is t' defend our world. No enemy ha' ever penetrated more than a few hundred meters afore bein' trapped an' destroyed."

Thinking of Freya, Jerry asked, "What about the elves? They're Little People, too. How come they don't live with you here in Svartheim?"

"Th' elves be forest dwellers down below, in Midgard. Livin', as they ha' fer a thousand generations among th' creatures o' th' forest, th' elves ha' learned t' communicate wi' th' beasts an' th' birds t' a certain extent. They live in hollow hills called Elf Mounds fer which they ha' their own defenses."

Brokk was vague about these defenses, hinting at elfin magic. When pressed, the dwarf repeated that the elves had power over animals and that this power extended to inanimate objects.

"For instance?" Jerry persisted.

Brokk grinned. "Fer instance," he said, "when attacked, 'tis possible fer an elf t' turn th' assailant's own weapons against him."

"What? How?"

"Th' Elfin Gift."

"That explains nothing," Jerry snorted, "Exactly what happens?"

"What happens," Brokk grinned, "is that an attacker's sword might leap from his hand, turn an' run him through, or his chain mail might squeeze him t' death, or his axe chop off his leg. Elfin magic. . . ."

"Psychokinesis!" Jerry blurted.

"Eh?"

"Psychokinesis. That's what 'elfin magic' would be called in the world I came from, if anybody could get it to work."

"They can't?"

"No."

Jerry was fascinated by the little man's dissertation. "Tell me more."

Brokk scratched his head. "Where to start? Many months journey t' th' north in th' Norden Bergen, th' Northern Mountains, lies th' land o' th' giants, Jotunheim. 'Tis a bleak place o' eternal ice an' snow, wi' freezin' mists an' treacherous, shiftin' glaciers that can open a crevasse under yer feet wi'out warnin', an' close up just as quick, swallowin' ye up like a hungry beast.

"Betwixt th' Southern an' Northern ranges lies th' land o' men, Midgard. Midgard starts at th' foot o' Svartheim an' ends at Ginnungagap."

"Ginnungagap?"

"'Tis th' Chasm o' Chasms that divides th' Land o' Men from th' Land o' Giants, a vast abyss wi'out bottom. Th' only way t' cross it is wi' th' help o' th' Ice Elves an' their flyin' dragons. Once across, ye've only t' cross Jotunheim t' th' foot o' th' Ultimate Peak, climb yer way up it through th' clouds, an' ye reach Asgard, th' City o' th' Gods. . . ."

The dwarf chuckled. "An' that, son Jerry, is where my lovin' wife proposes I take ye t' ask th' help o' th' gods in findin' yer lost Janet."

"You're kidding!"

"If that means ye think I'm makin' sport o' ye, 'tis not so. That one ha' been at me, natterin' an' natterin' that ye must be rejoined t' yer Janet, until I had t' agree just t' get some rest."

The dwarf gave Jerry a sour look. "I'm sore fond o' ye, lad, but I misdoubt I'm *that* fond o' ye."

Freya's musical laugh sounded from the doorway. "Never you fret, Jerry dear. He's only grumping to hide his delight for the adventure."

The elf-woman put her arm around her husband's neck and rubbed her cheek against his. "I know you, Brokk Hammermacher, you're as eager to go as Jerry is to find his Janet."

The dwarf grinned. "If ye say so, my dear."

Jerry looked at the two of them. "Just like that. We just mosey down our mountain, sail across a bottomless pit, wander across a land of giants, and shinny up a topless peak. Piece of cake." Jerry snorted.

Brokk chuckled. "Th' way you put it, it sounds easy enough." The dwarf scratched his head and grinned. "Mayhap I *did* leave out a detail or two. Did I mention the perils o' th' land o' men? Robber Barons? Rovin' bands o' thievin', murderin' mercenaries?"

"I believe you forgot to say anything like that."

"Did I touch on th' subject o' a forest o' flesh-eatin' plants? Trolls?"

"No," Jerry smiled, "I don't believe you mentioned any of those things."

"Careless o' me."

"Yes."

"Ah, but don't let it worry ye, lad. All in a day's work, eh? All in a day's work."

Jerry laughed. "You really think there's a chance to find my way back to Janet?"

"Aye lad, I do."

"Then bring 'em on!"

Brokk chuckled. "I knew ye'd see th' right o' it."

CHAPTER FIVE

Jerry wheedled and tried cunning. He employed every trick that used to work on his mother, but to no avail. Freya was adamant. He stayed in bed.

He squirmed, pouted, and verged on open rebellion. To put the cap on his impatience there was the constant tap-tap-tap from Brokk's forge.

"I told ye there's plenty enough o' that arm left t' strap a shield to," the dwarf said, "but I've somethin' t' show ye I think ye'll find interestin', when ye're a little more steady on yer feet."

Jerry tried to pry more from the little man. Brokk only grinned and said, "Patience, lad, patience. All in good time. It's almost finished."

What was almost finished? Brokk wouldn't say.

Then one morning Freya drew aside the curtain and looked at the sulky boy on the bed. Her lips curved in a smile. "Well," she teased, "do you intend to spend the rest of your life just lying around?"

Jerry sat up. He could do that now without his head spinning. "You mean. . . ."

"I mean you might try walking around for a few minutes if you promise not to overdo. Promise?"

Jerry grinned broadly. "Yes, mother." He hesitated.

"Well," Freya demanded, "You've been whining for days to get up. What's keeping you?"

"You."

The elf-woman looked puzzled. "Me? I just said you could get up."

Jerry blushed. "Aw, come on, Freya. I don't have anything on."

The tinkle of elfin bells filled the room as Freya laughed. "Oh for. . . ." Still laughing, she left the room.

Jerry swung his legs over the side of the bed, and stood up. The rock walls swayed, and the stone floor undulated under his feet like the deck of a ship.

He sat back down.

Bryn whined questioningly, while Odin's Messenger pointed his beak at the ceiling, and cackled mockingly. Jerry eyed the chortling raven sourly. "Oh, shut up," he growled.

Odin's Messenger chuckled.

After a few moments the room returned to normal. This time he rose more slowly, and except for a slight wavering, solidity remained solid.

His first few steps were uncertain, however by the time he reached his trousers hanging from a peg in the far wall he'd gotten the hang of it. The blue wool trousers were new, the product of Freya's needle. The slashed and blood-soaked garments of Jar Haz had been little more than tatters.

Jerry would never have believed that something as simple as putting on a pair of pants could be such a hassle with one hand. After having gotten his feet tangled in the pantlegs and nearly falling, much to the amusement of Odin's Messenger, he returned to the bed and sat down to get them on and hitched up.

Then came the insoluble problem of cinching them about his waist. Had the garment fit snugly, he might have managed the broad leather belt, but there was no way he could hold up the pants and buckle the belt at the same time.

Bryn watched with a puzzled expression on her scarred face, and Odin's Messenger uttered a series of mocking squawks from his perch. "Don't you ever get tired of laughing at me?" Jerry asked sourly. The big raven cocked its head to one side and chuckled.

"Who asked you?" Jerry growled.

He stood there with the waistband of his trousers bunched in his one hand and stared at the belt hanging uselessly on its peg. He sighed. "Mother," he called wryly, "Junior needs help."

Finally, trousered and girdled, Jerry stepped out into the passageway. The rock floor was smooth and cool under his bare feet. He looked about him curiously. To his left the passage ran off into the distance, to his right were several skin-hung doorways. He could hear the sound of Brokk's hammer coming from the one at the end of the tunnel. He looked at Freya.

"Go ahead," she smiled, "Brokk is waiting for you." The elf-woman waved him on, and returned to her kitchen.

Gaining strength with each step, Jerry entered the dwarf's workshop. He gazed about in wonder. From pegs driven into the walls hung scores of helmets, breastplates, and weapons of all description.

There were swords and daggers of a dozen designs and sizes. Maces, some simply smooth iron clubs, some with spiked heads, several Morning Stars.

The weapons ranged in size to accommodate dwarf, man, and giant.

Jerry stared at the latter. Swords with blades six or seven feet in length, and two-foot hilts. A Morning Star with a spiked ball larger than his head, and a four-foot length of chain attached to a three-foot handle.

For the first time the word 'giant' took on real meaning.

Several of the helmets and pieces of body armor were finished. Some with gold, copper, silver, or brass inlays, and all polished to a glistening brightness. Many more were simply roughed out in various sizes, waiting to be fitted to a buyer's special contours.

There were a number of anvils of different sizes and shapes for the forming of arm and leg protectors, others for the shaping of helmets. Coats of chain mail, painstakingly constructed of interlocking iron rings, hung from wooden mannequins. In the center of the room was the forge with its glowing coals and bellows.

Brokk was stripped to the waist. His face was sweating, red from the heat, and smudged with soot. He was using tongs to lift a white-hot sword blade from the fire.

Ignoring Jerry for the moment, the little man placed the blade on a flat anvil and worked it with light taps of his hammer. Jerry marveled at the strength revealed in the knotted muscles of the dwarf's bare back and shoulders. He handled the heavy sledge as Jerry would have handled a tack hammer.

The metal cooled from white to red to orange to black. The dwarf held the blade at arm's length, looked at it critically. With a grunt of satisfaction, he plunged it into a vat of water. Hissing clouds of steam all but obscured the little smith.

Brook laid the now cool blade on a work table, and turned, wiping his hands on his leather apron.

"So, son Jerry," he grinned, "'tis happy I am t' see ye up an' about."

He waved an arm to encompass the shop. "What d'ye think o' my toys?"

Jerry was impressed. "I've never seen such beautiful cutlery," he said, lifting down a two-handed broadsword to examine it more closely.

The hilt was of walrus ivory banded with silver. The pommel was an intricately carved hawk's head with rubies for eyes, and the cross guard resembled the outspread wings of an eagle. The blade was etched with runes and arcane symbols that Jerry knew were supposed to protect the wielder.

"Ach, that," Brokk snorted. "A piece o' frippery fer th' vanity o' an insignificant little man o' Midgard who fancies himself a king. I'd not ha' wasted my time on it, but he paid handsomely."

Jerry tapped the flat of the blade lightly against an anvil. The air was filled with a high pure note. "Frippery? It's as fine a blade as ever was forged."

"Well," Brokk growled, "I ha' my pride."

He cocked his head and looked at Jerry. "I see ye've a passable knowledge o' th' subject."

"A little. I was on the fencing team in college."

"Ye were what?"

"Fencing. A type of swordplay."

"Ah? A swordsman? 'Twas an axeman littered that hillside wi' corpses."

"Jar Haz was the axeman. Though I'm sure I could call on his reflexes if needed, I, myself, prefer the blade."

"Oh, Aye. I keep fergettin' ye're not one man, but two."

"Not exactly. Jar Haz, his spirit, is gone. . . ."

Jerry looked thoughtful, remembering the impression of mounted maidens in the sky, the fading sound of triumphant singing. "I think he must have gone to Valhalla. . . ."

"I doubt it not, lad, seein' how he acquitted himself in his final battle."

"Well anyhow, although his spirit has left, some of his knowledge and skills remain, it is as though there were two of us in here. Damn! This is weird!

The dwarf chuckled. "It is that."

He eyed Jerry. "Well, a swordsman should have a blade. D'ye see one that takes yer fancy?"

Jerry examined the fabulous collection of swords. All were masterpieces of the armorer's art, all typical of the period. That is, they were essentially crafted to hack and chop rather than thrust. The edges were keen, but the points too broad for easy penetration.

Brokk watched Jerry's face. "None suit ye, do they, lad?"

"They're great. But none's a fencer's weapon."

"Why?"

"I'll try to show you."

Jerry took up one of the lighter swords. He went through the various fencing positions, illustrating parries, feints, and thrusts, while the dwarf watched with keen interest.

"Ah," said Brokk, "I see. A whole different style! Ye rely more on th' point than th' edge."

"Exactly."

Brokk looked thoughtful. "I'd hate t' be th' one t' face ye in battle," he said slowly. "I see what ye mean about th' blade's design. Hah! Well, gi' me a drawin' o' th' sort o' weapon ye're trained to, an' between us, we'll craft ye a blade t' yer likin'. But first, I've somethin' t' show ye, lad. Somethin' I think will please ye greatly. I finished it only this mornin'."

The dwarf led the way to a workbench in one corner. He pointed to the object lying on it. "What d'ye think o' that?"

Jerry goggled at the articulated steel hand that lay on the bench. It was socketed to fit over his stump, and powered by a system of leather straps, steel wires, springs, and tiny pulleys. It looked extremely complicated.

He glanced at Brokk, his admiration showing in his face. He could hardly contain his excitement.

The little man laughed delightedly. "I told ye I had a surprise fer ye. That's it."

"It works? It really works?"

Brokk looked hurt. "O' course it works. D'ye doubt my skill?"

Jerry was apologetic. "Not a bit. It just looks impossible!"

Taking care not to foul the straps, Jerry picked up the device. The softly padded socket felt comfortable on his stump. Brokk ran the control straps up Jerry's arm, buckled them in place, led them across his back, to loop over his opposite shoulder. He tightened and adjusted until he was satisfied. He stepped back.

"Now lad, t' make th' dingus work, give a slight hunch t' yer right shoulder."Jerry lifted the steel hand to eye level and twitched his shoulder.The cunningly articulated fingers snapped shut. Brokk chuckled. Jerry relaxed his shoulder and the hand opened. He looked at the dwarf. "Son of a gun!"

Brokk picked up a large hammer with a thick oak handle. "Here," he said, "take it from me."

Jerry reached and twitched his shoulder. The steel fingers closed. The stout oak popped, crackled, and splintered, crushed.

Brokk let his breath out in a long whoosh. "I misdoubt I'm ready t' shake hands wi' ye yet, Jerry lad!"

Jerry stared at the splintered wood. "Holy **Jehasophat!**"

Though Jerry would have spent more time in the workshop, Freya insisted that he had done enough for his first outing.

"You can practice your new hand just as well lying down," was her edict. "Back to bed, young man."

Next morning the elf-woman relented, and struck a bargain with him. If he would promise to pace himself, and not push too hard, he could get up when he liked. Ready to promise anything that would get him back to Brokk's shop, Jerry agreed.

The as yet unmastered steel hand proved to be a *little* more of a help than a hindrance, and Jerry managed to dress himself without having to call on Freya for help. The minor triumph put him in high spirits as he hurried to the workshop.

At Brokk's suggestion, Jerry drew a sketch of a sword that was neither epee nor rapier, but a bastard relative.

It was cup-hilted with a cross guard hooked at each end. The blade was just over three feet in length, three quarters of an inch wide, with razor edges that tapered to a needle point.

"And it should be flexible," Jerry explained.

The dwarf looked at the drawing and shook his head. "'Twill never stand against a broadsword, even less against axe or mace. 'Tis too frail altogether."

Jerry explained that the use of this weapon depended not on brute force or strength, but on speed, agility and lightning thrusts.

"Most of all," he grinned, "it depends on not being where your opponent thought you were."

Brokk scratched his head. "Lad, ye're not makin' any sense."

Jerry laughed. "Look," he said, picking up a slender rod about four feet long. "Take that broken spearshaft and pretend it's a broadsword. Come at me as a broadswords man would."

Brokk hesitated. "Ye're askin' fer some painful bruises."

Jerry smiled. "Let's see."

"Very well. Guard yerself."

The little warrior attacked, using the heavy spearshaft in the manner of a broadswordsman, a technique that utilized a sword as little more than a sharpened club.

Jerry met the assault in the manner of a fencer.

More accurately, he faded away before it, giving little ground, but ducking and weaving to right and left, parrying the dwarf's cuts and slashes with twists of the wrist.

Jerry grinned at the startled expression that came over Brokk's face as the dwarf's bone-breaking blows, instead of landing squarely on Jerry's weaker rod and reducing it to splinters, slid along it to one side or the other, never coming close to his opponent's body.

Jerry let the dwarf have time to appreciate his defense, then laughed. "See what I meant about not being where your opponent thought you were? Now, guard yourself."

Jerry went on the offensive, parrying Brokk's blows and retaliating with swift ripostes that stung the little man wherever he chose.

Brokk gave a little gasp as Jerry's point gouged him in the solar plexus, and fell back, crying, "Enough! I yield!"

Jerry was immediately contrite. "I'm sorry. It was an uneven contest. I have the reach on you. And the height."

Brokk sputtered indignantly. "Why ye young puppy, I'll ha' ye know height an' reach ha' nothin' t' do wi' it. If ye'd stand still an' fight, I'd carve ye t' dog meat." He broke off as Jerry burst into laughter.

"I'm sorry, Brokk, I meant no disrespect."

The dwarf's face twisted in a sour grin. "I know that, lad. 'Tis only that I'm mortified t' be bested by a bit o' a twig! Whoosh! 'Twas like fendin' off a swarm o' hornets! Seemed like no matter where I struck, ye were somewhere else! An' that troll-curst point o' yers was everywhere at once!"

CHAPTER SIX

Over the next weeks Jerry practiced constantly, learning to master his new hand. At first it was a real hassle. He broke a lot of Freya's dishes, and ruined a lot of wood before he gained control of it. Eventually, the time came when he could pick up an egg without damaging it. In the beginning, he had to flex his shoulder consciously to activate the prosthesis, but eventually the action became reflex.

The steel hand had become a part of him.

As he learned to use his new hand, Jerry haunted Brokk's workshop, fascinated by the skill of the little smith. The dwarf showed an enthusiasm for the new sword that was as great as Jerry's own.

The morning after the fencing demonstration, Jerry hurried to the forge.

Brokk had already selected a long slender rod of high grade steel, and thrust it into the coals, where it was beginning to glow cherry red.

The dwarf worked the bellows, sending clouds of sparks and soot swirling up the flue. Jerry marveled that the little man could bear the heat radiating from the roaring forge. His arms, face, and upper torso were smeared with soot and sweat and reddened from the temperature.

Using long tongs, he prodded and turned the metal bar, insuring even heat throughout. The rod turned from red to blue-white. Brokk fished it out and turned to a large flat anvil, where he began to flatten it with blows of his hammer.

Time after time, the dwarf returned the iron to the fire and continued his hammering. Before Jerry's fascinated eyes, the iron rod changed to a flat, tapering blade. To Jerry's amazement there were no marks of the hammer on the metal, so great was Brokk's skill at his trade. It took hours, but Jerry's interest never lagged.

At last the dwarf held the rough blade up in the tongs and examined it carefully. He grunted.

"'Tis my thinkin' that 'twill be a monstrous fine bit o' work when finished." He allowed the metal to cool then subjected it to a final scrutiny and gave a nod of satisfaction. "Not a single flaw from one end t' th' other. Ye'll ha' a weapon that'll not let ye down, lad."

Jerry felt like a kid who'd met Santa Claus in person. "Great. What's the next step?"

Brokk removed his leather apron and hung it on a peg. He picked up a wad of rags and, wiped his arms and chest. "Th' next step, son Jerry, is t' ha' our supper an' get some sleep."

At Jerry's look of disappointment the dwarf chuckled. "Ye look like I just took yer honeycomb away. Buck up, lad, ye'll get yer blade."

Crafting a fine sword was not, Jerry discovered, something that happened overnight. It was several days before Brokk placed the finished weapon in his hands. Jerry followed each step in the process with avid interest.

First the blackened metal was scoured with coarse sand to remove scale and rust. Then came hours of filing and shaping to make the edges keen, the point needle sharp, and to assure that the slim sliver of steel remained perfectly straight. The hilt was of bronze, had a cup-shaped guard to protect the hand, and a cross-piece that hooked at either end.

Jerry explained the use of the cross-piece, and demonstrated how an opponent's blade could be trapped in the hooked curve, and sent flying with a twist of the wrist.

Before the hilt could be riveted to the tang, however, the blade had to be tempered. For this process Brokk sent Jerry from the workshop.

"'Tis a method known only t' us o' th' dwarf kind," he explained. "I hope ye'll take no offense, lad, but 'tis a secret we're pledged t' keep.

"I can tell ye only that th' process consists o' many heatin's an' quenchin's in water an' oil, an' other, secret, steps that take most o' a day. Then th' blade must remain buried o'er night in a closed metal chest filled wi' hot coals an' other things. . . ."

Brokk continued to exclude Jerry from the shop most of the following day, and at last, called him in to view the finished product.

The dwarf pointed to a workbench and said, "There ye are, lad. Does it meet yer fancy?"

Jerry felt goose bumps. The weapon lying on the scarred table was a swordsman's dream. A slim tongue of glowing steel. The bronze hilt gleamed like gold. He picked it up. The balance was perfect. It felt as though it grew from his hand. He could almost sense the entire length down to the tip. The sword was light, but had heft. Jerry cut a few figure eights through the air. He took a deep breath and looked at the dwarf. "It's a magnificent blade!"

"Aye, an' it's more than a point, lad. It has an edge as well." The dwarf set an unfinished helmet on the table. "Strike. Strike it wi' th' full force o' yer arm."

Jerry struck with an overarm swing that sliced through the iron, cleaving the helmet into two pieces. The air of the shop was filled with a high, pure singing from the vibrating blade. Jerry examined the edge. Not a nick! "Gor!" he marveled.

Brokk laughed delightedly.

Now Jerry had two activities to engage him. Learning to use his new hand, and practicing with his new sword. Gaining mastery over the steel hand posed no problem, but fencing against imaginary opponents was something less than satisfactory.

Brokk watched the youngster restlessly going through the moves of attack and defense. He chuckled. "Wouldn't that be more effective if ye had someone t' oppose?"

Jerry grounded the tip of his sword, and looked at the dwarf. "It couldn't hurt," he grinned.

Brokk buckled on his breastplate, and tossed Jerry a target shield. "Pick a helmet t' yer likin' an' we'll visit th' Tradin' Glen. 'Tis time ye saw th' sun again."

Jerry shrugged into an ill-fitting mail shirt, and donned a conical helmet that more or less fit. He had been made aware that only serfs and villagers went abroad in this world unarmed and unarmored.

Brokk looked at him. "Ye need mail an' helm t' fit ye. We'll set about outfittin, ye proper tomorrow. Come. Let's see what th' Glen has t' offer in th' way o' interest t' ye."

Although, during his recovery, Jerry had met a number of the Little People of Svartheim, this would be his first encounter with the humans of Midgard, World of Men.

The Trading Glen was a bowl-shaped clearing just outside the entrance to the dwarfholm, where dwarf and man met on terms of armed truce to conduct commerce. Armed truce, because men were looked on with suspicion and distrust in general, and with reason, Jerry learned.

The world of men feared and hated the dwarfs. The fear and hatred generated, as is most hate and fear, through lack of understanding.

Brokk explained. "Men hate us because they believe us to be abductors o' human children which we use fer dark an' evil rituals. The truth is that we Wee Folk rescue deformed children who have been abandoned or mistreated by their own kind, an' raise them as our own. The Little People return their hatred because o' th' persecution."

The dwarf shook his head. "'Tis a shame."

But the misconception maintained. Men traded with the dwarfs only because nowhere else could they obtain such fine weapons and armor.

They traded also for the gold, silver, and precious stones that the dwarfs, a race of miners, had in such abundance that they held them to be of little value.

It was here that Jerry encountered his first giants.

They were hulking, surly brutes, nine to twelve feet tall, clad for the most part in the skins of seal and walrus, and the white fur of the ice bears that roamed their frozen homeland. Vile tempered and hostile, they nevertheless curbed their natural enmity for the sake of bartering for the superior weapons of dwarfen manufacture.

The journey from Jotunheim to Svartheim was one of many months, but the weapons thus obtained, Brokk said, gave the buyer a great advantage over his fellows. It was to gain this advantage that they made the trek.

Jerry eyed the surly giants dubiously. "I don't know that I think much of the idea of putting weapons in their hands."

Brokk grinned. "Nor would I, except that centuries ago 'twas made a condition o' th' trade that th' weapons thus obtained would never be used against dwarf or elf.

"Strangely enough, lad, 'tis a promise that's never been broken."

Jerry, whom the dwarfs knew to be close to Brokk, was allowed to come and go at will, something unique for one of the human kind in the underground dwarfholm.

Accompanied by Bryn, who never let him out of her sight, he visited the Glen often. There he hired some of the trader-warriors to spar with him. In sparing with the traders, Jerry developed a bewildering fighting style.

In the beginning, he used the standard Viking round target-shield strapped to his arm. As he gained mastery over the steel hand he forewent the shield. Instead, Brokk forged for him a small round plate less than a foot in diameter, which he secured to his forearm above the metal fist. With this to parry anything short of a full-arm swing of axe or mace, combined with his flashing point and the steel hand to rip chunks from shield or armor, the one-time Salesman of the Year of Nationwide Insurance Corporation was a formidable battlefield presence.

Jerry began to take on adversaries in groups of three to five. All went away muttering thanks to their various gods that they would never meet the red-bearded youth in actual combat.

Within three months it became apparent that word of the invincible young warrior with the hand of steel had spread among the traders, and he could find no one who would spar with him even for gold.

Jerry traveled with Brokk on many of the little man's errands about the underground world. He learned much about the way of life among the Little People. He visited other forges including that of Sindri, Brokk's brother, who was acknowledged as the second best armorer in Svartheim.

Brokk, Jerry discovered, was a man of considerable importance in the subterranean world. When he brought it up, the little man shrugged it aside. "Ye make too much o' too little, lad. I'm a fair hand at th' craftin' o' metal, but then so are th' most o' us."

From others, though, he got a different opinion. Brokk was high amongst them, many looking on him in the light of a king.

Once again, Jerry's mind turned to the Norse mythology he'd read as a kid. According to myth it was Brokk, King of the Dwarfs, who had made the magic golden armlet worn by Odin, Father of the Gods. The magic bracelet that each nine days dropped eight golden bracelets in its own image. Brokk, the Dwarf King, who had forged the blade of the god Tyr, known as the Swordsman of the Gods.

And it was the Dwarf King who had made Thor's hammer, the magic hammer that when thrown by the God of Thunder, returned immediately to his hand.

Thor's hammer, the most powerful weapon possessed by the gods. . . the lightning. He remembered that Freya had called her husband Brokk Hammermacher.

Brokk Hammer-maker!

He broached the subject. Just once. The little man turned red in the face, and stamped his foot in rage. "Odin's bellybutton!" he growled, "Not ye, too? Am I never t' be quit o' that silly tale?" He waved a knotted fist in Jerry's face. "If ye'd be my friend, never mention that bit o' nonsense again."

Although there was much to engage his attention, Jerry was beginning to get restless. The underground kingdom contained no lack of marvels, but he missed the trees, the sun and the open sky.

He was in the forge, putting the final touches to the helmet he was fashioning for himself under Brokk's supervision. A last tap of the hammer, and he lifted it to eye level for inspection. Not bad. Okay, it was good. Now it needed only to be rolled back and forth in a barrel of sand to cleanse it of scale and rust, and Brokk could temper it for him. Then webbing and padding, and he'd have a skull of steel to protect the one of bone. A simple round steel cap to which he would attach a bit of chain mail to hang down the back and protect his neck.

Brokk entered the forge. He took the casque from Jerry, and inspected it. "Well done, lad, well done. I'll make a smith o' ye yet."

He laid the helmet on a workbench. "I've a surprise fer ye. Come along. Ye're about t' meet yer first goblin.

"Goblin?"

"Aye. 'Tis fer him I've been waitin'. He's called Ulf th' Far Traveled. A rover by nature, he's made th' journey t' Asgard half a dozen times. He knows trails an' bypaths that can get us safely through th' perils o' such an adventure, especially through th' land o' th' trolls."

Jerry looked blank. "Trolls? Asgard?"

Brokk grinned. "Aye, lad. Asgard. Th' City o' th, Gods. Where we must go if ye're t' see yer Janet again."

CHAPTER SEVEN

The 'gods' were mentioned, it seemed like, in every other breath by the peoples of Skandia, and Brokk had spoken of visiting them for aid in returning to Janet. But Jerry had never really taken either the gods or Brokk's proposal at face value. In his mind, Jerry had rationalized the various races of this strange world into which held been precipitated.

Dwarfs, elves and giants were self-explanatory. Malfunction of the pituitary, the gland that promotes growth. All three deviations from the norm were present in his old world, dwarfs, elves (midgets), and though rare, giants.

Goblins he reckoned to be the more unfortunately deformed, the hunchbacked, the clubfooted. Sufferers from a rare bone disease that caused the bones of the skull to continue growing until the victim's face resembled a nightmare of bulging brow and cheeks, a jutting prognathous jaw. Combining all these unfortunate features would produce a creature that Jerry had no difficulty in accepting as a goblin.

Brokk had told him how the Wee Folk had gotten the reputation of child stealers. In the far past a number of the deformed children who'd been abandoned by their folk had survived to band together. As they grew, they developed a pity for others of their kind, and rescued those who'd been cast out or abused by their own folk.

It is unfortunate, that even among outcasts, class distinctions arise. The midgets looked down on the dwarfs who were not so finely formed. The giants were contemptuous of all smaller folk. The ugly goblins were despised by all, and came to hate all. The outcasts formed separate tribes and by breeding with their own kind, became distinct races.

Gods and trolls, however, refused to fall into such easily labeled slots.

For generations dwarf and elf had warred on one another, but several centuries back the Little People, being so nearly alike, buried their differences and became friends and allies.

"So we go to see the gods," Jerry smiled.

Brokk chuckled. "Ye doubt me, eh?"

"Well, you don't mean Odin, Thor, Tyr, Loki and that bunch, do you?"

"Ye seem t' know o' them."

"Well, yeah, but they're only creations of the ancient Scandinavian mythology. . . ."

Brokk raised his eyebrows. "Are they, now? Ancient Skandia, ye say. 'Ancient' from what perspective? Yers? Or mine?"

The question jolted Jerry right down to the ground. Up until now he'd just been drifting, accepting the oddity of his situation, but never really coming to grips with it. But there it was, face to face: the fact that the little Hindu really had scooted him back along time! This wasn't 'ancient' Skandia. This was *now* Skandia. This was *today* Skandia. *Modern* Skandia, if the word 'modern' could be said to have any meaning.

How had the little mystic put it? He was riding the tip of the spear! There was nothing ahead of the spear point until it was lived. *There was no future, only the past!* The wind left Jerry's lungs in a cry of grief.

There was no Janet!

There would be no Janet until he had lived her. And he'd never live her, because he would have been dust for centuries by the time the nineteen nineties rolled around. No Janet!

Jerry's knees buckled, and he would have sunk to the rock floor had not the dwarf leaped and caught him, half-carried him to a bench. Brokk's face flooded with concern. "What is it, lad? What ails ye?"

Jerry looked at the little man with dull eyes, and in a dead voice explained.

The dwarf paced back and forth, stumping agitatedly on his short thick legs. "Na-Na, that can't be th' whole o' it, lad. There's some'at we're o'erlookin'. Look ye, lad, *ye* came from th' future, did ye not? Then it must exist, or how could ye be here now?"

Jerry lifted his head with hope, but his half-formed expression of joy faded. "I came back into my own *past*, not from your *future*, do you see?"

"No lad, I don't see. There's some'at amiss here. Oh, I don't doubt yer magician's knowledge o' th' way o' it, but somethin's akilter."

The little man gnawed at his thumb. "Ah!" He brightened, and clapped Jerry on the shoulder. "Buck up, son Jerry. Ye say ye came back along th' line o' yer own past. Well, th' thought comes t' me that if *ye* had a past, then this Janet o' yers must ha' one also, d'ye not agree?"

Hope blazed up in Jerry. Of course! The dwarf was right! The bright fire dimmed a little. "Yes, but how the devil does that help?"

Brokk laughed and pounded Jerry's shoulder again. "That, my boy, is what we'll learn when we reach Asgard."

The flame of hope flared up again, and this time continued to burn brightly. "Right. Let's go meet this fabulous guide of yours. When can we start?"

The dwarf chuckled. "Gently, lad. All in good time."

The goblin seated at the table in Freya's kitchen was the ugliest being Jerry had ever seen. His first impression was of a huge hunched and evil spider. A twisted hump caused the hideous head to thrust forward on a slim stalk of a neck. The bloated torso sprouted abnormally long arms and legs, spindly and frail appearing, that enhanced the impression of a giant spider. Seated, the apparition's knees rose above the level of his shoulders, and his arms were proportionate to his legs.

The creature was clad in a close-fitting jerkin of green-dyed leather and brown wool trousers cross-gartered to the knee. Its bulbous chest was protected by a battered steel breastplate. From his belt hung a braided sling and a pouch of leaden bullets. A short, broad-bladed sword was strapped crosswise of his hump with the hilt protruding above his right shoulder. A conical helmet with an oversized nasal lay on the table. An assegai, or short stabbing spear, and a target shield lay on the floor beside him.

The goblin turned his head in Jerry's direction and Jerry just managed to suppress a shudder of revulsion. The face was a nightmare. Its brow was a ledge of bone that left the eyes hidden in caverns of shadow. Instead of a nose, a short trunk lifted, questing the air inquisitively above a mouth that was a lipless slit filled with crooked, wicked-looking fangs.

"Ulf," Brokk said, "I'd have ye meet a young friend o' mine. Jerry, ye've heard me speak o' Ulf th' Far Traveled."

The goblin half-rose and extended a long-fingered hand. As he did so, the light revealed his eyes. At sight of the humanity, compassion, and bubbling humor mirrored there, Jerry never again thought of Ulf as being ugly.

Jerry took the proffered hand extended in friendship and made a discovery. The fragile looking arms were deceiving. From Ulf's handclasp, those arms seemed to be muscled with steel cables.

The goblin chuckled. Like his eyes, his voice was at odds with his appearance, being deep and musical. "I greet you, friend Jerry." He chuckled again. "And congratulate you. Many of the human kind, on seeing me for the first time, faint."

Jerry had the grace to blush.

Brokk, joining in his friend's laugh, pulled out a stool, and sat, motioning for Jerry to do the same. Freya brought drinking horns and a small cask of ale. She winked at Jerry. "It's always a long night when Ulf comes to visit."

The little elf-woman seated herself at one end of the table with a basket of mending, eager to hear the goblin's account of his voyaging.

Ulf had a droll, entertaining way of relating his adventures, that held his audience rapt. He had a knack of sketching vivid little word pictures that put the listener right there in the heart of the action. Although the goblin modestly downplayed his own part in the risks involved, it was easy to see that the misshapen creature was a being of high courage, with a real concern for others.

Jerry shot Brokk a puzzled glance.

The dwarf chuckled. "I see ye're questionin' my description o' th' goblin kind. Ye'll mind I told ye there be some among 'em not poisoned wi' th' hatred." The little man gave his friend a look of affection. "Nowhere will ye find a stouter companion nor a faster friend than Ulf."

If the goblin's fanged and snouted face could be said to reflect embarrassment, Ulf's did so. He turned to Jerry. "Those of the dwarf kind are prone to exaggeration, friend Jerry. It's a failin' of their breed."

The goblin's face twisted in a frightening grimace. It took Jerry a moment to recognize it as a smile. "It's my belief that they deal in tall tales t' make up for their lack of height."

Brokk scowled. "Why, ye spindle-shanked, twig-armed blatherer, I'll show ye height. I. . . ." He broke off as Ulf's deep laugh and Freya's elfin tinkle joined.

The dwarf blushed. He grinned at Jerry. "D'ye see what I must endure fer th' sake o' friendship?"

Jerry grinned back at the little man and patted him on the arm. "There, there," he said with mock solicitude, "*I* don't think you're short."

Brokk eyed the grinning Jerry balefully. "Short, eh? How'd ye like me t' shorten yer *other* arm?"

"Ouch!"

"Just ye mind yer manners, ye young puppy. I don't want t' be put t' th' trouble o' craftin' ye another hand."

Jerry grinned. "Yes, Father."

Brokk spoke to the goblin in a confidential aside. "Ye ha' t' remind these children how t' show th' proper respect fer their betters or they begin t' think too highly o' themselves."

Ulf chuckled. "Oh, absolutely," he agreed, winking at Jerry.

The goblin's smile faded. "Brokk's quite right about my folk. Only Odin knows why the goblin kind carry within them this hatred of all other races. Only the trolls out-do us in that, and that's because trolls are truly monsters without a flicker of any other emotion."

Ulf shuddered. "Monsters!" he repeated.

A thrill of horror coursed up and down Jerry's spine. What nightmare creatures these trolls must be to excite fear and disgust in even the hideous goblin!

Jerry looked at Brokk. "You've mentioned trolls several times, but you never said much about them."

Ulf's revulsion was mirrored in the dwarf's face. "He's right. Monsters be what they are. Soulless. Wi'out a trace o' humanity or pity. 'Tis my belief that even Hel, Dark Goddess o' th' Underworld bars them from her Realm o' Death, an' makes 'em wander forever between th' winds." The dwarf shuddered violently.

Jerry licked dry lips. "You've seen them?"

"Aye lad, once. When I journeyed t' Jotunheim in my youth." He shuddered again.

"Bein's wi' two heads. Some wi' three or more arms or legs. Some wi' tentacles like a squid, in place o' arms. One abomination wi' two bodies joined t' th' same head. Two o' our party fell into their hands an' were eaten."

"They're cannibals?"

Ulf answered. "Aye. They don't eat their own sort, but any stranger wanderin' into their land is meat for th' pot."

Jerry shivered.

Brokk's face cleared, throwing off its look of horror, and he laughed. "Well lad, are ye still eager t' travel t' Asgard t' seek yer Janet?"

Jerry growled. "It'll take more than trolls to stop me."

Ulf chuckled. "Oh, there's more, all right. But I've made th' journey safely several times. 'Twon't be easy, but with th' blessin' of Odin and a lot of luck, we'll make it."

"You'll guide us, then?"

"Of course. Didn't Brokk tell you?"

"Not in so many words." Jerry was curious. He looked at the goblin. "Why?"

Ulf's hump convulsed in a shrug. "Why? Because I am Ulf the Far Traveled." The goblin chuckled. "How can I be Ulf the Far Traveled if I don't travel?"

Jerry laughed.

"Besides, Brokk told me of your lost Janet. What sort of adventurer could resist such a challenge?"

Jerry looked at the hideously hunched and twisted, spidery-limbed gargoyle. "By the pink beard of the Prophet," he grinned, "Ulf the Far Traveled is a romantic!"

The goblin accomplished the impossible, he blushed.

"My reasons are my own," he snarled. "D'you want my help or do you not?"

Jerry was immediately contrite. "I meant no offense, friend Ulf," he said formally. "I trespassed on short acquaintance to presume to tease you. Please accept my apology, though I assure you my laughter was directed equally at myself. I recognized a fellow dreamer."

The goblin's face relaxed into his horrifying smile.

"Well spoken, lad," he said, "If fellow dreamers we be, then fellows in all else we'll be as well, and here's my hand on it."

Jerry clasped the spidery fingers warmly, deeply moved.

Brokk cleared his throat. "Humph," he grunted, dipping the drinking horns into the ale cask, and handing them around. "Here's t' good companions," he said.

Jerry and the goblin echoed the words. The warmth Jerry felt flowing through him was not caused by the strong ale.

Bryn padded into the room. As she caught the goblin's alien scent, she crouched, quivering. The hair along her spine rose, and her haunches bunched to spring. Her lips pulled back from her fangs, and a growl rumbled in her throat.

Jerry shouted, "No, Bryn! Down!" The big dog ignored him, preparing to leap.

From Freya's lips came a low, penetrating note. The war-dog's cropped ears lifted. She relaxed slightly, and looked at the elf-woman.

The weird sound rose and fell.

Tension went out of the bristling dog. She whined, and straightened from her attack mode. Her stump of a tail wagged, and she went to Ulf and licked his hand. Jerry stared at the tiny beauty, goggle-eyed.

Both Brokk and the goblin laughed.

"I told ye, did I not, o' th' Elfin Gift? O' th' ability o' th' elves t' communicate wi' th' beasts?"

Jerry was beginning to suspect more and more that whenever this was that the little Hindu had sent him back to, it was definitely not along his original space-time line! "But. . . ." he stammered.

The dwarf chuckled. "But. . . ." he mimicked. "Mayhap ye thought I was exaggeratin' or makin' sport o' ye?"

"I guess. . . . I suppose I did. Things like this just don't happen back where I came from."

He looked at Ulf. The goblin chuckled. Brokk folded short, knotted forearms on the table and leaned toward Jerry. "Lad," he said soberly, "I know nothin' o' th' world ye came from, but I suspect it t' be vastly different from th' one ye're in now.

"I ha' no doubt that ye've yer own magic an' wonders that would leave Ulf an' me gawkin' as ye do from time t' time."

The dwarf laid a hand on Jerry's arm. "But lad, ye'd do best t' ferget that world, an' take heed o' this world in which ye'll live. Or die. It comes t' me that ye've doubted much o' what I've told ye. Doubt me not, lad.

"I took an immediate likin' t' ye, boy, when first I clapped eyes on ye on that blood-soaked hillside. A likin' that's grown t' lovin' ye like a son."

He looked at his wife. "As has that one."

The elf-woman laid aside her mending, rose, and rounded the table. She took Jerry's face between her hands and kissed his cheek.

"It is as he says, dear. You've come to fill an emptiness. Odin, in his wisdom, has seen fit not to bless us with children of our own, but has, in his charity, sent us you to take their place."

Jerry's eyes stung and tears spilled down his bearded cheeks. He tried to speak, but couldn't. He could just look from the elf-woman to the dwarf.

Freya laughed warmly. "Your eyes say it all, my son."

Brokk harrumphed. "There," he said gruffly, "Enough o' this twaddle. D'ye see, lad, what I'm tryin' t' tell ye? Ye've got t' lay aside th' way o' thinkin' in yer old world, an' think in th' terms ye'll find here.

"From what ye've said, I get th' belief that ye've no gods where ye come from. But here th' gods are real. Th' trolls are real. Th' robber barons an' rovin' mercenary bands o' Midgard are real, an' death at th' hands o' any o' them is real!"

Brokk looked at Ulf and chuckled. "An' as ye can see, goblins are real."Jerry smiled sheepishly.

The dwarf went on. "I know not th' perils that might beset such a journey as we propose in yer old world, but in this world, my son, ye'd best take t' heart what Ulf an' I tell ye t' be th' way o' things."

Jerry listened to the little man, looked at his concerned face, and motivated by Jar Haz's instincts, went to the dwarf and knelt. He raised the little man's hand to his lips, then rested his forehead on its back. The ritual words rose from the Viking's memories to his lips.

"Guide me, Father," he said, "for I am thy child."

"Get up," Brokk grumbled, "Get up, ye hulkin' great lout. I'll not have ye slobberin' all over me. . . ."

Smiling, Jerry rose, and kneeling before Freya, repeated the rite. "Guide me, Mother, for I am thy child."

The elf-woman stroked the kneeling boy's head. Instead of words, a low crooning sound came from her lips.

In Jerry's mind rose pictures of a sparkling waterfall, of a doe nuzzling a spindle-legged fawn, of dew-spattered flowers. Leaping exaltations of larks, of sunlight on the laughing faces of children, and he knew the depth of her happiness.

Ulf cleared his throat noisily and his trunk of a nose waved from side to side, a mannerism that Jerry grew to recognize as a sign that he was deeply moved.

The goblin spoke. His words were formal as he completed the ritual."Before a witness, the lad known as Jerry Jar Haz has declared his submission to the will of Brokk of Svartheim and the Lady Freya, his wife."

He looked from one to the other. "Do you accept his homage, Brokk of Svartheim, and accept Jerry Jar Haz as your adopted son?"

The dwarf grinned and waved a negligent hand. "Oh aye, I take responsibility fer th' puppy."

Ulf's formality cracked, and he laughed. He looked at Freya. The elf-woman hugged Jerry and smiled. "You know I do."

Jerry's heart swelled at the love he felt surrounding him.

Ulf cleared his throat, honked, and wiped his trunk on a swatch of cloth.

Brokk uttered a bray of laughter. "By Odin's one eye!" he chortled. "A sentimental goblin!"

Ulf glared at him. "Do you think it possible that we might now get down to the business at hand?"

Brokk smothered his chuckles "Oh aye, t' business it is, old friend." He waved a hand at Jerry. "Sit ye down, lad. Ulf would t' business."

The goblin snorted.

"I've all my charts in my head," he said. "Well enough for my own reference, but of little use to young Jerry here. D'you suppose you could curb your mirth long enough to fetch out a map or two so as t' show our young friend something of what lies before us?"

Brokk stood up. "Aye, I can. If ye'll fergive me fer accusin' ye o' havin' a heart."

Ulf grinned sourly. "I'm a goblin. It's well known that goblins have no hearts."

Brokk winked at Jerry. "T' be sure. An' 'tis equally well known that the Little People are stealers o' children."

Ulf laughed.

The dwarf went to a brass-bound oaken chest against one wall. He rummaged through it for a moment and returned to the table with several rolls of parchment. He studied each briefly, and selecting one, he spread it on the table.

Jerry and the goblin moved around to his side.

"Here," the dwarf explained, "ye have Svartheim." His finger jabbed down on the chart.

Jerry studied the finely detailed and illustrated map. All Skandia was laid out before him.

To the south, in the Southern Range was his present position. He noted that from the public entrance to the underground world of the dwarfs, only one steep cleft in the crags led down to Midgard, the world of men. Circling Midgard was the beautifully detailed representation of a snake holding its tail in its mouth.

Jerry looked questioningly at Brokk.

The dwarf smiled. "'Tis Jortmungand th' Serpent ye see," he said. "One o' th' children o' Loki, God o' Mischief, th' Doer o' Good an' th' Doer o' Evil. He's th' Sly One o' th' gods. Th' one ye can never foretell. Even Odin Allfather cannot predict which way Loki's humor will send him. He's unpredictable as th' winds o' chance, capable o' great good or unspeakable cruelty, as his fancy takes him.

"Loki has three children. Hel, half livin' woman. . . half rottin' corpse, who rules th' land o' th' dead. The second is Fenrir the Wolf, who ever stalks th' sun an' th' moon, ready t' gobble 'em up on th' Gotterdamarung, th' final war 'twixt th' gods an' th' giants. An' Jortmungand th' Midgard Serpent who, as ye can see, holds th' world o' men in his coils, ready t' crush it when th' final battle begins."

Jerry grinned. "Nice bunch of kids." He looked from Brokk to Ulf. The goblin shrugged. "Th' tales of th' ancient gods," he said. "Whether they're true or not," He shrugged again. "who knows?"

It was as Jerry had read in the Norse mythology he'd studied as a child. He recalled that in an effort to restrain the great wolf, Fenrir, the gods had tricked him into allowing them to bind him.

Suspicious, the wolf agreed on condition that he hold the right hand of Tyr the Swordsman in his mouth. When Fenrir found that he could not free himself, he bit off the Swordsman's hand, thus weakening the gods when the Gotterdamarung should come.

"Yeah," Jerry repeated, "nice bunch of kids." Brokk chuckled.

"'Tis told that Odin, tired o' Loki's pranks, had him carried down into th' underworld where his daughter reigns, an' had him chained t' a rock.

"Over his head, Odin caused a great snake t' coil, and' from its fangs venom drips onto Loki's face. Venom that burns like fire.

"Hel, bein' a dutiful daughter, holds a bowl t' catch th' fallin' poison, thus savin' her father from pain. But when th' bowl is full, she must turn aside t' empty it, an' th' burnin' venom strikes its mark. 'Tis then that Loki's roars o' pain shake th' earth, causin' great tremors that open chasms an' precipitate avalanches, landslides, an' tidal waves. . . ."

Jerry laughed. "Seismologists back home would have a ball with that explanation!"

"Eh?"

"Magicians known as scientists, who claim to predict earthquakes," Jerry grinned.

"Oh."

Brokk's finger moved across the map.

"Here in Midgard are th' robber barons. Yarls an' Thanes an' petty kings who war constantly on one another. They attack an' despoil any who enter their territory lackin' th' strength t' defend themselves.

"In addition t' these thievin' nobles are th' rovin' bands o' mercenaries offerin' their swords t' any who'll pay their price. They roam th' land between times takin' what they will. Rapin', robbin', an' murderin, fer sport."

"Sounds like the Middle East," Jerry said dryly.

At Brokk's blank look, he waved a hand. "Never mind," he laughed, "A local joke."

The dwarf grunted. His finger moved again. "Now here," he grinned, "is where we leave th' easy part an' th' venture begins t' take on aspects o' interest."

Jerry stifled a mock yawn. "I was wondering when it might start to get interesting."

Brokk chuckled. "I misdoubt ye'll find much o' it borin', ye young puppy, but in truth this be th' chanciest leg o' th' journey."

His blunt finger stabbed an area colored bright blue. "Here," he growled, "Here be th' Glowin' Earth. . . Trollheim." The fearless little man shuddered. "Here," Brokk said tensely, "yer very soul be in danger."

The horror plain in the faces of the others crept into Jerry's consciousness, and he felt a cold hand clutch at his guts. "What do you mean?"

The dwarf said slowly, "I mean, lad, if ye tarry o'erlong in that blighted place ye may, yerself, turn into a troll."

The little man's voice sank to a whisper. "Far worse, Jerry lad, ye may become later on, th' *father* o' trolls. . . ."

Brokk shook his head in horror. "But," he said more cheerfully, "it's been proven that if ye linger no more than three days in th' curst land ye've no danger o' that."

Jerry looked at the blue colored sector. "Do you mean the 'Glowing Earth' actually glows?"

"Aye, lad."

Jerry no longer doubted the existence of trolls.

'Glowing Earth'. . . radiation!

'Trolls'? Mutants!

'Father of trolls?' Jerry had no doubt at all that extended exposure to the radiation would result in genetic changes that could produce monstrosities.

What if they were unavoidably delayed in that hellish place? What if he were exposed too long to the damnable rays? What? There was only one answer.

If he spent more than seventy-two hours in Trollheim his search for Janet was over.

It ended there. He would not, *he would not*, seek her out if any possibility existed that their union might produce a monster.

He would abandon his search, and join Ulf on his endless travels, if the goblin would have him. Jerry kept this resolve to himself.

Brokk was continuing his talk. "Beyond Trollheim we come t' Ginnungagap, th' Chasm o' Chasms, a cleft left in th' earth by th' axe o' Ymir, th' first giant. So deep is it, it has no bottom, an' as I told ye, must be crossed by th' help o' th' Ice Elves an' their flyin' dragons." The little man looked at Jerry and grinned. "An' that's always a chancy thing. Th' Ice

Elves be a moody folk, an' it's odds one way or th' other, whether they'll let ye ride their dragons, or feed ye to 'em.

"If we be still alive at this point, we reach Jotunheim. 'Tis that land o' never endin' snow an' ice I told ye of, wi' swirlin' mists cold enough t' freeze yer lungs."

Brokk grinned. "Ye've seen a giant or two, lad, but only in their gentler moods. An angry giant. . . *an angry bent on makin' mincemeat o' ye.* . . well, ye can see how it could become fairly interestin'." The dwarf laughed. "D'ye still want t' go?"

"Piece of cake."

Brokk chuckled. "Th' rest is easy. We've only t' climb th' Ultimate Peak, cross th' Rainbow Bridge an' lay yer problem afore th' gods."

"Piece of cake."

CHAPTER EIGHT

Now that Ulf had arrived, preparations for the journey to the gods went forward quickly. Brokk fashioned Jerry a shirt of chain mail, and gave a final tempering to his helmet.

Ulf cast more bullets. The leaden balls weighing an ounce each were ammunition for his sling, a weapon that Jerry was to learn the goblin could handle with almost the speed and accuracy of a repeating rifle.

Their departure date was delayed by nearly three weeks by Freya's announcement that she was going with them.

"Ye'll *not!*" Brokk roared. "I'll not ha' ye exposin' yerself t' th' dangers o' such a perilous venture, an' that's an end o' it!"

The elf-woman's lips thinned. She put her fists on her hips and thrust her face into the red, scowling visage of her husband. "I go, Brokk Hammermacher, and *that's* the end of it."

"Ye'll *not!*"

"I *will!*"

A wheedling tone crept into the dwarf's voice as though he knew he'd already lost the argument. "I cannot let ye danger yerself, my darlin'. What if aught should happen t' ye?"

Freya smiled, knowing she had won. "You know quite well, husband, that I can protect myself with the Gift. I'll be no burden on you, dear one, as you also well know. The Gift is a powerful weapon that can be used to protect us all, or be thrown into a fray at your side."

The tiny beauty rose on tiptoes and kissed her husband on the mouth. "Now stop your braying, my dear. I'm going."

The dwarf threw up his hands in frustration. "Am I never t' win an argument in my own home?"

Freya giggled. "No, dear," she said.

Growling, Brokk conceded defeat. But he was as adamant as she, when he stated flatly that they'd not move a foot until he'd crafted armor fit to protect his treasure.

Night and day, the sound of Brokk's hammer could be heard in the forge as the little man interlocked tiny iron rings, no bigger than Freya's little fingernail, to form the mesh of a metal shirt.

Jerry and the goblin stayed away from the shop, knowing that the dwarf was too intent on his work to want distraction.

Word spread through the caverns of Svartheim that a large caravan of traders from Midgard had gathered in the bowl-shaped depression, too small to be called a valley, that lay before the principal entrance to the dwarfholm.

These gatherings occurred two or three times a year. They were the occasion for the Little People to stock up on the things unobtainable in the underground world. Wool, linen, hides. Fresh fruits and vegetables. Long straight shafts of yew and ash to be made into spear shafts and bows. Wine, ale, and the drink of fermented honey, called mead.

In exchange, the traders took away the fine dwarfen weapons, armor, jewels, and precious metals that the dwarf kind held in abundance.

The gathering was also a time for merrymaking and contests of arms. These contests were in the nature of a tourney rather than actual combat, but were fierce and competitive, and frequently ended in death or crippling injury. It was a way for the humans to get the feel of their new weapons and show off their battle skills.

There were archery competitions and spear-casting. There was swordplay, and axe and shield work. Less often, slingers would vie with one another, the sling being a weapon taking great skill to master.

Leaving Brokk to his forge, Jerry and the goblin traversed the miles of tunnels and caverns to reach the surface to join in the revelry.

"Maybe there'll be somebody in this mob who hasn't heard of me," Jerry grinned.

Ulf, who'd never seen Jerry's bewildering fighting style, was unimpressed. "Are you, then, a warrior such as none dare face?"

Jerry looked smug. "I've established some small reputation hereabouts as being moderately familiar with weapons."

The goblin grinned his nightmare grin. "I'm glad t' hear it. Now I can face Trollheim with less fear." He eyed the slim length of steel at Jerry's belt.

Jerry chuckled to himself. His unorthodox blade and technique would surprise the goblin as it had all his opponents.

The two companions passed through the many defensive checkpoints. At each, they were recognized as intimates of Brokk's, and greeted warmly. They emerged from the caverns into the sunlit world.

At sight of the tall goblin, men shrank back, and handled their weapons in the face of this traditional enemy.

Ulf eyed the hostile circle. The men muttered ominously, and Jerry moved to his friend's side, hand on swordhilt.

Jerry had been warned by Ulf and the dwarf of this reaction to the goblin's appearance at the gathering, and had been instructed as to how he should respond.

He stepped forward and raised his left hand. Sunlight glinted on the steel fingers as he flexed them. "Do any among you know me?"

There was a murmur in the crowd, and the sound of rueful laughter came from several quarters. A number of voices shouted, "Aye, we know you, Red-beard."

One laughing voice yelled, "Aye, I know ye, and I still bear th' scars t' prove it." The man's friends joined his laughter.

A barrel-chested, leather-clad axeman with a huge braided yellow beard stepped forward. He raised his half-moon in salute. "I know ye, Thor's Fist. I know ye as a man o' heart and a stout adversary. What is yer wish?"

Jerry placed a hand on Ulf's shoulder. "This is Ulf the Far Traveled. He is one of the Rover Goblins. Ulf bears enmity toward no man who'd be his friend. He is my true friend, and will be yours if you'll let it be so."

'The red-beard drew his rapier, and held it high. "Before Odin I pledge my sword and my life that this is so." He looked from face to face in the crowd.

The leather-clad axeman turned to his fellows. "Th' word o' th' Fist o' Thor be good enough for me. What say ye? Is th' goblin t' walk among us?

There were few dissenting votes. These from ones who had never matched weapons with Jerry or seen him in action. The main body of the traders accepted the red-beard's pledge, and disbanded, returning to whatever activities had been interrupted by the goblin's arrival.

However, a small group of hard-eyed ruffians, a trades band never before seen at the gathering, stood glaring at the goblin and his human companion.

"I've heard o' th' human scum who band with th' Twisted Ones against their own kind," muttered one, fingering the hilt of his broadsword.

"But never before have I laid eyes on one o' 'em." He spat on the ground.

Jerry stepped toward the grumbling broadswordsman. He smiled pleasantly. "Did you call me scum?"

"Aye. And all who'd make pact with th' goblin kind."

"Didn't you hear me say that Ulf is friendly to the human kind?"

"I heard yer lie."

Jerry sighed. "Now you call me liar. Are you determined, then, to make an enemy of me?"

Most of the traders who had wandered off, began to drift back, forming a circle of grinning spectators. They'd seen Thor's Fist in action before.

Ulf looked uneasy. The grumbler was backed by three of his comrades, and the goblin feared for Jerry's safety, but he could do nothing to second the red-beard.

Any hint of goblin-against-human would turn the entire mass of traders against them, insuring not only his own death, but Jerry's as well.

The goblin glanced about, taking in the faces of the spectators. All were grinning broadly, and eyeing the four newcomers with looks of pity. He looked at his friend. It would seem that his worries for Jerry might be groundless.

The traders jostled one another, elbowing for a better view.

"Two silver marks on th' red-beard," shouted one.

"Four silver marks. . . ."

"Ten. . . ." Ulf's confidence rose as the betting grew spirited.

The burly axeman who had accepted Jerry's pledge on the goblin's behalf roared with laughter and whirled his half-moon in flashing figure eights.

"One *gold* mark, and all my goods, on Thor's Fist!" Ulf looked at the men with amazement. His friend was outnumbered four to one, and not a single one of the traders offered to bet against him!

Jerry took from his belt the ten-inch disc of steel that served him as ward, and strapped it to his left forearm above the steel hand.

Word of the impending fracas passed back into the tunnels, and a number of grinning dwarfs lined the ledges above the arena.

Ulf, observing the expressions of all about him, stood back to observe his friend in action. Jerry, still smiling pleasantly, took a step forward and drew his blade. "I ask you again. Are you determined on being my enemy?"

"Aye!"

"All of you?"

"Aye!"

"Then draw."

Of the broadswordsman's three companions, two were axemen and the third fancied the longspear. All carried shields. The broadsword cleared its sheath, and what followed happened so quickly that Ulf barely followed the action.

The red-beard struck in two directions at once The steel hand shot out to the left, and ripped the broadswordsman's shield from his arm, spinning him half around.

At the same instant, the slim tongue of steel in his right hand parried a thrust of the longspear, feinted high, and when the spearman raised his shield, the flashing point darted under it to skewer the lout through the knee. Screaming, he dropped both spear and shield and fell writhing to the ground.

Jerry whirled back to the swordsman who still tottered off balance. He grinned and lunged, running his blade through both of the man's unprotected buttocks. The roar of laughter from the spectators drowned out the wretch's howl of pain.

The two axemen, who had been crowding close behind their companions, suddenly found themselves confronting the darting tip of Jerry's rapier.

Their eyes crossed comically as they tried to follow the flickering circles and figure eights. Then as one man, they turned tail and ran, amid shouts of derision from the onlookers.

Traders crowded around the victor, clapping him on the shoulder, pounding his back and thrusting on him jacks of ale and horns of mead.

Ulf stood shaking his head.

The friends of the vanquished dragged their fallen comrades away, casting glances of grudging admiration at the red-bearded youth.

The crowd of congratulators thinned as the traders went back to their pursuits.

Ulf clapped Jerry on the shoulder. "*Thor's Fist*, eh?" The goblin chuckled. "The name fits you, friend Jerry. You strike as swiftly as the lightning!" He looked at what remained of the broadswordsman's shield where it lay on the ground. A large chunk of the iron-banded target of thick oak was missing, torn away by Jerry's steel hand.

The goblin chuckled. "'*Thor's Fist.*' That axeman's just given you a name that'll be sung around many a campfire before long, I have no doubt."

Ulf looked at his friend. "By Odin's one eye, if you'd had Bryn at your side, I doubt not that you could have routed th' lot of them!"

Jerry grinned. "I have a dim memory of Jar Haz's battle on the hillside. Brokk tells me that between us, Bryn and I left twenty three corpses there." He laughed. "And one hand."

The two looked around at the activity. At butts set up at one side, archers were vying with one another. Several pairs of swordsman hacked away. At a distance a number of axemen, among them the trader who'd dubbed Jerry Thor's Fist, were showing their skill at flinging the short-handled throwing axes that supplemented their heavier long-hafted weapons. Ulf looked unhappy.

Jerry noted the goblin's expression. "What's got *you* down?"

Ulf laughed shortly. "Th' opportunity t' impress *you* with *my* skill. I see no slingers t' compete against."

Jerry grinned. "Friend Ulf, a swordsman needs an opponent. One whose forte is missiles needs only to exhibit his aim in order to draw gasps of adoration from a crowd of worshipful admirers."

The goblin snorted, lifting his trunk-like snout. "Brokk's right. Ye are a young puppy overly full of yourself."

He grinned his fang-filled grin, and studied the traders and buyers milling about. Being taller than most of the human kind, he looked over the heads of the crowd and studied the various items for sale.

"Come, puppy," he grunted.

Jerry followed, grinning. The crowd gave way before the fearsome spider-man. They showed no enmity since he was friend to Thor's Fist, but a group of the curious began to follow the stilted form as he went from booth to booth.

Jerry watched, as puzzled as the rest, while the goblin purchased five tough gourds of the kind used to make bowls, each roughly the size of a man's head. Dangling the string bag the seller had provided, he next bought several feet of light rope and two trestle boards.

Followed by a growing crowd, the goblin took his purchases to a spread-limbed tree. Ignoring the crowd and the questions in Jerry's eyes, Ulf leaned the trestle boards against the trunk of the tree, and borrowing a piece of charcoal, sketched the rough outline of a man on each. He cut the light rope into lengths and looping one about the stem of each gourd, hung them a few feet apart from a branch.

The tall goblin stooped briefly and whispered to one of the onlookers. The man nodded. Ulf motioned the crowd back, and stepped off a hundred paces. He waved a spidery arm. The man set all five gourds a-swing, and moved hastily to one side.

In a swift series of smooth fluid movements, the goblin snatched the sling from his belt, dipped a hand into his pouch of bullets, and dropped one into the pocket of his sling.

The braided thongs whistled loudly as the spider-man whirled the sling twice about his head and let fly. Almost more quickly than the eye could follow, he had re-armed the sling and a second missile hummed through the air just as the first of the swinging gourds exploded. The other four burst in quick succession then came a series of loud, rapid thwacks, and the trestle boards jumped and fell over.

The crowd rushed back to the tree while Ulf coiled his sling, and replaced it on his girdle. He grinned at Jerry, and sauntered toward the jabbering mob exclaiming over the fallen trestle boards.

Jerry followed, slightly awed at his friend's speed and accuracy. When he saw the two-inch-thick oaken planks, his awe increased at the killing power of a couple of strings and a pocket.

He knew that David had conked Goliath with one of those things, but little David hadn't had the goblin's over-long, steel-cabled arm to add the hundreds more feet per second muzzle velocity that Ulf had put behind his whizzing bullets.

Anyway, David had only stunned his giant, and had had to finish him off by cutting off his head with a sword. Any one of Ulf's shots would have taken out the big guy on the instant.

There were three splintered holes in each board. One each where Ulf had marked the eyes, and one each where he'd marked the heart. Holes that went all the way through two inches of solid oak!

The crowd fell back at the tall spider-man's approach. Oddly enough, their faces showed no fear of him, only respect and admiration for the awesome power behind the goblin's arm and his uncanny accuracy.

Ulf eyed his handiwork critically. "Not too bad. For an exhibition," he said dryly to Jerry.

Jerry estimated the time it had taken the goblin to get off his eleven rounds and put it at just over eighteen seconds. The red-beard whistled.

An expert rifleman with a bolt-action sniping piece couldn't have done it any faster!

Jerry grinned at Ulf, and removing his helmet, swept the goblin a deep bow. "Friend Ulf," he said, "you have no concept of just how glad I am that in battle I shall be at your side and not facing you!"

The spider-man chuckled. "Odd," he said, "I had the same feeling as I watched you against four adversaries."

The clamoring mob of traders pressed horns, bowls, and leather jacks of wine, mead, and ale on them. It was past sundown before the mismatched pair of warriors stumbled through the entrance to the dwarfholm, and went reeling down the maze of corridors to Brokk's domain.

Freya made them stop their singing, and shooed them off to their beds.

Jerry sank down into a foaming sea of ale with the tap-tap-tap of Brokk's hammer in his ears.

At some point during the night Jerry began to dream.

CHAPTER NINE

Maybe it was all the ale that sparked Jerry's memory, maybe not, but Jerry remembered.

Remembered what it was he'd been trying to recall just before he woke up in Brokk's cavern to discover that his wounds were healed. Remembered word for word the conversation that had taken place between Janet and the little mystic just before he left his charred and broken Jerry Haskins body and arrived in his hacked and one-handed Jar Haz body.

"How can you be sure where he'll wind up?"

"It's not easy to explain, Memsahib. I must detach my karma, my aura, my consciousness, and search along your husband's life-thread to find the proper time and body that will serve him best. . . ."

"You mean your soul?"

"Again, little one, that is one of the words."

"But isn't that awfully dangerous?"

"Very. But I shall be safe."

"Are you sure?"

The mahatma smiled. "I shall be quite safe, little Memsahib."

"Won't it take a long time? To search over centuries?"

Mukkergee lifted his hands and let them fall. "How to make you understand? Time, as I said, is not at all what it is believed to be. Time does not flow on just one level, one plane, nor does it necessarily advance at the same pace on the different levels. . . ."

He made that helpless gesture again. "It is impossible for me to put into words. Let it suffice to say that when I leave my body, time as you know it, will not apply to me, nor will space.

"It will be as though I am looking down on the whole tapestry of life, and shall be able to see the life-thread that is your husband. I shall search along that thread to find the optimum time at which to reinsert him. That is as nearly as I can express it."

Janet's face showed bewilderment. "You lost me. But I guess *you* know what you're talking about."

Jahawarlal Mukkergee smiled.

Janet looked pensive. "I wish there were some way I could go with you. I'd give a lot to know where Jerry's going to be, and that he'll be all right."

The girl saw something stir in the little mystic's eyes, something that was immediately suppressed.

"What? What are you thinking?"

"It is unthinkable, Memsahib."

"What? What is it?"

"No. No, it is out of the question. Out of the question."

"What? Tell me."

"No. Little one, it is far too dangerous. Impossible."

"You're saying that there is a way I can go with you, aren't you?"

"You must not ask. You must forget it. The danger to you is beyond calculation. There are too many factors involved. The risk is too high. Much too high. I cannot allow it."

"But there is a way?"

Mukkergee sighed. "Yes."

"I'll take the risks."Janet looked into his eyes. "I'll risk whatever I have to to see that Jerry's all right."

"You don't know what you are saying, little Memsahib. Listen to me. I can assure my own safety, I cannot guarantee that even if everything went well, I could protect *you.*

"Listen to me. There are so many variables, that I cannot even be sure I could return you to this time and this place. No. I cannot. The danger to you is too great."

Tears welled up in the girl's eyes. "I have to know," she said, "I have to know."

Mukkergee laid his hand on Janet's wrist. "Memsahib, listen to me. You must understand. If you were to accompany me, your consciousness would be loosed from its anchors in the here and now, and you would be afloat on the void.

"An entity adrift between worlds, between time. There are forces at work in the universe that tend to urge such an entity into corporate form.

"These forces would be at work on you in ways unpredictable. I can influence these forces to a small degree, but only to a small degree." Mukkergee looked into the girl's eyes. "You are thinking that you could find a way to stay with your husband."

The little swami sighed. "In truth, the possibility exists, but consider the odds. "I must find an ancestor of yours along your husband's life-thread who is at the brink of death. One not imprisoned, ancient, or riddled with disease.

"Consider that, even should your own life-thread have crossed with his in past centuries, the odds against the two of you being together, at the same time and place, both at the point of death. . . . in suitable bodies. . . . No, Memsahib, it is not to be considered."

"You said that time moves at different paces and on different levels. Isn't it possible that on some other time-line we. . . ."

"Memsahib, I have told you of the forces in the cosmos that urge a drifting soul to incorporate. These forces are strong, and should there be no ancestral body for you to enter, it is possible that your consciousness could be infused into a tree, a stone. You would be alive but *unable to live*, aware but *unable to be!*

"I am not sure my powers could protect you long enough to return you here. No, Memsahib. I cannot permit it."

"I'm willing to take the chances. I don't really expect to be able to stay with him, but I have to know that he'll be all right."

"Memsahib. . . ."

"Please."

The little mahatma threw up his hands.

"At the lamasery in Tibet where I trained, the High Lama said that there is only one force in the universe against which it is useless to struggle. . . a determined woman! Very well, Memsahib, it shall be as you wish."

CHAPTER TEN

Jerry jerked upright in his bed, stone sober and drenched in sweat. That *had* been Janet's voice he had heard while pinned beneath the rock on that blood-soaked hillside.

Gods! What if the little mystic's fears had come true? What if Janet were infused into that hellish place? Trapped in a boulder? Unable to speak, unable to live, but aware?

Still shaking with his fears for Janet, Jerry rushed to the forge, where the sound of hammering told him he'd find the dwarf. He got himself under control, and told the little man of his recovered memory, and Janet's possible fate.

Brokk put down his hammer. "Gently, lad, gently. Ye don't know that t' be th' way o' it. 'Tis just as likely yer magician brought th' lass safely home."

"Yes, but what if she's. . .?"

"Aye lad, I know yer fear. If aught were t' happen t' Freya. . . aye, I know well yer feelin'."

Jerry paced up and down the smithy. "It's the not knowing," he exclaimed over and over.

"If only there were some way to find out for sure."

"Find out what, dear?"

Freya, apparently awakened by the voices, came into the workshop. Jerry saw the look of concern on her face as she moved quickly to his side.

"What is it, my son?"

Jerry sank down on a bench with a groan. The elf-woman held his hand while he told her. Freya smoothed the distraught boy's hair, and put two fingers to his lips. "Hush now," she soothed. "Calm yourself. Nothing's to be gained by dewlling on possibilities. Time enough to worry if the facts prove unfavorable."

"Facts? How will we ever know?"

"Simple, dear. We'll go and look."

"I don't understand."

Freya smiled gently. "Elfin Magic," she said. "We elves have an affinity with living things. If your poor Janet is trapped there, I'll feel her presence."

"Oh, Lord." Jerry looked at the elf-woman with stricken eyes. "I don't know which is worse. Not to know and be able to hope, or to know for sure that she's. . . . Oh, God. . . ."

Freya stroked Jerry's cheek. "Keep hope, my son. Even if it should be as you fear, all is not necessarily lost."

She raised the boy's face, and smiled into his eyes. "As I said, we elves have many secrets."

The elf-woman stood, and looked at Brokk. "Husband, can you lead us back to the place where you found our Jerry?"

"Certainly, my dear." The dwarf removed his leather apron, and wiped his hands.

"Whenever ye say."

"I say now."

Brokk eyed his wife. "In yer nightdress?"

"I'll be ready by the time you two arm yourselves."

Jerry returned in a few moments, accoutered and anxious to start.

Bryn padded at his heels, a worried look on her scarred face. She kept nudging his thigh and uttering soft little whines.

At last, Jerry came out of his self-involvement enough to notice. He knelt and took the massive head in his arms. "It's all right, old girl," he reassured her, "It's all right." Thus soothed, Bryn lost some of her worried look.

When he rejoined Brokk, he was happy to see that Ulf had joined the venture. The tall goblin offered his hand. "Brokk told me of your fears, friend Jerry. 'Tis my hope that they're unfounded."

Jerry looked his thanks.

Freya appeared almost immediately, and the little band set off down the winding corridors.

As they passed the door to Jerry's niche, there was a flutter of wings and Odin's Messenger lit on Bryn's shoulder. The big dog turned her head, and eyed her passenger. She seemed to shrug and accept the situation.

The journey took longer than Jerry thought. They tramped for miles through a maze of tunnels and vaulted caverns. The red-beard's respect for Brokk's stamina grew as he realized just how far the little man had dragged him and the wounded Bryn. He remarked on it.

The dwarf just shrugged. At last they reached a short corridor and arrived at a dead end.

This time Jerry's senses weren't clouded, and he examined the machinery that activated the rock that concealed the exit to the upper world. He was surprised to see a system of polished silver mirrors that gave a panoramic view of the outside.

Brokk determined that all was clear, and operated the lifting mechanism. The huge boulder rotated and lifted, and the little party stepped out onto the hillside.

The ravens and wolves had taken care of the fallen that had littered the scarp. All that remained of that wild slaughter was a few smashed shields and broken weapons, a few scraps of cloth and a bone or two. As was to be expected, all serviceable clothing, arms, and armor had long since been carried off by scavengers.

As Bryn emerged on the one-time field of battle, her cropped ears rose, and she crouched, massive head swinging from side to side. Apparently having reassured herself that no enemies remained, she straightened.

Odin's Messenger gave an ear-piercing caw of joy at sight of the open sky, and flung himself aloft on ecstatic wings. Jerry felt a pang of loss as the ebony bird disappeared from sight. The red-beard studied the familiar hillside closely. "That's where I was lying and that's the rock that pinned my arm and stopped the bleeding," he told Ulf.

He searched for the spot he'd been unable to see from his supine position, and from which had come the murmur of voices. Choking back his fear, he pointed it out to Freya. "There's where I heard her talking."

The elf-woman touched his hand reassuringly, and moved slowly about the area. Her face held a look of intense concentration and a low penetrating note vibrated in her throat. She lifted the oddly shaped quartz pendant that she wore around her neck, and held it before her face.

Jerry was startled to see the amulet begin to glow. A pale amber shaft of light emanated from the yellow crystal, and touched the ground. Freya turned slowly, scanning the area foot by foot with the glowing beam. She moved away from them, searching.

"'Tis a part o' th' Elfin Gift," Brokk whispered. "All livin' things give off an aura that touches their surroundin's. Th' crystal concentrates th' power o' th' Gift, an' gives it th' strength t' amplify th' vibrations left. If yer Janet's here, that one will find her."

Jerry was aware that even back in his old world, quartz possessed many properties not completely explored.

The vibration of quartz molecules were utilized in the accurate measurement of time, micro chips, and in other branches of electronics. Jerry's knowledge of physics was limited, he'd majored in Business Administration. But he guessed that the psychokinetic powers of the elves could cause the quartz to resonate to produce the result he was observing.

Oh hell, call it 'elfin magic' and let it go at that. He watched the little elf-woman with his heart in his throat.

At last Freya turned and came back toward them. Her face wore a wide smile. "Set your fears to rest, dear Jerry. Your loved one is not in this place. I sensed that she *had* been here, but that she safely departed. It appears that your magician returned her home after all."

Jerry knelt and hugged the tiny sprite. "Thank you, Mother. Thank God." Jerry's relief left him weak.

CHAPTER ELEVEN

State Trooper John Beame spotted the burned out car just after sun-up.The rain had stopped, and the day was dawning bright and clear. He could see where the heavy vehicle had slid on the treacherous curve, and plowed through the guard-rail. The road surface was still dangerously slick, as he discovered when the big Harley nearly slid out from under him as he eased around the turn onto Maple Lane.

The Trooper dismounted and booted the kickstand. He kept his footing with difficulty on the steep, slippery, pine-needle covered slope.

Half way to the car, he spied the two figures under the tree, some hundred yards from the wreck. He altered course. John Beame stared for a long time at the man and the girl, then returned to his motorcycle. He lifted the microphone from its bracket. "Five Mary Twenty one to Central."

"Go Five Mary Twenty one."

"Roll a meat wagon and tow truck to Highway eighty-seven and Maple Lane."

"What ya got, Johnny?"

"One-car smashup. Two dead at the scene. Male caucasian, twenty-four-twenty-five, six-one, one eighty five. Female cauc, twenty two-twenty three, five-two, one-five. Funny. . . ."

"What's funny?"

"Charlie, the guy's busted all to hell and fried to a crisp, but the girl. . . ."

"What's wrong with the girl?"

"That's just it, Charlie. Nothing. She's just dead. Just sitting there with a sweet smile on her face, holding the guy's head in her lap.

"Dead. No cuts. No bruises. No evidence of internal injuries. Nothing."

CHAPTER TWELVE

The weight of fear for Janet having been lifted from his shoulders, Jerry felt light-hearted and eager to get started. It was nothing he could pin down, but he was filled with the conviction that, somehow, things would work themselves out.

When looked at sensibly, the problems facing him seemed utterly insurmountable. The journey to Asgard, while definitely not a piece of cake, fell within the realm of possibility. Ulf had made the trip several times, twice unaccompanied.

If the goblin could do it alone, Jerry had no doubts that his well-armed little band of seasoned fighters could weather the venture. Not only were he, Ulf, and the dwarf adept at the use of their weapons, they had the added protection of Freya's elfin magic.

They might not make it, but the journey to Asgard was within their capabilities.

The seemingly insurmountable wall of impossibility rose up when he tried to see how he could be returned to a future that didn't exist. That's when his head began to swim.

How could Janet have returned to *her* future? Or *did* she? Could it be that she returned not to her future, but to her present? In the future?

If so, wouldn't that mean that he, too, had a present somewhere in his own future?

Or, maybe because Janet had no avatar on this plane into which to enter, she had not really left her future/present, but he, in taking over the body of Jar Haz, had created his own 'present' here and now for which there was no 'future' until he lived it?

Or. . . .

It was at this point that Jerry's mind generally threw up its hands and ran, screaming, off into the woods.

'What?' 'If?' 'How?' 'Future?' 'Present?' Whoa! Knock it off!

Impossible. But he was here. *That* was impossible, but it was fact.

And he was on a different time level, time line, space-time-continuum, watever, from the one he'd existed on back there. *Ahead* there?*Hell, wherever he'd left the burning car.* He knew that now.

Word came down that a horse trader had come to the Trading Glen. Brokk, engrossed with Freya's armor, sent Ulf who was a shrewd bargainer, to dicker for mounts for the journey.

Jerry accompanied him. Jerry watched as the goblin made a close appraisal of the trader's herd.

Ulf selected three of the sturdy mountain ponies that were renowned for their sureness of foot, their strength, and their fleetness on level terrain. He also chose two mules and a stout cart to carry provisions and baggage.

The goblin was accustomed to the hardships of the trail, but since Freya was to accompany them, Brokk insisted she be made as comfortable as possible.

While Ulf went into the long process of haggling with the trader, Jerry climbed to a pinnacle from which he could view the misty lowlands thousands of feet below, the land of men, the place called Midgard.

There wasn't much to see.

From thirty to forty thousand feet of elevation about all that he could discern were layers of cloud, drifting mists and an occasional patch of hazy green through a rift. He was about to turn away when a movement above the clouds caught his attention.

Jerry shielded his eyes with one hand. There. No. Yes, there, a flying shape coming towards him, His jaw dropped as the creature became distinct.

A long, fang-filled beak like the snout of a crocodile. A forty-foot span of leathery wings clumsily thrashing the air. An illustration from the Encyclopedia Britannica rose before his mind's eye. A *pterodactyl.*

A flying dinosaur!

That confirmed what he'd come to believe.

There could no longer be any doubt. He had left his original time-line. In his world dinosaurs had died out millions of years before the advent of man.

The nightmare creature swept into a lazy descending spiral and vanished into the cloud layer.

Great, Jerry thought. Just great.

Not only do I have to find a way into a nonexistent future, I have to find the correct time-line on which this nonexistent future doesn't exist.

And Columbus thought he had had problems!

Even so, Jerry still had this irrational feeling that things would sort themselves out. After all, this world had a set of real, live, working, gods, didn't it?

Who knew?

Well, there was a way to find out, if Brokk ever finished Freya's mail shirt.

The red-beard refused to be downhearted.

What seemed to Jerry to be half a lifetime, was, actually, only a bit over three weeks.

At long last the dwarf emerged from his workshop with a metal miracle in his hands. The steel mesh was so light it could be crushed together in the dwarf's two hands, yet so strong as to be impenetrable to point and impervious to edge.

It occurred to Jerry to ask why, since Freya possessed the Elfin Gift, she should need body armor.

"As wi' any weapon, lad," Brokk explained, "th' wielder must be given time t' unsheathe it. Just as th' finest o' swordsmen can be taken by surprise an' slain before he can draw, so could Freya be taken unaware. 'Tis very unlikely, 'tis true, but 'tis remotely possible an', lad, I take no chances wi' my treasure."

Jerry's impatience was nearing the boiling point by the time Brokk announced that they

would leave the following morning.

The dwarf had fitted Jerry out with a mail coat that hung to mid thigh and was slit before and behind to allow the wearer to sit a horse. It belted at the waist with a broad girdle from which hung Jerry's rapier, a leather wallet, the steel disc he used as a shield, and an eighteen inch poniard.

Thus helmeted, mailed, and armed, Jerry examined himself in Freya's large mirror of polished silver.

Boy, he thought, if the guys at good old Nationwide Insurance could see me now! What the well-dressed Viking will wear!

CHAPTER THIRTEEN

At last!

They were finally on their way! Jerry was in fine fettle. His spirits soared. He was on the first leg of the journey to Janet. Okay, so there were insurmountable obstacles. So what? He'd bridge those crosses when he came to them.

To the folk of this world, who believed in omens, the day was one of the most propitious. Bright sunlight and a cloudless sky smiled on them. It augured a good beginning.

The little band moved across the grassy swale of the Trading Glen toward the narrow gash in the cliffs that led down to Midgard. Even at this elevation the sun's rays were warm. Jerry tossed back his cloak of red wool, and removed his helmet. Sunlight flashed fire from his red-gold braids and silvery chain mail. He sat straight in the saddle, and felt like singing.

His satisfaction was made complete when he heard a series of mocking squawks overhead, and looked up to see Odin's Messenger descending toward him. Jerry uttered a glad cry, and raised his left arm. The big raven braked, and settled on the uplifted forearm, clucking and chattering. Jerry stroked the glossy head and the bird rubbed its bill against his hand.

"Where the hell have you been?" Jerry demanded, "I thought you'd run out on me."

The raven hopped to Jerry's shoulder and butted its head against the man's cheek. Again Jerry felt those waves of affection and comraderie emanating from the black bird. He was beginning to suspect that Odin's Messenger understood human speech.

Both Brokk and the goblin hailed the raven's return as a good omen.

Freya chirped, and Odin's Messenger left Jerry's shoulder, to land on the ridgepole of the covered cart. He began to twitter and chirp and the elf-woman answered in kind.

She laughed.

"What?" Jerry wanted to know, "What's he telling you. He *is* talking to you, isn't he?"

"Yes, dear."

Freya rumpled the black feathers affectionately. This mischief maker brings news that will help ease your anxiety. He has taken your problem to Asgard. He reports that the gods look on you with favor."

"Can they get me back to Janet?"

"You must realize, Jerry dear, that Odin's Messenger is only a bird. While he is trained to carry back battlefield reports accurately, his understanding is limited.

"From what I gather, Odin is intrigued by the challenge, but the variables are so many that not even he can guarantee success. Be of high heart, my dear son. The Father of the Gods is moving on your behalf. It quite well may be that by the time we reach Asgard a solution will have been found."

She smiled happily and Jerry's spirits rebounded. He felt full of hope. *The Father of the Gods is moving in your behalf. . . .*

How 'bout that!

Odin's Messenger complained querulously, apparently annoyed at the jouncing of the little cart, and lifting his wings, sailed to rest on Bryn's broad back. The war-dog seemed to welcome her passenger,

The one-time salesman of insurance looked at his companions, and felt pride at being accepted as one of them.

Ulf rode point as pathfinder.

A few rods to his rear Freya drove the little cart. She used no reins, controlling the two mules by elfin communication.

He and Brokk rode drag, fanned out to right and left a short distance behind Freya's cart.

Bryn, her tongue lolling redly, trotted along beside Jerry with Odin's Messenger perched on her back. Jerry shook his head in amused contemplation of his situation.

Here he was, Jerry Haskins of San Diego, California, crackerjack insurance salesman. Owner of a nice split-level home in the suburbs. One wife, two cars. Okay, one car and a station wagon. Well thought of by the higher-ups in the company. On his way up, career-wise. Quiet, relatively unimaginative, dependable. Good old Jerry Haskins. Hoo-boy!

Look at good old Jerry Haskins now!

Hair plaited into thick braids that hung to his waist. Neatly trimmed beard. Clad from chin to knee in gleaming chain mail. Flashier than a paisley vest, he chuckled to himself, but a hell of a lot more practical. Hanging from his waist was three and a half feet of sword and a foot and a half of dagger. Jar Haz's axe dangled on its thong from his saddlebow, and at his side trotted almost two hundred pounds of war-dog.

Jerry lifted his left hand, opened and closed his steel fingers. He laughed aloud. He'd scare the ever-loving hell out of the guys back at the office!

And look at the company he kept! A dwarf, an elf, and a *goblin* for pete's sake! He choked back another fit of laughter.

He'd caught a mental picture of him and his friends walking into one of Mr. Wilson's cocktail parties.

'Mr. and Mrs. Brokk Hammermacher, I'd like you to meet my boss, president of Nationwide Insurance. Mr. Wilson, may I present my foster parents and our friend Mr. Ulf? Mr. Ulf is a well known jet-setter. Travels quite extensively. Oh yes, Mr. Ulf has been all over. Midgard. Jotunheim. He is a frequent visitor to the capital city, Asgard. He's even met President Odin, I believe.'

He tried to picture the tall, hunchbacked goblin in a three piece suit and tie, sitting on a barstool as he now sat his pony, crouched like a giant spider with his knees level with his shoulders. Somehow Ulf just didn't seem to fit in with the three-martini-lunch-bunch!

Jerry eyed the spider-man with affection. Brokk had said it: "Ye'll never find a truer friend nor stouter companion. . . ."

The goblin wore his battered steel cap with its specially formed nasal, and his equally battered breastplate. His sling and bullet pouch hung from his girdle, as did a poniard similar to the one Jerry wore. Strapped across his hump was his short, broad-bladed sword with its haft protruding above his right shoulder. His assegai nestled in a saddle-sheath beneath his right leg, ready to hand. A round target shield of iron-banded oak hung from his saddle horn.

Brokk also sported full battle harness, the same scarred and dented accouterments he wore the first time Jerry saw him. Armor as battle-scarred as Ulf's. Mace, shortsword, paired throwing knives and target completed his armament.

Tiny Freya sparkled in her chain mail that glowed like buffed silver. Her hair was braided and wrapped around her shapely head. For travel she wore scarlet trousers cross-gartered to the knee, and soft doeskin buskins. On the seat beside her rested her special helmet. Brokk had forged it to cover her entire head. A panoramic slit permitted unrestricted vision. The little elf-woman was armed only with a small dagger and the elfin pendant of quartz around her neck.

Ulf's deep pleasant voice lifted in a bawdy drinking song, and Brokk joined in. The words rose out of Jar Haz's memory, and Jerry picked up the refrain.

Ulf reached the fortified gates at the cleft in the cliff walls, and passed through to enter the steep descent. His voice cut off as he rounded a curve.

Brokk heeled his pony into a canter and followed the goblin. Jerry closed up on Freya's cart, and they passed through the gates. The dwarfs on duty waved cheerfully. Twice more they passed through defensive checkpoints. It was plain that the Little People had no intentions of being taken unaware.

The last of the defenses had been left behind hours ago. The descent was steep, but Freya had no difficulty controlling the sure-footed mules. The little wagon bumped and ground along without incident.

Ulf, in the van, rounded a sharp turn and disappeared from sight. Almost immediately there came a deep bellow, followed by the high-pitched ululation of Ulf's war-cry.

The dwarf shouted to Jerry, and urged his mount into a gallop. Jerry followed on his heels, clapping on his helmet and drawing his rapier. Bryn, racing at his side, gave vent to a howl of challenge, and Odin's Messenger flung himself into the air.

They rounded the curve and slid to a halt.

Jerry quickly sheathed his sword, and snatched Jar Haz's axe from the saddlebow. Fighting giants called for a bit more firepower than the slender blade, and giants were what they faced.

Three of them.

The hulking brutes stood shoulder to shoulder, two armed with axes and the third with a spiked iron club Jerry wasn't sure he could even lift, never mind use as a weapon. Although only one of the monstrous trio was over eleven feet, it looked to be a pretty hot few minutes!

Ulf had dismounted, and stood wide-legged with his charged sling dangling from his right fist, waiting for one of the enemy to make a hostile move.

Giants on their way to Svartheim were usually on a peaceful mission to buy dwarfen weapons, but where giants were concerned, it was generally the best policy to take no chances.

The tallest of the trio snarled and raised his spiked club.

Bryn crouched to spring, and Jerry took a two-handed grip on the haft of the razor-edged half-moon. He threw one leg over the saddle and slid to the ground, moving quickly to the goblin's side.

Ulf's sling whistled once about his head, and the giant had never been closer to death.

Brokk leaped from his mount and shouted, "Ulf! Hold! I know this giant!" The deadly sling slowed, and the goblin lowered it to his side. Brokk turned to the behemoth. "Lower yer weapon, Hrimgrimnir o' th' Frost Giants. D'ye not know me?"

"Aye, I know thee, Brokk Hammermacher," the fiercely bearded

Frost Giant rumbled, "'Tis thee I've come t' see."

He rested the tip of his club on the ground. His two companions relaxed their guard.

Odin's Messenger, circling overhead, flew off to report to Freya.

Hrimgrimnir squatted politely so that the dwarf and his friends wouldn't have to crane their necks.

"Where be thee away to, Dwarf King? 'Tis many long months I an' my kin have traveled from Jotunheim just t' see thee."

"We're fer Asgard."

"Must thee? I crave thy skill t' forge me a sword t' gain back what is mine. Ask what thee will."

"'Tis not a matter o' barter, friend Hrimgrimnir. 'Tis a matter o' first priority. My son must meet wi' th' gods on a thing o' prime necessity t' him."

"Thy son?" the giant inquired politely.

"Aye, my godson."

Brokk looked at Jerry. "Th' red-pated lout ye see here. Jerry Jar Haz called Thor's Fist."

Jerry stepped forward.

The dwarf smiled at him. "Jerry lad, I'd like ye t' meet Hrimgrimnir th' Frost Giant, who's been friend an' more t' me in th' past."

The huge creature rumbled. "'Twas a thing of little note an' more than repaid by thy godfather. We'll speak no more on it."

Jerry offered his hand, and the giant took it in his vast paw gently. "In this world, friends are to be treasured," Jerry said.

The giant's beard parted in a smile. He looked at Brokk. "Thy godson speaks well," he said.

The giant looked at the steel hand. "Crossing Midgard, my brothers and I heard tales of a young warrior demigod among th' dwarfs, with a hand of death. Thy fame goes before thee, Jerry Jar Haz."

Freya's cart entered the little amphitheater, and the grinding of its wheels on gravel drew the giant's attention. "One of thy party, friend Brokk?"

"Aye. My wife, Freya o' th' Black Forest elves."

Hrimgrimnir indicated his two shorter companions squatting behind him. "My brothers, Hradalfar an' Hradnir."

The companions acknowledged the introduction, and Brokk presented Ulf. The goblin and the giants eyed each other warily but without open enmity.

Hrimgrimnir returned his attention to the dwarf. "Thy wife accompanies thee t' Asgard?"

"Aye.

The giant looked troubled.

"Friend Brokk, thee go at a chancy time," he rumbled. "Th' whole of Midgard is beset with turmoil. There be much warrin' between thane an' baron, an' th' Free Companies rove about, burnin' an' lootin' an' doin' as they will. Thy lady will be exposed t' much danger."

"Our fates be in th' hands o' th' gods, friend Hrimgrimnir."

"Aye, that be so. But I must warn thee also, friend Brokk, that Jotunheim, never a friendly place t' outsiders, is even less so these days."

"Why so?"

The giant growled. "Thrym, th' Frost King, Odin's curse on him. Thee know how it is among the giant kind, friend Brokk. We give our alliance t' our king, but 'tis more custom than servitude."

"Aye, that's so."

"True it is, we giants be unfriendly in th' main." The big man looked at Ulf. "In that we be not unlike th' goblin kind."

Ulf grinned.

"We be mostly just as unfriendly t' each other as t' those not of our folk, so 'tis not our way t' bend t' th' will of another."

Hrimgrimnir scowled. "But Thrym, th' goblin-souled. . . . Thy pardon, friend Ulf. Thrym has decided that all who live within what he has decreed t' be his kingdom will bend th' knee t' him an' woe t' those who refuse. Thee hast known me, Brokk Hammermacher, an' thee know me t' be not too unreasonable. . . ."

"Fer a giant," Brokk chuckled.

Hrimgrimnir's beard twitched in a smile. "Aye, for a giant," he conceded. "But I an' my brothers bend th' knee t' no man."

The big man growled. "Thrym, Odin's curse on him, came down on my steading whilst we were a-huntin'. They burned my holdin', slaughtered my servants and my kine, and took captive our sister Hulda."

Hrimgrimnir raised his spiked club and shook it. "Th' swine left us as thee see us, with th' furs t' our backs an' near weaponless."

The giant dipped a hand into his wallet. "But what we were a-huntin' when th' whoreson struck, was these."

Hrimgrimnir withdrew his hand and opened it. On the broad palm lay a score of large pearls. "Tears of th' Sea," he said. "Th' one jewel thee dwarfs cannot dig from th' earth, an' so hold t' be of great value to thee, is't not so?"

Brokk took one of the lambent orbs, and examined it almost reverently. "Aye, Friend Hrimgrimnir, 'tis as ye say. An' never ha' I seen Sea Tears t' match these. Ye've a fortune here t' buy ye th' half o' th' dwarfholm!"

"'Tis weapons I crave, Brokk of Svartheim. Weapons as only thee can forge. Weapons t' return t' Jotunheim an' reclaim what's my own."

Brokk stared at the big man.

"Th' three o' ye? Three against yer bloody-handed king?"

Hrimgrimnir laughed. "Nay, friend Brokk. Afore leavin' Jotunheim, I bespoke a number of my kin an' friends. They've agreed that, properly armed, they'll back my cause. Th' most of them have been scurvily treated by curst Thrym, an' have scores of their own t' settle."

Brook looked at the big man questioningly. "An' how d'ye propose t' transport such a mort o' weapons back t' yer homeland?"

Hrimgrimnir smiled. "A day's march behind is a troop of our kin with wagons. 'Tis why my brothers an' I came ahead. T' reassure th' dwarfen folk that we mean no mischief. 'Tis no war-party. We come t' trade only."

The giant stood and looked down at Brook who barely reached the big man's hip. "'Twas why I sought thee, Brokk Hammermacher. Thee knowest me well, Dwarf King. Is th' word of Hrimgrimnir th' Frost Giant sufficient t' assure thy folk we come in peace?"

The dwarf raised his hand and touched that of the giant. "Aye, friend. Yer word be as a bond o' iron."

Brokk searched his wallet and came out with a golden medallion. "Here, friend Hrimgrimnir, take this t' my brother Sindri an' he'll know ye come from me. Ye'll ha' yer weapons."

"'Tis thee who's known as th' finest armorer in all th' Nine Worlds. . . ."

"Softly, friend," Brokk broke in, "'Tis Sindri, as eldest, t' whom our father passed down th' art, an' 'twas my brother taught me all I know o' th' smithy. Ye'll have naught t' displease ye wi' th' arms from Sindri's forge. Take ye this token t' my brother an' tell him what ye'd have o' him."

The giant took the tiny medallion and stowed it carefully in his wallet. "Thee have my thanks, Brokk Hammermacher. It may hap that th' day will come when I may repay thee."

"Ye owe me naught, friend."

"I owe thee th' trust thee have in me." The big fellow started to turn away.

"Stay," Brokk said suddenly, "Tell my brother t' go t' my forge. There he'll mark a sword I think ye'll find t' yer likin'. 'Tis not completed, but say t' Sindri I said t' finish it fer ye as a gift o' th' Dwarf Folk. An' may it aid ye in th' retakin' o' what's yer own."

The giant's gratitude showed in his face. He looked long at the dwarf, and raised his club in salute.

Hradalfar and Hradnir, who'd spoken no word, lifted their axes, and followed their brother up the declivity toward Svartheim.

CHAPTER FOURTEEN

The descent into Midgard although short in miles, took a good three days to complete.

This was due to the steepness of the trail, and the treacherousness of the footing. For these reasons the narrow fissure was widened at two points into small amphitheaters where ascending and descending caravans could rest themselves and their beasts.

It was late afternoon of the third day when the companions debouched from the crack in the cliffs onto the High Meadows of Midgard. Here in the upper grasslands, were rolling hills and broad meadows dotted with groves of beech, ash, and oak. Here the flocks of sheep, goats, and great herds of cattle grazed and grew fat, to fill the cookpots of the land of men.

On three sides Midgard was bounded by similar grazing lands that sloped up to meet the eastern, western, and southern mountain ranges known as the Osten Bergen, The Southern Range, and the Westen Bergen.

To the north, however, no such pleasant country was to be found. The dense forest that covered all of the central part of the land of men ended abruptly at Ginnungagap, the Chasm of Chasms, the bottomless abyss.

From the far edge of Ginnungagap rose the towering northern range, the Norden Bergen, land of eternal ice, snow, and freezing mists.

Jotunheim, Land of the Giants.

The Central Forest was crisscrossed with broad trails which connected the villages that dotted the vast wood, and along which the drovers from the High Meadows brought their herds and flocks to the marketplaces of the World of Men. Through the greenery also ran many lesser known paths and byways.

It was by these that Ulf proposed to lead the little party, it being unsafe for goblins and Little Folk in most of the land.

Freya had sent Odin's Messenger ahead to scout the terrain. The black battle bird had returned to report no hostile concentrations within miles of the exit.

The day being well on, the little band camped for the night in a pleasant grove beside a clear cold brook. Jerry, a fair fisherman, augmented their supper with a dozen fat trout.

The meal was finished and Freya had tidied up. Brokk broached a small skin of mead and the drinking horns were broken out.

Ulf took a long draft of the honey-wine, staring into the fire, his hideous face wrinkled in concentration. "Thrym," he muttered, "I've heard that name before. . . ."

He sat up and uttered a snort of laughter. "Ah, of course!"

The goblin turned to Freya. "I remember now. 'Tis one of the accounts of th' doin's of th' gods long ago, and it concerns you, friend Freya, or rather your namesake of Asgard, th' Goddess of Flowers, Queen of th' Elves.

"A tale of Freya, Goddess of Spring, Thrym the Frost King, and the hammer of Thor, God of Thunder."

Brokk growled. "I've heard th' silly tale," he said sourly. "'Tis meant only t' amuse children. Bah!"

Ulf chuckled and looked at Jerry. "'Tis because the story is about somethin' Brokk chooses not t' discuss, that he grumbles so, Thor's hammer."

Jerry perked up. "Really? About how. . . ?"

"Nay lad, not about th' forgin' of it."

The goblin shot a teasing glance at the glowering dwarf. "That's something our friend guards as a secret. . . ."

"'Tis no secret," sputtered the dwarf. "'Tis a lie born o' th' waggin' tongues o' chatterin' addlepates. I ha' nothin' t' say on th' subject."

The little man glared at the goblin. "Ye'll please me, friend Ulf, by speakin' no more o' it."

Jerry grinned. "Touchy, isn't he?"

Ulf chuckled. "Well, well. I'll say no more of th' craftin' of Mjollnir, th' hammer of Thor, God of Thunder."

"What about Freya and the giant?"

"Ah, that." Ulf looked at Brokk. "You've no objection t' th' telling' of that, have you?"

The dwarf waved his hand. "Oh, if ye must waste yer wind."

With the firelight flickering over his fanged and snouted face, Ulf related the tale of Freya the Goddess of Spring, Thrym the Frost King, and Mjollnir the hammer of Thor.

The Thunder God awoke one morning to discover that his hammer, the mightiest weapon possessed by the gods, was nowhere to be found. This was a matter of deep concern to all the Aesir, as Thor, armed with his hammer, was their one invincible defense against the giants who plotted ever to destroy the gods. Mjollnir must be found before the giants heard of its loss, and attacked the City of the Gods.

Odin called the gods and goddesses together in the great meeting hall, Gladsheim.

It having been determined that Loki the Mischief Maker had had nothing to do with the disappearance, the Sly One was deemed to be the most likely to find the missing hammer, since he was familiar with the devious places in all the Nine Worlds.

He was ordered by Odin Allfather to search until Mjollnir was found.

The mischievous god borrowed from Freya her magic dress of falcon feathers, and transformed into a falcon, flew high and low over Midgard and Jotunheim.

From the beginning, Loki suspected Thrym the Frost Giant of the theft, and came at last to the Frost King's castle deep in the frozen mountains of Jotunheim.

Thrym readily admitted that he had the hammer.

"I've hidden it where it'll never be found, friend Loki," he said, "but I'll strike a bargain with thee. Bring me the fair Freya as my bride, an' I'll return th' hammer."

Loki flew back to Asgard, and presented the giant's demand to the assembled gods. Odin was furious. "**Never!**" he roared. "Never will I permit she who brings the beauty of flowers and the warmth of spring to be condemned to the frozen wastes of Jotunheim!"

There was much agitated discussion among the Aesir. All agreed that giving Freya to the giant was unthinkable, but how was Asgard to be defended without Thor's hammer?

Loki listened to the arguments then spoke. "I have a plan," the Sly One said, "whereby to retrieve that which has been stolen."

The assembly listened to the Mischief Maker's scheme and roared with laughter. All but Thor.

"Nay!" the Thunder God sputtered, "Never! I'll not do it!" Odin calmed his son's anger.

"It's the only way," he said, "and we must be defended."

In the end the Thunderer agreed. Amid a good deal of laughter, Thor was dressed in womens' clothing, and a bridal veil concealed his bristling red beard. He journeyed to Jotunheim with Loki, and was presented by the Sly One to the prospective bridegroom.

Thrym was eager to see the face of his bride, but Loki explained that the tender goddess was too modest to reveal herself until after the marriage.

At the urging of the Sly One, Thrym sent for the hammer and it was placed in the bride's lap.

At once, the God of Thunder tore off his disguise, and once again armed with his invincible hammer, laid about him, slaying Thrym and all the wedding guests. So it was that Thor and Loki returned to Asgard with Mjollnir.

Thus the beauty of flowers and the blessings of spring were saved for the world.

Jerry laughed. "I'll bet Thor isn't any more anxious to discuss that, than Brokk is to talk about his hammer."

The dwarf said sourly, "Can we now drop th' entire subject?"

Ulf gathered his cloak about him and lay back. "Oh, aye," he chuckled.

Jerry looked at the elf-woman. "Freya in Asgard cannot be as beautiful as you, Mother," he said.

The tiny sprite blushed. "Hush, flatterer."

Brokk harrumphed. "'Tis th' first sensible thing that's been said this night."

CHAPTER FIFTEEN

Jerry was worried, and he could see that Brokk shared his concern.

It had been over three hours since Ulf had gone ahead to scout the wood, and the goblin had yet to return. Jerry cursed the evil luck that had robbed them of the services of Odin's Messenger. Two days previously, the big raven had been set upon by a hawk. At a piercing warning cry from Freya the hawk had veered off, but the damage had already been done. The ebony battle bird fell to earth with a broken wing.

He now perched on Freya's ridgepole muttering querulously to himself.

Jerry kneed his pony and rode toward the dwarf. "It's been too long."

"Aye. My thought as well."

"I'm going after him."

Brokk scrubbed his beard with one gnarled hand. "Aye. I don't like it, but ye'd better."

Jerry knew that the dwarf would prefer to take the danger himself, but had Freya to consider, and was reluctant to leave her side. The red-beard nodded. He whistled to Bryn, and with the big war dog at his side, rode into the forest.

For the first few hundred yards the wood was open, a sunlit place of wide-set trees, green grass, sunlight, and flowers. As the thicket deepened, the trees came more closely together, the sunlight dimmed, and the flowers disappeared. The place took on an atmosphere of gloom and menace. Jerry strapped the warding disc to his forearm and drew his sword. He rode warily, alert for attack from any direction.

The little mountain pony, sensitive to its rider's mood, grew skittish. Jerry considered dismounting. The pony was no war-charger, and in an action might prove more of a hindrance than a help. He stepped down from the saddle and tied the reins to a tree. With Bryn testing every breeze, he proceeded warily afoot.

Ulf, a seasoned pathfinder, had left his mark to blaze the trail. Jerry looked for, and found, three almost invisible parallel cuts on treetrunks pointing the way. Bryn's scarred head swung to right and left as she tested the air for danger, but she gave no indication of anything amiss.

The man and dog struck a broad shallow stream, followed it as indicated by Ulf's blazes. Several hundred yards downstream the waterway widened to seventy or eighty feet, still it was no more than thigh deep.

Jerry spotted a tiny islet in midstream. On its minuscule beach sat a disconsolate Ulf. The goblin sat hunched with his knees to his ears and his spidery arms resting on them. He was staring at the water rippling past. He looked up as Jerry stopped on the bank opposite him.

The red-beard hooked a thumb under the rim of his helmet, and shoved it to the back of his head. He stared at the goblin. "Are you all right?" he asked, "What the hell's wrong? Are
you wounded?"

Ulf looked embarrassed. "Not wounded. Marooned."

"Marooned? What are you talking about? The water's barely
knee deep."

"To you. To a goblin, it might as well be th' bottomless chasm of Ginnungagap."

"I don't get it."

"'Tis a lengthy tale. Can we go into it at a later time? D'you see that tree leanin' at your side? Could you, d'you think, chop it down so as t' bridge th' stream? I tire of this place."

Jerry looked at the goblin's woebegone face. "Hang tight, friend Ulf. I'll be right back." Jerry jogged rapidly back to where he'd tied the pony. He retrieved Jar Haz's battleaxe from the saddlebow and returned quickly to the streamside.

He made an undercut in the side of the treetrunk in the direction he wanted it to lie, then fell to. The tree leaned toward the islet and began to pop and creak. "Heads up," Jerry warned, "Thar she blows!"

With a series of sharp reports, the treetrunk snapped, and crashed to earth, bridging the gap between islet and bank. Ulf gathered up his spear and shield and hurried across. Jerry was taken aback to note an expression of fear on the goblin's face.

Ulf stepped down from the makeshift bridge with a loud sigh of relief. "My thanks. I'd have another favor of you, Jerry lad, if you'll oblige me."

"Sure, pal. Anything."

"That troll-curst, lackbrained pony of mine. He's somewhere on th' other bank. Would
you. . .?"

Jerry grinned. "I don't get it, but sure old buddy, I'll go find him for you." The goblin looked relieved. "Again my thanks. With your permission I'll await you here."

Puzzled, Jerry waded into the stream followed by Bryn who splashed playfully at his side.

On the opposite bank he had no difficulty finding the pony's hoofprints and following them the short distance to where the little beast was grazing in a small glade. He gathered up the reins and led him back to where Ulf waited,

He looked at the goblin. "What happened?" he wanted to know.

Ulf eyed the pony sourly. "This scatterpate shied at somethin' and bolted into th' stream. He tripped on yon islet and I lost my seat. He continued on his hairbrained flight, leavin' me stranded until you came along."

Jerry looked at the shallow brook and shook his head. "I still don't get it."

The goblin cleared his throat. "We'd best be gettin' back t' Brokk and Freya. They'll be frettin' at our absence."

"Yeah. We were pretty worried about you."

Jerry paused, but when Ulf offered no explanation, he started off in the direction of his tethered mount.

Ulf followed, leading his pony. Both mounted up, and cantered back to where Brokk and the elf-woman waited for them. Brokk's relief at sight of the tall goblin was plain on his face. "What befell ye? We were sore afraid fer yer safety."

Looking embarrassed, Ulf explained what had happened. Brokk clapped the goblin on the shoulder. "'Tis sorry I am fer yer predicament, but happy 'was no worse."

Still lost at sea, Jerry repeated for the third time, "I don't get it. The water was barely knee deep."

Ulf sighed. "'Tis a curse placed on th' goblin kind. "In ancient times Odin tired of th' vile temper and needless cruelty of th' Twisted Folk. He drove th' goblins into a barren area, and decreed it t' be their land. T' keep them from minglin' with other kinds, th' Allfather caused th' land t' be surrounded by streams and rivers, and laid a deathly fear of runnin' water in th' hearts of my people.

"'Twas centuries before th' fear was conquered enough for th' Twisted Ones t' break from their prison. That was ages past, still th' dread is heavy on us. Where bridged, runnin' water can be crossed with only slight qualms."

Ulf shuddered violently. "T' actually *enter* a runnin' stream. . . ." He shuddered again. "It *can* be done, but th' terror it invokes can paralyze one of my kind."

Jerry laid a sympathetic hand on the goblin's spidery arm.

"I'm sorry, Ulf. I didn't understand."

Brokk glanced at the sun. "We've a couple hours o' travel time afore us. What d'ye think? Be th' wood safe?"

The goblin nodded. "I saw no sign of any passin' recently. Th' last time I came this way th' baron of this shire held th' peace, and permitted none of th' rovin' bands of mercenaries t' ravish th' countryside as they do in other parts. It should be safe enough if we stick t' th' smaller trails."

"Bryn didn't act like there was anyone around," Jerry put in. "It's pretty gloomy, that's all."

The dwarf looked at his wife. "What say ye, my love? Does th' Gift tell ye aught?"

Freya clasped the quartz amulet in both hands and closed her eyes. "I can't tell," she said a little uneasily, "the Gift is unreliable at great distances. . . there's something. . . something wrong. . . ." She shook her head. "I can't say."

"Well," Brokk said briskly, "We'll camp here. I'll not ha' us benighted in th' wood until we've scouted more thoroughly."

At daybreak, while Jerry and the dwarf struck camp, Ulf disappeared into the forest. He returned a couple of hours later to report no sign of anything amiss.

Brokk looked at Freya. "D'ye still feel th' wrongness, my love?"

The elf-woman concentrated on her amulet. She shook her head, undecided. "I feel there's evil astir, but cannot bring it into focus."

She looked at Brokk. "It is confused, husband. The evil seems to be directed not at us, but at others. . . . I cannot say."

Brokk scrubbed his beard and eyed the forest. He came to a decision. He looked at Ulf.

"We'll remain closed up. Ulf, ye keep nigh."

He turned to his wife. "My love, bespeak ye th' dog an' we'll ha' her range ahead. Can ye maintain elfin contact wi' her?"

Freya nodded. "To a certain extent."

For the next several hours the little band proceeded cautiously through the dense forest with Bryn scouting a mile ahead. Freya rode with her eyes closed, holding telepathic contact with the war-dog. The elf-woman would immediately be aware if the great mastiff should encounter anything out of the ordinary.

The little cart bumped along, Odin's Messenger clinging to the ridgepole favoring his splinted wing, complaining fretfully. There was no indication from Bryn that she had met with anything of interest.

There came a loud crack as one wheel jounced into a hole and splintered. On examination of the damage, Brokk found that the axle had also split. He removed his helmet, and wiped his brow on his forearm. "Not so bad," he announced, "a matter o' a couple o' hours. Ulf, if ye'll lend a hand here, I'll get my tools from th' cart."

"Can I be of any help?"

"Nay, Jerry lad. My thanks, but Ulf'll be all th' help I'll need."

Jerry felt charged with energy. He paced about, and finally approached the dwarf. "I can't sit still, Father," he declared, "I think I'll go up ahead, and help Bryn look for bad guys. I'll be careful." Brokk looked doubtful, but made no objection.

Half an hour later, Jerry reined in his pony. Bryn, who'd been trotting ahead of him, crouched abruptly, and the hair along her spine rose stiffly. Her cropped ears stood up, the scarred head swung back and forth as she tested the wind. The big dog looked back at her master. Jerry lighted down, and tethered his mount to a sapling. Adjusting his wrist shield and drawing his rapier, he moved up to the crouching dog.

For fifty yards Jerry flitted from tree to tree, Bryn moving silently at his side. From ahead came the chattering of ravens.

The red-beard parted a screen of leaves, and a silent curse rose in his throat.

He counted twelve bodies dangling from trees surrounding a small clearing, of the twelve, three were children. Nothing live moved in the glade except the black birds of death feeding on the corpses. Jerry figured the atrocity had been committed less than an hour before, as blood still flowed where cruel beaks tore flesh.

Jerry stepped into the open. Bryn stayed close to his side, hackles raised and teeth bared in a snarl. No one challenged him as he moved across this place of death.

On the far side he found where a troop of horses had milled around, a broad track of hoofprints leading off to the west. He studied the signs and estimated eight to ten riders. He went back for his pony, and followed warily after the murderers.

Once again Jerry dismounted as the war-dog bristled and pointed. Peering through a thick bush, he beheld three men-at-arms lolling beside the trail, while five others lashed a young girl to a tree. Laughing, they tore off her tattered rag of a dress. The girl looked to be about fifteen.

Jerry felt a red tide begin to rise in his belly.

He recognized it as the start of the berserker rage Jar Haz had felt on the hillside, and prepared to open himself up to it.

Even as the first tremors ran along his limbs and the breath caught in his throat, one of the lounging trio stood up and walked toward the five tormenting the girl.

"What a scurvy brute you be, Ragnar Ragnarssen," he said in an insolent drawl. "First a whoreson hangman, now a filthy rapist."

The one addressed turned toward the long-limbed youth. "Ye talk tall fer a milk-fed cub," he sneered. "I marked how ye and yer faint-hearted mates arrived late, an' shirked th' work in th' clearin'."

His four companions turned from the bound girl to watch their leader wring the neck of this young cockerel. All were grinning expectantly.

The lanky youth's friends rose lazily to their feet. The older, shorter one of the two scratched his chin. "Milk-fed cub?" he asked of no one in particular, "Faint hearted?"

The stocky mercenary gave his younger companions a pained look. "Surely that unwashed butcher o' children can't be referrin' t' you, Olin Longshanks. Or t' me."

He looked at the boy at his side. "He must be talkin' about you Orm Thorwaldssen." The older man eyed the fresh-faced boy. "Aye, that's it. Now that I think on it, you do look a bit maidenish and faint of heart."

The one called Orm gave his friend a grin, and looked at Ragnar.

"Do you think so? Do you really think that that spit-lickin' lackey of Baron Thurgild's could find th' courage t' insult me?"

The mild-looking youngster gave Ragnar a contemptuous stare. "Nay, Lars, th' mangy dog has th' guts only t' hang defenseless thralls and rape little girls." The youth laughed. "And he needs th' aid of four scum t' help him do *that*."

Ragnar's face turned purple with rage, the grins of his henchmen disappeared. The enraged Ragnar snarled wordlessly and grabbed for the longsword at his side.

The left hand of the youth called Olin Longshanks seemed to blur as he snatched a poniard from his belt and hurled it underhanded, simultaneously drawing his sword with his right.

The hilt of Olin's dagger protruded from under Ragnar's chin, a foot of blade extending from the back of his neck.

The dead man still tottered on his feet when Orm flung his axe, and Lars and Olin lunged.

In the space of a breath, the opposition had been reduced from five to one. It was easy to see that these three had fought shoulder to shoulder before now. They seemed to think and move as one.

The remaining thanesman dropped his weapon, and fell to his knees. Jerry was left gasping at the speed and precision with which the trio had concluded the encounter.

Orm placed a foot on the chest of one of the fallen, and wrenched his axe from the man's skull. Lars wiped his shortsword on a handful of his victim's tunic, and Olin retrieved his dagger from its sheath in Ragnar's throat.

He looked at the kneeling churl. "Faith, ye deserve t' die," he said thoughtfully. The thanesman fell on his face, crying for mercy.

"Ar-r-gh," Olin cleared his throat and spat. "Get up. I wouldn't soil my blade with such muck. Get mounted an' get ye gone afore I repent my charity."

The pitiable wretch scrabbled away, caught up one of the horses, and galloped off.

The grizzled Lars looked at the dead men-at-arms. "Well," he sighed, "it appears we're masterless once more. 'Twas a short commission. . . two days only."

"Aye," Orm laughed, "I misdoubt Baron Thurgild will welcome us with feasting and maidens for our work here,"

Olin slashed the ropes holding the terrified girl to the tree. She sank to her knees and raised clasped hands. "Please, my lord, please don't kill me."

"Get up, lass," the boy said roughly, "I'm no lord, only a rovin' man-at-arms. Get up, get up. Ye've nothin' t' fear from us. We're not like those butchers' lackeys. We had no part in what happened t' your kin back there."

The tall youth picked up the tattered remains of the girl's dress from the ground, examined it, and threw it aside. He tugged the cloak from one of the fallen, and tossed it to her. "Here, girl, cover yourself," he said gently.

"Aye, lass," Orm said, "We'd have stopped th' swine if we'd known their intent. We thought only t' return you t' th' castle."

Jerry had heard enough to convince him that the trio were men worth knowing. He was sure that Brokk would welcome the addition of three such stout swords to Freya's protection.

With Bryn at his side, he stepped into the open. Immediately the three friends whirled, hands to weapons. "Whoa!" shouted Jerry, "Hey, hold on, guys. I'm a friend."

He raised both arms over his head, keeping a wary eye on Olin's left hand where it hovered near his belt.

Bryn looked at her master for guidance. "No, girl," he said, "Stay."

Jerry had gathered that, although the youngest of the three, Olin Longshanks was obviously their leader.

It was to him he spoke. "Looks like you guys just quit your job," he smiled. "You looking for another?"

The tall youth stepped forward, and examined Jerry closely. He seemed particularly interested in the long slim rapier at Jerry's side.

"Your speech is odd," he said, "Where be your holdin', and what are ye called?"

"I have no holding. I'm on my way to Asgard with my godparents and a friend, to ask a favor of Odin. I'm called Jerry Jar Haz, and I'd feel a lot safer if your hand were a little farther away from that knife." Jerry jerked a thumb at the late Ragnar Ragnarssen.

Olin's eyes widened a little at the name, but he didn't move his hand. "We've heard of Jerry Jar Haz. There's hardly a campfire in th' land where tales of Thor's Fist and his magic sword aren't heard. How know we that ye be he?"

Jerry grinned. He stooped, and picking up a rock the size of a man's fist, crushed it between his steel fingers.

The three eyed Jerry's left hand. Orm's voice was tinged with awe at the power thus exhibited. "Then 'tis no gauntlet ye wear, but th' iron Fist of Thor visitors t' Svartheim speak of."

He looked at Jerry's face. "But 'tis said Thor's Fist be godson t' Brokk, th' Dwarf King. What manner of man would claim kinship t' one of th' Little People, th' stealers o' children?"

Mention of the Wee Folk caused the girl to gasp. Jerry noted that the frightened maid was trying to construct a makeshift dress from the cloak Olin had given her.

Olin followed his gaze, and went to her. He drew his knife, and cut a hole in the center of the cloak. The girl looked her thanks, and slipped it over her head poncho-wise. The boy removed a belt from one of the fallen, cut it down, and punched holes to fit the girl's slender waist. She looked pathetically grateful.

The young mercenary eyed Jerry up and down. "Aye, Orm speaks true, yet ye've not th' look of a child stealer, nor one who'd be party t' th' vile practice."

Lars, the grizzled mercenary, waved a hand. "Olin, lad, that be naught but an old wives' tale. 'Twas started t' frighten naughty children into behavin'."

"It be well known that. . . ." Olin began.

The old warrior snorted. He looked at Jerry and back at Olin. "Jar Haz can tell ye that it
be true th' Little People do, at times, take a child of th' man kind. . . ."

Olin grimaced. "Ye see?"

Lars chopped the air with a hand. "Let me finish. I, too, know this t' be true. But, boy,
th' only ones they take are those who, by some reason known only t' Odin, were born stunted, and be abused or abandoned by our kind. "Poor little tykes who are taunted and maligned even by their own parents. 'Tis only for them that the Little Folk come. T' take the poor unfortunates and give them a better way."

Jerry nodded. "That's so. Any child taken is raised with love and tenderness."

Olin and Orm looked at their older companion. "How know ye this t' be th' way of it, Lars o' th' Battlefield?"

"I'll tell ye. . . ."

Orm, ye were six when I found ye and Olin, and I was th' same age th' night th' elves came t' my village. (Lars said.)

I was returnin' from fetchin' water from th' village well when I spied three elfin warriors movin' silently up on th' house of Hans Adler, th' stone-cutter.

Before I could scream th' alarm, I was seized from behind, and a hand over my mouth cut off my cry. Ye can imagine th' terror in my heart! I was bein' stolen by th' Wee Folk, even as my Da had warned me would happen unless I mended my ways!

I near swooned from terror.

Then a wave of peace rolled over me, washin' away my fright, and a voice spoke softly inside my head. "Calm yourself, boy. You've naught to fear from us."

I don't know how I knew, but I knew that this was so. The elf released me, and I stood gawkin' at him. The little warrior, only inches taller than myself, laughed softly at my look of confusion. "You've naught to fear from the Little Folk," he repeated. You're a strong lad who'll grow to fine manhood. You're loved by your parents, are you not, boy?"

Confused even more, by this question, I nodded.

"Can you say the same for the son of the stonecutter?"

I knew what he meant. Eric Adlerssen, th' stone-cutter's son, was sickly and under-grown.

Though four years older than I, he stood no taller. He was th' butt of cruel jokes, teased by us children, despised and beaten by his father.

The' elf touched my shoulder. "'Tis he we come for. The wee lad is more the elf or dwarf kind than the man kind, and with us, he'll not be mistreated, but given the love withheld by his father. Will you keep our secret?"

Shamed by my own treatment of th' stone-cutter's son, I nodded. "Aye."

Next day th' villagers wondered at th' disappearance of Eric Adlerssen, but none really cared. Th' lad's own father was relieved t' see th' last of him.

I held my tongue.

Jerry shot the old soldier a grateful look. "Lars is right. I've lived among the dwarfs for over half a year. Let me tell you something of their true nature."

He held up his iron hand. "This is the gift of a man who, though a dwarf, stands taller than any of us."

Jerry told them of the battle on the hillside, and the resultant loss of his hand. He told how Brokk the dwarf had saved his life and taken him home, where Freya the elf-woman had sewn him back together and mothered him.

He told how the dwarf and his wife had adopted him as their own son. Of his lost Janet, and how his new godparents insisted on taking him to Asgard to ask Odin's help in finding her.

"And that's where we go, Asgard. It's a long and dangerous journey, and I think my godfather would welcome three such stout fighters."

At this reminder of Asgard, Jerry saw the eyes of the younger mercenaries light up. Lars, making the same observation, chuckled.

"Asgard, lads! Asgard! The name of Brokk, th' Dwarf King, is legend throughout all th' Nine Worlds, and he sounds more th' man of honor than most of th' barons we've sold our swords to. And he goes t' Asgard! Think, lads, think!

"Mayhap th' chance t' visit Valhalla! Mayhap t' see again old comrades-in-arms! What say ye?"

Jerry watched as the three talked among themselves.

He really wanted these men, and he knew that Brokk would welcome three such stout swords to add to Freya's protection.

Orm and Olin were quick as cats, and Lars was older than Jerry had thought, at least forty-five, which spoke much about the grizzled warrior's worth as a fighter.

Mercenaries seldom lived so long.

He turned to the girl, who, after listening to Lars's tale of his encounter with the elves, seemed to have lost some of her fear of the Little People. Jerry smiled at her. "My godmother would delight in caring for you, girl, tending your bruises and healing your inner pain. You should see her. She's the most beautiful woman in all the Nine Worlds, beautiful as the Goddess of Spring, herself, and she's as loving as she is beautiful."

The companions completed their discussion, and Olin spoke for them all. "Never did we think t' take service with one of the Little Folk, but Lars has said th' tales of them be not true, and never has Lars lied."

He grimaced, then grinned. "Nor is it every day that comes th' chance t' journey t' Asgard. We'll go with ye, and talk with your godfather."

"Fair enough."

Jerry reckoned that now was not the time to spring Ulf on them. He'd just have to wait and see what happened when the mercenaries saw the goblin.

Jerry chose one of the captured horses to substitute for the battle-shy pony, which he collected on the way back. The party avoided the glade of death to spare the girl the sight of her kin dangling there.

Jerry, in the lead, spotted the little cart. He noticed that the broken wheel had been replaced and camp set up.

Ulf and Brokk, at sight of the approaching riders, drew weapons and waited, Ulf with his sling, and the dwarf with a throwing knife in either hand. They recognized Jerry, and relaxed.

The red-beard was alert for hostile reaction on the part of the mercenaries at sight of the goblin. Olin yelled, "Betrayed! Ye've tricked us!" The three whipped out their weapons.

Jerry reined his horse against Olin's, caught the young mercenary's sword in the quillion of his rapier, and sent it flying with a twist of his wrist.

"Ulf!" he roared at the top of his lungs. "Disarm them!"

The goblin's sling whistled, and Orm's axe flew from his hand. In like manner, Lars's sword was struck from his hand. The startled trio milled about in confusion, trying to assimilate what had happened.

Brokk stepped forward. He looked from Jerry to the mercenaries. The dwarf sheathed his knives. "Calm yerselves," he said gruffly, "if any here were yer enemy, ye'd be dead, instead of disarmed, would ye not?"

The three eyed Ulf, more confused than ever. Lars was first to recover.

"A Rover!" he exclaimed. "'Tis one of th' Rovin' Goblins."

He turned to his companions and echoed Brokk's words. "Calm yourselves, lads. As th' dwarf has said, had th' Twisted One wished, we'd be dead."

Brokk nodded. "Aye. Ulf ha' no quarrel wi' th' human kind. He's enemy t' none except those who'd make him so."

The dwarf turned to Jerry. He removed his helmet and grinned. "Did ye not tell th' lads about us?"

Jerry laughed. "I told them about you and Mother Freya," he said, "I'm afraid I forgot to mention Ulf."

Brokk grinned. "Aye. 'Tis easy t' ferget a little thing like a goblin."

He turned back to the three. "Stay yer fears, lads. None here ha' any quarrel wi' ye." He waved a hand at a boar roasting on a spit nearby. "Light ye down an' share our fare."

The companions hesitated, looking at one another. The two younger men still eyed Ulf with hostility, though Lars seemed not to share their suspicion.

The grizzled soldier pointed to Orm's shattered axe lying on the ground, and his own sword a few yards distant. "Use your wits, lads. Can ye not see that th' dwarf speaks true? Th' goblin's bullets that struck our weapons could just as easily have struck our heads, but they did not. There's no ill-will here."

He looked at the roasting boar. "I, for one," he said, "am hungry, and accept th' invitation t' share meat."

Olin still hesitated. He looked at Jerry. "Why did ye not mention th' Twisted One afore now?"

Jerry laughed. "Would you have come this far if I had?"

A reluctant smile touched the young mercenary's lips. "Nay," he admitted, "if ye'd said Little Folk *and* a goblin, Odin himself could not have dragged us here!"

Olin looked the goblin up and down. "By Thor's hammer, 'tis a strange life, t' be sure. Only this mornin' we served a man who is a monster, and now I'm told t' look on a monster as a man. All th' gods must be laughin'"

Ulf chuckled. "Youngster, you could have phrased that a bit more gently, but I'll take no offense. Let there be truce between us until we know each other better. Agreed?"

Olin grimaced. "Lars has said it. Ye could have killed us, but ye did not. Aye, then, a truce."

Brokk repeated his invitation. "Light down, then, and share meat wi' us."

Olin nodded, and the three dismounted.

Freya had been watching the interplay from her cart. As Olin and his mates alit, the battered girl, who'd ridden at the rear, was revealed. The little elf-woman uttered a sharp cry of pity, and jumped to the ground. "Jerry, you addlepate, why did you not bring this poor child forward at once?"

She swung on Ulf, who stood nearest the girl's horse. "Ulf," she demanded, "bring that poor lamb to the cart."

The goblin looked at the girl, who cringed back in fear. He made no move toward her, his deep, mellow voice tender as he said. "I know I appear in your eyes a monster, but ye've no reason t' fear me, lass."

The frightened girl stared at the horrifying visage confronting her, terror twisting her features.

Freya raised her voice. "Child," she said.

The girl looked at the little elf-woman.

From Freya's lips came that eerie trilling. The fright faded from the maiden's face, and the three mercenaries gaped in disbelief as the girl ceased her fearful trembling, and extended her hand trustingly, allowing the goblin to lift her from the saddle.

They watched, still gawking, as Ulf carried the battered girl to the covered wain. Freya took charge of her, murmuring little sounds of reassurance. They disappeared into the cart.

Olin, Orm, and Lars stared at one another, their faces reflecting their perplexity at the actions of the girl. . . her, to them. . . inexplicable trust in the goblin.

Olin shook his head, his face a comical mixture of emotions. He studied the gangling Spider Man.

"This day has been most confusin'. I meet a warrior famed from one end of th' Nine Worlds t' th' other. I meet th' King of th' Dwarfs. 'Tis not enough. I meet one of th' goblin kind who does not attempt t' kill me. 'Tis still not enough. Th' goblin is trusted by a small slip of a girl. . . ."

The young mercenary shook his head again. "I can make no sense of it, but if a girl fears ye not, then how should I?"

Ulf chuckled. "As you say, most confusin'."

Brokk laughed. He filled drinking horns from a small keg of ale, and passed them around. He indicated the roasting boar. "'Twill be ready shortly, sit ye down."

Orm retrieved his companions' swords and his axe. The haft had been shattered by Ulf's bullet. He looked at it ruefully.

"One moment I was armed with an axe, the next I held a piece of splintered wood." He looked at Ulf with respect. "I'd not like t' face your sling as an enemy, friend Ulf," Orm laughed, "Consider me a companion."

The goblin grinned.

Orm whispered to Brokk out of the side of his mouth. "Why is he barin' his fangs at me?"

The dwarf chuckled. "'Tis a goblin smile. Ye'll get used t' it. Ye'll find Ulf a friendly fellow, if ye'll have it so."

Orm grinned. "If that's his smile, I've no wish t' see his scowl."

Ulf, overhearing, joined in Brokk's roar of laughter. Brokk took the young mercenary's axe. "I'll replace th' handle fer ye on th' morrow."

Ulf reached a long arm and turned the spit. Juices dripped from the roasting boar onto the coals, and filled the air with a mouthwatering aroma.

Brokk addressed Lars, the oldest of the trio. "Tell me, friend," He wiped foam from his beard. "d'ye serve a lord hereabout?"

Lars spat. "No longer," he growled. The old soldier looked at Jerry. "Your godson can tell ye why."

Jerry described his meeting with the three. "I offered them service under you, Father, if you approve."

Brokk studied the three men. It was plain from the dwarf's expression that he approved what he saw.

He turned to Olin since it was obvious that the youngster spoke for all three. "That ye quit Baron Thurgild shows that ye're men wi' honor. 'Tis in yer favor. If ye've no objection t' takin' service wi' a dwarf," he said, "'tis pleased I'd be t' ha' yer swords t' add protection fer my wife."

He looked at each again. "Though in truth, ye'd be regarded more as companions than as liegemen."

The dwarf leaned forward. "I know not th' goin' pay fer men-at-arms. I offer ye yer keep, fifteen gold marks a month each man, a dangerous journey, perils, hardship, an' my friendship. If ye'll see us through t' Asgard an' back t' Svartheim, ye'll ha', as a bonus, all th' gold ye can carry. Fair enough?"

The three looked at one another in amazement. Olin spoke for all of them. "Fair? Lord Brokk, 'tis far too much! Fifteen *silver* marks per *year* be a princely sum for a hired sword! We cannot, in honor, accept any such riches. For what ye offer for one month, ye could hire an entire troop of Free Companions t' serve ye for years!"

Brokk waved a hand. "Lad, ha' ye any concept o' how much gold a race o' miners can lay up in a few centuries? Think no more on it.

"As fer a troop o' Free Companions, I'll ask ye this. Ha' ever ye served wi' one such where ye could trust all yer messmates t' be depended on at all times?"

The three looked at each other and grimaced.

Olin shook his head. "Ye've th' right of it, Lord Brokk. Most hired swords be brawling drunkards, fit only for the sort of work Ragnar and the others performed this morning."

Orm spat into the fire. "With one exception only, they're bands of hangmen, th' most of them."

Lars and Olin nodded agreement. "Aye. With one exception."

Brokk smiled. "Ye see? We be a small, tight band o' friends. Friends guard one another."

Olin cleared his throat. "How know ye that we be not of that stripe?"

The dwarf smiled. "How'd I know ye'd refuse my gold?"

CHAPTER SIXTEEN

Darkness had fallen by the time Freya stepped down from the cart. She came to the fire and accepted a trencher of pork sliced for her by Brokk.

"The little lamb is sleeping," she said. "Poor child. To have lost all her kin. She is called Maryam. Her father was Hafrin, steward to Thurgild, baron of this shire called Gildholm. Maryam told it thus. . . ."

Hafrin served the old Baron Thurgild who was a hard master, but fairhanded. The old baron had freed him as reward for battlefield courage. Eventually, Hafrin was made steward of Gildholm Castle, a position of honor and respect usually reserved for some minor noble, as it was the steward's duty to see to the smooth running of his lord's household.

When Hafrin fell in love with the daughter of one of Thurgild's knights and she with him, the baron spoke in his behalf to the girl's father, and marriage was arranged between them. Thus Maryam was no daughter of thralls, but a gentle with servants of her own.

The old baron had died the year before, and Thurgild Thurgildssen had come into the title and the lands.

The new master of Gildholm was the opposite of his father, harsh and cruel, with strange appetites. The carnal nature he had had to suppress while his father lived, he now gave free rein.

No girl in the holding above the age of puberty was safe from her liege lord's bestial desires.

The castle's dungeons were filled with fathers, brothers, and lovers who'd been so foolish as to object to the baron's seizing of their loved ones.

The torturer and his lackeys were kept busy with branding iron, rack, and strangling cord.

Hafrin managed to keep Maryam from his lord's attention until by chance Thurgild spied the girl from a castle tower.

The baron sent at once for Hafrin to learn her identity.

When it came out that she was the steward's daughter, Thurgild flew into a rage at Hafrin's duplicity in keeping from him such a tidbit. He ordered the steward and all his family to the dungeons with the exception of Maryam who was to be brought to his bed.

Two of the baron's men-at-arms were loyal to Hafrin, and with their help an escape was arranged before Thurgild's orders could be carried out.

Hafrin, his wife, his four children, and his servants, fled the castle, only to be overtaken in the wood by Ragnar and his men.

Among the bodies dangling in the glade were Maryam's parents, her two younger brothers, and a sister. The rest were servants loyal to the steward.

The elf-woman touched Olin's cheek. "She told me how you came to her rescue, and what a mighty warrior you are."

The tall youth turned deep red.

Freya's elf-bell laughter tinkled. "Like Tyr the Swordsman, is how she described you."

The little elf-woman examined Olin critically. "I see little likeness to the god, but then I'm not fifteen, and in love."

Lars slapped his knee. "Aye. Olin Longshanks, defender of ravished maidenhood! Like Tyr, like Sigurd battlin' th' dragon, Fafnir!"

He nudged Orm. "What say ye, Orm? D'you not feel honored by his presence?"

Orm grinned. "Aye, Lars, I'll feel less terror next time we face an enemy, knowin' I've a war-god at my elbow."

Olin stood up, anger in his face. Brokk reached and laid a hand on the boy's arm. "Easy lad, they're only chafferin' you."

The dwarf chuckled. "Is it, then, such a bad thing t' ha' a pretty female o' your kind t' look on ye wi' gratitude?"

The young mercenary looked at his grinning companions, then at Freya's smiling face. The affection plainly mirrored in the elf-woman's eyes cooled his temper. The young man looked long at her.

His voice was filled with admiration as he said, "Thor's Fist spoke less than the truth, my lady, when he said only that you were th' loveliest woman in all th' Nine Worlds. If ye'll not be offended by th' words of a common hired blade, Lady Freya, no goddess in Asgard could possibly be your equal in beauty or kindness. 'Twill be an honor t' serve you."

Lars cleared his throat. "'Tis a windy speech, my lady Freya," he said, "but th' lad speaks for all of us."

"Aye," Orm agreed, "'Tis what I'd have said," he said with a sly dig at his friend, "only I've not th' silver tongue of th' young god."

Freya smiled. "It was a very pretty speech, Olin Longshanks." She gave a little laugh.

"I'm glad I'm no longer an impressionable maid, or my heart would be fluttered by such flattery."

Olin looked hurt. "My Lady," he protested, "I meant my words."

Freya's smile soothed. "I know you did, Olin Longshanks." She patted his hand. "And I am pleased."

The elf-woman looked at all three. "I feel like a queen with such defenders."

"An' so ye are, my love," Brokk said gruffly. He turned to Jerry. "Ye've done us all a service this day, son Jerry."

He scooped a horn of ale and held it high. "T' stout comrades." The dwarf placed the horn to his lips and lowered it empty.

Freya eyed her husband. She rose, and moved toward the cart. "Brokk Hammermacher, I want to hear nothing, not one word, concerning the state of your head in the morning." She looked at each of the others, a little smile at one corner of her mouth. "My lack of interest on that subject extends to you all. Good night."

They sat until late, discussing the destination of the journey and its reason. Though the level of the ale-cask went down considerably, none of the six had a head to complain about in the morning.

The three comrades looked at one another. Asgard! Olin voiced their awe at the thought.

"T' visit th' gods! 'Tis even more bogglin' t' th' mind than learnin' that Lord Jerry comes from another world and another time!"

While the mercenaries' attitude showed that they had lost some of their preconceived notions about goblins, and ceased to look on Ulf as a freak, accepting him as a comrade came a little more slowly.

The talk touched on how the three had come to be such close companions.

Lars heaved a great sigh of self-pity. "It's been my burden t' wet-nurse this pair ever since I pulled them as squallin' brats from th' flames of their village. These two and a dog were all that was left alive after a neighborin' thane swept down on their liege lord. Th' dog died, but I've been saddled with these infants for nigh fifteen years."

Orm nodded. "That's th' truth of it," he affirmed. "With one or two minor mis-statements. True it is that grandfather here passed through our village at a time of strife. But it was Olin, bein' a strappin' lad of four, and my humble self, a sturdy wight of six, who guided his feeble, falterin' steps t' safety, and we've had t' protect th' dodderin' gaffer from hurt and cut up his meat for him. Other than that, his account's accurate enough."

"I see," Brokk chuckled.

Olin looked curiously at Jerry's rapier.

"Never have I seen a blade like that carried by Jar Haz. 'Tis much too light t' be of great use is my thought. Why does he bear such a feeble weapon? Th' traders t' Svartheim carry tales of an invincible whirlwind called Thor's Fist. I cannot see. . . ."

Brokk chuckled. "Jerry, lad," he called.

"Yes, Father?"

"Young Longshanks thinks yer blade a mite frail."

Ulf grinned his goblin grin. "Aye, Jerry, th' splinter you carry does excite laughter amongst th' warrior kind. Why don't you carry a real weapon?"

Jerry stood up, smiling. "Friend Olin," he said, "arm yourself."
"I meant no offense."

"And no offense taken. It's to be a demonstration of fighting style, nothing more. No blood will be drawn, I promise you."

Looking a little uncertain as to just what he'd gotten himself into, Olin picked up his shield and drew his longsword.

Smiling, Jerry strapped on his wrist-ward and unsheathed.

"Have at me, Olin Longshanks. Don't hold back, attack as though the maid, Maryam, were at risk."

The gentle taunt drew laughter from Orm.

Cheeks reddening, Olin charged. He was no more surprised than were Lars and Orm when his overhead cut slid along Jerry's slender blade, and was caught in the quillion. The sword, wrenched from his hand, was sent flying by a twist of Jerry's wrist.

Jerry stood back, grounded his point and rested both hands on the pommel. "You seem to be weaponless, friend Olin," he grinned. "There's little honor for me in fighting an unarmed man."

The young mercenary looked from his empty hand to his sword lying yards away. He stared blankly at Jerry for a moment then broke out laughing.

"'Thor's Fist,' indeed! My weapon was struck from me by the lightning of Thor!"

He laughed again. "And that is how I will tell it, when I relate the tale of my first encounter with Jerry Jar Haz called Thor's Fist!"

Olin lowered his shield. He looked at Orm and Lars who were still staring, open mouthed. He grinned. "I guess I learned what I wanted to know."

He retrieved his longsword from where it lay several yards away. "Lord Jerry, could you teach me that trick?"

"Not with the sort of blade you carry." He held out the rapier.

The young mercenary took the light sword and examined it almost reverently.

"Ah-ha," he exclaimed, "now I see how you managed it." He ran his fingers over the curved ends of the crossguard.

Olin looked at Jerry and grinned. He looked at his empty hand and his grin widened. "It happened so quickly I had no idea where th' blade had gone! One second I was holdin' it, th' next I was empty handed! Never have I felt so much th' fool."

"Don't. You faced a totally unfamiliar fighting style. And a totally unfamiliar weapon. That's what gives me the advantage."

Though the boy's fascination with the rapier was obvious, he handled it as if it were a broadsword. Jerry took it from him, and flashed through a series of cuts, thrusts, and parries.

"It's used thus," he explained." He saw the longing on Olin's face. "I'll teach you," he said, "as soon as we can rig up something approximating a rapier for you."

Brokk overheard.

He patted Olin's arm. "There are elves in th' forest a few days march ahead who ha' some knowledge o' th' forge. I'll bespeak Freya t' communicate wi' them when we get farther along, an' if they agree, I'll craft ye a blade t' yer likin' lad."

The three mercenaries looked at their new employers incredulously.

Olin, ever their spokesman, cleared his throat. "Lord Brokk," he said in a low voice charged with emotion, "never have we been treated as equals by other than rough men-at-arms. But here we are accepted as comrades even as ye have said."

He looked at the other two. "My Lord, we pledged ourselves t' your service, but only as all Free Companions pledge their swords t' any who buy their skill."

The young mercenary looked from Brokk to Jerry. "Yet you, who've paid for the right t' treat us as hirelings, do instead treat us as friends."

The wonder of this showed in the faces of all three. "'Tis a new experience for th' likes of us." He scanned the faces of his mates and nodded.

"I say for all of us you have th' pledge not only of our swords but our hearts. We serve ye, Lord Brokk, for as long as you will have us, be it in this world or th' next!"

Brokk blew out his cheeks.

"Whush!" he snorted. "Lars ha' th' truth o' it. Ye are a windy one, Olin Longshanks. I'd correct ye on two points. Ye serve not *for* us but *with* us. An' fer as long as *ye* like, not th' other way 'round. Now, my long-winded young friend, if ye're through speechifyin', there's ale t' be drunk."

CHAPTER SEVENTEEN

Jerry threw back the corner of his cloak from his face and sat up. The sun not quite up, the glade was filled with a kind of pearly glow, and a light ground mist.

Freya had stirred up last night's campfire and was baking bread in a covered iron pot while chunks of the boar re-heated on a spit. On another spit at one side of the fire a number of trout were grilling.

There was movement from the direction of a small stream, and out of the mist came the tall figure of Ulf with more fish strung on a willow switch.

At the goblin's side walked Maryam, her makekshift dress gone, clad in one of Freys'a gowns let out to fit her. The girl's face turned up, laughing at one of Ulf's humorous sallies. Gone was the fearful, pathetic captive of yesterday. . . terrified by rapists, goblins, dwarfs, and the murder of her family.

In her place, a lissome young miss radiating happiness. The overnight change in the girl was stunning to anyone not familiar with Freya's elfin magic, the elf-woman's ability to telepathically communicate love, to calm, to soothe, to wash away pain, hurt, fear, and to heal a troubled heart.

Jerry knew that the little elf-woman had held the frightened child in her arms, and crooned her healing magic until all pain and fear had been cleansed from Maryam's soul.

The bright-faced, happy young woman skipping along at the goblin's side was proof of that.

Jerry stretched and stood up.

To one side the three mercenaries were rising from their cloaks, and Jerry grinned at the expression on Olin's face as his eyes followed Maryam's trim figure across the clearing. The girl knelt and began helping Freya at the fire.

Jerry's grin broadened as he watched the girl pretend that she was not aware of the young warrior's interest.

Brokk finished hitching the mules to Freya's cart, and beckoned for

Jerry to come help him round up the ponies and the captured horses.

Lars, Orm and Olin joined them. In a short while the beasts had been brought in and six of the horses saddled. The remaining horse and the three ponies were roped together in a line and tethered to the rear of the cart.

Bryn sprawled lazily under the wain, and Odin's Messenger walked back and forth on the ridgepole, keeping a bright golden eye on the bustle, and making derisive remarks. Freya called them to breakfast.

They were finished eating when Ulf returned from scouting the trail.

The goblin took the trencher of pork, fish, and black bread Freya handed him. He reported that all was well for the next few miles. Mercifully, the trail he had chosen lay far to the east of the glade of death.

The little band mounted up, and began the day's trek. Ulf scouted well out ahead. Brokk and Jerry rode point. Orm and Olin covered the flanks and Lars guarded the rear. Freya and Maryam chatted as the little wain bounced along.

Brokk had just called a halt for the noon meal when the baron's men broke from the surrounding trees and charged down upon them from two sides.

Orm flung his axe at the nearest rider, and drawing his sword, fell back toward the cart.

Olin's flying poniard emptied another saddle and he, too, went to the defense of the women.

Brokk, roaring like an angry bull, reined left as Jerry pulled right, Bryn racing at his side.

Jerry Haskins, the insurance salesman, had never fought on horseback, but to Jar Haz the Viking it was an old tale. Jerry let the Viking rise up inside him and take charge. Jar Haz's war cry burst from his lips.

He looped the reins over the saddle horn, steering the battle trained mount with his knees, and drove full into the charging horn-hats. The long rapier darted right and left like a striking snake. The terrible steel hand ripped away chunks of shield, armor, and flesh.

The steed, trained to fight, whirled this way and that, ironshod hooves dealing death to man and horse.

Bryn's almost two hundred pounds of fighting fury dragged rider after rider from the saddle to gory end with slashing fangs.

The baron's men were obviously seasoned warriors, but the speed and utter fury of Jerry Jar Haz's counterattack caused panic among them. They fell back before that darting steel snake, that terrifying steel hand, and the blood-covered thunderbolt that fought at his side.

The attackers broke and stampeded from the field.

Jerry wheeled his mount and galloped to assist Brokk and Lars who were facing a considerably larger number of the enemy.

The dwarf crouched on his horse's back, laying about him with his Morning Star. Men flew bodily from the saddle wherever the whistling spiked iron ball struck. Lars was proving himself a formidable sword-and-shield man.

Bryn, racing ahead, leaped up onto a horse's rump and sank her fangs into the back of the rider's neck. The big dog flung away from the terrified horse, struck the ground, and like a huge bouncing rubber ball, knocked another rider from the saddle, ripping out his throat as they fell together to the ground.

Jerry Jar Haz, a screaming berserker, attacked, the terrible steel hand again striking terror. Only here, one sergeant held his men to discipline, and the fighting was hot and heavy.

Then Olin and Orm were there laying about with their longswords. Still, victory teetered on the balance.

The red-beard saw Brokk fall from his mount and grief overwhelmed him. The distraction caused him to miss a parry, and a glancing blow from a broadsword sent him reeling in the saddle, off-balance and unprotected. The broadswordsman yelled in triumph, and raised his weapon for the kill.

The stroke never came. A round hole appeared in the center of the man's forehead and he disappeared from Jerry's view. All around him foemen were tumbling from the saddle as leaden bullets whizzed. He regained his balance.

Ulf's ululating cry rose above the sounds of battle as the goblin rode to the assistance of the three mercenaries, who were being hard pressed.

His assegai turned the balance as the four fought shoulder to shoulder. In a matter of moments the battle was over as the survivors fled the field.

Jerry shot one glance at the cart to ascertain that Freya and the girl were unharmed then searched for Brokk.

The furious dwarf stood spraddle-legged, shaking his fist at the now vanished enemy. Blood covered one side of his face but there was no doubt that the enraged little man was not seriously wounded. Jerry's relief was such that he felt lightheaded.

Jerry assessed their casualties. Orm, Olin and the goblin were uninjured. Lars's shield arm hung limply, Brokk's scalp bled freely, Jerry had taken two shallow cuts, and Bryn was favoring her left foreleg. At sight of the limping dog, Jerry leaped to the ground to examined her. To his relief she appeared no more than bruised.

Jerry accounted their hurts exceptionally light as he totaled up seventeen enemy bodies and six horses.

Brokk stumped by, headed for the cart and muttering curses.

"Th' whoreson scum ha' had their bellies filled wi' fightin' fer this day," he said with satisfaction.

The defenders gathered about the little cart. Brokk looked at his wife. "Why'd ye send yer guard away, my love? Th' lads had orders t' remain at yer side an' they'd not ha' left ye unless ye bade 'em do so."

The two young mercenaries looked relieved. "Then you blame us not, Lord Brokk?"

The dwarf shook his head. "Nay, lads. Ye but obeyed yer mistress."Brokk gave his wife a stern look.

The elf-woman returned her husband's scowl. "Now hear me, Brokk Hammermacher. I told you before we left Svartheim that I'd not be a burden on you. I've the Gift to protect myself and the child. You know that well. I'll not have you weakening your forces and endangering us all, by keeping two stout fighters tied down to guard that which needs no guarding. Do you hear me, husband?"

The dwarf grinned. "Aye, my treasure, I hear ye. D'ye think, my love, that ye could find yer needle? Yer husband an' yer son ha' need o' yer skill."

A smile played about the elf-woman's lips. "Aye, husband. Maryam dear, fetch my sewing kit."

"Yes Mother."

Lars, gripped his shoulder, and looked at the goblin.

"How is it ye can live your whole life believin' a thing," he said, "only t' find 'tis not so?"

The grizzled mercenary gave Ulf a long look. "Life is one surprise after another. You know th' feelin's of th' man kind toward your race. 'Tis true you're as fearsome a man as I've been told, but lookin' past your fearsomness, I see a friend who came to my aid. Aye, life is indeed a strange adventure, and I owe mine t' what you did back there, friend Ulf."

Olin spoke for Orm and himself. "Aye, goblin, Lars has said it. We all owe our lives t' your timely arrival. Without your help, we'd have been o'erwhelmed."

He extended his hand. "We'd be your friends."

Ulf gripped the proffered hand. "It is good to have friends."

Olin examined Lars's dangling arm. "The shoulder's been dislocated, 'tis all," he announced, "Orm, lend a hand."

Ulf asked if he could be of any assistance.

"Nay, friend, we're accustomed t' tendin' each others' hurts. I thank ye for your concern."

Orm grasped the older man about the chest, and Olin gave the arm a sudden yank. With a loud pop the bone snapped back into its socket. Lars rubbed his shoulder and moved it gingerly.

"Nicely done, infant."

Jerry and the dwarf sat stoically while Freya stitched up their cuts. Maryam gave Olin a shy look. "I'm glad you weren't hurt," she said softly.

Orm grinned at her. "What about me, little sister? Are you not glad that I be unharmed as well?"

The girl smiled at the young mercenary. "With all my heart, Orm Thorwaldssen."

She looked at all three. "I haven't thanked you for all you did in my behalf. If not for you, I'd have been shamed and left as food for the ravens."

It was Orm's turn to blush.

He cleared his throat. "'Twas no great thing we did, little sister, 'was only a thing that needed be done."

He touched the girl's cheek and walked away to round up the horses.

Freya finished her needlework, and Brokk called a council of war. He looked at the three.

"Did ye mark who th' whoreson were?"

"Aye," said Lars. "'Tis Baron Thurgild again."

The dwarf grunted. "I thought so. 'Twas t' be expected."

Olin spat. "I knew I'd repent lettin' that whimperin' craven live. 'Twas he set th' baron after us, and now we've brought his anger down on ye and your lady. . . ."

Brokk cut the youngster off with a peremptory wave of his hand. "Olin lad, d'ye think th' possibility had escaped me when I heard Jerry's account o' yer affray wi' Ragnar an' th' rest? Nay, lad."

The young warrior still looked troubled. He fingered the hilt of his sword. "I should have run th' dog through. But my Lord Brokk, 'tis one thing t' cut down a man in th' heat of battle, quite another t' do so whilst he blubbers on his knees. I. . . ."

"Ye did right," Brokk said gruffly. "I'd not ha' offered t' take ye into my service had ye done elsewise."

"You had no choice, Olin," Jerry said, "the question, is how many men will Thurgild sacrifice to his ego?"

"D'you mean will he attack again?"

"Yes."

"'Tis quite likely. It's not th' girl he's after. 'Tis plain Ragnar had orders t' hang her with th' rest. 'Tis his pride's been stung."

Maryam gave a little cry and shrank against Freya. The elf-woman put a protective arm around the shivering girl.

Olin looked uncomfortable. "Your pardon, lass. I was only tryin' t' answer th' Lord Jerry's question."

Jerry grinned. "About this Lord business. I'm not your lord. I'm trying hard to be your friend."

Olin looked pleased.

"Very well," he said, "*Friend* Jerry, then. I cannot answer with certainty. We had no chance t' gauge th' whoreson up close. 'Twas th' lass's father who engaged us only the day before you met up with us. But we've known many a dog of his kidney afore, and if Thurgild be as th' rest of th' breed, his pride's been wounded and he'll care little how many swords-for-hire get broken so long as he can mend it."

"Then," Brokk said thoughtfully, "we're t' expect all-out war."

"Aye, Lord Brokk. That's how I see it."

Freya spoke. "Husband, I know little about war, but it's my thought that to wait to be attacked is to lose. Is that not so?"

The dwarf nodded. "Aye, my love. In th' main that be so. What's yer thought on th' matter?"

"To win one must attack."

"Aye, but we six cannot attack a castle."

"Not the castle. Lay an ambush for them when they come tomorrow."

"We're still but six t' th' baron's many."

"That may be so, but. . . . Brokk, have you ever seen elves make war?"

"What's in that lovely head o' yers, my love?"

"When I was concentrating on the amulet during the melee to protect Maryam and myself, I sensed others of my kind not too far away. It is possible that they would come to our aid. I could contact them."

"'Tis too much t' ask. If they war on th' humans they chance arousin' th' ancient fear o' th' Little People. It could bring down a war o' extermination on 'em. We can't ask that."

Freya smiled. "We can ask, husband. They do not have to agree."

Brokk looked at the others. "What a wonderful thing is th' direct logic o' a woman. Who can argue wi' it? Well, what say lads? Shall we ask th' help o' th' elves?"

Jerry shrugged. "The worst they can do is turn us down."

Olin, speaking for the three, looked uncomfortable. "Lord Brokk," he said uneasily, "'Tis a fact that Ulf has shown us that what we believed about th' Goblin Folk be not so. But, t' be surrounded by elves. . . ."

The boy took a deep breath and straightened his shoulders. His tone firmed.

"My lord, we've sworn you our lives and our hearts. We follow where you lead."

Brokk chuckled. "I take it ye'd be more comfortable among giants?"

Lars grinned. "I wouldn't go quite that far, Lord Brokk." The grizzled mercenary sobered. "We be uneasy, my lord, but th' lad has said it. You lead, we follow."

Brokk looked at the goblin. "Ulf?"

"I think as Jerry. They can only refuse us."

The dwarf turned to his wife and grinned. "Well, my dear, it seems female logic takes th' day."

Freya cast a look about. "Let us be away from this place. The ravens are arriving, and soon the wolves will come."

"As ye say."

Brokk turned to the others. "Mount up. We'll put a few miles betwixt us an' this carrion." The dwarf leaped, and catching the saddlehorn, swung himself into the saddle.

Ulf, grinning sourly, rode off to scout. "This time I'll bypass no ambushes," he growled. Though no one had said anything, the goblin's face reflected his mortification at having missed the trap.

Orm and Lars fanned out as outriders. Brokk and Jerry flanked the cart and Olin rode drag.

Half way across the glade, the dwarf reined in and leaped to the ground. He picked up a fallen sword and examined it closely. He uttered a grunt of satisfaction, and handed it up to Jerry.

"I thought I recognized th' workmanship," he said. "'Tis one crafted by my brother, Sindri. If Bjorn th' One Eyed o' th' Falconholm Elves will lend me th' use o' his forge I can fashion it into th' rapier I promised young Longshanks."

He remounted and caught up with the wagon.

Jerry reined around and cantered back to where Olin covered the rear. He handed the sword to the mercenary. "Throw away your blade. Here's a real top grade weapon. It was made by Brokk's brother. Brokk says it will make a number one rapier when he gets the chance to work on it"

The youngster shook his head in wonderment. "It is hard t' get used t' havin' my employer treat me as a son! No wonder you call him Father." Olin smiled. "'Tis a good feelin'."

"Aye, Olin, it is."

Half an hour later Brokk signaled to pull up. All but he remained on guard while he spoke to Freya. "Call yer kin, my love."

The elf-woman clasped her amulet in both hands and closed her eyes. She concentrated on a vision of the glade where the fighting had taken place, then visualized the clearing where they now waited. The visual message was accompanied by an urgent summons.

A voice sounded in her head. "I hear you cousin, and answer. Expect Gorm of the Woods Elves."

Freya opened her eyes. "Gorm of the Woods Elves will be here shortly, husband."

The dwarf nodded. "'Tis well, my dear. We'll see what comes o' it."

A quarter of an hour later Lars shouted, "Lord Brokk! A rider approaches."

Brokk wheeled his mount, and galloped to where the sword-and-shield man sat his horse, peering down the grassy trail. Ulf and Jerry closed in but the dwarf waved them back.

"Guard ye th' wain," he called, "Mayhap 'tis th' one we expect, or mayhap 'tis a trick o' th' baron's."

The approaching horseman was a slender youth in green doublet and trunk hose. Jerry would have described the costume as a sleeveless jacket over a leotard. A green tam-o-shanter with a scarlet-dyed hawk's feather sat cockily on one side of a thick mass of golden curls, and on his feet were calf-high boots of soft, red-dyed buckskin.

The handsome face wore an expression of merry mischief. His only armament was a short dirk at his belt.

The small harp slung at his back explained his lack of weapons. The jaunty rider was a skald, a bard, a wandering minstrel. A composer of Sagas, a singer of History.

None but a troll would dare harm such, for to do so would guarantee his name to be reviled down the ages. Should one such be harmed, every skald in Skandia would sing of the crime in every castle in the land. The little stringed lyre was surer protection than the heaviest armor. The Singer rode easily, one hand holding the reins, the other fist resting on his hip.

Brokk grinned. "All is well, friend Lars. Yon's an elf."

"Be you certain sure? He looks human t' me."

The dwarf chuckled. "'Tis one o' th' Tall Elves. Many such dwell amongst th' human kind. But he's an elf. Trust th' Little Folk t' recognize one o' their own."

Lars drew in a sharp breath. "Now there's a comfortin' bit o' news! How's a man t' know if he's speakin' t' a man or an elf?"

Brokk chuckled. "Ye can't."

He punched the mercenary on the arm. "There be one thing o' which ye can be certain."

"What might that be?"

With a straight face, Brokk answered, "There be no tall dwarfs."

Lars grinned. "Aye, Lord Brokk, that be so."

The Singer neared, and Brokk raised a hand in greeting. "Ye be Gorm o' th' Wood Elves, friend?"

"Aye. Where is she who summoned me?"

Brokk led the Tall Elf to the cart. Both Jerry and the two young mercenaries on guard were as puzzled as Lars had been. They, like Lars, had been expecting someone Freya's size. Brokk waved an arm, signaling all to fall back on the wagon.

"This be Gorm o' th' Wood Elves. He assures me we need fear no further attack this day. His scouts report th' baron's lackeys be lickin' their wounds at th' castle."

The Tall Elf's voice was fluted and pleasant. "You've given them much to think on, but Thurgild's livid with rage, and determined to see you all food for the ravens."

Gorm addressed Freya. "You summoned me, cousin. What would you have of me?"

"I seek your aid in fighting our way clear of Gildholm that we may continue on our way to Asgard."

The Singer rubbed his chin. "Why must there be fighting?" He swept one arm in a circle, indicating the peaceful, sunlit sward. "D'you insist on littering this pretty place as you left the one you showed me with your summons? Are you, then, so bloodthirsty, cousin?" There was a tiny twinkle in his eye.

Freya's look was puzzled and Gorm laughed.

"You've been long away from our people, have you not, kinswoman?"

"Aye, cousin. I was but a girl when I married my lord Brokk."

The Tall Elf gave the dwarf a friendly look. "Your fame is great, Brokk Hammermacher.

'Twill be a pleasure to aid you and. . ." He turned to Ulf. ". . . my old friend the Twisted One."

The goblin's grin widened. "Ho, Gorm-Who-Cannot-Carry-A-Tune," he jibed, "'Tis good t' lay eyes on ye once again."

The Singer clasped hands with the goblin. "So you're off to Asgard once more."

"'Tis a long tale and dull. But 'tis apt t' be considerably shortened without your help."

The Tall Elf laughed and turned back to Freya. "You've been long from your people, cousin, and so have not practiced over-much the Gift, is it not so?"

"It is so, cousin."

Gorm winked at Ulf who grinned broadly.

"Why strive with weapons when it be not necessary?"

He pointed a finger at Ulf and the goblin vanished.

Gasps and cries of amazement went up from the onlookers. Maryam clutched at Freya, trembling, and the three men-at-arms fell back, handling their weapons, and muttering protective charms.

Brokk and Jerry looked at each other and Freya laughed.

Olin, his fear of magic showing in his face, nevertheless stepped forward and demanded, "What have ye done with our friend?"

"Aye," growled Lars and Orm, "Where be th' goblin, sorcerer?"

The Tall Elf eyed the three companions, and the respect was plain in his look. More than any, Gorm knew the courage it took for the three humans to confront him at that moment. When he spoke the respect in his eyes was echoed in his tone.

"The Dwarf King is well served by such stout hearts," he said, "but be easy, your companion has not been harmed."

"Nay," Ulf's voice came out of the air, "naught's happened t' me." The goblin chuckled. "I've not moved."

Gorm waved a hand, and Ulf stood once more before them.

Freya said soothingly to Olin, "It's no magic, lad. 'Tis only the use of the Elfin Gift in the hands of an adept. I see now what Gorm meant about the needlessness for weapon play."

Brokk scratched his beard. "I'm happy th' affair's plain t' ye, my love, but th' rest o' us seem t' be in some'at o' a muddle."

Gorm chuckled. "I did nothing to the Twisted One. I but placed in your minds the thought that he was not there, and your minds, believing this, told your eyes that it was so. So you saw him not."

Gorm laughed. "The hand gestures were merely frumpery to impress you with my mystical powers."

Brokk grinned. "I see. When th' baron's hangmen come at us again ye'll wave yer hand an' we'll disappear from their sight!"

A small smile quirked one corner of the Tall Elf's mouth. "Not exactly. It's not as simple as all that."

Gorm looked at them. "To plant a thought in the minds of a small party about one man is no great feat. But to convince the forty or fifty who'll be sent against you on the morrow that eight folk, their horses and a wagon be not before them is quite a thing again. It will take more than my power alone."

He looked at Freya. "Even with your Gift and the power of our two crystals, 'twould be no certain thing, cousin. 'Tis why I've sent for more to aid us."

Gorm glanced at the sun. "Our cousins will join us near sundown." He smiled. "And they'll be hungry. Come, friend Ulf, bring your sling, and we'll fetch meat for the pot."

Freya descended from the wain. "Thank you, cousin. We're grateful."

Gorm laughed. "Thank me not, my sister. I shall make the vile master of Gildholm a laughingstock in every castle in the Nine Worlds with the tale of how the Wood Elves of Gildholm Forest threw Fairy Dust in his eyes, and allowed the Dwarf King to slip from his grasp.

'Twill make a merry tale."

Just before sundown Orm, on guard, reported the approach of a small troop of horsebackers.

Into the glade rode the elfin band. Two were Tall Elves, the other five only little taller than Freya. All were dressed in the forest green of the Wood Elves.

Any uneasiness felt by the three mercenaries at the presence of so many of the Little People was quickly dispelled by the friendliness of the newcomers. The elves whooped boisterously at sight of the stag roasting on one spit and the dozen partridges on another.

One chubby green-clad sprite kneed his mount over to where the stag turned under the supervision of Lars. He drew a long breath and expelled it explosively.

"I know not your name, friend," he grinned broadly, " but the aroma of your cooking has won the heart of Krupp the Round!"

The grizzled man-at-arms grinned back. "Ye've put your heart in th' hands of Lars o' th' Battlefield, so called because that is where my foster-father found me squallin' under a shield."

The tubby elf leaned from the saddle and clapped the sword-and-shield man on the shoulder.

"'Tis as safe a place as any in Midgard, I doubt it not." Krupp eyed the crisply browning carcass. "How soon will your cooking be ready to sample?"

Lars grinned. "It but waited your arrival. Th' Lady Freya will call us t' meat shortly."

Chuckling, Krupp rode to tether his horse with the rest.

The sun set and the meal concluded, firelight flickered over the faces of the assembled company. It revealed the rumps and switching tails of the horses tethered nearby to a rope stretched between two trees. It highlighted the boles of the trees crowding the small glade, and glittered on the edges of axe-blade, sword, and dagger.

Dripping horns and leather jacks filled from the goatskins of ale and mead brought by the elves were passed around, emptied, and filled again.

The plan of the morrow's battle had been explained by Gorm, and was simplicity itself. The plan was to do nothing.

At dawn Brokk and his party would set off along the trail flanked on all sides by elfin outriders. At the approach of the baron's men the elves would link forces and blanket the minds of the enemy, so that they would see nothing. The elfin escort would be maintained until no longer needed.

"Not th' way t' glory," Lars growled to Krupp. The old warrior grinned. "But I must admit 'tis much less exertious."

The mood of the assemblage was light.

It was discovered that Maryam had a sweet singing voice, and Gorm accompanied her on his lyre to shouts of approval.

Ulf regaled the party with a slyly humorous account of his prior meeting with the elfin skald, and a bawdy adventure he and Gorm had shared in a Midgard tavern.

Jerry was called on to explain his metal fist. Jerry's tale of time travel and his quest to find his lost Janet fascinated the elves.

Krupp the Round declared his intention to join the Company, and learn the outcome of the venture.

Brokk surveyed the rotund elf appraisingly. The little man's dimensions were due to hard muscle rather than fat, and the shortsword in its battered sheath looked well used.

The dwarf nodded. "We'd be happy to add one wi' th' Gift t' our defenses," he chuckled, "if ye still be so inclined on th' morrow when th' ale's left yer head."

Krupp's companions whooped with laughter.

"Aye, Krupp," one shouted, "They can always use you to roll down upon an enemy to sweep the feet from under him!"

Krupp grinned at the dwarf. "Ignore them, friend Brokk. 'Tis but the prattle of children." He emptied his alejack and accepted another from Maryam.

"Skald," shouted one of the Tall Elves, "sing us a tale."

Gorm stood and cradled his harp. He looked around the company, and struck a chord. Immediate silence fell on the glade.

"I sing the Saga of Sigurd, and the Sword of the Volsungs."

The bard's voice rose and fell as he sang. Now low and intense. Now ringing with triumph and passion as he retold the story of the Hero Sigurd, and how he slew Fafnir the great dragon, and of Gram, the Wondrous Sword of the Volsungs.

As he listened, Jerry was sure he was hearing the origin of the English legend of St. George and the Dragon.

In his world, the Vikings had struck as far south as Rome and North Africa. They had settled large portions of Ireland, Scotland, and Northern England, and they had apparently brought their myths with themm to be incorporated into the body of English lore.

The band of comrades was on the move at daybreak. Krupp the Round, despite complaining of the pounding of his head from last night's ale, reiterated his intent to accompany the Companions on their quest.

Brokk confided in Jerry his satisfaction in having Krupp add his elfin gift to the band's defense.

It was mid-morning before Gorm raised his arm to halt the troop.

"They come," he said.

The Tall Elf waved to right and left, signaling the party to split and move to trailside. The elfin escort closed ranks and brought out their amulets. The human members of the band looked at one another questioningly.

Nothing happened. Yet when the baron's men rounded a turn in the trail, they simply rode on, passing between them, to disappear around another turn.

CHAPTER EIGHTEEN

Gildholm was four days behind them, and the band, with its new recruit, was nearing the dwelling of the elf-clan Brokk had mentioned as having a forge.

The past four days had gone without incident. Ulf had chosen trails through the endless forest that were known to the Woods Elves, the roving goblins, and very few others.

Brokk reined in alongside Olin. "By noontide we should be t' Falconholm, th' Elf Hill so called because th' elves o' this steading claim brotherhood t' th' swift hunters o' th' air.

"'Tis here, if Bjorn th' One Eyed will lend th' use o' his forge, I'll turn that longsword o' Sindri's into a rapier such as th' one o' young Jerry's here ye admire so much. That's if ye still wish it so."

"Oh aye, Lord Brokk." The young mercenary's voice still held an echo of wonder at the dwarf's generosity. "'Tis a wondrous fine weapon. Ye've my eternal thanks. . . ."

"Oh tush, lad, 'tis only a sword. T' tell th' truth o' th' matter, Jerry sees in ye th' makin' o' a prime blade in th' style he calls fencin'."

The dwarf chuckled. "'Tis a matter o' selfishness, if ye must know. Th' deadlier ye become in yer craft, th' safer will be my heart's treasure."

The dwarf winked at Jerry. "An' th' lass, Maryam," Brokk added slyly. Jerry chuckled, and Olin reddened.

A short time later the hunting scream of a falcon was echoed by one deeper in the forest. Krupp kneed his mount alongside Brokk. "'Tis a Falconholm sentry announcing our arrival," he said.

"Be that you, Krupp the Round?" a voice asked from above their heads.

The four looked up at the elfin sentry lounging comfortably in the fork of a tree.

"Ho, Grokk," Krupp greeted. "'Tis good to see you again, cousin. Be all well at Falconholm?"

"Aye. We've been expecting your party since sun-up. Gorm the

Skald sent word of your coming."

The elf eyed Jerry up and down. "Be welcome to Falconholm. We be particularly interested to meet the Dwarf King's godson, Jerry Jar Haz called Thor's Fist. Gorm the Singer has composed a saga about him, and his travels from another world and time. 'Twill be a novelty to meet a Hero who's still living."

"You've a long tongue, cousin Grokk," Krupp grinned, "Take care it doesn't get tangled in the iron fingers of Thor's Fist."

Grokk looked at the dwarf.

"Bjorn the One Eyed is anxious to greet you, Brokk of Svartheim. He has questions on the matter of the working of certain metals to ask of you, master armorer."

The elf shrugged. "I leave such things to you dwarfs, but Bjorn has a drop of dwarfen blood so the subject interests him."

"An' I leave th' use o' th' Gift t' elves too lazy t' lift a hand at honest work," Brokk shot back.

Grokk laughed. "Pass in peace."

The dwarf lifted a hand, and rode on.

Despite the flippancy of the sentinel's greeting, the band was warmly welcomed in the Elf Hill.

The elf village inside the hollowed hill was lighted, as was the dwarfholm, by phosphorescence that emanated from the walls. The symbol of the falcon was everywhere to be seen, and scores of the birds flew freely about.

Odin's Messenger prudently kept to the interior of Freya's cart. His cranky mutterings never ceased. Not even the elf-woman's reassurances had any effect on the battle bird's ill humor.

Being grounded with a broken wing was bad enough, he seemed to say, but to be grounded amid a flock of hawks was asking too much of his sweet nature.

Freya looked at Jerry, laughed, and gave it up. The raven continued to complain.

Jerry and the other humans gasped in amazement at the camouflage that concealed the entrance to the hollow hill.

Here it would be called sorcery. In the world Jerry had left it would be called holography. There were three-dimensional shrubs and rocks and trees that just weren't there. Jerry was at a loss to discern any projectors, and had to put it down to his universal expaanation.

Elfin magic.

The time spent with the Falconholm Elves was pleasant in the extreme. Grokk the sentinel had not exaggerated the elves' interest in Jerry's story. The time-traveler with the hand of steel was treated as the Hero of a Saga. Had he been less amused by the adulation, it could have turned his head.

Brokk disappeared with Bjorn the One Eyed into the elf's forge, and emerged four days later with a twin to Jerry's rapier. The young mercenary's delight with the gift was conveyed in his shining eyes, and the reverent way he handled the new weapon. He tried to express his thanks, but Brokk harrumphed and walked away.

Jerry had early recognized in the lanky, long-limbed youth the potential of a deadly fencer. His poise and balance, his long reach, his agility and strength of wrist, made Olin a natural master of the foil.

From what Jerry had seen of the youngster's expert left-handed use of his poniard, he decided to train him in the Italian method of rapier and dagger. The two-handed fighting style was a natural for the ambidextrous youth.

During the final days of their visit, the elfin villagers congregated in the central common to watch the bewildering swordplay between Thor's Fist with his metal hand, and the lanky youngster who used a dagger as a shield.

While it was apparent to both student and teacher that it would be months before Olin achieved his full potential, in three short days the boy became an opponent to be respected. He caught on quickly to the wristflick that disarmed, and twice in the three days Jerry came close to losing his blade. Only his years on the college fencing team saved him from embarrassment.

Krupp the Round watched the flashing, darting blades wistfully. He assumed Jerry's fencing stance and ran through a comical parody of the red-beard's graceful moves. The chubby little man sighed and sheathed his shortsword. He patted his rotund middle with both hands. "If this were height instead of breadth it's tall enough I'd be to handle a blade like that."

Jerry grinned and Olin laughed. The young mercenary clapped Krupp on the shoulder.

"'Tis tall enough you be as ye stand, friend Krupp. 'Tis heart, not height, that weighs th' most, and 'tis my wager, ye've plenty of that."

Krupp grinned. "I'll try to remember that it's not height that counts when I fight my next giant."

On the following morning, the band set forth with an escort of Falconholm Elves to see the travelers safely to the border of their steading.

Ulf, Brokk, and Jerry conferred with the Falconholm scouts as to the safest trails leading north. Malcolm, called Surefoot, the leader of the elfin scouts, sketched on Brokk's chart several unmarked ways.

"You must understand, friend Ulf, that these paths I've shown you, while secret from most, do take you through territory belonging to folk of your kind who've not your tender heart. There's no guarantee that these trails be unknown to them."

The elf's face showed concern. He traced a route with one finger. "This way would take you around the goblin country, but would add weeks to your journey."

Ulf smiled his fang-filled smile. "'Tis understood, friend Surefoot. All trails be beset with danger of one sort or another. If not goblins, then somethin' t' be equally unenjoyed."

Ulf rolled up the chart and thrust it into his belt. "At least with goblins, I'll know what to expect and mayhap a way t' deal with it." He clasped hands with the elfin scout. "You've our thanks for all your help."

As they rode, Ulf remarked, "Two of the robber barons of this shire have castles nearby, but they raid not in this direction!"

Jerry looked a question.

Brokk explained. "This close t' th' steadin' o' th' Falconholm elves, Jerry lad, th' danger be minimal. The humans o' the district avoid this part o' th' forest out of their ancient fear of the Little Folk 'cause they know 'tis haunted by the elf kind."

Ulf, as usual, rode well out in front, but now his post was not so lonely. Orm, the mercenary, frequently rode beside him.

The little band of travelers had much to learn about each other. The hours of trail time which could have been boring, were not.

The members of the party beguiled the time in various ways. Lars, the greying sword-and-shield man, felt an interest in Krupp, and pressed the chubby elf with questions about the Elfin Gift, a subject that fascinated the old soldier.

"Why, friend Krupp," he wanted to know, "is it that ye need t' bear arms when you could use th' Gift as we saw it used in Gildholm and simply make yourself invisible t' your foes?"

The rotund elf tried to explain. "'Tis possible to do as you say. But you must understand that the magic has its limitations. It is indeed a powerful weapon of both offense and defense, and one used by elfin warriors in battle along with their weapons of steel."

The little green-clad man rode for several moments in silence. Finally he spoke again. "Let me put it to you thus, friend Lars. In single combat I can, and do, use the Gift as you proposed. By planting the thought, I simply vanish.

"That leaves me the option to just walk away, leaving the enemy bemazed. If the situation warrants, for instance to avoid unnecessary battle as in Gildholm Wood, I do just that.

"I have also the option to pursue the action. If the enemy be like unto the breed that hanged Maryam's folk, I can run the dog through at my choosing, and on several occasions have done so. Still it's without pleasure that I look back on it."

Lars eyed the little man. "Ye do what is necessary on the field of battle," he shrugged.

"But," Krupp went on, "Where it's simple to do one-on-one, it becomes difficult to impossible in the heat of a melee to hold the thought in the minds of several men at once.

"Even Gorm the Skald, who is one of the Old Ones and has great power over the Gift, had to call on assistance to control the fifty who were sent against you in Gildholm.

"Sure it is that I use one power of the Gift to vanish from the sight of one foeman, and another part to turn another's own weapons against himself. But in the cut-and-thrust, hack-and-slice of a lively engagement the Gift is only one of the weapons in my sheath."

Krupp looked at his companion. "It's always a good thing to have a comrade to guard your back in battle, friend Lars. Be not offended, but your age, alone, testifies to your fighting qualities. . . ."

Lars chuckled. "I intend to get older." Krupp echoed the chuckle.

"It's a thought worth exploring. I could add to your protection with the Gift and your sword and shield could guard my back. The Gift, while powerful, has no great range when diffused in several directions at once as used in a melee.

"If you agree, come nightfall and we camp, we'll practice, you and I, on how to guard each one the other. You'll learn just how far you can part from me and still be covered by the elfin shield."

Lars grinned broadly. "I agree. And friend Krupp, you may be sure that I'd not stray far from your side. T' be sure, I'd likely cling t' ye like a frightened maiden."

The elf laughed.

Lars had another question. "It's my understandin' that readin' thoughts be a part of th' gift. Why, then, in th' midst of battle can ye not read th' thoughts of a foeman and bestall him?"

Krupp laughed. "You've the same mistaken belief of the elfin magic that besets the most of the human kind, that it's infallible. Not so. The Gift has, as I told you, its limitations.

"Aye, thoughts can be read, but only those sent deliberately. If you are worried that I can see what's in your mind, rest easy. The only thoughts I can read are those sent by another elf, and then only if he wishes it so.

"'Tis true I could place a thought in your head, you've seen that done, but we elves have a code that prevents us from doing that to a friend. Gorm the Singer vanished Ulf before your eyes only to prove that you had nothing to fear when he closed the eyes of Thurgild's men."

Lars, turning from scanning the trees on his side of the trail, had another question. "Can you not feel th' approach of danger?"

Krupp made a little gesture. "At times, aye. But it's not something to rely on. 'Tis much too vague and chancy though it has been of help on occasion."

Jerry and Olin rode thigh to thigh, the young mercenary listening intently as Jerry explained the tactics and theory of swording with the tip in preference to the edge, yet using the edge to advantage.

Olin nodded. "There's practically no defense against th' dartin' thrusts unless one is trained in fencin'. It's no wonder you're such a deadly fighter, Jerry Jar Haz!"

Olin fingered the poniard at his belt. "When we camp tonight I'd like ye t' show me again th' counterstroke with th' dagger. I feel I'm missin' somethin' there. Th' balance feels wrong."

"You bet I will," Jerry said, "being off balance in the slightest can be fatal."

The red-beard chuckled. "I sure don't want my star pupil to be flunking the course because of a piece of iron through the gizzard."

Olin grinned. "Since I be your *only* pupil, I'd not like it if you had t' close your school on my account."

A little while later Olin spoke again. "That block with th' crossed sword and dagger against a downstroke, think you 'tis enough t' ward a broadsword?"

Jerry shook his head. "You don't try to block a blade that heavy by taking it head-on. Tonight I'll show you how to meet such an overhead cut, give with it, and turn it aside. But remember what I told you, one of your best tactics in fencing is not to be where your opponent strikes. Avoiding contact as much as possible, looking for your opportunity to get in your thrust.

"A fencer's blade is only half his weapon, the other half is his agility. His ability to move, move, and keep on moving. Razzle-dazzle 'em, buddy. Keep 'em off balance and bewildered."

Jerry rode on, pleased with his young pupil, and pleased that he was proving himself to be a capable tutor.

The camp that night had the look of a salle-de-armes. To one side Lars and Krupp the Round were feeling out the perimeter of the elf's psychokinetic reach. On the other side of the fire Jerry put young Longshanks through a slow-motion runthrough of attack, defense, and counterattack. Since the mercenary would not be facing another fencer, Jerry was armed with broadsword and shield which he used in the manner of the day. They were rehearsing a certain maneuver over and over.

There were basically only two ways to attack with a broadsword, the overhead downward cut like chopping wood, and the sidewise swing from right or left, only an occasional thrust with the nearly blunt tip.

There were two ways to meet a broadswordsman. Head on with brute force, taking the blows on shield or swordblade and returning in kind, or Jerry's way.

To counter the sideswing, Jerry had shown the youngster how to leap back, let the blade go by, lunge before the foeman could stop his swing. Then, depending on how the enemy used his shield, counterstrike with either sword or dagger. It was the dagger stroke that Olin felt needed improvement.

Jerry detected the flaw in the boy's footwork. When he struck left handed with the poniard, a little misstep put him just a trifle off balance. That little trifle could prove fatal in a real fight. They went over the move again and again until Olin mastered the tactic.

Student and tutor dropped beside the fire, and accepted the jacks of ale offered by Maryam and Freya.

The girl looked up shyly from under long lashes as she handed Olin the leather tankard, and the young mercenary reddened as his tongue stumbled over his words of thanks. Jerry grinned and rescued him by continuing to lecture.

"Now. In attacking with the rapier your best bet is to threaten always the face. No man wants to be blinded. He will unconsciously raise his guard. Then you go in under the shield to pierce groin, lower belly, knee, slash the femoral artery here. . . ." Jerry placed his fingers on the inside of his thigh.

"This stroke is not instantly fatal, but rapid arterial blood-loss will quickly weaken him for the deathstroke. Or, if you can, just walk away from him and he'll bleed to death in a matter of minutes. . . ."

The red-beard fell suddenly silent, a strange expression on his face. "What is it, friend Jerry? Somethin' troubles you. . . ."

The former insurance agent lifted his cup-hilted sword and stared at it. Half a dozen emotions warred with one another in his face. He raised his left hand and flexed the steel fingers.

He seemed suddenly bemused, disoriented.

Brokk was instantly on his feet. He rounded the fire and dropped to one knee at Jerry's side. He gripped the red-beard's shoulder. "What ails ye, lad?" The dwarf's voice was thick with concern.

Jerry looked blankly at the burly little warrior. He groped for the dwarf's hand and clung tightly to it. He stared into the little man's face, his eyes filled with confusion.

"Brokk. . . ."

Jerry's voice was husky and uncertain. "Father. Who am I?"

The red-beard shook. "Who am I? I'm Jerry Haskins of San Diego, California, U.S.A. I sell insurance. . . . I never even got into a fist fight in the schoolyard. The most violent thing in my life was High School football!

"Fencing is just a fun sport to develop poise and coordination. The tips of the foils aren't even sharp, for pete's sake!

"And I just heard myself telling a nineteen year old boy how to gut somebody or slice an artery and leave him to bleed to death. . . ." The agony in his face deepened. "*Brokk, who the hell am I?*"

Bryn, her scarred face corrugated with concern, reared up and put her head in Jerry's lap, uttering worried little whines. The red-beard bent and took the massive head in his arms, and hugged her. "It's all right, old girl. Nothing for you to worry about."

The big war-dog licked his face. Jerry straightened and looked at Brokk. The dwarf placed a hand on Jerry's knee. "Gently, lad, gently. 'Tis th' way o' things here. Th' one who fights th' best, lives th' longest. This is not th' world Jerry Haskins grew up in. 'Tis th' world Jar Haz grew up in, an' *ye* be Jerry Jar Haz.

"'Tis th' fencin' skill o' Jerry Haskins, an' th' battle knowledge an' fury o' Jar Haz that makes ye th' finest fightin' man o' two worlds.

"If ye'd not had th' Viking's instincts, ye'd not ha' survived yer first playful crossin' o' swords in th' Tradin' Glen. In this world men do not play at swordin'. Even in th' mock fights ye saw there, th' combatants were serious about winnin'. Though Jerry Haskins knew it not, each o' yer opponents was earnestly strivin' t' kill ye. But Jar' Haz th' Viking knew this, an' wouldn't let it be so. Jar Haz defended ye, an' Jerry Haskins let it be a game.

"'Tis a harsh an' brutal world ye've come t' live in, my son, an' without th' Viking ye'd be as helpless t' cope here as Jar Haz would be without Jerry Haskins if he were caught up in *yer* world."

Across Jerry's mind flashed a picture of axe-armed Jar Haz trying to cross Market Street in downtown San Diego during rush hour. It helped to put things in perspective. He laughed.

Brokk patted Jerry's shoulder. "D'ye see, lad, 'tis th' Viking's knowledge o' this world an' yer knowledge o' th' world o' Jerry Haskins that makes ye Thor's Fist, able t' survive in either.

"But as I pointed out t' ye once, this be th' world ye've t' live in, an' if ye live not by its rules, ye'll not live long, nor would th' Viking long survive in th' world ye left without Jerry Haskins t' guide him."

Something ran through Jerry mind. 'Cross at the green, not in between.' The dwarf was right. Jar Haz would have succumbed to his first attempt at street-crossing without Jerry, just as certainly as Jerry would have succumbed to his first attempt at sword-crossing without the Viking.

Brokk had said it. Skandia was a harsh and brutal world, and it took harsh measures to stay alive in it. Jerry would have to understand and accept that if he intended to live and find Janet.

And he did intend to live and find Janet.

Here, knowledge of bloodletting was on a par with knowing how to cinch a big corporate insurance policy back in California. A simple matter of making it from day to day.

And he was no longer Jerry Haskins, supersalesman for Nationwide Insurance. He was the adopted son of Brokk of Svartheim, the Dwarf King. He was Thor's Fist, the world's only tall dwarf! Jerry laughed out loud.

The red-beard straightened his shoulders, and looked at Brokk. "Thank you, Father. I've got it clear in my head now."

He turned to Olin Longshanks. "Okay, buddy, you ready to run through that dagger bit one more time?"

CHAPTER NINETEEN

Days, miles, and green forest flowed past uneventfully, as Ulf kept to the back byways marked for him by Malcolm Surefoot the Falconholm elf. The little band had been on the trail for six weeks. Every night mock battles were fought to keep each warrior keen, and to sharpen battle skills.

All looked to Brokk, as unquestioned leader, but as fighters, they had gravitated naturally into three pairs, drawn together by mutual fighting style. It was not only that soldiers traditionally fought in pairs, it was just plain common sense to have a matelot you could trust to cover your back in a melee.

Lars and Krupp the Round made a comical looking duo, but the mismatched pair usually took top honors.

The others cried foul since Krupp used the Gift as their third weapon. Jerry would never forget the first time he charged down on the rotund little man, only to have him flick out like a popped balloon. But that wasn't nearly so traumatic as having his rapier fly from his hand, turn, and make playful thrusts at him. Lars laughed so hard he had to sit down.

Jerry made no more humorous remarks at their expense.

Orm and the goblin also made a formidable pair. Shoulder to shoulder, Orm with his axe and Ulf with his assegai, shields locked rim to rim, taking them was like storming a castle.

Jerry and Olin, each guarding the other's back, were ever on the move. Ever on the attack. Dancing, lunging, retreating, turning swordstrokes with their darting rapiers, and dodging and weaving to evade axe or mace, pressing with their points, threatening face or groin or knee.

Freya discovered to her chagrin that she had only a marginal command over her heritage, the Elfin Gift. She'd been Maryam's age when a handsome, self-assured young Brokk, not yet called Hammermacher, came to the elf-mound that housed her village.

The young dwarf had come to dicker with her father for a supply of elfgold. Elfgold was not gold at all, but a rare element only the elves knew how to find, and was one of the ingredients used by the young metalsmith in his secret tempering process.

That had been so many years ago that Jerry, when he heard, had difficulty believing it.

Lifespans were long in Skandia if one avoided the everyday hazards, and Freya, for all her youthful beauty, was over a hundred years old. Womanlike she wouldn't say just how much over.

Brokk was nearly two hundred. Jerry found that in the body of Jar Haz, he could look forward to a couple of centuries himself, always providing, as Brokk had said, he remained alive in a land where he who fought best lived the longest.

But even in Skandia a century was still a hundred years. That's a long time to be away from one's culture, and the elf-woman had had little contact with her kind after marrying Brokk and moving to Svartheim.

Her command of the Gift was only such as came instinctively. She had not had the training she would have received had she grown up among the elves.

Krupp undertook to correct this.

Brokk relieved the little man from trail duty, and he rode beside the cart instructing the dwarf's wife in the use of her heritage. Maryam was fascinated to learn the many ways in which the Gift could be used.

Krupp had no reservations about speaking of these secret things before the girl. Firstly, she was a friend, and the adopted daughter of Freya and the dwarf, and secondly she was human and lacked the power to utilize what she learned.

The sunny-natured girl laughed delightedly when Freya playfully caused the cart to seem to disappear, leaving herself and Maryam apparently jogging along in midair. The illusion was for Maryam's eyes only, as the elf-woman had not yet mastered the difficulty of holding more than one mind at the same time. But every day Freya's power over the Gift grew.

Night had fallen and the meal ended. Ulf sat studying the chart unrolled on his knees. The goblin tossed a bone into the fire, and wiped his fingers on the log beside him to cleanse them of grease. His brow wrinkled. With a taloned finger he traced one route after another. The creases in his forehead deepened.

Brokk glanced at the goblin. "What causes ye t' look like a lovesick stork? Ye resemble a worried goblin, an' meanin' no disrespect friend Ulf, a worried goblin's no sight t' delight th' eyes."

Ulf grunted. "'Tis an improvement over th' sight of a dwarf, worried or otherwise, meanin' no disrespect, friend Brokk."

The dwarf chuckled. "What's troublin' ye, Ulf?"

The goblin held the chart to the fire so Brokk could see. "Here," he said, his finger indicating the spot, "Here's where we are this night."

"So?"

"So." The finger moved. "Here's where we'll be at sunfall two nights hence."

Jerry, as second in command, peered over Brokk's shoulder. "What is it, Father?"

The dwarf fingered his beard. "'Tis th' borderland o' Ulf's kin. We be enterin' goblin country."

Ulf's hideous face held an expression of indecision. "Old friend, I have no more desire than you t' run upon those of my kind. In their eyes I be renegade, a traitor t' th' hatred they hold for all otherkind. I can expect no better treatment than any who fall into their hands."

The other members of the party drew closer. They knew that this was a council of war that affected them all. Brokk looked around the circle of firelit faces. "Yer friend Ulf th' Far Traveled ha' somethin, he'd place afore ye. I know not what he proposes, but I charge ye t' listen well an' consider his words."

The goblin looked into the faces of his comrades. He indicated the chart."Were I alone," he said, "I'd turn here t' th' west and follow this route."

The long finger marked a trail on the map. "But," he continued, "were I alone, I'd care not whether th' venture took another month or another year."

The finger traced an alternate route. "Malcolm Surefoot of th' Falconholm Elves told me that this path be known t' only a few, and that it would carve some ninety sunrises from th' journey. It is th' trail taken by th' elves when they must journey t' th' north. But it leads through th' goblin land. Malcolm seemed sure that this trail was little used, but warned that elfin magic guards elfin travelers, and could make no guarantee for any not of th' elfin kind."

The goblin looked at Krupp and Freya. "D'you think you've power enough over th' Gift t' cloak us from goblin eyes?"

Krupp spoke. "Nay. 'Tis like in the forest of Gildholm. It would take more than our combined command to cover us all with the cloak of invisibility. What's your alternative?"

Ulf indicated still another path. "This way t' th' east be shorter, but most of the territory is marked incognito. 'Tis thought that somewhere in this area is th' forest of flesh-eatin' trees, though 'tis unknown whether th' trees actually exist or are merely travelers' tales of cock and bull.

"Also 'tis said that trolls have been seen here, though it is far from Trollheim. That, again, is open to speculation. It may or may not be true.

"Th' question afore us is this. Do we go north along th' trail possibly beset by goblins. Do we swing west, th' longest but by far th' safest way. Or do we turn east, avoidin' th' Twisted Ones and shortenin' th' trek, but facin' we know not what?

"So, comrades, turn we west, east, or continue as we go?"

Ulf looked at the firelight flickering over the faces of his friends. "This is a decision I care not t' make alone, so I drop th' scorpion in your laps t' deal with as you will."

There was much discussion and much examining of the chart. In the end, it was decided to take the shortest route and follow the elf-trail through the goblin land.

For the first seven days after the band crossed into goblin country all was well. Krupp and Freya used their Gift to the utmost to detect and foretell any danger that threatened.

Bryn, bespoken by Krupp who had even more command than Freya over animal communication, ranged far and wide, in constant mental contact with the round little elf.

Odin's Messenger, freed at last from the restraint of his splinted wing, added air support to the reconnaissance team on the ground.

But as Brokk had told Hrimgrimnir the Frost Giant, "Our lives be in th' hands o' th' gods." And despite their vigilance, the four goblins were not detected until Ulf rounded a curve and, literally, bumped into them.

Tired of the saddle, Ulf had dismounted and was leading his horse, when he rounded a bend in the trail, and ran bodily into the group of his clansmen.

Startled, the Far Traveled One leaped backward, voicing his ululating cry. The goblins, recognizing Ulf as one of the outcasts, drew their swords and, screaming, charged.

Taken utterly by surprise, Ulf would have been slain on the spot had not Jerry and the chubby Krupp, responding to their friend's war-cry, come pounding round the turn at full gallop.

The encounter was short and deadly.

The descending blade of the leading goblin was almost in contact with Ulf's skull when the heavy weapon flew from the spider-man's hand, circled in a tight arc, and plunged its length into its wielder's chest.

Ulf's assegai dispatched a second. Orm, joining the fray, hurled his axe, accounting for the third.

The remaining goblin ran, his, long spindly legs covering the ground at a great pace.

Ulf's hand shot up to the shortsword hilt protruding above his right shoulder, and in one smooth flowing movement, drew and flung. The sword whirled end over end to sink to the hilt in the hump of the fleeing goblin.

Brokk and Olin Longshanks galloped into sight, and reined to a halt. Jerry sheathed his unused rapier. "Well! That didn't take long!" He searched the
surrounding forest. "Any more of them?"

Ulf retrieved his shortsword. "Nay, that be all of them. And a good thing. Had one escaped, we'd have th' whole village down upon us."

"Th' village must be near," Krupp remarked. He cawed loudly, and Odin's Messenger glided down through the trees to land on the elf's shoulder. Krupp placed a finger on the bird's head. "Find the goblin village."

The battle-bird flew off, rose and began circling. His orbits got wider and soon he was out of sight.

Olin reined his mount around. "I'll inform th' Lady Freya."

"No need, friend Olin," Krupp said, "I've sent the thought to her."

Jerry laughed. "I keep forgetting the elfin telegraph."

"Th' what?"

"Never mind."

The red-beard looked at the sprawled bodies. He pointed to the one with his own sword in his hear"This guy makes you look like a Queen of Love and Beauty, Ulf."

The goblin wiped purple blood from his blade with a handful of grass, and returned it to its sheath across his hump. He grunted. "I'd have you know that I'm considered quite handsome
amongst my kind."

Jerry grinned. "That's what I said."

Guarded by Lars, Freya's cart rounded the bend. The dwarf looked around. "Well," he grunted, "This calls fer th' layin' o' plans."

The big raven descended, and landed on the ridgepole of Freya's cart, chattering. Freya chirped and nodded to Krupp. The little green clad elf turned to Brokk.

"The goblin village lies no more than three leagues to the west," he reported. "Now we know in what direction to lay those plans."

Ulf had a guilty look on his face. He took Brokk's chart from his belt. "'Tis t' th' east we should have gone a week past. I've not been completely open with you, friend Brokk. If ye'll light down, I'll show you on th' map."

The dwarf dismounted, giving his friend a puzzled look.

Ulf looked unhappy. "I didn't deceive you, exactly. . . ."

Brokk eyed the spider-man. "What in th' realm o' Hel be ye blitherin' about?"

The goblin squatted and unrolled the chart on the ground. The company gathered close. Ulf's finger indicated their position. "D'you mind th' night a week agone when I bade you decide th' route we'd take?"

The dwarf nodded.

"D'you recall that I remarked I'd take th' western route and laid little stress on th' time lost by doin' so?"

"Aye."

"I also remarked on how little was th' likelihood of this path bein' known t' others of my kind. And ye'll likely remember how I dwelt on th' unknown, th' possibility of trolls and th' forest of flesh-eaters t' th' east."

"What's yer point?"

"I'd not deliberately deceive ye, old friend, but did hope t' influence you t' take any trail except that t' th' east."

"Why not to the east?" asked Jerry.

Ulf hung his head. "'Tis th' shortest route, and mayhap th' safest for all I know, but t' my shame, I let cowardice sway my recommendations."

Brokk looked keenly at the goblin's face. "Tell me, friend Ulf, did ye lie t' us?"

Ulf shook his head. "Nay, Brokk."

"No. Ye did not. Ye did but tell of th' choices an' let us make th' decision.

"I tell ye this. Th' name 'coward' fits ye not, Ulf th' Far Traveled, an' I'd not have it applied t' ye even by yerself."

The dwarf chopped the air with his fist. "Now, my friend, what troubles ye about th' eastern way?"

Silently Ulf pointed to the map. The dwarf studied it for several minutes. He looked up at Ulf and nodded. "I see," he said softly.

Jerry broke the silence. "What is it, Father?"

Brokk's stubby finger indicated the scores of blue lines that crisscrossed the land to the east of them. The dwarf looked up. "There be all streams an' rivers, rills an' brooks. . . . Runnin' water."

Freya, Krupp, and Jerry nodded their understanding. Maryam and the three mercenaries looked puzzled.

Jerry explained the horror of running water held by the goblin kind.

"If we head east, there's no way the goblins would come after us, but the trip would be a hellish nightmare for Ulf."

The humans looked at Ulf, understanding and compassion growing in their eyes.

The goblin was unable to meet their eyes for shame. "'Twas a craven thing I did t' conceal a shorter and possibly safer way out of cowardly fear."

Brokk struck the goblin roughly on the shoulder. "I told ye once that I'd not have a hint o' th' cowardly laid t' yer name, ye spindly lout. 'Tis no fault o' yers that Odin laid a curse on yer people. Th' only thing t' discuss is t' decide whether we continue this trail or d'we seek a path t' th' west."

"You don't hold me responsible for. . . ."

Brokk broke in. "Ye'll anger me if ye continue t' talk like a fool." Jerry growled agreement with the dwarf's sentiment.

Ulf stood up and eased the strap of the sword sheath athwart his hump. "We go east," he said.

There came an immediate clamor of protest. Brokk spoke for them all. "'Tis askin' too much o' ye."

The goblin put a foot in the stirrup, and swung himself into the saddle. "Mount up. We go east," he repeated.

CHAPTER TWENTY

By the fourth day of their trek through the stream-filled terrain, the band saw Ulf's terror of running water diminish to only uneasiness, and by the ninth day it had disappeared entirely. He now waded waist deep without a qualm.

On the twelfth day, the band was halted by a sluggish river both wide and deep. Jerry, who had seen the maneuver in many a western movie, took charge of the river crossing.

He had Ulf and the three mercenaries fell designated trees, and chop the trunks into several long logs. These were roped to the sides of Freya's cart, and proved well able to buoy up the little wain. The elf-woman, with Maryam beside her, urged her mules into the gentle current.

Ulf eyed the river, and his face showed a return of his old fear. The far bank had been scouted, and was being held by Krupp and two of the mercenaries. The goblin had watched the three swim their horses across, paddling alongside and clinging to their saddlehorns.

While the fear of wading shallow streams had been conquered, it was obvious by his attitude that the thought of going into that broad sweep with no bottom under his feet brought back a rush of the old terror.

Jerry watched Ulf as the goblin eyed the little cart bobbing off behind its mules, with Brokk and Olin Longshanks in attendance.

The red-beard knew what was going through the Twisted One's mind. He moved to the Goblin's side. "Ulf," he said softly, "Good friend. I know your problem. In my old world it's called a phobia. That means the irrational fear of something that doesn't bother most other people. There are all sorts of phobias. The fear of heights. The fear of closed spaces. The fear of open spaces. Fear of strangers, of spiders. . . . Even one called hydrophobia, the fear of water.

"That's what was planted in the minds of your people ages ago. By Odin? By something else? Who knows for sure?

"My problem was acrophobia, fear of high places.

"When I was a kid, a child, I went climbing with some friends up into a half-finished skyscraper. That's a building tall as the High Seat of Odin in his palace Valaskjalf in Asgard from which he can see into all the Nine Worlds.

"We climbed into the framework of beams above where the walls ended. I was nearly blown off by a gust of wind, when suddenly, I realized how far it was to the ground.

"Ulf, old buddy, I really do understand how it is with you and water. Exactly as it was with me and heights. I wrapped my arms around a vertical beam and there I sat for hours until some workmen found me and got me down. They practically had to break my arms to get me to let go of that beam!"

The goblin looked at Jerry. "How did you rid yourself of the fear? I've marked no squeamishness in ye on that score."

"Years later, when I was grown, another kid got himself in the same fix. There was nobody else around, and I could see he was going to fall any minute. I had to force myself to go up and get him. Once I'd done it, I had it licked. . . ."

Jerry abruptly broke off, and shading his eyes with one hand, stared at the opposite bank.

He pointed.

Across the river, the party was closed up around the cart, and looking to the wood, weapons at the ready. Brokk waved an arm, signaling the others to fan out. With a quick move, the dwarf drew and flung his throwing knives at something in the trees, and snatched his Morning Star from his belt.

Jerry swung into the saddle. "It looks as though they're under attack!"

He urged his mount into the river.

Ulf hesitated only a moment before following the red-beard into the flood.

The goblin clung with a death grip to the pommel of his saddle, and kicked his long legs. Only he could know the effort it took to fight down the terror raging within him. As he emerged on the far bank, he grabbed his spear and shield from the saddle, and loped toward where the others were gathered.

"What's amiss," he called breathlessly.

His comrades turned to him, smiling. Brokk said, "Nothin' now. Ye're this side o' the river."

Ulf dashed his shield to the ground in fury, and shook his assegai threateningly. "A trick. A low, deceitful. . . ."

The goblin's rage made him speechless. He stammered. "Is this the way you treat one who's fought at your side? Is this what you think of me?"

"Aye," Brokk said, "This be what we think o' ye, old comrade. We think ye'd charge headlong into Niffleheim an' face down Weird himself, if so be ye thought any one o' us stood in need o' yer help. We counted that yer love fer us would be stronger than yer fear o' th' river.

"Tell me, old friend, were we wrong?"

Jerry watched Ulf's rage drain out of him. The goblin looked from face to face. The same was plain to be read in each, the warmth of comraderie.

The goblin jabbed his spear into the ground and put his hands on his hips.

"Tricked! 'Tis a fine set of friends *I* have!"

From that day it was apparent that Ulf's fear of water was gone.

Toward the end of the second week they lost one of Freya's mules. They camped for the night, and stretched a picket rope between two trees as usual. During the night a disturbance broke out among the tethered animals.

Lars, who was on watch, sounded the alarm, and all turned out to investigate. Nothing was found in the surrounding woods, but when they checked the picket line, the mule tethered at one end was found to be missing, its halter broken. Orm joined Lars on guard for the rest of the night, but nothing further occurred.

The little cart had never really needed two mules, and the remaining animal was not overburdened doing the job alone.

The loss they suffered three days later was much more serious. They lost one of the riding horses. That was bad enough but, could have ended in real tragedy.

They almost lost Maryam and two of the mercenaries.

The band halted for nooning, and as usual, loosened saddle girths, and looped reins over shrubs or branches to restrain the mounts while they ate the noon meal.

With no warning there came a wet popping sound, and the wide trunk of the tree to which one of the mounts was tethered opened vertically like a huge mouth.

A tangle of vine-like tentacles shot out, and wound rapidly about the horse. The doomed animal screamed in fear as the tentacles withdrew, pulling it toward the gaping maw.

Lars and Jerry, who were closest to the terrified beast, leaped to their feet, whipping out their swords. Jerry slashed one of the ropy tendrils and Lars hacked at another with his longsword. The others rushed to aid, but the poor horse was dragged kicking and neighing into the foul smelling opening and the treetrunk snapped shut. They could faintly hear the animal's screams from within the tree.

The shocked, frustrated warriors stood helplessly by while the monstrous plant digested its meal.

A shrill feminine shriek jerked them around. Another of the hellish things had opened, and its tentacles held Maryam in their coils, drawing her toward a similar doom.

Olin Longshanks loosed a wild berserker scream, and rushed headlong into battle with the carnivorous plant, Lars close on his heels, and the rest a heartbeat behind.

The lanky young mercenary stood among the writhing vines, slashing right and left with his keen rapier, lopping off tentacle after tentacle. But there were too many of them. One, then more, of the living ropes twined about him, and he and the girl were being steadily pulled to a hideous death.

Lars was howling his warcry, and hacking away then he, too, was enmeshed in the coils. All three seemed doomed.

The campfire roared up suddenly, and several blazing brands hurtled through the air into the opening in the tree. The first few were quenched by the copious digestive juices in the hollow. More and more of the flaming brands flashed through the air and into the tree. An elfin breeze fanned them into a roaring bonfire.

Thick acid sap began to bubble and boil. Steam gushed from the opening. Writhing tentacles loosened their grasp, and dropped lmply to the ground. The flames took hold, and the tree began to blaze. Its limbs shook and quivered, its leaves began to fall. The quaking branches went limp and sagged.

Maryam and the two mercenaries lay bruised and exhausted among the now dead tentacles. The girl raised herself on one elbow. Freya, uttering little cries of distress, rushed toward her, but it was Olin Longshanks who reached her first.

The young swordsman caught her up in his arms, and cradled her to his chest, laying a cheek on the flame-red head. Maryam clung to the boy, sobbing.

The elf-woman dropped to her knees beside them. She crooned a soothing note as she stroked the girl's hair and Maryam soon got over her fright.

"Come, dear," Freya said, soothingly, "Come to the wain and let me cure your hurts."

"Yes, Mother," Maryam murmured, but her eyes were on Olin's face, and the light in them left no doubt as to how she felt about the long-limbed youth.

"I'll carry her, Lady Freya." The girl's arms clasped tightly around Olin's neck as he rose and carried her to the cart.

"I can walk," Maryam said, her arms maintaining their hold.

"I know," Olin replied.

The girl snuggled closer, smiling happily.

Brokk clapped Krupp the Round on the shoulder. "'Twas a most impressive fire-show ye whipped up, friend Krupp. Ye saved th' day."

"'Twas Freya thought of it," the elf disclaimed, "I but aided her. It did work wondrous well, didn't it?"

All the band were closely surveying the surroundin woods to ascertain if any more of the flesh eaters were near. None were.

"Well," said Jerry, "now we know what happened to Freya's mule."

"Aye, an' now we know where not t' pitch camp henceforce," Brokk said.

Orm was tending to the several cuts and bruises Lars had suffered in the encounter. "Lars o' th' Battlefield," he chortled. "Mighty warrior! I think I'll compose a saga t' th' Hero Lars, and his epic contest with a tree. . . ."

Lars grinned. "At least I didn't lose my mount t' one."

Olin joined the group. Lars chuckled. "Now here's th' one who deserves a saga, friend Orm. A rousin' tribute t' Olin Longshanks, and how he rescued th' fair Maiden, Maryam from th' embrace of an amorous vegetable. Now there's a tale t' set th' walls of Valhalla a-ring with shouts of praise!" The old warrior's grin broadened. "And did ye mark, friend Orm, how th' grateful maiden clung t' her hero? Her Swordsman o' th' Gods? Aye, it be a proud day in Odin's Mead Hall."

"Let be," the red-faced Olin growled.

Brokk touched the young mercenary's arm. "Be it tree, or Fafnir th' Dragon, lad, yer Maryam'd been eaten had ye not got t' her so quick."

The dwarf's face creased in a grin. "But ye will ha' t' admit t'would sound a merry tale t' any who were not here this day t' see th' fullness o' it."

A reluctant grin moved Olin's lips.

The band was now shy one riding horse. Krupp the Round solved the problem by giving his mount to Orm. "I be light, and if you've no objection, friend Lars, I'll mount up behind you."

The company moved out, this time on the alert for squat, wide-boled trees with broad shiny dark green leaves.

Now that they were looking for them, they were awed by the phenomenal luck that had protected them for so many days. The deadly plants were disturbingly numerous, and were becoming dangerously more so as they progressed.

During the post-action discussion following what Orm persisted in calling 'The Saga of Tyr and the Tree,' it had been agreed that the tentacle reach was approximately thirty feet. They added a safety factor of ten feet and were careful not to come any closer than that to one of the leafed monsters.

This necessity to avoid the flesh-eaters resulted in slow going and a sinuous route that Ulf described as the track of a drunken snake.

More and more often they were forced to back-track as the deadly plants crowded more closely together.

Three nights later Ulf was, as usual, poring over the chart. Suddenly the spider-man ripped out a colorful oath, and slammed one balled fist down on his knee. "Of all th' troll-witted dunderheads, I be chief!"

"Hoy!" Brokk exclaimed, he and Jerry startled by the goblin's outburst, "What in Hel's realm ails ye?"

The goblin slapped the map with the back of his hand. "This," he almost shouted. "This! Look ye. What do you see?"

The dwarf took the chart and studied it closely. "What?" he asked at last. "I see nothin' t' upset ye."

Ulf jabbed the chart with a taloned finger. "Here, oh wisest of dwarfs, this. Tell me, what do you see?"

Brokk looked again. "'Tis th' river we crossed. What about it?"

"What about it? D'you not see how it flows?"

The goblin traced the river's course with a talon that nearly cut through the parchment. The dwarf's eyes widened. "T' th' north. It flows t' th' north."

"Now d'you see?"

"Aye," Brokk said slowly, fingering his beard. "Aye, I take yer meanin'."

Ulf snorted. "It's my thought that you should elect another t' pathfind this expedition."

The goblin's voice was filled with self contempt.

Brokk stared at his old friend. He removed his helmet and ran a stubby hand through his hair. "That's yer thought, is it?"

The others had gathered at the goblin's outburst. Brokk replaced his helm. "An' why, if th' question be not too impertinent, would we do somethin' that daft?"

"Because anyone else would have seen days ago that t' escape this curst place all we had t' do was t' build rafts, and advance our journey easily on that north-flowin' river. But I, blinded by th' ancient fear of runnin' water, saw it not."

"Until now," Brokk said, "But ye saw it."

"Three weeks late."

"So? Look ye, Ulf, ye say any else would ha' noticed th' route. Did any mark it? I marked it not. Did Jerry? Orm? Olin? Any of us? I've studied th' chart as closely as yerself. Old friend, I've not even th' excuse o' ancient fear. I've no excuse at all."

"Near a month and a half lost." The dwarf shrugged. "That be th' cast o' th' runes."

He cocked an eye at the goblin. "Tell me, friend, think ye that ye must needs be infallible? Ha' ye, then, drunk from th' Well o' Mimir th' Water o' Knowledge o' all things?"

The dwarf looked at Ulf's face and grinned. "Ugly as ye be, I make note that ye ha' two eyes, an' th' price o' a drink from Mimir's well be yer right eye. So far as I know, only Odin Allfather ha' paid that. Be ye assumin', then, th' wisdom o' Odin?"

Jerry burst out laughing.

"Ulf old buddy, I think what my godfather is trying to say in his long-winded way, is that we all make mistakes. Don't take it so hard. Hey, I even made a mistake myself once. I think. . . ."

Ulf grinned. "I find that hard to believe, oh Master Swordsman."

The goblin turned to Brokk. His fang-filled grin widened. "And I remind you, oh shortest of dwarfs, that amongst my kind I'm considered handsome. 'Tis th' rest of you who are a blight to the eyes."

Brokk chuckled.

The trek back to the river was uneventful. They merely followed their own backtrail and avoided the carnivorous trees. It took them six days to build three rafts to carry themselves, their mounts, and Freya's cart and mule. Two weeks later they were clear of the flesh-eating horrors.

"From hence forward," Orm remarked, "I'll keep an open mind about tales told over an alejack, no matter how unlikely they seem."

None disputed him.

CHAPTER TWENTY ONE

Despite the report of Hrimgrimnir the Frost Giant of widespread unrest in Midgard, the little band of adventurers encountered no problems over the next five weeks. The seeming tranquillity of the land, however, in no way tempted them to relax their guard.

The ambush in Gildholm Forest, and the near tragedy in the forest of flesh-eaters had taught them that the price not only of liberty, but of life itself, was eternal vigilance. And vigilant they stayed.

Whenever possible, Krupp the Round contacted elf clans in the vicinity, and gathered news of the conditions prevailing in the district.

He and Jerry spoke with a gray and wrinkled elf in the shire of Ethelstane. The news the old elf imparted was not encouraging. "My advice is to swing wide to the west, and stay clear of Ethelstane Keep. Gymar the Thane is one to avoid even when his mood be merry, and lately he's been a bit testy."

"Has he now?"

"Aye, cousin. Only a week agone he demonstrated his displeasure with one of his villages by hanging two entire families, every man, woman, and child. One a mere babe in arms. Fourteen there were, dangling in the wind for the ravens to pick."

Jerry settled his sword belt, drew his rapier half-way out of its sheath, and slammed it back in. A growl of anger rumbled in his throat.

Krupp scratched his chin, and looked up into the sky. "What upset the thane's sweet nature?"

The old elf shook his head. "One of the villagers had the audacity to slay a falcon of the good lord's for slashing out the eyes of his infant son.

"Gymar hanged the lot, then he hanged the family of the child's mother for daring to protest the atrocity."

Krupp spat. "Why, that's understandable enough," he said dryly.

"What's the sight of the child of a mere thrall, to compare with the loss of a well trained hunting bird?"

The gray elf shrugged. "'Tis the way of the human kind, and no affair of the elves. Steer ye a course well to windward of such evil is my advice."

"Aye, cousin, your words deserve much consideration."

Jerry and the rotund elf reported the conversation to the assembled company that evening.

"The old one's advice is sound," Krupp said.

The little man controlled his anger with difficulty. "Although, strictly speaking, 'tis none of our affair, it sits ill on me to have to bypass without lifting a hand to avenge such cruelty."

Brokk laid a hand on the elf's shoulder. "Aye," he growled, "All here echo yer feelin'. But there be nothin' we can do. Th' old elf's advice be sound. We'll take it."

Shortly after noon on the second day of their westward detour, Orm, riding point with Ulf, spied a mercenary outpost keeping watch on the road.

They reined in and Ulf drew his sling. It was his intention to pick off the sentry before the man could alert his troop, and allow the band to retreat undiscovered.

Orm leaned from his saddle and placed a restraining hand on the goblin's arm. "Hold your missile, Ulf. Lars, Olin, and I once served with that lad in th' Free Company of Hjalmar th' Axeman. All Hjalmar's men be of like mind t' us. They'd never serve a butcher. Wait here whilst I bespeak him."

The goblin remained concealed while Orm rode toward the sentry. He raised a hand in greeting. "Ho, Guntar Ingmarssen, 'tis Orm Thorwaldssen."

"Ho, Orm. It has been long since our last service together. Be you seekin' service with th' Axeman?"

Despite his show of friendliness, the sentry remained keenly alert.

"Nay, brother. I've taken service with a private party bound for Asgard. So you're still with Hjalmar?"

"Aye."

Guntar relaxed the tiniest bit. He knew Orm, and treachery was not a trait of those who served the Axeman.

"Where be your employer? How big is your party?"

Orm shoved his helmet to the back of his head. How to tell this human that his employer was a dwarf? That he served with elves and a goblin? The problem was taken out of his hands as Olin rode up accompanied by Brokk.

Guntar reined his horse back a few paces at sight of the dwarf. He unlooped his axe from his saddlebow and laid it across his knees.

"Ho, Olin Longshanks. How come you t' be in th' company of th' child stealer?"

Olin glanced at Brokk and kneed his mount closer to the outpost. The dwarf sat his horse quietly, and let the young mercenary handle the situation.

"You know me, Guntar Ingmarssen," Olin said, "Do I lie?"

Guntar looked the younger man in the eyes. "Nay, Olin Longshanks, I've never known you t' lie."

"When I served as your lieutenant under th' Axeman did you ever know me t' do aught dishonorable?"

"Nay, Longshanks."

Olin eyed the mercenary coldly. "We've had reports of th' lords hereabout. Now I ask you, Guntar Ingmarssen, is Hjalmar still th' leader of honest fighters, or has he become a butcher?"

The sentry's eyes narrowed and his friendliness dropped away. He braced his feet in the stirrups and handled his axe. Guntar's voice was hostile as he asked, "What mean you by this insult?"

"Mark you, Ingmarssen, I intend no insult, but we've heard how some in th' pay of Gymar of Ethelstane hanged two whole families down t' th' last babe over a troll-curst falcon. "I ask you again, how stands th' Axeman?"

Guntar drew himself up angrily. "Mayhap ye intended no insult, but th' question itself be insulting. You asked if I know you, then I ask if ye know me? If you do, then you know that I, nor none of my mates, would take service under a dog like th' Thane o' Ethelstane."

Guntar glared. "I'll have your apology, damn ye, Olin Longshanks, or by Thor, I'll have your blood."

Olin raised one hand placatingly.

"My apology you have, brother. My deepest apology. 'Tis only that Orm, Lars, and I unwittingly took th' service of one of th' same kidney as this troll-curst butcher and 'twas two days before we discovered th' whoreson's true nature.

"If ever ye hear that we served Thurgild o' Gildholm. . ." He turned to Orm. ". . . tell Guntar how we quit th' service of th' merry Thurgild."

Orm related the circumstances of their encounter with Ragnar and his lackeys, and of their meeting with Brokk and his party.

"And ye took service with th' dwarf?"

"Aye, and a kinder master has never been served."The sentry looked at Brokk.

"Never before have I encountered one of th' Little Folk."

He looked at Olin. "As ye say, your master has none of th' look of a demon about him."

"Will you then, brother Guntar, ask Hjalmar th' Axeman t' ride out t' meet with us?" Olin smiled. "You'll understand that we'd rather not ride into your camp unless it be under th' protection of th' Axeman."

The sentry nodded. "I'll send word. "Where'll you be if Hjalmar agrees?"

"We're camped not a quarter league down th' trail."

Guntar looked at Brokk who had taken no part in the talk. He hesitated a moment, then raised his axe in salute. The dwarf smiled and returned the gesture with an uplifted hand, then he and the two mercenaries turned their horses and rode back to where the others had laid camp.

Less than an hour had passed when Orm signaled the approach of a horseman, and Hjalmar the Axeman rode into camp. The mercenary captain had expressed his trust in Olin by coming alone.

The chieftain was not overly tall. He made up for his lack of height by being overly broad. His shoulders were wide as an axe-handle and his chest bulged beneath his shirt of chain mail. The conical helmet sported a pair of hawks' wings. His face was ruddy, with a heavy sweep of gray-blond mustache, and his eyes were a penetrating blue. A broad white scar ran from over his left eye down across his nose, over his right cheek and ended at his jawline.

Carried across his thighs as he rode, was an axe too heavy for most men to lift, yet Olin, Orm, and Lars had seen the mercenary chief roar into battle swinging the massive cleaver one-handed.

Hjalmar the Axeman halted his mount and looked down at the group awaiting him.

Any tension was dispelled when the burly warrior addressed his first remarks to Bryn. He looked at the war-dog and touched the scar that ran across his own face. He chuckled. "Well, old girl, it appears that we ran into the same swordsman."

He looked at Brokk and raised his axe. "Ho, Brokk o' Svartheim. I ask yer permission t' light down an' share yer fire."

There was in the mercenary's face no trace of the usual reaction of human to Wee Folk, and he recited the formal request as politely as he would have asked it of one of his own kind.

"Light down, friend, and welcome," Brokk completed the formula.Hjalmar swung down from the saddle. He showed no reaction at seeing Ulf."Ye be th' first goblin I've met who raised no weapon against me at first sight. Ye must be one o' th' Rovers."

"Aye, friend Hjalmar. I bear no ill will toward any except those who'd be my enemy."

The mercenary chieftain raised his axe in brief acknowledgment, and spoke to Brokk. "I know o' ye, Brokk Hammermacher. 'Twas one o' yer kin crafted me this cleaver."

Brokk looked more closely at the oversized axe. "Aye," he said, "'Tis th' work o' my brother Sindri. Ye've been, then, t' th' dwarfholm?"

"Aye, an' spilled many a horn o' mead wi' yer brother. 'Tis a small world, Brokk o' Svartheim."

"It seems we're well met, Hjalmar o' th' axe. Olin an' th' others speak o' ye wi' respect, an' o' th' pride o' servin' under ye. What know ye o' th' bestial atrocity committed hereabout a week agone?"

The scarfaced mercenary growled.

"'Tis only one o' th' outrages that be happenin' in Midgard these days."

Hjalmar paused to pat the head of Bryn who'd come to his side. "All over th' land th' barons an' thanes war on one another. Th' spillin' o' blood ha' become a sport."

The scarface spat. "Gymar, th' dog o' Ehtelstane Keep, be one o' th' bloodthirstiest. It ha' become a bit o' a problem findin' employment fer my Company. I lead fighters, not trolls, an' we'll not serve a master fer gold only. Th' times be hard fer any not willin' t' play th' hangman."

Brokk made a quick decision.

"How'd ye feel toward takin' service wi' a dwarf?"

"Ye're offerin' a commission?"

"Aye, if th' offer be not offensive t' ye."

"I was told ye're fer Asgard."

"True."

Hjalmar looked thoughtful. "I've never been t' Asgard."

"Then ye accept?"

"I do."

"I offer ye th' same terms that I offered Olin an' th' lads. Fifteen gold marks fer each man each month, an' thirty fer yerself as leader. A bonus if ye see us through th' venture an' return t' Svartheim."

The scarfaced chieftain shook his head.

"'Tis too much." He looked at the three. "An' I'll wager my entire pay fer th' journey that these three said th' same."

Brokk chuckled. "Ye've just doubled yer wages."

"I cannot accept that. We serve ye fer th' same scot as we'd serve another."

The dwarf turned a bland face to the mercenary leader. "Ye accept my service then?"

"Aye.

"An' ye'll take my orders?"

"Aye."

"Then, friend Hjalmar, hear my first order t' ye." Brokk laughed. "'Tis that ye accept th' gold I offered ye wi' no further hagglin'."

"I cry foul, Lord Brokk," Hjalmar grinned. "But as I've taken yer service, I obey yer orders."

"Yer men," Brokk said. "Will they take orders from a dwarf?"

The scarface smiled. "My men take orders from me an' I from ye. Have no fear on that score, my lord. My men follow where I lead, an' trust me t' lead 'em in th' right. Ye'll find 'em loyal t' a man."

The dwarf presented the rest of the band. Hjalmar bowed to Freya. "My Lady," he acknowledged.

To Maryam he smiled and preened his long mustache. "If only I were forty years younger," he sighed.

Maryam giggled.

The Axeman clasped hands with Krupp the Round and Jerry. Lastly he turned to Ulf.

"'Tis strange t' serve wi' a Twisted One, but if ye be friend t' th' Dwarf King, I offer my hand."

Ulf grinned, and they struck hands.

The bargain sealed with a horn of ale, Hjalmar suggested that his new employer move his entourage to the mercenary camp.

Brokk agreed. "Ye'd best go before, an' prepare yer men fer th' sight o' Ulf. I'd not want anythin' untoward t' happen."

"Aye, Lord Brokk, it shall be as ye say."

The mercenary chieftain departed, and the others broke camp to follow.

The Free Companions were less than half a league distant and Brokk expected no danger, but did not lower his guard on that account. It was due to that watchfulness that the whole band was not overwhelmed when Gymar's cutthroats rose out of foxholes on either side of the trail, and fell on them.

Ulf, in the lead, was felled unconscious by a thrown club, and Freya's cart was overset in the first rush. The two women were spilled out onto the ground, and nearly trampled in the savage melee raging around them.

Freya threw a protective cloak of invisibility over herself and the girl, but Maryam, scrambling out of the way of pounding hooves, disappeared into the choking cloud of dust.

Brokk, roaring with fury, laid about with his Morning Star, crushing skull after skull trying to force his way to where he'd last seen his wife and the girl.

Lars had Krupp mounted behind him, and the two were taking heavy toll of the attackers.

Jerry and Olin, whirling this way and that, thrust and slashed, sending many a soul screaming down into Nifflheim.

Orm's axe hacked and slashed, taking his share of the enemy.

But the little band was too heavily outnumbered, and would have been massacred except for the arrival of Hjalmar the Axeman and his mercenaries. Fifty of the Free Companions of Hjalmar's Company quickly cleared the field.

When heads were counted, Maryam and the goblin were found to be missing.

CHAPTER TWENTY TWO

When Maryam regained consciousness, her head throbbed painfully and the whole left side of her face was purple where the thanesman had struck her with his fist. She realized that she was head down over the shoulder of a running man. Every jolt caused searing pain.

The girl raised her head as much as she could, and looked round.

She saw a number of men-at-arms darting through a grove, dodging between trees and leaping over bushes, as though fleeing in terror for their lives.

She cried out at the sight of two of the men dragging the limp body of Ulf by his long arms, without heed to the stones and shrubs that battered him.

At the sound of Maryam's cry, her captor tightened his grip. "So ye're awake." He laughed shortly. "'Tis good. There be little pleasure in takin' a wench who's not conscious t' enjoy it."

His chuckle was harsh with cruelty.

Terror rushed through the girl. She was once again in the hands of a brute, and no Olin Longshanks to rescue her this time.

She groped for the small dirk at her belt, but it was gone. She gave in to despair. Overwhelmed with grief and hopelessness she fainted.

When next Maryam opened her eyes she found herself alone on a rough cot of straw in a dank stone cell with iron bars at a small window in the door. She drew up her knees and curled up into a frightened shivering ball.

There was the sound of a footstep in the corridor outside the barred door, and yellow light from a torch flickered over her. The girl shot a fear-filled glance at the door. The torchlight wavered on a brutal face staring at her through the bars.

"Ye were right, Eric Ragnarssen, it be th' same wench what got yer father killed. I were torturer t' Thurgild of Gildholm an' seed th' doxy many a time. Why be Gymar holdin' th' bitch t' ransom? She's no kin t' pay it."

Maryam recognized the voice that answered. It was the man who had run with her through the woods. "Rolf Bjornssen overheard th' dwarf, Brokk o' Svartheim, offerin' fifteen gold marks t' each of Hjalmar th' Axeman's Company t' serve him.

"It seems th' wench is adopted daughter t' th' filthy child-stealer, and if he'd pay gold like that t' mere blades, Gyrnar reckons he'll lay out a mountain o' gold t' ransom th' girl."

There was the sound of coarse laughter. "Just my filthy luck t' grab a tender bit like that, and have it taken from me by th' thane."

The torturer leered obscenely. "Why not have yer sport of her? Twas you found her." Eric Ragnarssen snorted. "Be you daft, man? Gymar'd have me down here for you t' work on."

The torturer chuckled. "An' I'd welcome ye right joyfully, friend Eric. I've always been fond of ye."

Eric hastily changed the subject. "What be th' fate of th' goblin?"

"Gymar plans t' roast him fer th' delight o' th' troop on th' feast day of th' goddess Idun, five days hence. I'm t' entertain th' Twisted One afore th' burnin', an' ye can be sure that by th' time th' flames get him, he'll welcome their embrace."

"Ye're a-torturin' him now?"

"Nay, not yet. Gymar wants him strong an' hale t' endure th' longer for his pleasure."

The voices moved off down the corridor, and Maryam was left alone with her terror, her fear for Ulf, and the rats.

CHAPTER TWENTY THREE

It took eight men to restrain Olin from assaulting the castle single--handedly when he discovered that Maryam was missing.

The boy went berserk, and blood would have been spilled, had not Jerry disarmed him immediately with a quick twist. By super effort, and no few bruises, the mercenaries managed to truss the youth like a pig for market.

Several helmetfuls of icy water from a nearby stream had to be thrown in his face before the mad look of the berserker faded from his eyes.

At last he looked up at Jerry. "You can loose me now, friend Jerry. Th' madness is past." Olin's eyes were filled with agony as he searched Brokk's face. "We must find her, my lord."

The dwarf gripped the young man's shoulder hard.

"We will. Never ye fear, lad, we will. We'll find her an' take vengeance. Ye can loose him, son, he'll do no hurt."

"'Twas some o' Gymar's scum," Hjalmar stated. "Th' lass'll be in th' Keep."

"What about Ulf?"

"I like it not t' have t' tell ye, Lord Brokk, th' goblin bein' such a near friend t' ye."

"Ye're sayin' he's killed already?"

"Nay, 'twould be better if 'twere so."

The Axeman's face was cold. "Lord Brokk, I've soldiered in this part fer nigh two years."

He turned to Olin. "I brought th' troop here shortly after ye parted from us."

The Mercenary chieftain turned back to Brokk with a look of pride in his eyes. "Th' lad was sixteen only an' one o' my best lieutenants." He returned to his original statement. "As I said, I've been in th' neighborhood nigh two years. Hired swords talk a-plenty o'er ale. Th' sort o' scum hired at Ethelstane Keep e'en boasted o' watchin' th' cruelties in th' torture chamber. Lord Brokk, 'tis my thought that yer friend is intended t' supply entertainment in th' castle yard fer th' thane an' his troops."

"Torture, ye mean?"

"Aye."

Agony twisted the dwarf's face. "E'en now he may be on th' rack."

The Axeman tugged at his mustache and shook his head. "I think not," he said slowly.

"I've learned much about th' troll-hearted Thane o' Ethelstane in th' past two years. Th' whoreson dog loves well t' mock th' gods, an' it comes t' me that th' feast day o' Idun, th' sweet goddess o' youth, falls five days' hence.

"'Tis my thinkin' that the bloody-handed bastard will hold 'til then. 'Tis like him t' desecrate th' tender goddess wi' such blasphemy."

"Then ye think we've five days t' mount a rescue?"

Hjalmar nodded. "Five days, aye. A rescue?" The scarfaced captain shook his head slowly. "'Tis impossible."

"Why say ye so? Know ye this castle?"

"Aye, Lord Brokk." The mercenary's tone was unhappy. "Aye. 'Tis impregnable."

"Explain."

Ethelstane Keep, the Axeman explained, was built atop a natural stone pedestal in one of the few canyons in Midgard.

The great pillar soared upward two hundred feet from the canyon floor, and stood an equal distance from the canyon rim. It was connected by a narrow stone causeway that could easily be defended by a few archers. Even if an enemy should force the causeway, he'd face a fifteen foot gap with drawbridge and portcullis, and the added defense of an overhanging balcony with trapdoors through which pots of boiling oil and melted lead could be dumped on the heads of the attackers.

"'Tis hopeless, my lord Brokk. Th' only way t' take th' castle be from th' air, an' we're not birds. Yer friend be doomed, an' th' lass."

Jerry shot the Axeman a sharp look. "Answer me this: Is there any high ground near the Keep? Ground higher than the walls?"

"Aye, Lord Jerry. There be one steep hill. I take yer meanin' but 'tis o'er a thousand yards from th' walls, an' no catapult could cast that far, e'en if we had one."

"It's not catapults I'm thinking about," Jerry said, "I'm thinking of your remark about birds."

"Birds?"

"Aye, friend Hjalmar," Jerry laughed, "birds. Mount up, Hjalmar the Axeman, and take me to see this impregnable castle."

Jerry and the mercenary leader returned some two hours later.

"Well?" Brokk asked, impatient over his godson's air of mystery.

"Well?"

"Softly, Father, softly," Jerry smiled, "I have to know a couple of things more, then if my idea can work I'll tell you."

He turned to Hjalmar. "Would the villagers hereabout help us if I could practically guarantee to put the merry Gymar out of business permanently?"

Hjalmar grinned. "'Tis my guess they'd do anything t' rid themselves o' that butcher."

"Good. Send some of your best men to find out. If any of Gymar's men are about, scrub 'em."

"Scrub 'em?"

"Erase 'em. Wipe 'em out. Dammit, man, kill them. No word of what we're doing must reach the castle."

The scarface laughed. "Oh, we were plannin' that anyway, but there'll be none o' th' whoreson in th' village.

"After th' defeat they suffered this day, th' scurvy dogs will all be in th' Keep, safe from our swords. My guess is that they'll stay, lickin' their wounds, until they think we've left th' shire."

Jerry grinned. "All the better. See if you can find a big supply of parchment and/or hides and see if the villagers will scrape them so thin you can almost see through them."

Puzzled, Hjalmar went to issue the orders.

Jerry turned to Olin."Remember that swamp we passed about three hours back down the trail?"

"Aye."

"Take ten men and bring back all the reeds you can carry. Get the longest ones you can find."

"Aye, Jerry." As puzzled as the Axeman had been, Olin ran to round up his men.The dwarf grabbed Jerry's arm. "Will ye tell me what ye're about, or must I hammer it out o' ye wi' my mace?"

Jerry chuckled. "No need for violence, Father, this is where you come in."

The red-beard took a sheet of parchment, and borrowed Freya's quill and inkhorn. He sat at the rough table in Hjalmar's tent, and with Brokk looking over his shoulder, began to sketch.

"What's that ye're drawin'?" growled the dwarf, "A bird?"

"Not quite. It's called a hang-glider. With one of these, and a place to take off from, a man can soar like a bird.

"Look, I scouted the hill Hjalmar spoke of. It's perfect for launching a hang-glider."

Jerry made a quick sketch of the castle on the pedestal, the canyon rim, and the steep hillside. He used little arrows to indicate air currents. He explained how the updrafts along the canyon rim would give the flier the altitude to clear the castle walls.

He completed his drawing of the hang-glider. "You're the master builder, Father. Do you think you could construct fifty or sixty of these? In three days?"

The dwarf studied the sketch. He noticed the arrangement of the body harness and steering bar. He pulled at his beard. "Aye, lad, 'tis none so difficult wi' enough hands t' help."

"I'll need at least one by tomorrow morning so I can start my gliding school. There's a super tall tree not far from here that's just right for launching short flights.

"With a lot of luck, Hjalmar's men should learn enough to get them through one thousand-yard flight without killing *too* many of them. I hope."

The chatter of many voices drew Jerry and the dwarf from the tent. The Axeman's men had returned from the village, and it looked as if the whole population had come with them. Many of the villagers had armloads of parchment. The rest carried sheepskins.

Jerry stopped one of the men-at-arms. "Hey," he said, "all that parchment. That's exactly what we need. Where'd they get it?"

The mercenary grinned. "Out of every window in th' dorf. They were willin' t' give up anything for a chance t' rid themselves o' Gymar."

"Good. Get them to scraping. I want those parchments as thin as they can get them without putting holes in 'em."

"Aye, Lord Jerry."

Olin returned with the reeds, and Brokk put him and his men to work splitting and lashing them together according to Jerry's sketch. He, himself, and the village blacksmith, set to work fashioning the body harnesses.

The labor continued throughout the night, and in the morning Brokk presented Jerry with eleven completed frameworks.

Jerry put several of the women to stitching together the paper-thin parchments. When a piece large enough to cover a frame had been fabricated, the red-beard supervised the women as they wet the sheet, stretched it tautly over the frame, and sewed it firmly into place. It was set aside to shrink and dry and the women went back to join the others in piecing together more skins.

A men-at-arms brought Jerry the first completed harness, and he attached it to the first completed glider. He hefted the contraption. It was light enough for a child to pick up, but sturdy and solid. He looked around at the throng of curious men-at-arms.

Jerry grinned. He motioned for the troop to follow, and carried the glider to the tall pine he'd marked earlier.

Since it was impossible to climb and carry the glider, Jerry had had a pulley attached to the topmost limb and a whip rove through to hoist the single-wing aloft.

The red-beard had the men sit, and he explained the bird-like wing. "Ordinarily you need a running start to launch one of these things."

He pointed to the treetop.

"But since the wind is fairly strong and blowing in the right direction, I'm pretty sure I can get airborne from up there."

Jerry grinned. "If I can't, it's been nice knowing you."

He explained about air currents and how to use them. He didn't try to go into any aerodynamics, mainly because he had no idea of the field himself. He was lecturing strictly from one barely successful attempt that had left him with a broken collar bone.

The sword-and-shield men, the axemen, the spearmen, and the wielders of club and mace, seemed an unlikely group of aeronauts, but there was one thing going for Jerry's idea.

The men of the Free Company of Hjalmar the Axeman were not the usual run-of-the-mill drunkards and brutal hangmen that comprised the bulk of mercenary troops. These were all hand-picked by the Axeman not only for their fighting abilities, but for their intelligence as well.

That was what made Hjalmar's Company one of the finest fighting forces in all Midgard. All of these men had quick reflexes, or they died. All these men could concentrate on the immediate problem, or they died. All these men were able to adapt to rapidly changing circumstances, or they died. And all these men were brave to the point of recklessness, and none were afraid to die.

A pretty unbeatable combination.

Jerry looked around the circle of fascinated faces. "Is there anything I've said that you don't understand? If you've got any questions, ask now."

He pointed to the hang-glider dangling from the pulley a hundred feet overhead. "It's a long fall."

There were questions. A lot of them. All these men were fatalistic, but none were suicidal.

Jerry answered all their questions as fully as he could. "Any more? Anything?"

The men of the Free Company of Hjalmar the Axeman were satisfied that they understood as much as they could about what was being asked of them.

Jerry took a deep breath, and turning, began to climb up to the launching branch. The mercenaries watched as the red-beard mounted, reached the single-wing, and strapped himself into it.

From that height they couldn't hear the number or the fervency of the prayers Jerry was muttering that he had correctly guessed the number of square feet of surface area needed to support the weight of a husky warrior and the poundage of his iron weapons.

With a final crossing of his fingers, Jerry leaned forward and launched himself into the wind. The makeshift contraption worked. His stomach lurched as he dropped a few feet, then Jerry felt himself buoyed up and, swept into a long lazy turn that carried him out between the few trees, and soared for five hundred yards over an open field to a perfect running landing.

The men-at-arms had followed the glider, running full-tilt beneath their soaring leader, whooping their various war-cries, and already feeling the thrill of flight. They surrounded Jerry, nearly mobbing him with their congratulations and their exuberance.

All clamored to be first to duplicate the feat.

Jerry called loudly for Olin Longshanks. The youngster appeared almost immediately. "Aye, Jerry?"

The red-beard waved at the jostling soldiers. "Have you any control over these maniacs?"

Olin grinned. "Aye, Jerry."

He turned and began bellowing orders in a voice Jerry had never heard the kid use before. The tones were deep and full of command. It was the voice of a born leader of men who expected to be obeyed and obeyed immediately.

The milling crowd of mercenaries quickly fell into ranks, and ceased their hubbub. Olin gave a few more orders, and turned to the astonished Jerry.

He saluted by raising his rapier, and said loudly so as to be heard by all. "Troop assembled, Lord Jerry. What be your commands?"

Jerry understood that the young leader was reminding the men who was really in charge. Jerry looked at the boy he'd known for months and hadn't really known at all.

He said just as loudly, "Well done, Olin Longshanks. With men like these, the taking of Ethelstane Keep will be a piece of cake."

The men in the ranks did not understand the lord Jerry's reference to cake, but grasped its meaning, and a shout of affirmation rent the air.

With Olin to enforce discipline, Jerry began his jump school.

One after another the heavily armed mercenaries mounted the tall pine, and flung themselves into space. More of the single-wings were delivered, and the program was stepped up. There were many crashes and a few broken bones, but no fatalities.

By the third day, Jerry had a company of fairly competent airborne rangers.

Hjalmar the Axeman was determined to lead his Free Companions into the fray, but his rhinoceros-like build, together with the weight of his ponderous axe, was too much for the aerodynamics of the glider.

The mercenary chieftain fell like a stone, and only the cushioning effect of numerous breaking branches slowed his descent enough to prevent any really serious injury.

Jerry recalculated, and Brokk constructed a glider that would support the Axeman's weight.

By nightfall of the fourth day all had been done that could be done, to prepare for the assault on Ethelstane Keep.

A plan of the castle, obtained from the description by a deserter from Gymar's ranks, was studied until every foot of the edifice was driven into the consciousness of every member of the assault force.

Details were told off for special assignments. Who were to clear the outer walls. Who were to take the drawbridge and lower the defenses so the villagers could invest the courtyard. Who were to secure the overhanging balcony so that the pots of boiling oil and melted lead could not be thrown against the invaders. Who were to assail the Keep itself and engage the thane's bodyguard.

And, lastly, those who were to ignore all else, and drive straight for the dungeons to free Ulf and Maryam.

CHAPTER TWENTY FOUR

Maryam woke, and the terror rushed in as it had for the four mornings past.

Today was the fifth day, the feast day of Idun, Goddess of Youth. The day that Ulf the goblin. . . Ulf of the twisted body and great heart. . . was to be tortured and roasted over a slow fire. Ulf who was her friend. Ulf who was her protector.

An emotion that was totally foreign to the girl's gentle nature began to burn in her mind.

Hatred!

Something she'd never known before. Hatred for those who would maim and torture for the sheer enjoyment of it. Maryam felt an uncharacteristic passion to strike out, to hit back, to destroy such evil.

The girl was surprised to find her thoughts turn to the hours on the trail she'd spent listening to Krupp the Round as the chubby elf instructed Freya in the use of the Elfin Gift. The little man's words, so often repeated, began coming back to her.

If only I were an elf, she thought, it would be easy to be free of this horrible place and to save dear Ulf as well.

Maryam closed her eyes and concentrated on what Krupp had said about moving solid objects with the Gift. While Freya already possessed this ability, Krupp had shown her how to sharpen the faculty to use it the more keenly.

The method as described by the elf, was clear in her mind.

Her eyes fell on the filthy bowl in which Elford the torturer had brought last night's porridge.

Without thinking about it, the girl concentrated on the bowl as Krupp had taught. In her mind she pictured it rising into the air, sailing across the room and smashing against the far wall. She *willed* it to happen.

The bowl leaped aloft, and hurtled into the wall, splintering into fragments!

Maryam stared at the shattered dish, unable to believe what she had done.

She was no elf, yet she had exercised the Elfin Gift!

The girl had no way of knowing, nor did the elves, that psychic ability was also to be found, though rarely, in some humans.

It was inevitable that, from time to time, some isolated individual discovered in himself psychokinetic power, telepathy, or some other form of E.S.P. It is easily understandable that any such individual carefully concealed his abilities, for fear of being taken for a witch or an elf.

It was several minutes before the shock wore off, and the girl's brain began to work again.

Somewhat fearfully, she went over in her mind just what she had done. Could she do it again? Did she have the courage to try? She did. Maryam concentrated on the only other object in the room, the straw-filled pallet.

She visualized it rising and floating across the room, then *willed* it so. The flimsy mattress
rose three feet from the stone floor, and soared across the cell to thump solidly into the wall.

Maryam looked at the cell's iron barred door. Could she?

She drew in a deep breath. She had nothing to lose by trying. In her mind she saw the door burst from its hinges, then *willed*.

The heavy door bulged outward. She willed harder. With nerve-grating screechings, the long spikes holding the hinges pulled free from the jamb, and the door crashed outward into the passageway. Maryam hesitated only a moment, then stepped out of her cell into the corridor.

The hall was empty.

In one direction were more cells, and in the other it opened into the chamber of torture with its rack, its wheel, its branding irons and the other tools of the torturer's art. Where to find Ulf?

She was becoming panicky standing alone in that frightening place. Suddenly she threw all her chips into the pot. "Ulf!" she shouted, "Ulf, where are you?"

The answer came from a cell near the end of the hall.

"Here, little sister, I be here."
Maryam ran to Ulf's cell. The goblin was full of questions. "How did you. . .?" was as far
as he got.

The girl said tensely, "Get away from the door."

Ulf, startled by Maryam's peremptory tone, swallowed his questions, and moved to one side. Maryam *willed*, and the door burst inward.

The goblin stared at the girl, stunned. "Ye've th' Gift!" he stammered.

"But how?" Maryam grabbed him by the arm, tugging him from the cell. "I don't know. I just. . . . I don't know. What do we do now? How do we get out of this horrible place?"

The goblin stroked his chin. His trunk of a nose lifted and quested about, as it did when he was puzzled, then apparently put the question of Maryam's elfin ability aside.

"First, weapons. There must be somethin' in th' torture room. Quickly, little sister, I must arm myself."

They had taken only two steps, when a section of the wall swung open revealing a camouflaged door, and Elford the torturer stepped forth.

The master of the dungeon was a hulking brute both wide and tall. He was stripped to the waist, and revealed a bulging chest and massive belly hard with muscle. Thick black hair covered torso and arms, and a tangled black beard concealed the lower half of a face lined and seamed with cruelty.

The torturer uttered a brutal laugh at sight of his escaping prisoners.

"Where d'ye think you're goin'? You must be eager t' entertain my lord and his guests, goblin, t' break forth from your cell t' greet me."

His brutal chuckle sounded again. Elford hefted the heavy iron bar he carried, and took a step forward.

Maryam convulsed with terror, and struck out with her new-found and as yet uncontrolled power.

The raw energy released by the frightened girl seized the torturer in its grasp, and flung him against the stone wall with such force that the sound of cracking bones filled the corridor. Elford's limp body bounced forward, and fell face-down to the floor.

Maryam fainted.

Ulf leaped and caught the swooning girl before she struck the floor.

The goblin looked with amazement at the shattered body of the torturer, then down at the unconscious girl in his spidery arms. He was somewhat dazed, and no little shaken, by the awesome power released by the gentle child cradled to his chest.

He carried Maryam into the torture chamber and laid her gently on a bench. He checked her breathing and satisfied himself that she had merely fainted.

Ulf looked about for weapons. There were knives of all sizes.

Small ones for the cutting out of tongues or flaying a man alive. Larger, heavier blades for the lopping off of a limb. The goblin chose one of the latter, a blade two feet long, thick and sharp, similar in size to the shortsword he customarily carried athwart his hump.

He spied a longspear and a shield leaning in a corner. He hefted the spear. It was too long for his convenience. He laid it on one of the tables, and using the heavy knife as a cleaver, shortened the shaft to the length of the assegai to which he was accustomed. He tested the balance. and grunted with satisfaction. Further search turned up a rusty helmet to complete his makeshift armor. He picked up a small knife for Maryam.

A sigh from the girl brought the goblin to her side. Maryam opened her eyes and jerked upright. Her eyes darted fearfully about, filled with panic until she saw Ulf.

"Oh, Ulf," she whispered, "I'm so frightened."

"Rest easy, little sister. We leave this place now. Come." He handed her the little dirk.

Ulf explained as he led the way back to the cell corridor. "Every castle has a secret way to escape should it come under siege. Ethelstane Keep is impregnable to assault due to its causeway approach, but the causeway itself makes it easy to cut off the garrison from supplies. Therefore there must be an escape route."

The goblin ran his hands over the stones in that portion of the wall from which the torture master had emerged. Suddenly he grunted, and pushed. The stone under his hand sank into the wall several inches. There was a grating sound, and a segment of the wall swung inward. He turned to Maryam.

The girl was standing with both hands pressed to her mouth. Her face was ashen as she stared at the gory mess that had been Elford the torturer of Ethelstane Keep.

The goblin took Maryam's shoulder and turned her toward the spiral stairway revealed by the opening in the wall. "Waste no tears on that one, little sister. The world has been well rid of a monster equaled in cruelty only by the trolls. Come."

Maryam followed the goblin down the steep descent. The concealed door swung shut behind them, but the secret passage was lighted by torches in sconces every few yards.

The stair seemed endless. Maryam's legs were trembling with fatigue, and she was wondering how much longer she could hold out before having to call for a rest.

Ulf stopped in his descent, and signaled Maryam to wait and be quiet. The girl sank to the stone step gratefully.

Ulf moved downward on silent feet. What seemed to the frightened girl like an eternity passed. Maryam shuddered as the air was rent by a piercing shriek. There came sounds of a brief struggle, followed by silence.

Maryam's heart lurched, then raced furiously at a footstep on the stair below. Ulf rounded the curve and she almost fainted with relief.

In her eyes the goblin's fanged and snouted face was beautiful!

"The way is clear," Ulf said.

They stepped over the bodies of the three men-at-arms who'd been on guard, and thrust their way through the heavy growth of scrub that screened the portal from the outside. Once clear of the shrubbery, they found themselves at the foot of the towering pinnacle atop which sat Ethelstane Keep. The sky overhead was just beginning to lighten with the coming dawn, but here in the canyon it was still night-dark.

The goblin led the way, senses alert and snout questing. He came upon a faintly marked path and paused. Assured that it was safe, he beckoned Maryam, and set out briskly for the canyon wall. It seemed safe to assume that the path led to an ascent out of the gorge.

They came to a stop as faint sounds of fighting came from high over their heads.

While the light was still dim at the bottom of the canyon, it was full daylight above. The familiar noises of men engaged in mortal combat floated down to them. War cries, yells, the clash of arms.

"They're attacking the castle!" Maryam exclaimed. "Should we go back?"

Ulf shook his head. "I think not, little sister. The Keep is invulnerable."

The goblin was puzzled. Even if Brokk and Jerry were foolish enough to attack the Keep, which they were not, Hjalmar the Axeman was too veteran a campaigner to throw away the lives of his men in a foredoomed assault.

"Mayhap 'tis a diversion," he muttered, unconvinced. A diversion for what? Yet the sounds of battle seemed to be coming from within the castle.

CHAPTER TWENTY FIVE

The Free Company of Hjalmar the Axeman consisted of four lieutenants, six sergeants, and six squads of twenty men-at-arms. Three of the lieutenants commanded two groups each, and the fourth was aide-de-camp to the Axeman.

Four of the squads were drawn up on the brink of the takeoff hill in the faint light of pre-dawn, and Jerry was issuing final instructions.

"When you cross the canyon rim there will be a strong updraft at this time of day. Ride it. Ride it high. Get all the altitude you can. The castle sentries will be looking for attack by land, not from the air. You want to be high enough that they don't see you until we dive on them."

He looked at one of the sergeants. "Big Horst. Repeat your orders."

"Th' drawbridge. We're t' overpower th' watch, raise th' portcullis and drop th' bridge."

"Time?"

"We've no more than ten minutes t' complete th' task."

"Why?"

"Because th' rest of th' troop and th' men of th' village will charge th' causeway th' moment they see us over th' walls of th' Keep. We've that much time t' take out th' warders afore they can loose arrows and slings into 'em."

"What should you do if the men assigned to clear the walls should be repulsed?"

The burly sergeant grinned. "I lead my men against th' drawbridge, and leave it t' Little Horst t' do his job, as he's always done."

"And when you've dropped the drawbridge?"

"We join with Little Horst in clearin' th' walls."

"Right."

Jerry pointed to another. "Little Horst?"

The sergeant answered. "We're t' mount th' walls quickly, an' engage th' defenders. We've ten minutes also fer th' same reason." The sergeant grinned. "'Twill be done in less."

"Then?"

"We all join with Helmut o' th' Fjords in takin' th' Keep."

"Helmut?"

"'Tis our task t' assault th' Keep proper, under Hjalmar, and take th' Thane."

Jerry looked at Olin Longshanks who had been commissioned sergeant by Hjalmar for the duration of the action.

"Olin?"

The youngster's face was set and hard. "I go with you an' the lord Brokk straight t' th' dungeons, and Odin have pity on any who bar th' way."

"Lieutenant Bjorn Strongarm?"

"I coordinate th' takin' of th' gate and walls, then join th' assault on th' Keep."

"Lieutenant Olaf?"

"I be aide-de-camp t' th' Axeman and go where he bids."

Jerry looked at the Captain of the mercenaries. "Hjalmar, the lord Brokk and I go with Olin Longshanks to the dungeons. You've the vital job of securing the castle."

Hjalmar raised his ponderous axe. "I lead against Gymar th' butcher. Ethelstane Keep will be yers when ye come up."

Brokk eyed the mercenary leader. "I expect no less, Hjalmar th' Axeman," he said grimly.

Jerry noted the brightening of the sky in the east. "We jump off in five minutes. Squads try to keep together and land together."

The red-beard turned to Lars and Orm and Krupp the Round who stood a little to one side.

"You guys better join the villagers now." He shook hands with each. "Good luck."

Lars had been designated to lead the volunteers from the village, with Orm as his second in command, and Krupp as resident magician.

Freya had been left in the protection of the remaining two squads under the command of Ehelred the Lame.

The lieutenant known as Ethelred the Lame had been born with one leg shorter than the other. The resulting limp in no way impaired his abilities as a fighting man. He had earned his position in the Company by his ferocity on the battlefield.

The elf-woman kept Bryn at her side, and sent Odin's Messenger to bring her reports of the battle. The men-at-arms assigned to her protection had quite obviously lost their fear of the Little People, but just as obviously still stood in awe of Freya's elfin powers and her unearthly beauty.

"H-hour." Jerry checked his troops. All were snugged into their gliders awaiting his command.

The assault waves were thus:

Olin's squad and that of Hjalmar the Axeman were to jump off first. They would land in the castle yard, and engage those of the enemy who might descend into the dungeon, and harm the prisoners.

On touchdown they'd split, Hjalmar going for Gymar and the Keep, and Olin going directly for the dungeons. The second wave would take off thirty seconds after the first, to secure the walls and gate.

Jerry watched the sun clear the horizon. Its rays warmed the air, causing it to give lift to the single-wings.

All eyes were on Thor's Fist as he raised one arm, swept it down to point at the castle, and broke into a run for the cliff. The first line, pacing him, launched into space.

There was a momentary drop as they left the cliff-face, then the warming air buoyed them up, and they headed for the canyon rim on a slowly rising flight. Each had expected the drop and updraft, and the troop rose swiftly on the strong current, gaining altitude.

The open court of the castle below looked awfully small from their height. Jerry shouted the order and they began their descent.

Jerry saw one of the sentries on the wall below glance up and spot the airborne attackers. The man stood, frozen for a moment, then screeched a warning in a voice filled with hysteria. His fellows followed his pointing finger, and gaped at the sight of flying warriors.

Only two archers had the presence of mind to nock and loose. One of the arrows flew true, and Jerry was pained to see the man on his left take a shaft through the throat, and plunge earthward.

Then the wall was only a couple of yards beneath him, and the courtyard dead ahead. He leaned forward sharply and dropped his feet, to hit the ground running. He slapped the quick-release Brokk had devised, and leaped free of the glider.

All around him men were doing the same.

Brokk, cursing sulphurously, tore himself free and headed at a run for the door leading to the dungeons. Olin Longshanks overtook him, and disappeared through the portal.

Hjalmar the Axeman roared orders, and his segment charged the Keep.

Jerry pounded after Brokk, followed by the rest of the squad. Even as he entered the passage leading down into the bowels of the castle, the second wave was landing.

Jerry couldn't help grinning at the blasphemous oaths Brokk hurled in all directions as the red-beard's longer legs carried him past the dwarf.

Keeping the blueprint of the castle in the forefront of his mind, Jerry followed the proper twists and turns, the men of the squad hard on his heels.

Olin Longshanks was out of sight somewhere ahead of him. He encountered no opposition, nor heard any sounds to indicate that Olin had run into any. He burst through the door of what was obviously the torture chamber. From a corridor in the opposite wall came the sounds of banging doors, and Olin shouting Maryam's name.

Jerry crossed the chamber. Olin was standing in the middle of the empty passageway, looking down at the shattered body of the torturer. There was no sign of Maryam or the goblin.

Since the ones they sought were obviously not there, Olin swallowed his grief, and issued crisp orders. The squad double-timed back to the courtyard to join in subduing the castle's defenders.

When they emerged into the court, Brokk found Hjalmar the Axeman to be as good as his word. The castle was taken.

Brokk was pleased. "Where's th' whoreson Thane o' Ethelstane?" The Axeman pointed. "There."

Jerry and the dwarf followed the mercenary's finger. Impaled on a spear, the severed head of Gymar of Ethelstane grinned down at them. Brokk grunted. "Well done. How many prisoners ha' ye?"

Hjalmar shrugged. "In th' heat o' battle we'd no time t' take any."

"All be slain?"

"Aye."

Olin cried out. "Then there be none t' tell us what happened t' Maryam and th' goblin!"

Hjalmar stared at the young mercenary. "What mean ye? Did ye not find them in th' dungeons below?"

"Nay, th' dungeons were empty. None was there except th' body of a man who looked t' have been trampled by a herd of horses."

"Mayhap then they were never brought here." Hjalmar looked puzzled. "But I find that hard t' credit. Where else would Gymar take them?"

"They were here," Olin said grimly. "Two of the cell doors were burst open, and in one of th' cells I found this ribbon. 'Tis Maryam's."

The youngster clutched the bit of bright ribbon tightly. "Now who's t' tell us what happened t' Maryam and th' goblin!"

The Axeman rubbed the scar that bisected his face. "How could I have known, lad?"

He turned to Brokk. "'Tis my blame, my lord. 'Twas I gave th' order t' take no prisoners."

The chieftain gestured, angry with himself. "My first commission in yer service an' I handle it badly." He drew himself up and looked at the dwarf. "Ye owe me nothin' my lord Brokk. We've not earned yer gold. I take my men an' depart, cravin' yer pardon."

The dwarf growled and raised a hand. "Stay, Axeman. Be not so hasty t' condemn yerself. True, 'tis a blow, but ye yerself said it. Ye'd no more way o' knowin' that Ulf an' th' lass were not in th' cells below than did any o' us."

Brokk looked at the men-at-arms bustling in and out, piling up the loot from their victory. As was the custom, the victors were entitled to the spoils of the vanquished, to be divided among them according to strict protocol.

The dwarf pulled at his beard. "Th' castle's been combed thoroughly in search o' goods. No sign o' Ulf or th' girl?"

Hjalmar shook his head. "None's been mentioned, but then none ha' been lookin' fer them."

He raised a shout. "Olaf! Olaf Olafssen! To me!"

The aide-de-camp came running. "Aye?"

"Th' ones we came t' free be not in th' cells below. Begin a search immediately. Take ye all hands, an' scour this curst sty from tallest turret t' lowest level. Overlook no smallest nook nor corner on yer life. D'ye understand me, Olaf?"

"Aye, Hjalmar. Th' search will overlook nothin'." Olaf moved off, bellowing orders. The courtyard emptied quickly as the men swarmed through the castle.

With the yard cleared, a group of the village volunteers could be seen clustered about something or someone near the portcullis.

The crowd was oddly silent. There was a stir, and men backed aside to let Lars o' th' Battlefield pass. Cradled in the sword-and-shield man's arms was the limp and bloody body of Orm Thorwaldssen.

Lars approached, followed by the villagers. There was an odd look on the graying mercenary's face that was reflected in the faces of those behind him. A look of dazed awe.

Lars laid Orm's body gently on the cobblestones. The young warrior had sustained literally dozens of wounds. The deathblow had been a sword thrust through the heart.

Olin looked at his foster brother, and fell to his knees, a wild keening wail of grief, too deep to be put into words, pouring from his throat.

Lars knelt beside the stricken boy and put an arm around his shoulders. His grief for the young warrior he had raised from childhood was silent, but no less deep.

Jerry and the dwarf looked at each other, torn by the agony of their friends, and their own sorrow at Orm's death.

Krupp the Round emerged from the group of silent, awed peasants. The elf's normally jolly face was touched with sorrow, but held that same strange awe shared by Lars and the villagers.

Jerry looked at the little man.

"What is it? What the hell's going on?" He pointed to the group of silent churls. "What's the matter with those guys? What's the matter with *you?*"

Krupp smiled.

"A saga, friend Jerry. We have witnessed a glory! The saga of Orm the Hero. An anthem of praise for the bravery and glory of Orm, beloved of Odin, the Chosen of the Shining Maids! What a pity there's no skald here to compose it properly. But the story will be sung!

"The name of Orm Thorwaldssen will ring in every castle in Skandia! I have no harp to give it the music, nor can I sing if I had the harp, but I can tell it to you as I saw it happen."

It may be that the little elf was no skald, but no skald could have made his listeners enter more into the story than did Krupp the Round.

As he wove the tale, his command of the Elfin Gift, and the intensity of his voice placed pictures and snatches of the emotions felt by Orm into the minds of his hearers.

Orm watched as the airborne squads passed over the walls. Lars gave the command for the villagers to charge the causeway. The ill-armed but enthusiastic churls responded, and the assault was on.

Lars and Orm ran shoulder to shoulder ahead of the screaming mob. Orm's axe swung in flashing figure eights, and Lars shouted his war-cry across his shield and whirled his longsword over his head.

The squad detailed to secure the gate and drop the drawbridge did their job but there was a glitch.

A defense point that had not been shown on the blueprint they'd studied.

An extra gallery within the arch of the portal could not be approached from the wall, only by a stair from the courtyard. It was protected by the overhang from attack from above.

The result was that the ten minutes allotted to secure the gate stretched to eighteen, and those eight extra minutes proved disastrous.

The sergeant commanding the ten-man detail of the defense demonstrated that he knew his trade.

He held his men concealed until the attackers were well within bowshot then, began picking off those at the rear of the assault force. Any who turned to flee back along the causeway were struck down. They were prevented from advancing by a fifteen foot gap and the upraised drawbridge.

The helpless churls were being slaughtered.

Orm Thorwaldssen raged. He shook his axe at the laughing archers and screamed his fury. The shrieks of the butchered villagers rang in his ears, and the red haze of the berserker madness began to fill his eyes.

He snarled and searched for a way to span the gap. He studied the blank face of the upraised bridge and the blank stones of the wall. He noticed that the blank face of the bridge was none so blank. Big iron bolts studding the surface could provide hand and foot holds for an agile man, if only there were some way to reach them.

He had an inspiration. It was rash and foolhardy in the extreme with little chance of success, but little chance was better than no chance at all, and men were dying every second he hesitated.

Lars stared, a look of bewilderment on his face, as Orm dropped his shield and stripped off helmet and mail shirt. The young warrior kicked off his sandals and flexed his toes.

The older man shouted questions, but caught up in the rising berserker rage, Orm heard nothing. His mad eyes calculated the distance, and he flung his axe. The half-moon made one revolution, and sank deep into the wood of the drawbridge.

Lars watched helplessly as his foster son raced toward the end of the causeway, and leaped the fifteen foot gap. Orm's hands closed around the haft of his axe, and he sent up a prayer to Odin that the weapon would hold.

It did.

His body slammed hard against the wood. His feet felt for and found support on the protruding iron bolts. Orm loosed one hand from the axe and grabbed another of the bolts. Bracing himself, he wrenched free the axe-blade and looped its thong about his wrist.

Dangling the axe, he began to ascend from one bolt to the next.

Arrows from the defenders sang about him, none found its mark. He moved at an angle, across and up, and reached the end of the narrow balcony. The little platform was wide enough for only one man, so Orm could meet the enemy one at a time.

He received his first wound as he reached the top of the bridge, and came within swordstroke of the defenders. Clinging firmly to the handhold, Orm parried the second slash and counterstruck. The defender's sword arm, still clutching the sword, fell down past the causeway, down the hundreds of feet to the bottom of the canyon.

The swordsman stared in surprise at his armless shoulder. Orm, never really having felt the slash across his back, swarmed up and over the balcony rail. With a sweep of his left hand he sent the man tumbling after his arm.

In the melee that followed, the berserker cleared the gallery. In doing so he took numerous wounds, several that would have proved fatal in the long run, but the young Hero would not live long enough to die of them.

He struck down the last man between him and the windlass that raised and lowered the drawbridge, and slashed the rope with a stroke of his axe.

The bridge leaned outward, and crashed down on the causeway just as one of the wounded defenders rose to his knees, and with his last breath, thrust his sword into Orm's back and through his heart.

Both fell dead together.

Lars and the villagers stood rooted, unable to move, and stricken with paralysis born of awe, as a rainbow arced from a clear sky, and touched the corpse-littered gallery.

The area was engulfed in a brilliant glow within which could be seen shining figures on horseback, and from which came the sound of triumphant singing.

The awe-stricken company watched as the Shining Maids gathered round the crumpled body of Orm, then the glow lifted, following the rainbow as it receded back into the sky from whence it had come.

The ringing anthem faded.

Released from their paralysis, the group rushed after Lars as the old soldier raced across the drawbridge. They waited at the foot of the stairway revealed by the lowering of the bridge, while Lars o' th' Battlefield mounted, and brought down the Hero's body.

As Krupp talked, the courtyard had gradually filled, as the men-at-arms completed their fruitless search for Maryam and the goblin.

The hardbitten soldiers ringed silently around the body of Orm.

The elf looked around at the gathering. The men stared from the slain Hero to the awestricken villagers, and a tinge of the wonderment touched all of them.

They had all heard of the Chosen, the ones selected by the Shining Maids and borne to Valhalla, but only one among them, Jerry, had ever looked upon one such.

And *he* still had his doubts as to what he had actually seen.

Olin Longshanks and Lars o' th' Battlefield stood up, their grief assuaged by the elf's recitation of Orm's heroic deeds.

Lars lifted his face to the sky, and raised his longsword. His voice roared forth in a mighty shout,

"Odin! Odin!"

There came a great clashing of metal on metal as the entire company crashed swords on shields and echoed Lars's cry.

"Odin! Odin!"

The slain young warrior was known to most of the Free Company of Hjalmar the Axeman, from having previously served in their ranks.

The entire band, led by the Axeman, filed past Orm's blood-covered body and saluted with raised weapons, in praise and tribute to the companion who had been selected by the Shining Maids.

None showed sorrow for their fallen friend. Many showed envy.

The overpowering grief that had crushed young Longshanks to his knees was vanquished by exultation in his foster-brother's glory.

Hjalmar the Axeman bellowed for attention, and the courtyard fell silent. The scarfaced chieftain lifted his ponderous axe and spoke.

"Th' Chosen o' Odin shall be given a funeral worthy o' a Hero o' Valhalla. Clear out th' spoils o' th' castle an' ha' th' villagers gather wagonloads o' wood t' be stacked throughout th' Keep. Soak it well wi' oil.

"This lair o' th' troll-curst Thane o' Ethelstane shall become th' funeral pyre o' Orm Thorwaldssen, our comrade chosen by th' Maids o' Battle t' sit wi' th' Allfather.

"T'night we feast an' make merry in honor o' Orm Thorwaldssen. Wi' th' risin' o' th' sun, we send th' body o' th' Hero aloft in th' smoke t' join wi' his spirit in Odin's Mead Hall."

Hjalmar stepped down, and joined his employer while Olaf, the aide-de-camp, took charge of the preparations for the Hero's funeral.

Brokk clapped the scarfaced mercenary on the arm. "Well done, Axeman. Th' lad deserves no less."

Olin and Lars took up Orm's body, and carried it into the great hall where they would wash him, and dress him, and lay his weapons beside him on the long trestle table to lie in state.

Olaf reported to his Captain, and Hjalmar relayed the information to Brokk and Jerry.

"As ye ordered, my lord Brokk, th' Keep's been scoured from turret t' dungeon. No corner nor cranny, nor crack in th' walls, ha' been overlooked. There's no sign o' yer friend or th' lass."

It was evident that the Axeman still felt the weight of guilt. "If only I'd known. . . ."

"But ye couldn't," Brokk said in a tone that closed the subject. "No more could we. 'Tis th' end o' it."

That night the Company feasted in the great hall of Ethelstane Keep, toasting Orm the Hero as he lay with his weapons in state.

At the sun's first rays, torches were set to the piles of oil-soaked wood stacked throughout the castle.

The Free Company of Hjalmar the Axeman, rejoined by the two squads under Ethelred the Lame, stood in ranks on the canyon's rim, and watched the infamous Keep become engulfed in flames.

The intense heat caused huge cracks to appear in the castle walls. Large segments of masonry let go, and plunged into the canyon. A great pillar of smoke shot up from the conflagration, and rose high in the sky, carrying with it the mortal remains of Orm the Hero.

More and more of the crumbling castle fell into the depths until all that remained was a heap of smoldering rocks atop the pedestal. Officers shouted orders, and the Company stood to, wheeled, and marched back to camp.

CHAPTER TWENTY SIX

Standing in the slowly brightening gloom at the bottom of the gorge, Ulf listened to the diminishing noises of the battle overhead. Something had been decided, but what?

Who had fought whom, and who had won? And how would the outcome, whatever it had been, affect Maryam and himself?

Still puzzled, the goblin turned back to Maryam. "Come, little sister, we must make the canyon rim. There at least we'll be clear of the castle and can rejoin the company."

He shook his head. "I understand not what is happening."

Ulf quickened his steps, eaten by curiosity as to what was going on above. The goblin's long strides were too much for Maryam.

"Ulf," she called breathlessly, "Slow down. I've not your long legs!"

Ulf slowed his pace.

"Your pardon, little sister." It was hard to restrain his impatience to learn what was afoot.

The pair reached the base of the canyon wall, and as Ulf had expected, a steep trail led upward, angling zig-zag across the face of the scarp.

A waterfall tumbled noisily over a series of ledges. At one point, a narrow foot bridge spanned the stream as it boiled over the lowest of the ledges before plunging thirty feet into a deep pool from which it broadened into a swiftly flowing river.

The footway over the torrent was wet with spray, and proved to be treacherously slippery.

Ulf, in the lead, turned to caution the girl of the danger. He was just in time to see her feet shoot from under her, and send her plunging into the rushing water.

She disappeared in the wild welter of foam at the foot of the cascade. The girl's red head bobbed to the surface twice, farther and farther downstream, then vanished.

Ulf descended the trail in great leaps and raced along the bank of the stream. His eyes searched frantically, but there was no sign of the girl.

He spent more than an hour searching, unable to give up, although he knew there was no hope.

At last, with his heart heavy within him, the goblin resumed his climb to the rim of the gorge.

He rounded an outcrop, and came face to face with the largest bear he'd ever seen. The great bruin towered up on its hind legs with a roar, and struck with a claw-armed forepaw.

Taken by surprise, Ulf went down from a stunning blow to the head. Only the rusty helmet he'd found in the torture chamber saved him from a crushed skull. Spear and shield flew from his hands and the goblin plunged from the narrow footing to land with a bone-jarring crash on a ledge twenty feet below.

The spider-limbed goblin rolled onto his back, unconscious and with one leg doubled at an angle that proclaimed it broken.

The bear leaned over the brink of the footpath. Its upper lip peeled back to show yellow tusks, and an angry growl rumbled in its throat. It eyed the goblin's still form, massive head swinging from side to side. The unconscious Ulf lay unmoving. The bear lost interest and lumbered away down the trail.

Night fell and Ulf still did not move. The moon rose full, and shone down into the gorge. The goblin stirred and one arm moved aimlessly.

He groaned and opened his eyes. For long minutes he lay looking up at the moon, trying to piece together his thoughts and the events leading to his present predicament. His first memory was the loss of Maryam in the torrent, and a wave of grief went through him. Then he remembered the bear.

He made an effort to sit up and the agony stabbing upward from his broken leg threw him into a swoon.

When next the goblin opened his eyes, he remembered to make no sudden moves. He assessed the damage and found the broken leg.

Moving with caution, he gritted his teeth and slowly straightened the fractured limb. It was broken cleanly at the thigh.

Grunting with pain, Ulf dragged himself to a nearby bush, and drawing the torturer's heavy knife from his belt, lopped off two thick branches.

These he stripped of leaves and twigs and using strips cut from his jerkin, splinted the break. The effort left him bathed in sweat, and half unconscious from the strain. He was too weak to do more.

He slept.

The sun was well up when next he woke. Although he was still weak, the rest had restored enough of his strength to enable him to drag himself back up on the trail. There he rested for he knew not how long before beginning the long crawl up the canyon wall.

The goblin never knew how many hours it took him to drag his battered body up the steep trail. At last he was on level ground and sank once more into a semi-stupor. He heard voices, then gentle hands lifted him and carried him to a straw filled cart. There followed a bumpy ride, each jolt of which sent stabs of agony shooting up his leg. The ordeal proved too much and he sank into unconsciousness.

It was three days later that Ulf regained his senses to find that he was lying in a hammock stretched between two trees. He lifted his head, pleased to note only a slight dizziness, and glanced around at the bustle of the camp of Hjalmar the Axeman.

Olin Longshanks was first to notice the goblin's return to the land of the living. Not surprising since the young man had been at Ulf's side from the moment he had been brought into camp by the mercenaries who had found him.

It was Odin's mercy that it had been three members of Hjalmar's Company who had found the goblin. . . men who knew Ulf to be close friend to their employer. Had he been found by men of Midgard they would have, in their fear and hatred of goblins, torn him to pieces.

The spider-man had been suffering from shock and a raging fever. Freya had been in constant attendance, using her healing magic. The broken leg had to be reset, but was knitting nicely.

Olin loomed over the goblin's hammock, firing questions. "Where be Maryam? Did she escape th' castle? How did you. . . ?"

Brokk broke in. "Hold, lad. We all want t' know, but gi' th' poor man a chance!"

The dwarf's concerned face came into Ulf's view. "'Tis glad I am t' see ye recovered. Ye must fergive th' lad, Ulf, he's been near daft wi' worry o'er th' maid. Does she live?"

The pain in the goblin's face gave the answer before he spoke. Olin's voice broke from his throat in the keening wail of unspeakable grief he'd expressed for Orm.

Jerry, Lars, and Krupp the Round joined the group. Jerry placed an arm around the stricken youngster's shoulders. He wanted to say something comforting, but there was nothing to be said. Lars o' th' Battlefield showed his pain for the young warrior he'd raised as a son.

Looking at him, Jerry felt that the aging sword-and-shield man would have gladly traded his life for that of the girl's to wipe the grief from Olin's heart.

In halting tones, Ulf described their escape from the dungeons. The listeners were stunned to hear of Maryam's command of the Gift.

The goblin described how the girl had been swept away by the torrent, his fruitless search for her, and his subsequent encounter with the bear.

The group had been augmented by Hjalmar the Axeman and several of his men. The scarfaced mercenary chieftain berated himself roundly for not having arrived sooner on the field of the attack by Gymar's men.

"My lord Brokk, had I been handier, neither th' girl nor th' goblin would ha' been taken."

Brokk dismissed this. "Ye're too hard on yerself, man. 'Tis a miracle o' th' gods ye arrived at all. Ye'd no way o' knowin' we'd be attacked. 'Twas only by happenstance ye heard th' sound o' th' fray an' rode t' our assistance."

It was apparent by Olin's look that the boy had tuned out the conversation. He gripped the goblin by the shoulder.

"Friend Ulf," he said tensely, "ye did not actually *see* her dead body, did ye?"

"Nay lad, I did not. But th' poor maid went down into the water' and she came not up. Ye say I've lain here three days. Olin lad, if th' lass lived, she'd have returned t' us by now."

Olin shook his head. "I can't accept that. I want t' search for her." He turned to Brokk. "With your permission, my lord, I'd go t' look for myself."

The dwarf looked his commiseration. "Lad," he said, "'Tis hopeless, but ye'll never rest easy in yer mind 'til ye've turned every stone yerself."

He looked at Ulf. "Where'd ye last see th' lass?"

Ulf described the trail, the cataract, and the foot bridge.

"Th' poor child went o'er th' fall into th' caldron at th' foot. I saw her surface twice downstream, then saw her no more."

The goblin turned a pained face to Olin. "I did my best t' find her. I searched for o'er an hour, lad. 'Twas no use. I'm sorry."

The young mercenary clasped Ulf's shoulder. "I know that were there anything you could have done, 'twould have been done. Think not that I lay any blame t' you, friend Ulf, but don't you see? I'll never be able t' rest free 'til I've searched for myself.

"Mayhap she's lost t' me, but if I look not, then all down th' years I'd be wonderin' whether I could have found her."

Freya laid a hand on the boy's arm. "Of course you must go."

Brokk harrumphed. "We be all goin'."

Hjalmar the Axeman expressed his determination of never again allowing his employer to go anywhere unescorted. He told off a squad to accompany the dwarf and his inner circle.

The party rode to the head of the trail. The descent being too steep for horses, they dismounted and started down.

CHAPTER TWENTY SEVEN

Maryam screamed as she felt her feet go out from under her, and knew that she was falling. The breath was knocked from her when she struck the water, and she was only dimly aware of going over the verge and plummeting into the seething caldron at the foot of the falls.

The girl's slim form was buffeted violently about, water filling her mouth and nose. Just when she thought her lungs would burst, her head broke the surface and she sucked in a great gulp of air.

Submerged once more, wrenched and rolled and hammered by the violent eddies, she swept downstream. She was allowed one more breath then pulled under again. She was fast losing consciousness.

Her body hung limp below the surface as the current slowed and towed her into a deep, calm pool.

Maryam was barely aware of a dark shape swimming toward her. A webbed hand covered with rich brown fur seized her leg and dragged her toward the bottom of the pool.

That was the last she remembered until she opened her eyes in a cool, dimly lighted grotto. The light, as in the elf hill and the underground world of the dwarfs, came from phosphorescence in the walls. She was lying on a floor of clean dry sand a few feet from a small pool.

The girl raised herself on one elbow and looked around. Against one wall was a pallet of leaves and moss. Near the edge of the pool was a small mound of fish bones and mussel shells. She wrinkled her nose, but the air of the grotto was sweet and fresh.

She sat up, then shrank back in fright, as a circle of ripples appeared in the center of the little pool, and a sleek brown, fur covered head bobbed up from the water.

The creature that climbed from the pool was about the size of Freya the elf-woman, and resembled a humanoid otter. Rich, golden brown fur covered the river sprite from head to toe. The facial features were a blend of the human and the round muzzle of an otter. Small round ears clung closely to the sides of the head, and the eyes were bright and friendly. Maryam could see that the creature's nostrils had valve-flaps for swimming underwater. The hands and feet were webbed.

As the little water nymph emerged from the pool, it was apparent that she was female since she wore no clothing.

The fur-covered body approximated that of a human girl of about nine or ten years, and the round, almost-human face held an expression of friendly curiosity.

Maryam stared at the little apparition flabbergasted, her fright forgotten.

The little pixie exhibited the friendliness of a puppy, and the curiosity of a kitten. Maryam quickly discovered that the sprite spoke no human tongue, but burbled along in a chattering voice like the chittering of a squirrel. Maryam tried to convey that she wished to be returned to the surface.

The little water nymph dived into the pool and returned with a large flopping trout.

Maryam sighed and tried again. It was evident that the little ottergirl wanted to please, but couldn't grasp the human's meaning. She squatted, disconsolate, and looked at Maryam. Then the round face brightened, and she dived into the pool again. This time she came back with a double handful of succulent mussels.

Maryam gave it up.

The strain of the past several days, combined with her near-drowning, sapped her energy. She was tired, and she was sleepy. She was also hungry, but not hungry enough to eat raw fish.

She might be trapped here, but her jailer showed only the greatest friendliness, and she felt safe. She made signs that the little pixie did understand, and the gentle creature took her hand and tugged her in the direction of the of the pallet of moss and leaves. Maryam lay down, and free of terror for the first time in days, fell asleep.

The girl had no idea how long she slept, but when she woke the river sprite offered her another fresh-caught trout. The sleep had refreshed her, and her appetite was raging. Her stomach lurched at the thought of raw fish, but demanded something without delay.

Maryam screwed up her courage, and took the offered fish. She drew the knife Ulf had given her in the dungeon, and filleted the trout, cutting it into small cubes. She discovered that raw fish wasn't half bad when you're hungry enough.

Time passed.

The little otter-girl was as amusing as a frolicking puppy, but her inability to understand Maryam's need to be taken back to the surface was frustrating in the extreme.

The girl estimated by her sleep periods that three, maybe four, days had passed since she fell into the river. She knew that the band would be worried about her.

She wondered if Olin Longshanks were worried. She was *fairly* sure that the young warrior cared for her as she cared for him. But Olin, having been a mercenary soldier since he was big enough to swing a sword, was cautious about revealing his feelings. She couldn't be certain how deeply those feelings ran.

Had Maryam been able to see the hollow-eyed boy, with his grief-ravaged face, all her doubts would have been removed.

There were two things, however, of which she *was* sure: she wanted out of the grotto, and she was sick of raw fish.

The little water nymph was friendly as ever, and as eager to please, but unable to understand. It obviously never occurred to the little creature that the girl didn't know that she could just dive into the pool and swim to the surface whenever she wanted to.

As she learned later, Maryam could have done just that at any time.

The tunnel leading to the grotto was short, and the depth of the river not all that much, but the girl had no way of knowing that.

The sprite had left, and Maryam was staring hopelessly into the pool, when something stirred in her mind. At first she was unable to define the feeling, then a clear picture flashed into being. It was a vision of herself accompanied by a question.

There followed an alien, but friendly, thought, and Maryam knew it was the mind of the little water nymph. This picture wasn't so clear, but depicted herself again, this time showing the grotto in which she sat.

The other mind said distinctly, "*Maryam.*" It was Freya!

"Oh yes, Mother," Maryam sobbed, "Here I am!"

The elf-woman's thought came again. "*Maryam.*"

"I'm here, Mother."

A third time: "*Maryam, will your thoughts.*"

For a moment the girl was confused, then she remembered the dungeon.She formed the thought, *"Here I am, Mother."* And willed. She knew immediately that she had been successful.

Freya's voice sounded in her head. "*Don't be afraid, dear. The river sprite has told us where you are. She's coming to get you. It's only a short way. Take a deep breath, and follow her.*"

Maryam felt, as well as heard, the elf-woman's warm laughter.

"*Yes, dear, he has been worried about you.*"

Maryam blushed. She hadn't known that that thought had been so prominent in her mind.

The first thing she saw as her head broke the surface in the wake of the little water sprite was Olin Longshanks, and never would she forget the smile that washed the pain from the young warrior's face at sight of her.

A few moments later the boy grasped her upraised hand, and pulled her from the river into his arms.

By the time he released her, Olin had left no lingering doubts as to the depth of his feelings.

He knelt on the river bank, and thanked the otter-girl for rescuing Maryam, his thoughts being projected to her by Freya.

Maryam hugged the wet little creature, and with her new-found ability at thought projection, thanked her for all her kindnesses. The nymph waved goodbye with such a woebegone expression on her round little face that Maryam was almost reluctant to leave her.

It was near sundown when the band returned from the canyon and gathered around Ulf's hammock.

They. . . Brokk and Freya, Jerry, Olin and Maryam, Lars, Krupp the Round, and Ulf the Far Traveled. . . had begun to think of themselves as family.

The goblin had been told of Orm's death.

"I'll miss th' lad terribly, but who can feel sad that he was taken t' Valhalla?" He brightened. "Valhalla! Mayhap we'll see him there."

Ulf touched Maryam's hand. "I've yet t' thank you for savin' my life."

Maryam looked at Freya and shook her head. "To think I could have communicated with the otter-girl all the time!"

The elf-woman smiled. "Yes dear, you have the ability, but it needs developing."

"I feel so stupid, Mother. I let you all worry," Olin's hand tightened on hers. "and I could have been safely back here days ago."

Olin wanted to know why she hadn't used her psychokinetic power to free herself from the grotto.

"I didn't know how."

The girl made a helpless little gesture and giggled. "All I know how to do is throw things."

Ulf laughed from his hammock. "That may be, little sister, but you're passin' good at doin' that!"

He chuckled. "You should have seen what she did t' Elford, th' torturer. . . ."

The goblin broke off as he saw the girl's face go chalk white at the mention of the torturer's shattered body. "Your pardon, little sister."

Freya put her arm around the trembling girl and kissed her cheek.

"What you did was right and necessary. You saved Ulf from torture, and your own life as well. Think of it only in that way."

They talked into the night. Freya and Krupp voiced their decision to spend the time waiting for Ulf to recover, in tutoring Maryam in the use of the Gift.

It was discovered that Maryam's command of the power was far short of that of the elves, but more than sufficient to enable the girl to protect herself in a fray.

CHAPTER TWENTY EIGHT

Preparations went forward for the continuation of the journey as soon as Ulf was ready to travel.

With Brokk's approval, Hjalmar the Axeman appointed Olin Longshanks lieutenant to command the squads of Bjorn Strongarm, who had been slain in the assault on Ethelstane Keep.

At Hjalmar's order, Olin recruited from among the ranks of the villagers who had followed Lars in the attack. The taking of the Keep had not been without losses, and men were needed to replace those killed in the battle.

Every moment was spent in training the new recruits. Supplies were laid in, and unlike other mercenary bands, Hjalmar paid for them.

Many of the mercenaries, especially the recruits, were disturbed when it was learned that their commission would lead them through the land of the trolls, but none deserted. Of the Company, it transpired that only Hjalmar and Ethelred the Lame had ever been to Trollheim. These two, and Ulf, briefed the troop on what to expect.

"We've no more than three days t' pass through th' Glowin' Earth if ye wish t' keep yer humanity," Hjalmar emphasized over and over.

"If we've t' fight, ye'll fight like ye never fought before, d'ye hear me, ye worthless dogs?"

"Aye, we hear you, Axeman," the hard-bitten troopers shouted, none taking offense at Hjalmar's epithet. It was apparent that they knew their leader respected their abilities and loyalty as they respected him.

It took a week before Ulf's leg was healed enough to travel. In that time the new recruits had shaped up enough to tell the point of a sword from its hilt, and Hjalmar the Axeman proclaimed himself satisfied with their progress.

The scarface stood on a tall stump, and surveyed the assembled rookies. He planted his fists on his hips and bellowed, "Remember this. Those o' ye who survive yer first melee, can brag in th' alehouses that ye're a Free Companion o' th' Company o' Hjalmar th' Axeman. Those who don't, I expect t' be braggin' t' Odin an' th' Heroes in

Valhalla!"

The volunteers roared with laughter, and crashed their weapons against their shields.

"Hjalmar! Hjalmar!"

The morning they set out was pouring with rain. Such weather was often encountered on such a march, and no reason to delay.

Freya and Maryam rode in the relative comfort of the cart, and the rest wrapped their cloaks about their heads and rode stoically through the downpour.

Ulf, in charge of Hjalmar's scouts, sent advance men to the fore and outriders to the flanks.

Hjalmar the Axeman, aware of where Olin's heart lay, put the young lieutenant in command of protecting the women's cart.

The rain continued for several days but finally cleared off, and the travelers were gifted with perfect weather. They pushed steadily northward.

Every day the new recruits improved until even Ethelred the Lame, who had been promoted to aide-de-camp to Hjalmar the Axeman, conceded that they might not slay *too* many of each other in the heat of battle.

In the company of the human mercenaries, it was no longer necessary to keep to the back trails to avoid contact with the men of Midgard. Progress toward Asgard proceeded at an accelerated pace.

Tension mounted steadily as the company neared the borders of Trollheim. Then came the night when Brokk pointed out to Jerry a faint bluish glow which could be seen on the horizon.

Although the area of contamination was still several days march, the hellish glow was a grim reminder that here a man could lose his soul. They began to encounter evidence of how nature could be perverted.

Windborne seeds and spores from the Land of Glowing Earth had taken root and grown into indecent parodies of normal vegetation.

They saw common wildflowers that had petals of pulpy flesh that recoiled to the touch, emitting little squeaks of fright, while the stems retreated into the ground.

They passed through a field of sunflowers fifty feet high.

Grasshoppers a foot long, some with more than one head, a dozen or more legs. Butterflies that stung like wasps. Mushrooms three feet across.

A mutated gourd vine ran everywhere. It looped down from the trees, festooned bushes, covered the ground underfoot. In places, details had to be assigned to cut a passage with their swords. Jerry worked alongside the others, slashing with his keen rapier. The vines themselves were tough as ropes, but the fruit, the size of cantaloup, was dry and fragile, easily shattered to release a cloud of tiny spores.

Two days from the Trollheim border, Ulf, well out ahead of the troop, was informed by a scout of the discovery of a wounded giant a quarter league ahead.

The man wanted to know if the goblin wished to send forward a slinger or archer to despatch the creature. Ulf motioned for several of his men to follow, and rode to assess the situation.

The goblin spied the giant half lying, half sitting, leaning against the bole of a tree. There was something familiar about the big man. As he came closer, Ulf was startled to recognize Hradalfar, brother of Hrimgrimnir the Frost Giant.

To the amazement of the scouts, Ulf sent one of their number pelting back to fetch Freya, and himself rode to the wounded goliath and dismounted.

"Ho, Hradalfar of th' Frost Giants, be you badly hurt?"

"Ho, goblin. 'Tis not fatal, methinks, but I've lost so much blood I be too weak t' stand."

The giant eyed the mercenaries nervously sitting their horses at a distance.

He looked at Ulf. "Will thee have me killed?"

"No fear of that. Did not Brokk claim old acquaintance with your brother at our meeting near Svartheim?"

"Aye."

The big man looked at the mercenaries who were apprehensively handling their weapons. "But thee were not in th' company of th' human kind then."

"Rest easy, these be in th' service of Brokk Hammermacher. Th' elf-woman, his wife, is even now on her way here t' tend your hurts."

Hradalfar sighed. "Then 'tis well met. Th' dwarf, bein' friend t, my brother, may consent t' save him."

Before Ulf could question further, Brokk rode up with Freya riding pillion, Jerry pounding along close behind him. The dwarf dismounted and aided Freya to alight. Jerry swung from the saddle. The faces of all three held concern.

Brokk knelt beside the giant. "Ho, Hradalfar. What's amiss? Where be yer kin?"

Freya brushed past. "You can ask questions later, husband, the man's in need of care. Can't you see he's bleeding to death?"

The little elf-woman beckoned to one of the mercenaries. The man came forward, suppressing his fear of giants.

"Aye, my Lady?"

"I need your cloak."

The soldier removed his cloak and offered it.

"Cut it into wide strips for bandages."

"Aye, my lady."

Freya smiled. "My husband will replace it."

"Nay, my lady. My lord Brokk pays me more than enough t' replace a cloak. 'Tis my gift t' you and your friend th' giant." The soldier drew his sword and cut the garment into strips.

Freya cut away Hradalfar's jerkin to bare the gaping wound in the giant's side, and swabbed away the blood. She took out her needle, and Hradalfar sat stonily while she stitched him up. The little elf-woman bandaged the wound tightly, and issued instructions.

"Tell Hjalmar the Axeman to make camp here. We stay until the Frost Giant is fit. Cut enough soft boughs to make Hradalfar a bed."

"Aye, my lady."

Several of the mercenaries cut the necessary branches, and made the giant comfortable. Hjalmar the Axeman rode in, and ordered camp to be set up as Freya instructed.

He rode over and eyed the giant. "My lord Brokk, ye've some strange friends. First a goblin, now a giant!"

A crowd of soldiers gathered at a distance. It seemed that only three of them had ever seen a giant before, and Hradalfar, though just a bit over ten feet, caused quite a stir.

Brokk had waited impatiently until the giant had eaten. "What befell ye? How came ye by yer wound, an' where be yer brothers?"

The big man eased his wounded side, and related the disaster that had overtaken him and his brothers.

Hrimgrimnir had received the weapons they had come for, including the gift sword as Brokk had instructed Sindri. The Frost Giant was greatly pleased with the superb blade.

The wagons, following, had camped at the foot of the defile leading to the Trading Glen. In time they were loaded, and the giants began their return trek.

"Three days agone," Hradlafar said, "we met on th' trail, Skrymar, a giant friendly t' Thrym, our enemy. Skrymar told us of a group of Thrym's trusted friends who secretly plotted against him. They wanted to meet with my brother, Hrimgrimnir, and aid him in his war against the Frost King."

Hradalfar grimaced.

"Skrymar was convincing, Odin blast him, and Hrimgrimnir agreed to meet with the cabal."

Scrymar stressed secrecy, and suggested that Hrimgrimnir come alone, but the rebel, wary of a trap, said that his brothers would accompany him, or there'd be no meeting.

Scrymar agreed, and the weapons wagons were sent on ahead, while the three brothers went with the messenger.

The meeting was to take place just outside Trollheim, a place safe from Thrym's spies.

Not being fools, the brothers were on the alert for treachery and in the ordinary run of things would have acquitted themselves handily. But the blow, when it fell, was so foul that they were taken utterly by surprise, and overwhelmed.

Thrym the Frost King had done the unthinkable.

He had made a pact with the trolls!

Caught in a narrow defile, the brothers were fallen upon by a horde of trolls who leaped from above and attacked from front and rear.

Skrymar the treacherous watched while the disgusting creatures swarmed over his victims, then turned his back, and walked away.

"Hradnir be slain," Hradalfar said stonily, "and Hrimgrimnir taken. I alone fought my way free."

"Yer brother lives? Th' trolls have him yet?"

"Aye."

Brokk removed his helmet, ran his hand through his graying hair, and looked at Jerry.

"'Tis not th' way o' th' trolls t' keep prisoners." He looked back at the giant. "Why now?"

Hradalfar spat.

"After my escape, I crept back t' see if there were aught I could do for my brother, but I were too weak from th' loss of blood, and they were too many. But I o'erheard th' Soulless Ones speak of th' pact they'd made with accurst Thrym, may Hel take him. They were t' keep any of us taken alive, t' be turned over t' Thrym t' be tortured as an example t' others who might think t' rise against him."

"D'ye know where Hrimgrimnir be held?"

"Aye."

The dwarf stood up and struck his fists together. "Ye say this was three days agone?"

"Aye."

"Then yer brother's been in th' Curst Land too long. He's by now one t' father trolls. 'Tis likely Hrimgrimnir won't want t' be rescued."

Jerry, who had not forgotten his determination in the event of just such a thing happening to him, looked at the giant with pity.

But Hradalfar shook his head.

"Nay. We were never in th' land of th' Blue Earth. Th' cavern where he be held be only a few leagues from here. 'Tis not in Trolheim."

"That be it, then. I've no choice but t' free yer brother."

Brokk turned to Hjalmar and the mercenaries, who had gathered closer to hear the Frost Giant's tale.

"Ye heard," he said loudly. "Fer myself, I'm bound t' attempt t' rescue Hradalfar's brother. Yet I'll ask no man t' follow. 'Tis a personal debt I be repayin', an' none o' ye need risk. . . ."

Hjalmar the Axeman stepped forward.

"My lord Brokk," he said, "I crave yer fergivness fer interruptin' so fine a speech, but ye be fergittin' one small detail I beg t' bring t' yer attention."

The dwarf looked at the scarfaced mercenary. "Aye?"

"Aye, my lord. I be Hjalmar th' Axeman, an' these be th' finest soldiers o' fortune in all th' Nine Worlds. We don't take service then fail t' serve.

"Wherever ye lead, we follow." The chieftain drew himself up and lifted his axe. "We await yer commands, Brokk o' Svartheim."

There came a roar of approval, and the clash of weapons on shields from the ranks.

It gave Jerry a little shiver of pride to serve with such men.

Brokk raised one arm, and the men fell silent. "Very well, since ye'll have it so."

He turned to Hradalfar. "Be yer brother wounded?"

"Aye, and sorely."

"Ye say he's held in a cavern not far from here?"

"Aye. 'Tis heavily guarded."

"Know ye when yer brother's t' be given up?"

"Nay. But 'twill be soon."

Brokk motioned to Ulf. "Take th' best o' yer scouts an' bring me a full report o' th' situation." The dwarf smiled grimly. "D' I have t' remind ye not t' fall into their hands?"

The goblin grinned back. "I'll bear that in mind."

Ulf conferred with the Frost Giant, then he and his men struck out on foot to reconnoiter. The goblin returned several hours later with a detailed report.

Ulf squatted by the fire, his knees up to his shoulders, and sketched a map in the dirt.

The yellow fireglow highlighted the goblin's hideous features as he gave his report. Jerry and Hjalmar looked over his shoulder as he explained the situation.

"Here's th' cliff at th' foot of which is th' cavern. This line here," the goblin indicated with a talon, "is a natural wall of rock that screens th' mouth of th' cave. 'Tis about fifteen feet high and curves in at each end, leavin' only a narrow entry. 'Tis easily defended by only a few warriors."

Ulf drew a wavy line some distance in front of the wall. "This is th' tree-line, leavin' an area of bare ground some hundred feet wide t' be crossed before reachin' th' wall. Easy for archers behind th' wall t' decimate an attackin' force."

Ulf looked at Brokk. "'Twon't be an easy task, old friend."

Jerry studied the rough map. He shoved his helmet to the back of his head and looked at Ulf. "That's the only way in?"

"Aye, Jerry."

"Hjalmar could lose a lot of men."

The scarface grunted. "They be well paid fer takin' risks."

Krupp the Round interrupted. "Let me study more closely your sketch, friend Ulf."

The goblin moved aside and let the rotund elf examine the lines in the dirt. The little man pulled at his under lip, a look of concentration wrinkling his face. "Tell me more about this hill."

All eyes were on the green-clad elf. Krupp looked into space, still worrying his lip as he listened to the goblin's description.

"'Tis mostly rock with only a few shrubs, and of course these cursed gourd vines that run everywhere. It slopes gently on three sides and th' fourth be th' cliff wherein lies th' cavern."

Ulf looked at his drawing then, closed his eyes to visualize the terrain. "There's th' large open space as I said, and th' screenin' wall. . . ."

Krupp broke in. "Did you study closely the face of the cliff?"

"Aye. Why?"

"Describe it."

"'Tis straight up and down, smooth and blank except for one odd formation. . . ."

Krupp's eyes popped open and he gestured. "To your right as you look at the cliff?"

Ulf nodded. "Aye, t' th' right."

"Would it look like a wolf's head?"

The goblin started. "A wolf's. . . . Aye! As you mention it, it does!"

Several of the scouts who had accompanied Ulf nodded their heads. "Aye," said one, "Now that I think on it, it does resemble th' head o' a wolf."

"Looking to the left?"

There came a chorus of affirmation from the scouts.

"Aye. . . . Aye. . . ."

Krupp stood up and faced Brokk.

"It's Wolfhaven, an abandoned elf hill. I suspected it when Ulf mentioned the screening wall."

A look of wonder came into the elf's eyes. "It was so long ago that its existence was believed to be only myth." Krupp shook his head. "But there can be no doubt. It's Wolfhaven."

A murmur of interest ran through the assembled warriors. Brokk looked at the elf. "Ye be certain, then."

"Aye."

Krupp's voice took on the tone and cadence of one reciting by rune. "In the time of Halfin Wolfhead, over ten thousand years ago," the little man said, "the elves were many in the Valley of the River Om. Many were the hills made hollow to house their villages. Chief of these villages was Wolfhaven, seat of Halfin Wolfhead, the strongest of the elves and their acknowledged king.

"One night came there a mighty whistling in the upper air. The eerie sound grew and grew until it became a roar to deafen the ears. With it came such a rush of wind that flattened great trees, and blew away the very soil from the ground.

"The elves huddled in their mounds in mortal terror. Then was there a mighty concussion as some great object struck the earth, sending waves like the waters of the Salt Sea rippling through the very rock of the elf hills."

Sounds like a meteor, a big one, Jerry thought.

"The People cringed in fear for many days before any dared venture from the mounds. It was Halfin Wolfhead the King, who first sallied forth to discover what had happened.

"It was then that they found the forest leveled, and saw a great pall of smoke rising in the air many leagues to the north. At the base of the smoke was a frightening blue glow."

A radioactive meteor! Jerry shivered.

"Not even Halfin the King had the courage to venture into the Blue Land that glowed in the night.

"The elves of the Valley of the River Om hunted to the east and to the west and to the south, but none dared venture to the north.

"A generation passed. And another. And another.

"Halfin Wolfssen, great grandson of The Wolf, ruled in the Valley when the first of the monsters came down upon them. Nightmare creatures with more heads, arms, and legs than ever Odin gave to elf or dwarf or giant or goblin or man.

"More hideous than goblins. Without soul or humanity. It was Halfin Wolfssen who gave them the name of troll."

Krupp shuddered.

"For three generations the elves of the Valley of the River Om warred with the trolls, then abandoned the Valley to move south, away from the monsters, the Soulless Ones.

"Wolfhaven was the last bastion of the elves to be given up, and is remembered in the Runes."

Brokk fingered his beard.

"There's a point ye're makin' beyond th' telling' o' history, is there not?"

Krupp grinned. "Aye. To every elf hill there are many concealed entrances. We have only to find one."

The dwarf snorted. "Oh, aye. After ten thousand years o' bein' forgotten? As Jerry would say, 'tis a piece o' cake."

Krupp tugged down his tunic and settled his sword belt more comfortably. "Ten thousand or ten hundred thousand, the hill is still there, the cavern is still there, and the portals will still be there. Some of them.

"We've the night ahead of us to find one. It's safe enough. The trolls are as fearful of the dark as the goblin kind fear running water. We can search in peace."

The round little man drew himself up and squared his shoulders. At the gesture, a visible dignity fell over him like a cloak.

"I am not only your comrade, Krupp the Round, elfin man-at-arms. I am also Krupp the Seneschal, Steward of the Palace of Wolf Halfinssen, descendent of Halfin Wolfhead, King of the Elves, and as such, Keeper Of The Ancient Runes. In my head are clues that will make the finding of a portal only a matter of time."

Krupp looked at the moon. "We have five hours of dark." He turned to Lars. "Will you accompany me, Lars o' th' Battlefield?"

The grizzled sword-and-shield man rose to his feet, and picked up his gear. "Aye."

CHAPTER TWENTY NINE

Half an hour before sunrise, Krupp and Lars returned.

It was apparent from their faces that they had been unsuccessful in their search.

"We found two of the portals but they had fallen in years ago. Had we more time we could have located an entry."

The elf turned to Hradalfar. "At least I bring good news of your brother. Under cover of the darkness, we scouted close to the cave. We overheard the guard saying how Hrimgrimnir was recovering from his wound, and that it would be the third day hence before Thrym's lackeys arrive to take him in hand.

"We've two nights to essay a rescue."

The tiny elf patted the giant's shoulder.

"Fear not, friend Hradalfar, we'll have him free. I doubt not we'll find an entry this night."

The day was spent in formulating plans. One after another, ideas were proposed and discarded.

Given that a rear assault could be effected through a hidden passage, a diversion at the mouth of the cave was imperative.

Jerry studied Ulf's sketch of the cavern mouth's defenses. That wall was a real stopper. Combined with the killing ground cleared before it, it looked to be sheer suicide to mount a frontal attack. From the protection of the wall, slingers and archers could massacre any force charging across the open space.

Jerry sighed. "If only we had some gasoline," he said.
"Some what?"

"Gasoline. It's a highly flammable liquid in my old world that ignites easily, and spreads flames quickly."

Brokk scratched his ear. "Well, we've none o' that, but Hjalmar's men ha' a few kegs o' a distilled wine that'll gi' ye a pretty blaze."

"*Brandy!*

"Eh?"

"Brandy. The distilled wine. Of course! Half the waiters in America have singed their eyebrows serving crepes suzette!"

Brokk tugged at his ear and looked puzzled. "I don't take yer meanin', lad."

"Forget it, Father. Suffice to say the brandy just might work for what I've got in mind."

"What's in yer mind?"

"I'll show you. We'll see if it swims."

He turned to Hjalmar. "Send for a keg of the distilled wine. and have one of your guys bring me some of those gourds. . . and a piece of cloth of some kind."

"Aye, Lord Jerry."

A few minutes later, Jerry had all the items he requested. He took one of the fragile gourds and cut a small hole in one end. This he filled with brandy from the keg. Tearing a strip from the old shirt provided, he stuffed it into the hole. He saturated the wick and held it up for all to see.

"This, my friends, is what is called in my old world a Molotov Cocktail." He took a burning twig from the campfire and lighted the brandy-soaked rag. "Now we'll see if it works."

He threw the gourd at a nearby boulder.

The thin-shelled calabash shattered on impact, throwing liquid flame in all directions. Jerry let out a whoop of triumph.

"Voila!" he chortled.

Shouts and cries of delight went up on all sides. Hjalmar's mercenaries immediately approved the new weapon. They crowded around Jerry, clamoring for another demonstration. The red-beard accommodated, filling and throwing three more of the firebombs.

"Na!" Brokk laughed exultantly, "That's th' way t' deal wi' th' Soulless Ones!"

"Aye!" the Axeman roared, "We'll send th' Cursed o' Odin t' Nifleheim on th' fires o' Muspelheim!"

"There's your diversion, Kruppp the Seneschal!" Jerry grinned. "Only, my deceitful-little-friend-who-conceals-from-his-comrades-his-lofty-station, it won't be a diversion, it'll be an all-out attack! We'll burn 'em out from behind their wall, and force the entrance. Find your back door, my chubby buddy. It'll be your job to get to Hrimgrimnir and free him when we mount the assault. Can do?"

Grinning from ear to ear, Krupp clapped Jerry on the shoulder.

"Aye, Jerry Jar Haz Thor's Fist. Can do!"

Now that a means to initiate the action had been found, the briefing continued. Krupp the Round gave the Company a run-down on the elf hill.

"The entire hill's been hollowed out to contain the village." The elf laughed. After ten thousand years, it's doubtful if any of the houses still stand.

"Hrimgrimnir'll most likely be held at the rear of the cavern to keep him farthest from the entrance. If so 'twill make it that much easier to surprise those guarding him by coming on them from a concealed tunnel. And we will find a tunnel this night."

The elf stepped down, and Brokk took his place on the little rise. The dwarf shoved his helmet to the back of his head, and scanned the assembled men-at-arms.

"Ye're wonderin' why a dwarf would concern himself wi' th' fate o' one o' th' giant kind."

There was a murmur of agreement from the assembled men.

"Aye, my Lord," spoke one, "We are."

"I'll tell ye."

In his youth, as has been noted, Brokk traveled widely, gathering further knowledge of the art of metalworking to add to that already known to the dwarfs.

He journeyed once to Jotunheim to seek out a giant called Skrimm the Smith, one of the few giants with the knowledge. Skrimm was reputed to have a process for working gold that surpassed even that handed down by Brokk's father. The dwarf hoped to trade secrets.

"Skrimm," said Brokk, "bein' a creator rather than a destroyer, did indeed trade thoughts wi' me. I an' my three apprentices learned much from th' giant, an' taught him much in return.

"Th' trail home crossed o'er a great glacier. As we made our way up its side, one o' the sudden cracks that add t' th' danger o' travel in Jotunheim opened under our feet, droppin' us into a deep crevasse.

"My three companions were killed, an' I badly hurt.

"I were unconscious, wi' both legs broken, when Hrimgrimnir happened along. Th' giant descended into th' narrow crack wi' great difficulty, an' at great danger t' himself, t' carry me t' safety."

Brokk told how Hrimgrimnir had brought the dwarf to his castle, and bade his sister Hulda nurse the little man back to health. The giant maiden did all in her power to ease his hurts, and eventually Brokk recovered.

During his convalescence, Brokk made the acquaintance of Hrimgrimnir's two younger brothers, a pair of strapping giant teenagers full of fun and mischief, Hradnir and Hradalfar.

When the dwarf was fit to travel, Hrimgrimnir saw him safely to Ginnungagap, and bargained with the Ice Elves to fly him to Midgard.

Brokk paused and looked slowly over the faces of the men-at-arms in the ranks.

"When I asked him why a giant, my traditional enemy, would risk his life to save mine, he scratched his head, shrugged his shoulders an'said only, 'twas th' thing t' do."

Brokk drew himself up. "Rescuin' th' giant be th' thing t' do."

The dwarf's statement met with nods of approval from the mercenaries.

It was easy see that he had touched on a thing they could all understand, the repayment of a debt of honor.

It was equally apparent that by thus taking them into his confidence, he had bound the Free Companions even more closely to his service. Never had hired mercenaries been considered as anything more than swords to be used and broken. The thanes and barons who employed them, looked on them as nothing but useful dogs. Yet here was a patron who took them into his confidence. Who shared his feelings with them, treated them as companions. . . as men.

Jerry waited until the cheering stopped then, he stood up. He raised his steel hand. The Company fell silent and came to attention.

"Stand easy," Jerry said. "Sit down and listen up."

He grinned inwardly as he fought down the impulse to add, 'smoke 'em if you've got 'em.'

The men sat or squatted comfortably, and waited for their orders.

"You've all seen the effect of the Molotov Cocktail. . . ."

He was immediately inundated by a flood of cheers, shouts, and the clashing of weapons on shields.

He waited for the clamor to die down. He knew what fueled the mercenaries' enthusiasm. . . the same crawling horror of the mutants that lurked in his own guts.

Courageous and stoically fatalistic as these professionals were, Jerry knew all shuddered inwardly at thought of combat with the unclean trolls.

Nothing else in the Nine Worlds aroused more horror, or struck more terror anywhere, than the Cursed of Odin.

This new weapon of Thor's Fist's gave them the edge they needed to overcome this bone-deep aversion to contact with the Soulless Ones.

Jerry laid out the plan of battle for the coming engagement. Details were told off. Who would remain to guard Freya and Maryam. Who would participate in the attack on the gate. Who would accompany Krupp and Lars through the tunnel.

Jerry summoned all who claimed skill with the sling. He had a supply of the gourds filled with water for use as practice ammunition.

The red-beard walked up and down, observing the candidates as they lined up and hurled their shots at targets set up to test for range rather than accuracy. He picked the six who achieved the greatest distance, and turned them over to Ulf for intensive training.

Jerry watched his 'Field Artillery' practice for a while, grunting with satisfaction as their accuracy as well as their range improved. His Molotov Cocktails had upgraded the chances for a successful assault.

There was no hope of crossing the killing ground before the cavern without casualties, but a sudden rain of firebombs flung from the concealment of the forest's edge would clear the defenders from behind their parapet and drastically reduce the risk to the attacking force.

The red-beard had already briefed Krupp and Lars and the men who would go with them. The elf and the sword-and-shield man rolled up in their cloaks to catch a few hours sleep.

Hradalfar was recovering rapidly.

Two days of rest, Freya's healing magic, plus the giant's own recuperative powers, had returned enough of his strength to enable him to participate in the defense of the women in the event of an attack.

But when Jerry went to confer with him, he found that the giant had vanished. He reported the defection to Brokk. The dwarf's face reflected disappointment at Hradalfar's desertion, but he made no comment.

To the satisfaction of both Jerry and Brokk, Freya and Maryam, working in concert, had perfected the ability to hold themselves invisible to a greater and greater extent. It was amusing to watch the amazement of the soldiers assigned to their protection as they saw their charges disappear and reappear before their eyes.

Odin's Messenger kept constant aerial reconnaissance over the cavern entrance, and reported all activity to Freya, while Bryn remained glued to Jerry's side.

By nightfall, a satisfactory store of firebombs had been laid in, and the 'field artillery' exercised and instructed.

Everything that could be done had been done, and nothing remained but to wait until Krupp and Lars discovered a rear entrance to the elf hill.

Half an hour after sunset the elf and the sword-and-shield man disappeared into the night.

CHAPTER THIRTY

An hour before moonset the scouts returned, their faces beaming with triumph.

They had found a tunnel and checked it out, The secret passage looked down on the interior of the hill from a vantage point high up near the domed ceiling, and a series of descending ledges gave access to the floor.

"Hrimgrimnir's bound with ropes and guarded by at least two score of the unclean Cursed of Odin," the elf reported.

"Success will depend heavily on the distraction of the guards by the attack on the entrance, but depend on us to do our part."

Brokk nodded with satisfaction and gave the order to begin. Krupp waved to his contingent, and they trotted off into the darkness.

The others handled their weapons and inspected their gear. Each of the artillery pieces consisted of a slinger, and an assistant who would light the firebombs and keep them coming.

A short wait followed before the main body moved out, to give the elf time to get his detachment into position.

Brokk looked at Jerry. The red-beard nodded and signaled Hjalmar the Axeman to lead off.

Following their commanders, the mercenaries proceeded at a swift, silent trot, to take up preassigned positions fronting the cave mouth.

When the men were in position, Jerry pointed at Olin. The young lieutenant threw back his head and the long-drawn howl of a hungry wolf poured from his throat.

Points of light appeared along the edge of the forest, and a moment later half a dozen fireballs soared in sputtering arcs through the air to burst in great splashes of flame atop and beyond the protecting wall. Hardly had they landed before a second salvo followed.

Jerry allowed four flights before launching his attack.

As the barrage ended, Jar Haz's battle scream rang out, and howling men rushed both ends of the wall.

The slingers continued to pelt the area with liquid fire as they charged.

The attackers were protected by water-soaked cloaks and saturated wrappings about arms, legs, and heads.

They knew that the fight would have to be swift and victorious, if they were to survive the inferno of their own making.

Jerry, leading the assault to the right, rounded the barrier and skidded to a halt.

Flames there were in plenty. Unfortunately there was nothing else.

No defenders. Nothing to defend. Just the sheer, unbroken face of the Cliff.

He stared across the fire at Brokk and Hjalmar the Axeman at the opposite end of the wall.

The dwarf, bellowing curses, ordered his followers to use their water-soaked cloaks to beat out the flames.

Jerry followed suit, and in a few moments the cliff-face was illuminated only by the torches carried by some of the men.

Jerry sought for, and quickly found, the almost invisible cracks that delineated the camouflaged door, but there was no clue to the concealed mechanism that activated it. He hammered at the rock in frustration.

Inside, Krupp the Round and his detachment would even now be engaging the enemy, and be fatally outnumbered. The elf's command stood to be massacred unless a way could be found immediately to gain access.

In the midst of their frustration there came a gargantuan roar, followed by unfamiliar battle-cries, and a dozen giants, led by Hradalfar, burst from the forest.

The Frost Giant raised his huge axe to Brokk in greeting. "We have come to aid. What be thy commands?"

Jerry quickly outlined the problem.

Five of the goliaths were armed with spiked iron clubs. They began battering the cliff face with swings of incredible force. Chunks of rock flew in all directions. A club-head broke through, and in a few seconds the hole was enlarged enough to permit the passage of a giant.

Hradalfar stepped forward.

"Thor's Fist," he shouted, "'Tis my brother we seek. I claim th' right t' lead."

Brokk answered. "Ye're sore wounded, Hradalfar. Ha' ye th' strength?"

The giant shook his axe. "I failed my brother once. I'll not do it again!"

Brokk waved toward the breach in the cliff. "Lead, an' quickly!"

The giants threw themselves through the opening, with the

mercenaries close on their heels.

The interior was brightly alight and the sounds of battle echoed loudly from the rear of the cavern.

The longer legs of the giants carried them into the fray well in advance of the others.

Jerry, pounding at a dead run with Bryn at his side, was awed at the violence, the fury, and the sheer destructive power of warring giants.

The great spiked clubs and outsized axes swung, and shapeless red blobs of mutilated flesh flew through the air right and left. One eleven foot colossus snatched up a four-armed abomination, and tore the mutant in half with his bare hands.

Jerry plunged into the melee, the howling war-dog at his heels. A two-headed monstrosity wielding a two-handed broadsword faced him.

The red-beard took the stroke on his blade, turned it aside and ran the hideous creature through.

Both heads screamed.

Shuddering with revulsion, Jerry withdrew, and cut at the side of the troll's neck. One of the heads flopped forward limply, and the other screeched in agonized fury.

Sickened to the farthermost corner of his soul, Thor's Fist struck and struck again in horrified panic. . .

. . . then his mind went blank, as the red curtain of berserker madness fell over him.

When next, sights and sounds filtered through to his consciousness, he found that the battle was over.

He rubbed the back of his hand across his eyes, and looked around.

The ground was littered with dead trolls. There were a number of mercenary casualties, and one giant had been slain. Then it became borne upon him that all were staring at him.

Even the faces of the giants held looks of respect.

Brokk stepped up to him, fists on hips. He peered closely into Jerry's eyes. "Be ye Jerry, lad? Or be ye still Jar Haz th' Viking?"

Dazedly Jerry looked at the dwarf. "What happened?"

Hrimgrimnir thrust himself to the fore. "I say t' thee, godson of th' Dwarf King, 'tis glad I am that thee fought beside me, and not against me. Thee be well named Thor's Fist."

He looked at his fellow giants. The big men raised their weapons in salute.

Jerry stared at the solemn giants, looked around at the dead trolls, the awed respect mirrored in the eyes of the mercenaries, and back at Brokk.

"I'd love to hear about it some day," he muttered.

The dwarf grinned.

The rescue had been a success, though not without cost.

There had been casualties to Hjalmar's men, but in view of the odds, extremely light.

Only four had been killed and fifteen wounded. None of the wounded had lost limbs, and all were expected to recover. Such losses were the daily lot of the Free Companions, and accepted as part of the life.

The wounded were helped on their way, and the fallen placed on makeshift biers and carried out of the hollow hill.

The giants took up their own slain comrade and bore him out. The return to the camp was made in silence.

The dead mercenaries were laid out on piles of oil-soaked wood and their weapons placed beside them.

The giants, as was their custom, arranged their dead comrade in a sitting position. His head was braced upright with his helmet in place. His weapons were placed in his hands, and his fingers clasped around them. Oil-soaked wood was then stacked around him and his friends sat in a silent circle.

As the first rays of the sun touched the horizon, torches were applied to the pyres, and the spirits of the fallen ascended in the columns of smoke.

The rites for their dead completed, the Company, including the giants, gathered to hear Krupp narrate his end of the operation.

The elf had his detachment in place well before the appointed hour. Judging the time from the stars, the little man scouted ahead for one last look, and came out on the ledge overlooking the cavern.

"The guard around the open entrance at the opposite end of the hill was the same as before," Krupp said, "but there had been a change for the worse since Lars and I last were there.

"Hrimgrimnir had been moved. He was now some hundred and fifty yards farther from the wall of the cave, and the guard around him had been almost doubled."

Krupp looked at Brokk. "The sword that was your gift to the giant was thrust into the ground not far away, the Curst of Odin taunting him about it."

The chubby elf grimaced. "Not only did the added distance rob us of the element of surprise, the added guards left us outnumbered almost two to one. There was now two hundred yards of open ground to cover to reach the three score trolls guarding the prisoner. However there was no help for it. We would just have to move that much faster when the time came. I returned to the men to brief them on the change."

Krupp turned to Hjalmar the Axeman.

"Friend Hjalmar, you have boasted that you lead the finest fighters in the Nine Worlds."

Before the bristling mercenary chieftain could react to the word 'boast' Krupp laughed, raising a placating hand. "Nay, my fiery-tempered friend. 'Tis no boast. You do.

"When I told them of the increased odds, they merely shifted on their feet, settled their weapons, said 'The outcome of any battle lies in the hand of Odin. If we're to win, we'll win. If not, we've heard that the drink in Odin's Mead Hall be of the best.'"

Hjalmar roared with laughter and slapped his thigh.

Krupp grinned. "What could I do with such madmen? I did the only thing I could. I hitched up *my* belt, and led them into the tunnel.

"I paused on the interior ledge to assess the situation. It hadn't gotten any better. I caught each man's attention, and waved to right or left. Accustomed to storming an enemy position, each picked his route to the group of trolls guarding the prisoner."

The elf looked at Jerry. "Your firebombs came over the screening wall right on schedule. Hrimgrimnir's guards shouted in confusion, and looked toward the wall of flame blanking the entrance. They milled about, uncertain, their attention on the fire. We took advantage of their disorganization to launch our attack.

"Your mercenaries, Hjalmar the Axeman, like the professionals they are, quietly, with the swiftness of wolves, leaped down the descending ledges, and had covered half the distance to their objective before one of the trolls spotted us and screamed a warning.

"What happened next was not on the plan of attack.

"The gate guard, instead of defending the entrance as expected, fell back before the rain of fire and activated the counterweights that lowered the rock door, sealing off the outside and cutting us off from reinforcement.

"That ended our hopes of victory, but not a man-jack of them broke stride in the charge, all falling on Hrimgrimnir's warders in a desperate death struggle.

"All expected to die, to do no more than take as many of the Soulless Ones with us as we could before being cut down.

"We were surprised to find that most of the trolls were poor fighters, their deformities impairing their coordination. Their greatest weapon, we discovered, is the horror they inspire.

"Even so, we were fatally outnumbered to begin with, and the Cursed of Odin would soon be reinforced by those who had been guarding the gate.

"The Free Companions of Hjalmar the Axeman fought as though each were two men, hacking a path through the abominations, until one reached Hrimgrimnir and slashed his bonds."

Hrimgrimnir surged to his feet.

"Aye, friends," he affirmed, "Th' elf and thy warriors, Axeman, fought like a whirlwind. It is my sorrow that the brave one who cut me free is even now ascending aloft on the smoke of the funeral pyres."

He sat back down and Krupp continued his recitation.

The elf chuckled. "I'd never seen a giant at war before. Hrimgrimner snatched up his sword and laid about with unbelievable ferocity, hacking a troll in half at almost every stroke. Then suddenly there were a dozen giants, and the battle changed rapidly."

The elf caught Jerry's eye.

"I saw you engaged with a two-headed monstrosity, saw the look of revulsion on your face. Then, even above the roars of the giants, rang the battle scream of Jar Haz the Viking, as Thor's Fist went berserk!

"The flashing of his rapier seemed to weave about him an impenetrable cloak of scintillating death.

"The terrible steel hand wrought mayhem, rending and tearing, while that darting, slashing silver blade seemed to be everywhere at once. And as it flicked and danced, the bodies of trolls piled up around him. Even the giants stepped back and stared in wonder.

"Then there were no more trolls. . . ."

CHAPTER THIRTY ONE

When the funeral pyres had burned themselves out, Brokk called a council to determine their next move.

Hrimgrimnir spoke. "I be in thy debt, Dwarf King. Ask what thee will."

Brokk looked at the big man. "Then I'll ask that ye stop talkin' nonsense, old friend. I've but repaid ye fer th' life ye returned t' me these many years agone. I'll ask ye t' speak no more on it."

The Frost Giant nodded.

It was agreed that such a large party, especially one accompanied by giants, could cross Trollheim without fear of attack, and so it proved. They joined up with the giants' wagons on the other side of th Glowing Earth two days later, and proceeded to Ginnungagap.

Jerry had seen the Grand Canyon and had thought it a pretty big hole in the ground.

But when he looked into the Chasm of Chasms, the Grand Canyon shrank to the size of a crack in the sidewalk. He could hardly believe the sight of lightning flashes in thunderstorms twenty to thirty thousand feet below him.

Hrimgrimnir and Brokk dickered for days with the sullen, moody Ice Elves before a satisfactory bargain was struck.

The Little Men of the north were nothing like their sunny, easygoing cousins to the south.

Brokk had described them pretty well when he had said it was odds one way or the other whether they'd let you ride their dragons, or feed you to them.

The dragons were, as Jerry had suspected, pterodactyls.

The monster flying lizards were larger than described in the encyclopedia back home, most with a wingspan of up to a hundred feet. Some even larger. There was a special affinity between the huge saurians and their masters.

The Ice Elves dealt in two commodities, air travel and second hand clothing. Travelers to and from Jotunheim were in need of both.

The climatic peculiarity of the region was due to the prevailing winds, warm tropical air rising from the great chasm, and the frigid jetstream that coursed low above Jotunheim.

The winds blew south, carrying the warm air to the hither side, keeping the area comfortably temperate, while across the vast abyss the low-hovering jetstream made the homeland of the giants a place of iron-hard ice and drifting snow. The far rim of the Chasm of Chasms was eternally veiled in a curtain of mist formed by the meeting of warm and cold air masses.

This rapid transition from temperate to frigid necessitated a drastic change of wardrobe, and the little men of the mountains made a good thing of outfitting travelers both coming and going.

At length the bargaining was concluded, and the party exchanged their wool and leather for thick warm furs. The troop's mounts, Freya's mule and cart, and the wagons and beasts of the giants were all traded.

The weapons the giants had obtained from Svartheim were made into bundles to be strapped aboard the flying dragons. From their point of landing on the other side, all would travel on foot.

They were led to what passed for the local airport, a wide level stretch at the edge of the chasm. At the very brink was a tall tripod from which hung a monstrous curved horn. From mouthpiece to bell it was at least forty feet in length. The elfin leader drew in a deep breath and blew a long throbbing note.

The deep, gut-wrenching blast seemed to increase, rather than decrease, as it sank down into the depths of Ginnungagap.

Jerry waited expectantly, staring into the abyss. He made out a number of tiny shapes rising out of the clouds far below. The shapes rose in lazy spirals, growing larger and larger.

The first of the huge flying lizards soared up over the rim, circled overhead, and swooped to a lurching, stumbling landing in the open ground.

A foul reek of carrion was borne to them from the creature's breath.

The giant pterodactyl glared at them out of red eyes. It hissed, and gnashed the foot-long teeth in its crocodile beak.

A look of concentration passed over the features of the dragon-master as a silent command passed telepathically between him and the lizard. The behemoth folded its wings and stretched out its neck to rest its head on the ground. One after another, dozens of the flying monsters swept over the rim and landed, each assuming the attitude of the first.

The bundles of weapons were secured to certain of the beasts and others were designated as riding mounts.

Elfin dragon-masters mounted their charges, scrambling up and settling into a cockpit-like depression just behind the creatures' heads. The giants each chose a mount, and the Company disposed themselves aboard the rest.

Jerry discovered that the monster's knobbed spine formed a series of saddle-like notches down the leathery back, and provided firm seating. He took a grip on the vertebral knob that rose like a pommel in front of him, experiencing a twinge of the old acrophobia he had described to Ulf.

Seated just ahead of him, Olin Longshanks cradled Maryam's slight body in the safety of his arms. Brokk and Freya were saddled just forward of them.

He heard Ulf, behind him, mutter, "I've never *really* enjoyed this leg of th' journey."

The sentiment was echoed by the mercenaries completing the load.

A shrill whistle from the elfin convoy commander warned of takeoff. Jerry tightened his grip on the vertebraic pommel.

The pterodactyl waddled clumsily to the brink of the abyss and leaped into space.

Most of the troop, with the exception of the new recruits, had been airborne once before, at the taking of Ethelstane Keep. Even so, the lurching sensation produced a few howls of fright.

The flight across the Chasm of Chasms took twenty hours.

On arrival in Jotunheim the Company dismounted, stiff and aching, to be met by the contingent of Ice Elves who manned the Northern Station. At a little distance sat a small group of giants. Hrimgrimnir went to speak with them.

Hjalmar the Axeman bellowed orders, and the Company fell into ranks.

Hrimgrimnir the Frost Giant lumbered up, his cheeks ruddy from the cold, and rime sparkling in his dark beard. The big man raised his sword in salute.

"Ho, Brokk o' Svartheim. 'Tis much I owe thee, friend."

He gestured toward the giant newcomers who waved, smiled, and lifted their weapons in greeting.

"My mother's brother and his son bring me great news. In my absence many more have risen to join me in overthrowin' Thrym th' tyrant. They await only the weapons I bring. 'Tis thee whom we have t' thank for th' opportunity t' free ourselves once and for all from th' yoke of th' troll-curst oppressor."

The Frost Giant knelt in the snow and extended a vast hand.

"Dwarf King, best of friends, thy heart is as great as that of th' greatest giant, and thy name will be revered throughout Jotunheim as th' one who made our victory possible."

The big man stood and once more raised his sword. The other giants clashed their weapons against their shields and raised their voices in a shout.

Brokk, embarrassed, waved aside the thanks.

"Be ye certain there's nothin' more we can do t' aid ye?"

Laughter rumbled in Hrimgrimnir's chest. "I mean thee no disrespect, friend Brokk. In thy courage thee stand as tall as any in th' giantholm, but," the big man smiled, "in a battle between giants. . . ."

The dwarf grinned.

"Aye, I take yer meanin, my friend, we'd get trampled underfoot." Hrimgrimnir chuckled. "Aye." He pointed to Hradalfar in company with half a dozen of the giants.

"T' repay thee in part, I'm sendin' my brother and six of my companions t' escort thee and thy party, t' see thee safely across th' giantholm. May thee fare well in thy quest. Thee'll forgive me, but I must see t' th' transfer of our weapons."

The big man raised a hand in farewell and moved off.

Hradalfar approached with the giant escort. "My brother has placed us under thy orders, friend Brokk. We await thy commands."

CHAPTER THIRTY TWO

Since it had not yet been determined who was for, and who was against Hrimgrimnir, encounters with other giants might prove disastrous, so Hradalfar, who knew the country well, took pains to avoid contact with others of his kind.

This necessitated a circuitous route that added weeks to the journey.

Except for the struggle to stay alive in the bitter cold and howling winds of the giants' homeland, Jerry found the trek across Jotunheim uneventful.

The giants, in their own element, showed the mercenaries how to throw up igloos when camping for the night, and all, even Jerry, were pleasantly astounded at how snug and comfortable a house made of blocks of ice could be.

Jerry was also impressed at the amount of game to be found in the frozen wasteland. Although his diet had never before included items like fox, wolf, or bear, he learned to eat them. There were snowshoe rabbits in abundance, and since a great deal of the terrain consisted of frozen-over lakes, fish could also be had in plenty simply by chopping a hole in the ice. A type of rock lichen, adapted to the climate, provided a valuable substitute for vegetables.

The only things that broke the monotony of the trek were two close brushes with glacial cracks like the one that had nearly killed Brokk, and half a dozen encounters with the huge ice bears that roamed the frozen wilderness.

For three months they climbed laboriously up and down successive glaciers, slogging through thigh-deep snow, dragging heavy sledges laden with camp equipment. They plowed ahead in the face of howling winds fraught with ice crystals that tore at unprotected skin.

It was a tired Company that arrived at last on the Plain of Vigard, midway up the Ultimate Peak.

Here, according to myth, the last battle between the Gods and the Frost Giants would be fought.

Although at an altitude much greater than ice-bound Jotunheim, the Peak rose above the frigid jet-stream that gave the land of the giants its arctic climate, and the temperature of the Plain was quite pleasant. It was here that those who had business with the gods awaited summons.

The vast Plain was dotted with the tents of those seeking audition.

Hjalmar ordered camp to be set up.

Hradalfar and his companion giants, who had proved to be good friends over the past months, came to say their farewells. The mercenaries had ceased to exhibit amazement at having found themselves boon companions to these, their traditional enemies. They gathered to wish the giants well in their struggle to free themselves from Thrym's bonds.

The big men raised their weapons in final goodbye, and left to rejoin Hrimgrimnir in his revolt against Thrym.

Jerry was no less impressed than the others by what he saw.

The broad Plain of Vigard was covered with the camps of other visitors to Asgard. From the far edge of the Plain a shimmering bridge of multicolored translucence arched upward and soared away into the clouds. The Bifrost Bridge, the Rainbow Road that connected the City of the Gods with the world below. At the foot of the Bridge stood a gatehouse of the same opaline material.

Jerry, Brokk, and Ulf approached the Gatehouse. A massive figure stepped from the door. He was clad in a knee-length chiton belted at the waist, and wore sandals cross-gartered to the knee. His long hair and beard were white and elaborately curled. The Gatekeeper of the Gods was unarmed.

The big man smiled warmly at the goblin and raised a hand in greeting. "Ho, Ulf the Far Traveled. It has been long since last I saw you. it is always good to see a friend."

"Aye, Heimdall the Watcher. It is good to see you again."

The goblin indicated his companions. "I bring Brokk Hammermacher of Svartheim and Jerry Jar Haz called Thor's Fist. 'Twas said that Odin himself has expressed interest in th' lad."

The Gatekeeper looked at Jerry. There was a momentary pause and Heimdall said, "Aye."

Jerry noticed another tiny hesitation. "The lad's expected."

The red-beard examined the Guardian more closely. Something wasn't quite right. What? What? What didn't quite jibe? What was it that he sensed to be out of phase? Then he got it. Those almost imperceptible hesitations at questions as though he were receiving his answers from elsewhere. . . .

That and something more.

The way Heimdall moved. It was infinitesimal. Something, Jerry was sure, that couldn't be perceived by one who was not born in his time and his world.

It was the impression of a movie film running through the projector at the proper speed but clicking one frame at a time. Only a microsecond between clicks, but it was there. What would account for this anomaly?

Holy jumping Jehosaphat! Heimdall the Watcher was an android! And not from Jerry's time-frame, either.

This ultimate product of robotics, was from a civilization far in advance of the nineteen nineties! Jerry's mind went into a momentary tailspin.

As if from far away he heard the Watcher say, "Jerry Jar Haz called Thor's Fist will have to come alone. You, his friends, will have to await him on the Plain of Vigard until his return."

The red-beard made a herculean effort to shake off his confusion. "Sure, yeah. . . . Why not?"

Still dazed by his discovery, he heard Brokk say, "Go ahead, lad, we'll wait fer ye in th' camp."

Jerry waved a hand. "Yeah, sure. . . ."

Brokk and Ulf left, and instead of stepping aside for Jerry to mount the Rainbow Bridge, the Watcher motioned for him to enter the gatehouse.

Heimdall pointed to a door. "Step in there."

Jerry did so.

The door slid smoothly shut. Jerry felt a gentle pressure against the soles of his feet, and still in the grip of euphoria at this strange change in the way of things, felt only mild surprise to realize that he was in a high-speed express elevator.

The car slowed suddenly and the deceleration was so swift that he almost went into free-fall. The door slid open.

The red-beard found himself looking at a pretty girl in a silver lame leotard and body stocking. He became suddenly acutely aware of his rough furs, his armor, and the weapons that he had come to accept as part of him.

The girl smiled at his confusion, and held out a hand. "Please follow me, Jerry Jar Haz."

The hallway down which he followed his guide was walled and ceiled with the same translucent material as the Rainbow Bridge, and brightly lighted by overhead fluorescents.

They passed many gods and goddesses.

The women wore the body-stocking-leotard garment, and the men high-buttoned tunics and trousers. All were exceedingly handsome.

Jerry felt increasingly out of place in his Skandian garb.

The guide stopped at a large door. She touched a button and the door slid open. She motioned for him to enter. She smiled. "Welcome to Asgard, Jerry Jar Haz called Thor's Fist."

Still more or less in shock, Jerry walked into a large chamber that resembled the computer room at good old Nationwide Insurance, only bigger. A *lot* bigger!

The walls were lined from floor to ceiling with banks of muttering, clicking computers, and television screens that monitored a hundred areas all over Skandia, panning from one location to another.

Jerry recognized the 'airport' of the Ice Elves on one screen, the rocky spire that had once supported Ethelstane Keep on another. The volcanic land called Muspelheim. His vision blurred at the kaleidoscopic overview of the Nine Worlds. He shook his head.

At the heart of this vast information center was a raised command console at which sat a broad-shouldered, handsome red-bearded man. He stood up at Jerry's entrance, descended to the main floor, and advanced.

He waved a hand, indicating the flickering screens.

"Welcome to Odin's Tower from which he surveys all Skandia. Welcome to Asgard, Thor's Fist."

He grinned. "I'm Thor."

Jerry stared at the man, and his mind went into neutral.

Too much had happened in too short a time. Too quick a transition from harsh medieval Skandia to futuristic technology. The lighted screens seemed to sway and dance, and the floor under his feet lurched.

Jerry put out his hand of flesh to grasp at something that wasn't there. Darkness leaped at him from the corners of the room, and he fell with a crash of armor.

When he opened his eyes, he was lying on a comfortable couch in a small office off the computer room. The man who claimed to be Thor was pressing a glass to his lips.

"Drink this," he was saying, "It'll help."

CHAPTER THIRTY THREE

Jerry surged up off the couch, his hand automatically reaching for his sword. "What the bloody hell. . .?"

Thor laughed. "I don't blame you. I'd be a little puzzled myself."

"*A little puzzled?* Jerry laughed shortly. "Mister, you've got a black belt in understatement! Who *are* you?"

"Sit down, Jerry Haskins of San Diego California USA, and I'll tell you."

Jerry sat and Thor pulled up a chair.

"For starters," Jerry said, "I know it's the custom in this world to address everyone by his complete genealogy, but do you think you could cut it to just Jerry?"

Thor laughed. "It does keep the conversation a little crisper that way. My full name is Pe-Trok An Gund An-Tros of Vanir called Thor the Thunderer."

Jerry stared. "Pe-Trok An Gund. . . ."

The Starman grinned. "Call me Pete. Vanir is the seventh planet of a sun probably not yet discovered in the time from which you come."

"*Extraterrestrials!*"

"That's it."

"But how. . .?"

"Shipwreck."

"The Glowing Earth! Nuclear drive, right?"

"Unfortunately, yes."

"How'd you know that I'm from another time?"

"The raven you call Odin's Messenger.

"We've trained a number of the birds as battlefield observers. You'll learn why in time. There are a couple in every flock. He reported the upcoming battle. Jar Haz looked to be a likely candidate so I sent the Valkyries to preserve him."

"*Valkyries?* Okay, Valkyries. Why not Valkyries? I give up. What's going on?"

Pe-Trok. . . Pete. . . laughed.

"Easy, Jerry. Not all at once. It's much too complicated to explain in a couple of sentences. There are things you must see first, to understand any explanation.

"Trust me that all of your questions will be answered in full, but it'll take time."

Pete laughed again. "You're not the only one with a consuming curiosity, you know.

We are burning with interest in you, too. You're our first time traveler. We find you *very* interesting."

He grinned. "You wouldn't believe the stir you've made in Asgard!

"But, coming back to your question. When your Odin's Messenger returned to the field of battle after making his report, he saw the spirit of Jar Haz the Viking being taken up by the Shining Maids, but the body of Jar Haz continued to live.

"This was puzzling to the bird. This was something that had never happened before. Ravens are inquisitive creatures by nature, and this one had been trained to observe.

"He followed you down into the tunnel with the dwarf and filed away everything he saw and heard for future reference. When you brought him back to the open surface, he reported back here."

Jerry grimaced. "And I thought he was hanging around because of my irresistible personality."

Pete smiled. "Cheer up. The bird's adopted you."
The Starman gave Jerry a quizzical look.

"You, Jerry Haskins of San Diego California USA, known as Jerry Jar Haz called Thor's Fist, have a way of attracting loyal friends, be they bird, dog, dwarf, elf, man or goblin."

Pe-Trok raised one eyebrow. "Even giants! My friend, I envy you."

"I," Jerry said with feeling, "have a way of being a very lucky guy to have such friends."

He looked up. "Speaking of those friends, if I'm to stay here a while, I'd better notify them. They'll worry."

"It's already taken care of. The elf-woman and the girl are in the care of Sif, my wife, and the others are being welcomed by the Heroes of Valhalla.

"Olin Longshanks and Lars o' th' Battlefield are even now drinking happily with their old friend, Orm Thorwaldssen."

"Orm? He's here?"

The Starman smiled. "Yes, Orm and many another. The Free Company of Hjalmar the Axeman has attracted many who have become Heroes. The mercenary Captain is greeting many an old comrade."

"Jar Haz?"

"He's anxious to meet you."

Jerry's head was spinning. Too much, too fast! Pete rose and came to Jerry's side.

He laid a hand on the red-beard's shoulder. "It's a bit overwhelming, I know."

Jerry looked at the Starman. "If it's this mind-boggling to me, how are the others reacting to. . ." He gestured to the computer screens. ". . .this?"

Pe-Trok smiled. "They know nothing of this. They are seeing and living exactly what their mythology tells them about the City of the Gods. A piece of necessary theater."

He patted Jerry's shoulder. "Easy, Jerry. Everything you want to know will be explained in time. As I said, we're every bit as curious about you as you are about us."

Jerry eased his helmet, and looked around. "That's another thing. You seem to be in charge. Everybody seems to think some guy named Odin was running things around here."

Pete chuckled. "Oh, he does."

He pointed to a data plate set into the command console.

Jerry read: O.D.N. Model XIV-a323.

"He's a *computer?*"

Pe-Trok nodded, smiling.

"Hey!" Jerry jerked his head around and looked sharply at his companion. "What's going on here? How come guys from another planet use the Phoenician alphabet and Arabic and Roman numerals? Yeah, and now that I think of it, how come you speak English like a native Californian?"

The Starman chuckled. "Where do you think your Romans and Arabs and Phoenicians got their cultures?"

Jerry goggled. "You've been here that long?"

Pete nodded. "Yes. We've been trying to contact our home planet the whole while."

He gestured upward. "The Ultimate Peak is a giant radio beacon constantly broadcasting our distress signal."

A look of sadness flitted briefly across the Starman's face. "We've had no answer in over ten thousand years."

Jerry opened his mouth. "Ten thousand. . . ."

Pete smiled. "Later, Jerry. Take your time. We know that it's much too much to absorb all at once. That's one reason we let you make your way across Skandia, rather than simply sending the Valkyries for you.

"We needed the time to sort out how to acquaint you with the truth in an orderly way. Most importantly we needed time to marshal our resources to see if we could help you, and how.

"Rest assured that all your curiosity will be satisfied. How we Vanir got into the god business. How it works, and why it must."

The Thunderer laughed. "And the thing that is puzzling you at this minute, how it is that I speak to you in the idiom of your own time and place."

Jerry grinned. "Yeah. How about that?"

Pete took him by the elbow. "Come along, Jerry. We've had rooms prepared for you ever since you left Svartheim. Let me take you to them. A hot bath and some clean clothes, and you'll be in better shape to meet the rest of the gods. Relax, Jerry. We'll give you all the help at our command."

Thor led the way through several passages, arriving at a section that was obviously living quarters. He stopped before a door. "Relax," he said again. "Take your time and soak some of the chill of Jotunheim out of your bones. Don't be nervous about meeting the rest of the gang. Remember you're the most stimulating thing that's happened around here in centuries."

Pe-Trok grinned. "You may not believe this, but it's not always as much fun as you might think, being a god."

He opened the door. "Anything you want, just tell the attendant. I'll be back for you later."

Jerry closed the door and looked around. The furnishings were Spartan but looked comfortable. His gaze fell on one piece of furniture that caught his immediate attention. A wet bar against one wall.

"Yes," he said aloud. "I can most definitely, certainly, absolutely use a drink. A very large drink."

He investigated a number of cut-glass decanters. None smelled familiar, but all smelled delicious. He chose one at random, and poured a stiff three fingers into a crystal goblet. He took an appreciative sip. The immediate result was a warmth that spread through him easing tension. He took another and sighed.

At a soft sound behind him, he reacted instinctively.
His rapier was in his hand as he whirled, dropping into a fighting crouch.

A girl shrank back, a look of fright on her pretty face at his fierce demeanor. She stuttered, "I am Mora, your attendant, Lord Jerry Jar Haz called Thor's Fist."

Jerry straightened and sheathed his sword. "I'm sorry I frightened you, Miss," he said, embarrassed. "Please forgive me. I'm afraid I'm not quite as civilized as I used to be."

He smiled. "And for heaven's sake please drop all that formality. I'm just plain old Jerry."

The girl returned his smile. "All right just plain old Jerry," she giggled. "I've drawn your bath and laid out a more appropriate wardrobe."

She advanced and held out her hand. "Let me help you off with your weapons and armor."

Jerry allowed her to unbuckle his sword belt and help him out of his smelly furs. But when she started to undo his jerkin, he called a halt.

He eyed the pretty girl. "Miss, I don't know the customs hereabouts, but where I come from, grown men take their own baths. Just show me where things are, and I'll manage."

Mora dimpled and curtsied. "Would you feel more at ease with a male attendant?"

"Definitely!"

"I'll send a squire to attend you." Smiling, the girl withdrew.

A moment later a young man entered. "I am Mok-An, Lord Jerry. Let me help you, sir."

Disencumbered of his furs, mail, and weapons, Jerry unstrapped his steel hand, and stepped down into a huge sunken tub filled with scented water.

He stretched luxuriously and let the hot water ease the tension from his muscles.

Mok-An examined Brokk's cleverly constructed piece of work. He shook his head in

admiration. "Sir, with the science of the Vanir you could have a prosthesis powered by microchips and nuclear batteries, and it wouldn't work one whit better than this one made by a dwarf with access only to Medieval technology. I never cease to wonder at the peoples of this world."

He looked at Jerry's stump. "The Vanir can even regrow that hand if you want."

Jerry picked up on the phrasology. "You keep making reference to 'the Vanir'. Aren't you one of them?"

Mok-An smiled. "In a way, yes. I am an android."

Jerry started. "Mora?"

"Yes, sir. An android."

"I'll be a monkey's uncle!"

Mok-an looked puzzled.

Jerry laughed. "Forget it."

He held up his stump and examined it in the light of the android's statement.

Regrow his hand?

The decision was easy. "Thank you, but I've grown accustomed to my godfather's gift."

He grinned. "Besides without it, I wouldn't be Jerry Jar Haz called Thor's Fist. I'd be just Jerry Haskins called Jerry."

Mok-An laughed.

Jerry wallowed appreciatively in the warm water. The last hot bath he'd had was back in Brokk's cavern before they left Svartheim more than a year and a half ago. Bathing in cold streams, while invigorating, was no comparison.

Besides, he'd not been out of his furs for three months. The climate of Jotunheim bore no resemblance whatsoever to that of Southern California. To have removed his furs would have been to freeze solid in a matter of moments.

He gave a guilty start. None of them had been out of their furs, and all were fastidious about personal cleanliness.

"My friends. . . ."

"Ease your mind, sir. All of their wants have been provided for."

Jerry, bathed and relaxed, beard freshly trimmed, put on the clothes Mora had laid out for him.

He examined himself in the full length mirror. The high-buttoned tunic and trousers, made of some material that felt like silk, made him look like a sissy.

He hadn't realized just how much he had *become* Jerry Jar Haz called Thor's Fist. He missed the weight of chainmail on his shoulders. He missed his weapons. He missed Bryn. And most of all he missed having his friends at his side.

He'd been almost rude when Mok-An had suggested cutting his hair. He'd become very fond of those braids.

He grinned at his reflection and muttered, "*Barbarian.* That's what you've become, a complete barbarian and you wouldn't change a thing."

The android went to answer a knock at the door. Pe-Trok surveyed the renovated Jerry.

He chuckled. "You look a bit more civilized, and a little less like sudden death on the hoof."

Jerry grimaced. "I was just thinking that I looked like a sissy."

Pete laughed and gestured. "Come along. The others are anxious to meet you."

They entered a small banquet room. The score or so persons seated at the long table looked up with friendliness and poorly concealed eager curiosity.

Pe-Trok waved a hand. "Friends, our long-awaited guest, Jerry Haskins. Make him welcome."

There was a babble of greeting to which Jerry responded in the Skandian manner to which he had become accustomed.

"Ho," he said, raising a hand.

Once again he was surprised to find how much more at ease, and how much more at home he felt among his circle of strange friends, than among these kind and civilized people, but the assemblage quickly made him feel welcome.

Thor introduced his fellow gods.

Tyr, the one-handed Swordsman of the Gods, to whom Maryam had likened Olin Longshanks to the amusement of Orm. Contrary to myth, Tyr had two hands.

Frigga, supposedly the wife of Odin, was Tyr's mate.

Baldur the Beautiful God, a truly handsome man, and his wife Nanna.

Idun, Goddess of Youth, whose feast day had seen the taking of Ethelstane Keep, and her husband Braggi.

Sif of the Golden Hair, Thor's wife. Frey, god of spring and his wife, Freya.

Jerry took particular note of the Queen of the Elves, Goddess of Spring and Flowers. Freya the goddess was breathtakingly beautiful, but Jerry stood by his statement to Freya the elf-woman, 'Freya in Asgard cannot be as lovely as you, Mother.'

Jerry was seated in the chair of honor, and food was served. I n addition to the Skandian fare of roast boar, venison, and grilled fish, there were unfamiliar but delicious dishes of Vanirean concoction.

The gods and goddesses fired questions at him with the innocent curiosity of children. Though Jerry quickly lost his feeling of being an outsider, he realized that he had become Skandian to the core.

It was instantly evident that whatever it was that had caused the Vanir to go into what Pe-Trok had called the god business, it had not been conquest, arrogance, or any desire to lord it over a less sophisticated people.

The godly names by which they had been introduced were not, of course, the names their parents had given them.

Pe-Trok An Gund An-Thos called Thor the Thunderer explained . . . .

CHAPTER THIRTY FOUR

Jerry listened in fascination as Pe-Trok related the disaster that had brought the gods to Skandia.

The Vanir had a pressing problem. They were virtually immortal.

The birth-rate was low, but even so, it was imperative that they continually seek out new worlds to which to emigrate as the race expanded. As a consequence, the Secretariat of Interstellar Exploration constantly sent thousands of starships into space to probe the universe for uninhabited planets capable of supporting Vanirean life.

"We Vanir are a civilized people. Conquest is no part of our intentions," Pe-Trok explained.

"There are literally billions of planets which fit our needs. Therefore, no planet already containing intelligent species can be considered for colonization. It is, of course, inevitable that exploration parties occasionally come in contact with native populations, and specific rules of conduct are laid down to cover such instances.

"Extreme care is to be taken to avoid any actions that could interfere in any way with the locals. Landing Teams are strictly enjoined to do nothing that might disturb the existing ecology, or to introduce any anachronistic factors that might affect existing cultures, and they are to respect native mores and religious beliefs."

Pete grimaced.

"Unfortunately, in our case, we found it impossible to conform to Secretariat guide-lines.

"The Starship, on which I was Third Officer, was in the one thousand twenty fourth year of its voyage when we entered the planetary system shown on our charts as XII-AF-VIX.

"Trouble developed in the main drive-chamber and the danger of melt-down was imminent."

The Starman made a helpless gesture.

"As if that weren't bad enough, to complicate things further the steering drive also developed gremlins, and our doomed vessel proceeded at a lurching, chaotic pace.

"It was pure chance that the nearest planet of the tiny star system on the verge of a spiral galaxy was the third from that sun. This planet called Earth by its inhabitants. We managed to crash land, causing great damage and loss of life."

The other gods and goddesses nodded.

"Yes. Over half the crew perished," Tyr said.

Pe-Trok continued. "As it happened, it was three weeks before the core reached critical mass, and we survivors were able to salvage a gratifying portion of the ship's stores and equipment. We established a base camp well out of the possible fall-out zone, and set about creating a life-style to sustain us until contact could be made with the home world.

"I had been Third Officer, but the loss of the Captain and the Second and First Officers in the crash, catapulted me into command. As soon as our base camp was completed, my first order of business was to send out search parties on antigravity sleds to explore the planet, and to seek out the optimum location on which to build our beacon.

"It immediately became apparent that the Secretariat's ban on contact with locals could not be adhered to in our circumstances. By that one chance in fifty trillion, the whole planet contained intelligent life-forms that proved to be bipedal humanoids almost identical in genetic structure to ourselves.

"The exploration teams reported back on varying races within the humanoid population, with divergent levels of development. However their examination disclosed no peak higher than the one in the far north of the land in which we had crashed, known to the natives as Skandia.

"We moved the colony to a broad plain midway up the pinnacle. We named the place the Plain of Vigard, after the garden in Vanirean mythology where life had begun on our home world. We constructed a permanent city to house ourselves while we built our distress beacon, a project that took several centuries."

Pete explained that this posed no problem for the virtually immortal Vanir. Once the body of a Vanir reached maturity it ceased to age. They could be killed, but diseases did not affect them.

Barring accident or murder, the exact lifespan of a Vanir was unknown.

After several centuries, though, senility would encroach. In the normal order of things when this condition was detected, the individual was placed in suspended animation under controlled conditions, where he would undergo a battery of hypnotic and telepathic reconstruction to restore his faculties to normal.

Hypnosis and telepathy played a large part in the everyday lives of the Vanir. They were far in advance of the elves of Skandia in what Jerry would call E.S.P.

They were fully telepathic, but like the elves, were strictly ethical about invading another's mind.

Surface trivialities like speech patterns, were easily picked up, and posed no invasion of the individual's privacy.

That explained why the Vanir could speak with Jerry in his own idiom, though none would have thought of probing his mind to learn what they wanted to know about him.

They also possessed telekinetic powers superior to the elves. Their greatest power, however, lay in the field of hypnosis. This faculty was integral to the reconstruction of a senile Vanir.

"But the hypnotherapy," Pe-Trok continued, "is tied to a drug extracted from a plant that grows only on Vanir, and almost our entire supply of the drug was destroyed in the crash. When we ran out, there was nothing that could be done for those who succumbed, but to preserve them in cryogenic sleep while research teams sought an alternate method of revival.

"We confined ourselves mostly to Skandia, and for the first few decades all went well between us and the locals.

"Then the race known as goblins, who due to some genetic flaw, were constantly consumed with hate and bloodlust, ambushed and killed a large party of Vanir explorers. We tried to treat with the Twisted Ones, but our diplomatic mission was set upon and murdered." Pe-Trok told how the normally compassionate Vanir were infuriated. A General Council was convened to decide how to deal with the situation.

Some, outraged, advocated a war of extermination. The innate gentleness of the race, however, prevented any such response, and Pe-Trok evolved an elaborate plan.

Aware that even the goblins feared the wrath of their local hierarchy of gods, it was decided to dress the Vanir in the garb and trappings of Heroes, the Beloved of Odin, while he and the senior officers assumed the regalia of the ruling gods.

Pe-Trok's second in command, En-Kap An-Zok, was a tall, massive man of truly god-like proportions, and on him fell the mantle of Odin Allfather while Pe-Trok took up the hammer of Thor the Thunderer.

"We 'gods' and 'heroes' fell upon the land of the goblins, descending from the heavens on antigravity sleds, and striking with 'thunderbolts' from our laser weapons."

Jerry visualized a sort of helicopter cattle round-up, in which the goblins were herded west into a harsh and barren land encircled by numerous rivers and streams.

"We Vanir linked minds and laid a devastating terror of running water on the Twisted Ones that effectively isolated the murderous goblins from the rest of the Nine Worlds."

Pete smiled. "A fear, as you have learned from your friend Ulf, that persists to the present day."

The next crisis came several generations later, when horribly mutated humans began to appear out of the crash site.

"We had been completely unaware of any human population in that area, or we could have taken immediate steps to contain the situation. We have ways of dealing with radiation poisoning that, had we known in time, would have nipped the problem before it got off the ground. But by the time the plague was known, it was too late to reverse the damage.

"These two incidents, so contrary to our directive, together with our dismay at having had so disastrous an impact on the locals, caused us to withdraw to the city we had built on the Ultimate Peak, and sever all relations with the population.

"Even so, the effects of our unwilling presence on this planet resulted in one more catastrophe.

"Three centuries later, when we activated our monstrous signal tower, the initial burst of radio energy was so enormous that it triggered an unforeseen change in the upper atmosphere. One that diverted a stratospheric jet stream of super-frigid air into an irreversible course, low over the land known as Jotunheim.

"The Land of the Giants changed almost overnight from a pleasant temperate place into an arctic waste. Great glaciers formed. Snow began to fall and did not stop. Icy winds sprang up and lashed the snowscape with howling gales.

"The giants who lived there had been a relatively peaceful people, but after a few generations of battling their harsh environment, they became as harsh and hostile as the land. They became bitter, sullen, warlike and filled with seething anger.

"We Vanir looked upon the changes we'd unhappily brought about, and felt an enormous responsibility for the beings whose normal course of development we'd so disastrously disrupted. We began to effect small changes here and there with the technology at our disposal, in an effort to correct or alleviate some of the damage.

"Nothing spectacular, just little nudges that would change things for the better over the centuries and, hopefully, put the planet back on track."

The Vanir also aided indirectly in the rise of other infant civilizations outside Skandia as well, foreseeing the impact that future interplay would have on the development of the planet.

The Phoenicians, the Greeks, the Romans. The Hebrews, the Egyptians. On the other side of the world, the Mayans, the Aztecs, the Incas. The Chinese, Japanese, East Indians.

But a burden of guilt lay on them for the disasters they'd unwillingly wrought in the Northland, and there they stayed.

The peoples of Midgard and Jotunheim, of Svartheim, as well as the lesser lands of Niflheim (a frigid underground offshoot of Jotunheim) and the fiery, volcanic region in the far south known as Muspelheim, had observed the assault on the goblins coming from above.

They'd seen their gods descend and strike a blow that freed them from the horror of the goblins. They began to look on Asgard as a place where they might actually go to seek the help of their gods.

Delegations and individuals began to make the murderous trek to the Plain of Vigard from all parts of Skandia.

"We felt an immense responsibility toward these people," Pe-Trok said. "We could not just simply turn them away, so I called a general council. It was agreed that the unsophisticated folk of this planet could never grasp the reality that was Asgard, so we decided to give them something that they could relate to. . . their gods.

"It was further agreed that helping individuals here and there could certainly cause no more harm than we had already done."

Individual Vanir were assigned certain roles.

"En-Kap An-Zok, who had made such an impressive Odin during the goblin war, was confirmed in that part.

"I felt that I had made a marvelous Thor, so I continued in the guise of the Thunder God. As you see, other Vanir became lesser gods and goddesses in the hierarchy."

To the amusement of all, the role of Loki the Mischief Maker, the Doer of Good and the Doer of Evil, the Sly One of the gods, fell to a jolly, warm-hearted Vanir who had an unfortunate cast in one eye that gave him a sly, roguish appearance. Moko Aln Op-Jar, the Vanir under discussion, stood up, bowed to Jerry with a broad grin.

The details of the myths of Skandia were well known, so each god and goddess assumed the appropriate dress and accouterments of his role.

A great rough-hewn long-house was constructed and labeled Valhalla, the Mead Hall of Odin Allfather, where the spirits of the Heroes slain in outstanding battle drank and feasted and fought eternally.

Some of the younger Vanir took to the roles of brawling, roistering Vikings with enthusiasm. No great number of these could be spared from their duties so artificially intelligent androids were constructed to fill the Great Mead Hall with revelry.

Here the visitors to Asgard were brought to see what they expected to see. En-Kap An-Zok, enthroned on a tall dais, presided over the brawl with godlike presence.

Several more centuries passed. The seeds planted in other civilizations took root and began to bear fruit.

The Phoenicians took to the sea, and began to explore. The Romans expanded their empire. The Greeks rose and subsided.

Across the ocean, the Mayans discovered astronomy. The Incas developed a highway complex, and a mail system as good as any devised, but failed to make use of the wheel.

On the opposite side of the globe, the Chinese invented paper, gunpowder and spaghetti.

Christianity sprang up and began its inevitable march across the face of the planet.

In Asgard the cryogenic vaults were filling up with Vanir in need of rejuvenation.

The biologists and medical researchers worked in never ending, overlapping shifts to develop a drug with the properties of the Vanirean plant.

The breakthrough however, when it came, was found not by the doctors, but by the engineers.

San-Ka Kern Jom-Ak, a junior engineer in the laser laboratory, was working on a project suggested in jest by one of the senior scientists.

Kaf-Ra Kern Dap-An had complained bitterly one day that an idea had come to him while he was deeply engrossed in a project, and that by the time he found the time to develop it, it had faded from his memory.

"What I need," he said humorously, "is a 'think-net, to catch these ideas, and hold them until I can get around to them."

The Premise had intrigued San-Ka. A retaining chamber for thoughts. Why not?

Thought is an electrochemical process. That involved electrons. Why not a chamber of free electrons to absorb the ones created by the thinking process?

Why not a chamber that could absorb those thoughts and release them when needed?

Kaf-Ra had stared at his young assistant.

"I don't know why not. It's an interesting concept."

"Then I can work on it?"

"How near are you to completion of Project XO-10-a-KN?"

San-Ka scratched his ear. "A year. Maybe less."

"All right. Complete present assignment then have at it."

"It may take a while."

Kaf-Ra chuckled. "What's a century or two, eh?"

"Thank you, sir."

It did not take a century or two, but it did take twenty seven Years before San-Ka came up with a working model.

The device consisted of a helmet within which a tiny laser beam continually scanned the head of the wearer.

Like a compact disc player with a laser needle, Jerry would have said.

It transferred thought impulses via another laser to a coalescent globe about the size of a soccer ball, where the impulses were absorbed and recorded on a mass of free electrons.

By reversing the process, the stored thoughts could be re-experienced. In theory. Kaf-Ra examined the junior engineer's achievement. "Will it work?"

San-Ka scratched his ear. "I think so. There's only one way to find out. . . ."

The young scientist sat and placed the helmet on his head. The entire laboratory staff gathered to observe. San-Ka pressed the activating stud and the opalescent globe began to glow.

He looked at it. "So far, so good."

After a few moments he switched it off. He sat for a minute, crossed his fingers, and pressed the reversing stud.

The young man's eyes rolled back in his head, his body arched in a taut bow. He quivered alarmingly, then went limp. San-Ka was rushed to the Medical Center.

For three days he lay like a dead man. On the fourth he began to show signs of returning awareness.

On the sixth day he could talk, and Kaf-Ra was sent for. The older scientist looked at his young colleague.

"What happened?" he demanded.

San-Ka told him.

It wasn't just the recollections of the past few thoughts that had returned to him, it was his entire life.

In every detail.

All at once.

It was too much to handle.

The think-net was useless. It was shelved.

Fifty years later someone mentioned the failed experiment.

"I wonder what would have happened if someone besides yourself had put on the helmet and received all your life memories," a pretty chemist remarked in the snack shop.

A brain specialist sitting with them shuddered. "Catastrophe! It would have blown out every synapse in his brain."

San-Ka stared. He leaned forward and rested his forearms on the table. "What if the recipient's brain were blank?"

"What do you mean?"

"I mean what if the recipient's brain had no memories of its own? What if it were blank but still functional?"

The specialist sat up. "Like one that's been cryogenically preserved?"

"Exactly!"

The senior physician stood up. "Come with me. We have to propose this to Pe-Trok immediately!"

The Commander listened to the two scientists with rising enthusiasm.

He looked from one to the other. "Is it possible?"

The brain specialist laughed and slapped his hand down on Pe-Trok's desk. "Yes!" he said, "Yes!"

Pe-Trok flipped a switch on his console. "Call an immediate session of the Full Council. I want everyone there in half an hour."

The proposal was submitted, and the meeting laid open to questions.

Though the entire Council was enthusiastic about the breakthrough, one seemingly insurmountable obstacle kept coming up: where were the life memories to come from?

If a living Vanir were to volunteer his, he'd only be creating a clone of himself.

The society could not afford to be inundated with clones.

A dying Vanir could live again by having this life-essence transferred to one of the cryogenic sleepers, but that solved only one minor problem, few Vanir died.

So where were the elements that would revive their frozen brethren to come from? It seemed to be back to square one.

This obstacle was discussed and rediscussed over the next few years. The Possibility of regeneration so near at hand was frustrating.

Each year the expected number of Vanir succumbed, the cryogenic vaults became more and more crowded.

Pe-Trok and the other senior Officers were nagged by the fact that eventually the whole expedition would be doomed in lie in frozen sleep, their only hope being the fading possibility of a rescue ship from home.

Unless a solution could be found.

As it turned out it was Pe-Trok himself who found the answer, and in a most unexpected manner.

It had long been the custom, when the pressures of godhood became too great, that the god would don the trappings of Skandia, and go down into Midgard for a vacation. Since that savage world was not safe for any woman unless she had a protector, when one of the goddesses felt the need to go, she had to be accompanied.

Sif, wife of Pe-Trok, felt overwhelmed by her duties in the Chemistry Department, and persuaded her husband to take her for a brief holiday.

It was decided to go dressed as a wandering men-at-arms and his woman.

Clad in the steel and leather of a mercenary, and armed with axe and dagger, the Commander of the Vanir and his wife mounted an antigravity sled and traveled to Midgard.

To cloak the flying carpet in invisibility was no problem for two adepts at telepathic hypnosis, and they landed unseen in a small wood not far from a large village.

The grav-sled was concealed beneath a pile of leaves and the self-destruct activated. Should it be discovered by any who did not know how to disarm the device, any touch would cause the machine to fall into indistinguishable dust.

Pe-Trok checked his weapons, including the small laser pistol under his tunic, and he and Sif of the Golden Hair proceeded to the village tavern.

The place was filled with mercenaries of the better sort, and the atmosphere was one of conviviality. The newcomers were welcomed with boisterous hospitality.

One of the mercenaries, who looked from his accouterments to be an officer, approached their table before they had a chance to order.

"Ho, friend," he said heartily, "I be Lars Larssen, lieutenant t' Olaf Knudssen, an' by yer leave I'll ask ye t' drink a horn o' ale with me an' my mates as it be a special occasion we celebrate."

He looked down at Sif with respectful admiration. "I pray ye not t' take this amiss, friend, but yer lady's much too beautiful fer th' luckiest man alive!"

The mercenary lieutenant bowed clumsily but sincerely, and raised his ale horn in salute.

"T' yer beauty, my lady, which lights up th' room like th' sun."
He turned to the proprietor. "Innkeep!" he bellowed, "Ale! Ale fer me an' my mates and this Odin-blessed warrior an' his goddess!"

Pe-Trok grinned, and answered in the vernacular, "I thank ye, friend. 'Twill honor my wife an' myself t' share a keg or two in such company."

He accepted a dripping flagon. "T' what be we drinkin', friend?"

The burly man-at-arms lifted his drinking horn. "We drink t' Olaf Knutssen, our Captain, now dead, a warrior such as is seldom seen in this world. An' t' th' damnation of th' whoreson dog, Baron Knecht."

He drained the horn, belched, and wiped his beard with the back of his hand.

"Until yesterday I was second in command to th' finest Captain ever served. Then that black-hearted swine Knecht fell on us with four times our strength. Th' attack were solely fer sport, we havin' no quarrel with him.

"We lost half th' Company in th' first rush, taken as we were, unaware, in country we had every reason to think friendly land."

To the surprise of the two Vanir, Lars Larssen threw back his head and bellowed with laughter. The lieutenant's merriment was echoed by the two dozen others in the room.

"Aye," Larssen chuckled, "Cut t' half strength we were in seconds. But, friend, this be th' Free Company of Olaf Knutssen by th' hammer o' Thor, an' Olaf rallied us instanter t' counterattack. Bein, by now eight t' one against us, th' foul dogs thought t' finish th' game easily."

The assembled mercenaries roared out again, waving their drinking-jacks and pounding on the tables with the hilts of their weapons.

"Aye," shouted one, "Th' game was finished all right, but not t' th' likin' o' Baron Knecht an' his men."

Lars Larssen lifted his ponderous two-handed sword. "With this I clove th' treacherous dog, Knecht, from crown t' waist!"
Unexpectedly, tears ran down the rough warrior's cheeks. "But not before th' whoreson had slain our Captain with a foul thrust in th' back."

"Aye," roared one of the mercenaries, "Ye were lucky t' get in a blow, Lars Larssen. . . ."

"As were we all," shouted another. "Olaf nigh slew th' lot single-handed afore bein' struck down by a coward's blow from th' rear!"

Bellows of admiration for their slain leader went up from the band again.

"T' Olaf! T' Olaf Knutssen, who even now must be sharin' a horn with th' Allfather, an' entertainin' th' Heroes o' Valhalla with th' saga o' his last battle!"

An expression of fierce intensity darkened the face of Lars Larssen. He raised his ale-horn and a wild war-cry burst from his throat. The Company fell silent.

"Aye," he screamed, "If there be any justice in Asgard. . . if th' Gods have any honor, that be so. Fer none ever fought so valiantly, nor were more of a Hero than Olaf Knutssen.

"An' if th' gods be not false, they be greetin' him as a brother!"

Pe-Trok felt a stab of guilt at the mercenary's remarks. ". . . *if th' gods have any honor. . . if the Gods be not false. . . .*"

It suddenly struck him that the solution of the problem of the Vanir lay before him.

Why not?

Why not turn the make-believe Valhalla into a real Hall of Heroes?

Here was the supply of life-memories to fill the blank minds of the frozen Vanir. Memories not tainted with senility.

Awareness that could be re-educated, given time. . . and the Vanir had plenty of that. . . re-educated to reconstruct the sleeping Starmen.

Pe-Trok mulled over the thought.

It was certainly something to put before the General Council.

By midnight, Sif had been pledged by every man of the Company, and every man-jack of them had fallen in love with her.

Pe-Trok felt as if his shoulders had been pounded to pulp by the exuberance of the congratulations on his having such a wife.

Shortly after moonset they managed to slip away. The grav-sled had been undiscovered and they were back in Asgard in under an hour. Not even stopping to shed his leather and steel, Pe-Trok called an immediate council meeting.

The question was: could the essence of a dying human be infused into a cryogenically frozen Vanir?

In the opinion of the more knowledgeable, the Vanir would essentially then become that human.

Very well. But with time and hypnotherapy, could he be reoriented as a Vanir?

Possibly.

Would elements of the human remain?

Quite likely.

Then we'd be preserving both the Vanir and the human to the advantage of both?

Yes! Yes!

We'd deprive the human of nothing. Actually we'd be giving him a sort of immortality, and restore one of our brothers at the same time.

All right. But what would be the effect on the human mind to be yanked out of his body, carried around in a jar, then injected into a stranger?

He'd go insane.

Right.

What if. . .?

What if the human were to be convinced that all that occurred was straight in line with all he'd been taught to believe?

What if he were taken from a field of battle by the Shining Maids, and carried aloft on a winged horse, across the Rainbow Bridge to the Hall of Heroes?

Yes!

Simple enough to project these thoughts hypnotically, and keep the human under hypnosis until he awoke in Valhalla, where he could be slowly indoctrinated to accept the reality of his existence.

It would work!

All right, interjected one of the goddesses, but what about the women?

A similar scenario could be worked out for the dying woman. A goddess could appear and carry her to. . . where?

To the palace of Frigga, Queen of the Gods, where she could live a life of quiet happiness serving the wife of the Allfather until her indoctrination was complete.

But would that be reward enough?

You know the harshness of the life of a Skandian woman. Yes, the prospect of uninterrupted happiness would be enough.

Done.

Details?

We need scouts to notify us of impending battles. No consciousness is to be taken before the absolute certainty of death.

Understood.

Scouts?

Built in.

The mythology says that Odin's two ravens, Hugin and Munin, daily fly over the Nine Worlds and bring him news.

Breed intelligent ravens, we have the technology, put a few in every flock, and train them to spot a Hero and bring the report back to us.

Then?

Then we send out the Valkyries.

Some of our specially trained medical technicians on grav-sleds. Mass hypnosis can, if necessary, cause all the combatants to see Shining Maids on winged horses. In fact that's a good thing to work for us.

Let them see their Heroes being chosen.

It can be done.

Then?

Then they put the helmet on the fallen Hero, and transfer his being to the electron chamber and bring it back here.

The human thinks he's riding on a flying horse clasped to the bosom of a Valkyrie.

No trauma. No shock.

We induce a short blackout. The Vanir is infused with the memories of the Hero, dressed in the Hero's battle-trappings, smeared with synthetic blood, and taken to Valhalla.

There he wakes to find himself being bathed by the Battle Maids, his wounds miraculously healed.

He is clad in new armor and introduced to his fellow Heroes. Curtain. End of Act One. As the Mead Hall fills with actual Heroes, we phase out the androids.

It'll work.

No it won't.

Why not?

Too much time consumed in putting helmet on fallen hero. It'll weaken the illusion. We've got to find a way around that.

Back to the lab?

Back to the lab.

It didn't take so long this time. The basic elements were in place.

After a few failures, San-Ka modified his original concept of a helmet to a receiver that achieved the same result with a diffused beam.

They were ready for a field test.

It worked.

CHAPTER THIRTY FIVE

The history took several days to relate in its fullness.

Pete showed Jerry all around back-stage Asgard. "It was a little over eight and a half thousand years ago that San-Ka completed his electron chamber.

"There have been improvements since. Things go a lot more smoothly now, but it still takes severeal years in Valhalla to complete the transition.

"We must let the human absorb the reality slowly to insure the safety of his ego, and the safety of his sanity, for he must benefit as fully as the Vanir."

Jerry looked at the Commander. "You were the original Pe-Trok who was Third Officer on the Starship?"

"Yes, but I've been through Valhalla quite a number of times."

Jerry thought back. "Then you must have been one of the cryogenically preserved ones."

"No. The rejuvenation is necessary only every fifteen hundred to two thousand years. I had been through the process aboard ship shortly before the crash."

He smiled. "But I was getting pretty close to the edge when I came up with the plan.

"At the start, fifty years after reawakening were needed for the human to fully understand
and the Vanir to re-learn what he had forgotten.

"This is no longer necessary. We have caught up on the backlog of the preserved and now, when senility approaches, we can do what we did back home, place the Vanir in a state of suspended animation before the condition is too far advanced, and infuse him with a Hero before his own memories are lost.

"But we have to proceed slowly in letting the human become aware of the true state of things. To apprise him immediately of the presence of another mind would have the same effect as predicted when the question was posed as to what would have happened if San-Ka's life memories were absorbed by another person.

"It would destroy the human and that is unacceptable to us."

Jerry looked at Pe-Trok with a little frown of puzzlement wrinkling his brow. "I don't get it. I 'infused' the body of Jar Haz and I was immediately aware of what was going on. I didn't go crazy. . . or *did* I?"

Pe-Trok laughed. "No, Jerry Haskins of San Diego California USA, called Jerry Jar Haz Thor's Fist. You are not hallucinating all this.

"The situation is not parallel. You had knowledge beforehand that a change was coming. You are also more culturally advanced than the simple peoples of the Nine Worlds. Valhalla is still necessary to protect the barbarian from traumatic shock. The Vanir is immediately aware of the infusion, but holds back his own persona, allowing the barbarian to become aware of the truth slowly, in doses he can handle."

Pete said sincerely, "I am happy to be able to say that we Vanir aren't just rationalizing an act of selfishness.

"The melding of Vanir and human is truly of benefit to both. The human lives for hundreds of years beyond his life expectancy, and is as much a part of the experience as is the Vanir. The human comes to understand and accept that when the senility again approaches in one to two thousand years, he will be replaced by another Hero."

The Commander looked at Jerry.

"I am not only Pe-Trok the Vanir, but also Knute Ericssen, onetime Captain of a Company of Free Companions."

Jerry grinned. "I'm pleased to meet both of you."

He sobered. "I think I'm ready to meet Jar Haz face to face now."

Pete smiled. "The Viking has completed enough of his transition to be aware of his duality, and understand the bond between the two of you. Yes, it's time you met."

Pete stood. "We go to Valhalla. Resume your Skandian dress and weapons, and meet me back here in half an hour."

Jerry was reminded just how much of a Skandian he had become as he donned his steel and leather.

He felt more natural than he had in days, with the weight of chain mail on his shoulders and the comforting bulk of his rapier at his belt.

Tucking his helmet in the crook of his arm, Jerry returned to the Commander's office. As he entered he stopped abruptly and stared.

Pe-Trok of Vanir had vanished. In his place stood Thor, God of Thunder, Protector of the City of the Gods.

Jerry knew that it was an optical illusion, but the Vanir seemed to have grown larger. He looked wider and taller. His red beard bristled pugnaciously, and his red hair fell to his shoulders in ringlets. He was clad in a red wool chiton with short sleeves and his biceps bulged mightily. The chiton fell to just below his knees and his thick, muscular legs and feet were bare except for the cross-gartering of his sandals. About his waist was the Thunder God's magic girdle that doubled his strength. He wore the steel glove with which to catch the thunderbolt when it returned to his hand, and resting on his shoulder was the great iron hammer, Mjollnir.

Pete grinned and flexed his muscles.

"Pretty impressive, wouldn't you say?"

At sight of Mjollnir a question rose in Jerry's mind. "Why does Brokk get mad every time that hammer's mentioned?"

Pete laughed.

"I'm afraid I'm responsible for the little man's problem."

The Starman sobered. "You have lived with the Dwarf King for over a year and a half. You are even his adopted son. But you still have not realized the depth and scope of that hammered down little giant."

An expression of respect showed on the Vanir's face. "Brokk Hammermacher of Svartheim is truly King of the Dwarfs. He is a power not only in the dwarfholm, but acknowledged throughout the Nine Worlds as the master of all masters in the art of metalworking. His skill is legend.

"Look at your own hand. a small miracle of technology wrought under the most primitive conditions."

The Vanir smiled.

"Brokk's reputation is well deserved. Years ago on one of my holidays in Midgard I carelessly damaged my laser pistol. We Vanir carry Skandian weapons, naturally, but we're not really all that good with them, so we copper our bets by taking along a weapon we *can* use."

The Starman shrugged. "It's not *really* cheating. We avoid conflict as much as possible, and we fail to see why we should die just because some oaf wants to play rough."

Jerry grinned. "Makes perfect sense to me. I guess you could say that I'm cheating with this rapier and my knowledge of fencing in a world that knows nothing but brute force."

He mimicked the Vanir's shrug. "As you say, it's a matter of survival in a world where survival is all. Don't apologize on my account."

Thor matched his grin. "Anyway, to get back to the Dwarf King.

"I damaged my laser, and being not too far from Svartheim, decided to see if the reports of the dwarf's skill were grounded in fact. I decided to bring the weapon to the master armorer to find out if his reputation were justified.

"It wasn't easy to get in to see him. Beings other than dwarfs are not generally welcomed in the caverns of the underground world, as you know, so I had to use a little godly magic. By means of hypnosis I caused the dwarfs to see only a fellow dwarf, and was passed by the guardians and allowed to proceed to the master's workshop.

"Alone with Brokk, I reverted to my normal appearance, well, the appearance of Thor the Thunderer, and presented him with my laser gun. He was fascinated by it."

Pete's expression of respect deepened. "All I told the little man was that the device was broken."

The Starman's tone of voice proclaimed his admiration. "The dwarf took this piece of totally alien technology to his workbench and in a matter of minutes he disassembled it, and studied the various parts.

"He grunted to himself then, separating the damaged element from the rest, proceeded to fabricate a delicate replacement part with only his forge, his hammer, and the skill of his fingers!

"Two hours later he reassembled the weapon and took aim at a helmet sitting on the bench.

"Well, it worked. Of course the dwarf had no way of knowing the power of a laser blaster. It not only disintegrated the helmet, but blew a sizable hole in the wall of his shop as well."

Pete grinned. "He had just hurled one of Thor's thunderbolts! Scared the hell out of him!

"You can understand that there was no way I could leave and allow the little man to retain memory of this alien weapon.

At first I thought I'd play it cute, and leave him with the belief that Thor the Thunder God had come to him for a hammer. I even planted that thought before I came to my senses and erased all recollection of my visit. I left thinking that I had taken care of everything."

Pe-Trok grinned crookedly.

"All right. I admit that the whole adventure was an unforgivable piece of childish foolishness."

He laughed. "But then, we gods, like humans, are sometimes subject to acts of childishness. At any rate, I *had* been careless, and somewhere along the line my post-hypnotic suggestion slipped a cog.

"One night Brokk got severely drunk with some friends, and a partial recollection surfaced. He mentioned forging Thor's hammer. The next morning his friends questioned him about it, but the memory had vanished, and he flatly denied having said any such thing.

"You have seen the result. His friends teased him unmercifully about it, and the story spread. Now you know why he gets mad."

Jerry chuckled.

Pete hefted Mjollnir and grinned. "Ready to meet Jar Haz?"

The sprawling longhouse called Valhalla was constructed of rough-hewn logs. The interior walls were hung with the skins of bear, wolf, and boar, and brightened with the gaily painted shields of the Heroes.

Conspicuously absent were any weapons. The Vanir, aware of the volatile nature of their Heroes were taking no chances that their guests would kill each other a second time.

At each end of the long hall whole carcasses of boar, deer, and oxen turned on roasting spits in vast stone fireplaces, the dripping juices filling the space with a delicious aroma. Huge barrels of ale and mead stood open-ended, so that the android serving girls had only to dip the drinking horns and ale-jacks to fill them for the thirsty revelers that thronged the long trestle tables of the Mead Hall of Odin. The place was a-roar with shouts, raucous laughter, loud bragging voices, joyous singing.

A great shout went up as the god Thor and Jerry entered. Thor raised his hammer in greeting to his 'father,' Odin.

En-Kap An-Zok, enthroned on a fur-covered bench on a raised dais, and playing his role of Allfather with boisterous gusto, waved a huge overflowing jack of ale, and bellowed a return greeting.

It was some time before Pete and Jerry could break clear of the press of admiring warriors, many of whom had heard of Jerry Jar Haz called Thor's Fist.

Jerry, looking over the heads of the jostling Heroes, spotted Jar Haz, momentarily jolted to recognize himself in the Viking. He and Pe-Trok elbowed their way through the admiring crowd.

The Viking looked at Jerry out of the Vanir's eyes. "I've been told of you, Jerry Haskins called Jar Haz, Thor's Fist."

He grinned crookedly.

"I thought I was prepared, but 'tis sore strange t' be lookin' at myself lookin' back at me!"

"Aye, Jar Haz the Hero," Jerry replied soberly, "it takes a bit of getting used to."

Both laughed and struck hands. Jar Haz examined his former self. His eyes fell on the steel hand.

"I remember losin' that hand t' a whoreson swordsman with a great yellow beard."

He held up his left hand. "Th' gods have restored it." A wistful look came into his eyes. "'Twas Bryn's warnin' that saved me from losin' my head t' th' bastard. How be Bryn? Even in Valhalla I miss her."

Thor left the two warriors alone to get to know one another. Jerry brought his alter-ego up to date.

The Viking was fascinated by Jerry's tale of time travel, and the adventures of his trek to Asgard.

It was a strange encounter.

Happily, Jerry could see that the meeting was as inwardly satisfying

232   Frank O. Dodge

to the Viking as it was to him. At last they shook hands, Jerry feeling the warmth of the Skandian's friendship, and returning it in like measure.

On another occasion, Jar Haz and Jerry Jar Haz met with Olin and Lars, who were joyously reuniting with Orm.

The young Hero hadn't been long enough in Valhalla to as yet understand the reality, and was the same warm, slyly humorous Orm they'd known in Midgard.

It was as if they'd never been parted. They were joined by Brokk, Ulf, Hjalmar the Axeman, and most of the Company.

The goblin, who had fought so many battles shoulder to shoulder with Orm told how sorely he missed the young mercenary, and became rather emotional as the evening wore on.

It was quite a bash.

As the stay lengthened, Jerry neglected none of his friends. He visited frequently with Freya and Maryam at the palace of Frigga, Queen of the Gods, and kept in constant touch with Brokk.

He felt guilty and uncomfortable at withholding the facts from his friends, but could tell them only that the gods were working on his problem.

The day arrived when Jerry told Pe-Trok, that much as he enjoyed Asgard, he wanted desperately to get on with his search for his wife. Could the Vanir help him or could they not?

The Vanir could.

Pete chuckled understandingly. "Come on," he said, "I want to show you something."

The Vanir led the way. "It's a gadget that we fooled around with a few centuries ago. We decided that it didn't have enough practical value to waste a lot of time on, so it's been sitting on the shelf until we heard about you."

He laughed. "That's another of the reasons you were left to trek across Skandia instead of being contacted at once. We needed time to reactivate the thing and get it working."

The Vanir turned into a side corridor. He pointed to the sign over a **door: TEMPORAL DISPLACEMENT LABORATORY.**

Pete grinned. "Fancy way of saying Time Machine."

Jerry came to a halt.

"Time machine? *Time Machine*? What. . .?"

Pe-Trok laughed, "Jerry," he said, "What did you have in mind when you set out to seek the help of the gods?"

"What do you mean?"

"I mean just what sort of help did you propose to ask for? Just what did you imagine the gods could do to solve your problem?"

Jerry's face reddened. "Hell, I don't know. I guess I really didn't give it much thought. Looking for gods was. . . hell, I don't know. Everybody seemed to think you'd wave a magic wand, or toss Fairy Dust in the air and sing 'jim-jam-bonny-meecha-kambo' or something, and everything would come out peachy.

"Hell, Pete, I never went looking for any gods before. How the hell did I know what I expected? I'm an *insurance salesman*, for the love of Mike. What do I know about gods?"

The Starman chuckled. "Exactly the way we felt about it when your Odin's Messenger dumped the problem in our laps.

"It was much too intriguing a riddle to ignore, but to quote you, what the hell did *we* know about it?

"We were in the same dilemma as you. How do gods or anybody else go about locating somebody who may be drifting along an unknown timeline or who may be just across the street, two houses down? Most interesting.

"Look, Jerry. This god business gets awfully boring at times, *most* of the time, actually. Of course we have our routine research and development programs to pursue until we get word from home, but Jerry, *ten thousand years!*

"That's more than a long weekend even for the Vanir! To have a challenge like this come along was, if you'll pardon the pun, a godsend! Do you see why you became so important?

"*A time traveler!* Not only that, but a time traveler with a fascinating problem!

"We've been experimenting with this time device off and on for centuries, but as I said, it hadn't much practical application. The time-span was too short.

"Then you came along! Time seemed to be the obvious answer, so the project assumed new interest.

"Everybody wanted a hand in the game, but time travel was the jurisdiction of the time travel boys, and they've put everything they've got into the project. I think you'll be happy with the result."

Pete pushed open the door. "I'll let the Director explain it to you." Om-Jak Toth En-Mork, head of the time-study lab, shook Jerry's hand. "You've certainly stirred things up in here, I can tell you! I suppose Pe Trok has told you what we propose to try."

"No, he said he'd leave that to you."

"All right."

The temporal scientist waved his visitors to seats, and sat behind his desk. He steepled his fingers. "When the scout raven recorded his report of all he'd seen and heard in the caverns of the dwarfholm, we learned of a being who had transmigrated from another time and space, into the corpus of a dweller of this time and space.

"That, of itself, was something to stimulate the imagination. Something we *had* to know more about. But then, in continuing his report the bird told of yet another manifestation.

"He recorded seeing two other beings materialize at a short distance as you lay pinned. There was something about these two newcomers that is not quite clear. Something beyond the bird's ability to comprehend."

Jerry jerked upright.

Om-Jak paused and smiled.

"The surprises, friend Jerry, are not yet over. *An entire Company of Free Companions stepped out of the air!* The leaders of the mercenaries conferred with the other two. . . ."

The project head's voice trailed off.

"Don't quit on me now," Jerry yelped, "What *happened?*"

The lab director waved a hand. "We don't know. At that point, the stone on which the raven sat moved under him, and when he looked again for the other figures, they'd vanished. Odin's Messenger elected to remain with you, and followed you and the dwarf down into the tunnel."

Jerry drummed his fingers on the lab chief's desk. "Okay. So?"

Om-Jak smiled at the youngster's impatience. "So," he said, "it's safe to assume that the first two figures were your wife and the Hindu Mystic . . . you heard her voice, remember. Who the others, the mercenary troop, were, was a mystery.

"One thing of which we were sure, though, is that they were normal time travelers. . . ."

"Normal time travelers," Jerry said dryly.

The temporal expert grinned. "I keep forgetting that what is accepted as ordinary here in the lab, might seem extraordinary to others.

"What I meant was that they appeared in corpus. . . bodily. . . whereas you were a metaphysical manifestation such as we'd never encountered before.

"We went over and over the scout bird's report. We knew it to be accurate as far as it went, the ravens are trained to be accurate.

"But what to make of it? Puzzle piled upon puzzle! Can you imagine the excitement you've caused here?"

Om-Jak laughed.

"We went over and over it until our heads were spinning, then one of my young assistants came up with a viable theory. What if the mercenary Company were you and some friends arriving to rejoin you with your wife?"

Jerry let out an involuntary, and purely Skandian battle-scream of triumph, and immediately beet red, he apologized.

"Uh, sorry. . . . fellows? You can come out from under that desk. . . ."

CHAPTER THIRTY SIX

Things were moving along.

Jerry listened as the project director started a long technical explanation of the apparatus.

Pe-Trok came to the rescue. "Save it for your grandchildren," Pete said impatiently. "Jerry doesn't know what you're talking about, and I don't care. Keep it short."

The time machine consisted of a small chamber with a door on each side. It was surrounded by ultra-high-frequency electromagnets and impressive looking copper coils and other gadgets that defied description.

When activated, the magnetic field generated was so powerful that it warped the very fabric of time and space, opening a gate between the worlds through which one could step back into the past.

Bewildering banks of dials and vectors and flashing lights allowed the technicians to fine-tune the temporal displacer to the exact distance into time one wanted to go.

Om-jak, the Project Director, patted the control console of the time-warp machine.

"This," he said, "will transport you through time, but of itself, that's all it does. To move you from here, to where you want to go in terms of physical space, this is necessary."

He picked up a bulky helmet with coils and antennae, linked to the time machine by thick cables.

"This amplifier allows a trained psychokinetic technician to teleport you at the same time to a specific, pre-selected destination."

Jerry walked around the impressive mass of technology shaking his head.

"You sure this thing works?"

Om-Jak smiled. "It works. We can set you down when and where you want to go, within reasonable limits."

Jerry snorted. "Uh-huh. And just what do you consider reasonable limits?"

The Project director grinned.

"Well, we couldn't, for example, set you down on the moon seven thousand years ago."

Jerry grunted. "I don't want to go to the moon. Just how accurate *are* you?"

"We can put you within two feet of a given spot, and within a nano-second of a specified time."

The red-beard looked dubious. "I don't know as I'd care to miss the rim of Ginnungagap by two feet, or wind up standing knee-deep in a rock."

Pe-Trok laughed. "These lab types have a habit of not mentioning little things like that."

Om-Jak sounded a bit stuffy. "Very funny. Actually, we wouldn't consider sending anyone through if there weren't built-in safety factors."

Jerry looked at him. "Like what?"

Om-Jak grinned. "I could tell you," he said, "but unless you have about a hundred and fifty years of fourth-dimensional theory and quantum math in your resume, you wouldn't understand it."

Jerry returned the Director's grin. "Touche'."

"Stated simply, there are safeguards against a traveler's emerging within a solid object.

"Such an occurrence would result in an explosion that would rend the planet. You have no need to fear that. And as for falling into Ginnungagap, we allow leeway for things like that.

"At any rate there'll be no glitches in your case.

"We've cross-checked the information you've given us with the vectors given by the scout raven, and we've pinpointed the exact spot and optimum time to set you back at the foot of the hillside where the Viking fought his last battle."

Om-Jak paused. "I'll be going with you. I must talk with the Hindu about how he transported your consciousness extracorporeally from one time to another."

Pete snorted. "Why do all you lab boys have to talk such gobbelty-gook gibberish? *Extracorporeally!*" He snorted again. "Why in the hell can't you just say out of body?"

Om Jak grinned. "Then we'd have nothing to razzle-dazzle you administrative types with.

The Hindus's result is similar to our method of bringing up the Heroes, but he did it without technology, *and* across time! I have to talk to him!"

Jerry broke in impatiently.

"I don't care if you bring your Aunt Fanny and your Uncle Bud. All

I want to know is *when do we get started?*"

"Patience. Patience. It will take a little time to set up. From what we know now from the raven's report, all of Hjalmar the Axeman's Company go with us.

"Can you imagine marching them through here? We've got to make a few preparations."

Jerry fought down the urge to act like a sullen little boy. "Yeah. I see what you mean. But dammit. . . ."

Pete clapped him on the shoulder. "We'll make it as quickly as possible."

The red-beard grinned sourly. "I know. But to be this close makes every delay seem like a lifetime."

Om-Jak briefed Jerry on the scenario devised to preserve the Skandians' beliefs in their mythology, and protect the Vanir from exposure.

The Director looked at Jerry. "Sound okay to you?"

Jerry nodded. "Yes, it'll work fine, but I hate having to lie to my friends."

"I'm sorry. I fully understand your dislike but there's no other way. It's up to you to persuade them."

"Hold it," Jerry said. "There'll be no persuading. The men will make their own decisions."

Pe-Trok broke in. "This whole conversation's academic anyway. We already know that they went."

It was Om-Jak's turn to interrupt.

"If," he said. "If Han-Ok's theory is correct, and the Company is that of Hjalmar."

Jerry snorted disgustedly.

"Hell! You big brains can if all you want to. I'm going to talk to Brokk and the others. We'll find out what's what and when's when when the time comes."

He turned to Pe-Trok. "Pete, will you get me down to the Plain of Vigard?"

Jerry stepped from the gatehouse of Heimdall the Watcher, stopped and turned to Pe-Trok. "Dammit, Pete, I understand the necessity of keeping the truth from them, but I hate it. They're more than just friends. They'd never lie to me, and my keeping silent is just the same as lying to them. I feel like a traitor to their trust."

Pe-Trok cleared his throat and looked uncomfortable.

Jerry eyed him. "What?"

"Jerry," he said, embarrassed, "if it will make you feel any better, you couldn't tell them anything about us if you tried. Now I feel like the traitor, but if you'll reflect, you'll see that we have no choice."

"You planted a post-hypnotic suggestion."

"We had to."

Jerry laughed. "I should have guessed."

"You're not angry?"

"Under the circumstances? No. See you later."

Not being Heroes, the company had tired of the eternal revelry of Valhalla, and had returned to their camp. That's where Jerry expected them, and that's where he found them.

The breezes of the Plain of Vigard were cool and pleasant, while far below them the arctic wastes of Jotunheim continued to be lashed by the frigid jet stream. The broad Plain was well populated with the camps of those who had come seeking audience with the gods, but even if Jerry hadn't known where Hjalmar's tents were pitched, the camp would be easy to find.

One had only to look for the Axeman's personal standard, a huge red banner with a black axe, rippling proudly in the light air.

Jerry strode into the camp with his helmet under his arm, his red hair streaming loose. Maryam was first to spot him.

"Mother," she called excitedly, "Jerry's here."

The elf-woman emerged from her tent and smiled her happiness. "Jerry," she said, opening her arms. The red-beard knelt and kissed her hand. Freya laughed and hugged him.

Jerry rose and looked around at the others who had quickly gathered.

"Ye've news!" Brokk exclaimed. "I can see it in yer face!"

Jerry laughed. "Aye, Father," he said exultantly, "the gods have found the way!"

The dwarf harrumphed. "An' about time," he snorted.

Jerry looked at the assembled Company. The entire band had gathered, eager to learn their next step. The red-beard felt a surge of pride and affection for these rough soldiers-of-fortune who followed, not because of Brokk's gold, but because a bond had been forged out of mutual respect and comradeship. Down to the last men-at-arms they would stand beside each other.

Jerry stepped up onto an overturned camp kettle so as to be seen and heard by all. From their expressions as they waited for him to speak, all, even Brokk, were impressed by the special favor shown the red-beard by the High Gods of Skandia.

He looked at each man in turn, and was gratified by the loyalty and affection reflected in the faces of these fierce, tough followers. "I have just come from Odin," he said. "The Allfather has found a way to help me continue my search."

He paused and let his eyes rove over the assemblage. "I ask no man to follow where I must go. . . ."

He was interrupted by howls and shouts from the men. A stentorian voice bellowed from the ranks. "Ye lead, Thor's Fist, an' we'll follow ye straight into Nifflheim itself if ye wish it so!"

Roars of affirmation rent the air.

Jerry raised his hands for silence. "Hear me out, friends. The way I must go is one never before traveled, and is strange and filled with dangers. . . ."

He was immediately drowned out by cries of denial. Hjalmar brandished his ponderous axe. "Ye do us injustice, Lord Jerry. Ha' we not, every man o' us, proved our contempt fer danger?"

Jerry looked at the angry Captain. "Aye, Hjalmar. None have shown more clearly their bravery. Never accuse me of doubting your courage, or holding lightly the loyalty of your hearts."

The red-beard raised his clenched steel fist.

"Hear me. It's not doubt of your valor that prompts me to speak. It's that very valor that I must warn you against on the unworldly road I must take.

"The dangers that beset this path are not the dangers of combat where you can fight back, but the dangers that lie between the worlds. The dangers of Weird. . . the dangers of the unknown."

A hulking broadswordsman, with the skin of an ice bear he'd slain single-handedly thrown over his shoulder, pushed his way to the fore. "We'll hear ye, my Lord Jerry, then we'll follow where ye lead."

Jerry's eyes stung, and he had to wait a moment before he could continue. "And if I lead out of this world?"

The broadswordsman laughed and cut whistling figure-eights in the air with his sword. "In this world or out, my Lord, th' edge of my blade will be as sharp."

There came a mighty clash of weapons on shields, and a deep roar of agreement went up from the Company.

Jerry again raised his steel hand.

He grinned. "Never have I seen such a stubborn, unruly mob of ruffians."

This sally was greeted with fierce laughter.

"All right, then. I lead through the Land of Weird, through the tunnel of death, on a journey back through time to the place where I will find what I seek. D'you still insist on following?"

A hush fell over the ranks. The mercenaries looked at one another, then again clashed their weapons.

Hjalmar the Axeman spoke for all of them. "If death be where ye lead, then that be where we go."

"Aye! Aye!"

"You misheard me. I said *through* the tunnel of death. If you heed *my every word*, I'll lead you, and you'll not be harmed."

"What difference? Ye lead, we follow."

"What difference? Did you hear me say that you must heed my *every* command to the letter, or I'll not take you?"

His answer was another mighty clash of weapons.

Jerry looked at Brokk.

The dwarf grinned, and lifted his mace. "Ye heard, my son."

Freya and Maryam nodded, and Ulf shook his assegai.

"I've not come this far t' go back now," Lars o' th' Battlefield laughed. "Besides it can be no worse than facin' Jotunheim again."

This brought a gale of laughter from the men.

Jerry grinned.

"Very well, then. Listen closely to my commands. You must. . . you must. . . heed my every word. On this hangs your only chance of life. You must do *exactly* what I tell you and you must do *nothing* else. To deviate from my orders in the slightest can destroy us all.

"We journey back in time. Into our own past that has already happened. *If any single man of you should do anything that would alter that past in any way, we could all simply vanish as if we had never been.*

"That is the danger I warned of. It is not something that can be faced with courage, axe, and broadsword. It is not something you can fight.

"Therein lies the peril. "You are all men of action, and I'm telling you you cannot act. You *all* have to understand that or we are *all* doomed."

Jerry fell silent and studied the men. "Do you understand?"

"We're t' face a foe we're forbidden t' fight?" Hjalmar the Axeman's face was troubled.

Jerry shook his head. "The foe will be within yourselves. You will be tempted to lash out. It is this battle instinct that you have to fight. You must do nothing, say nothing, until I give you leave."

"Are we, then, settin' an ambush?"

"Not exactly, but that's a good parallel. You must act as though setting an ambush."

Ah.

This was something that, as trained warriors, they could all relate to. Having laid many a trap, all knew that silence and instant obedience were vital.

Jerry scanned the ranks.

"Let me tell you something of what to expect. You will enter the tunnel through time and Weird, and therein will see monsters in the mist, ghosts, and fearsome shapes.

"They will not harm you *if you obey my commands*. At the end of the tunnel you will step out onto the field that will still be littered with the fallen of a mighty battle. The last fight of Jar Haz the Viking, now a Hero in Val. . . ."

He was drowned out by cries of wonder and amazement.

Hjalmar the Axeman bellowed for quiet. "Silence! Silence, ye brayin' jackasses! Let Lord Jerry speak!"

The men fell silent. Jerry continued.

"When you step out on the field, find immediate cover. Go to ground, and remain silent and still. No matter what you see, no matter what you hear, *do nothing, say nothing until I give the order*. Do you understand?"

Again the clash of weapons. "Aye!"

Jerry shook his steel fist. "I ask you again, do you understand?"

Sobered by Jerry's intensity, the men fell silent. Hjalmar the Axeman spoke. "Aye, my lord Jerry, it shall be as ye say."

"Very well. Strike camp. We leave at once."

CHAPTER THIRTY SEVEN

Years of experience had made the Company proficient at striking camp, rolling tents, bundling personal belongings, and getting on the march in a surprisingly short time.

The Free Companions of Hjalmar the Axeman were ready to move out in fifteen minutes.

With Bryn trotting at his side, Odin's Messenger perched on her broad back as usual, Jerry led the way up a steep trail to a cave high up on the Peak. He paused, and faced the Company.

"From this point, comrades, the order to remain silent and take no action is in effect. Follow closely the path I take, and no harm will befall you."

He raised his clenched iron fist, and entered the cave. The men followed by squads, each squad leader muttering dire threats as to what would happen to any man who disobeyed the Lord Jerry.

The Company moved into a world of illusion created by Om-Jak.

All that they saw and experienced there, was the result of the mass hypnosis at which the Vanir were so adept, but that made it no less real to the men.

They were met just within the entrance by Om-Jak in the guise of a man-at-arms.

"This is Thorwald Thorssen," Jerry introduced. "He will guide us through the Land of Weird in safety. Obey orders and no harm will befall you."

To Om-Jak and Jerry, it was a walk down a long hallway.

To the men, who saw and experienced just what the Vanir wished them to see and experience, it was a trek through an underground world of cold gray mists which swirled eerily, and were filled with half-seen monsters and horrid phantoms that loomed and retreated.

More than anyone, Jerry knew that the Free Companions of the Company of Hjalmar the Axeman had never shown more courage than during the terrifying journey through the Land of Death.

Deprived, by Jerry's orders, of the use of their battle skills and weapons, only the rigid discipline of Hjalmar the Axeman, and their own iron nerve, so often displayed, saw them through the ordeal.

At journey's end they faced what they were led to believe was a formless wall of nothingness, through which they stepped to find that they were standing at the foot of a corpse-littered hillside.

In reality, they had entered the Time Lab through a long hall, and passed through the temporal displacement chamber.

Om-Jak had predicted accurately, and Jerry felt an eerie shudder as he looked at himself lying with his arm pinned beneath the boulder. Bryn lay across his legs, and Odin's Messenger perched on another rock.

The raven had its head cocked to one side, and fixed him with an inquisitive golden eye. But Jerry's attention was drawn and held by the sight of two not-quite-solid figures who stood looking at the wounded Jerry. . . the wounded Jar Haz. . . the man who lay with one arm crushed under a great rock.

Bryn at his side, looked from her master lying on the ground, to her master standing at her side, and emitted a low whine of confusion.

Jerry touched her head. "Quiet, girl."

The rest of the Company stepped out of the air, and obeying orders, found cover.

Jerry and Om-Jak approached the not-quite-solid figures. The red-beard looked at the Vanir. "Will she understand Skandian?"

Om-Jak smiled, and nodded. "No problem to plant the language in her mind."

At the sound of footsteps, Janet turned and let out a little squeak of surprise to find Jerry standing beside her.

Like Bryn, the girl swiveled her head from Jerry to Jerry. Neither was Jerry, but both were *Jerry.*

The girl's face was a sea of churning emotions.

There was a difference in both these Jerrys from the Jerry she had known. . . the Jerry. . . in her time-frame. . . she'd seen only moments ago. . . but despite the difference, she showed no doubt that he was Jerry.

With a glad cry, she flung her arms around her husband. But she was without substance, and to the dismay of both, her arms passed right through him.

Jahawarlal Mukkergee uttered a sigh of compassion. He had tried to warn the girl that such might be the case.

Janet looked at her husband and began to cry. "Oh, Jerry. Oh, Jerry."

"Don't cry, darling. Things will work out."

"But I want to kiss you."

Jerry's smile was a little crooked.

"I've a few thoughts along that line myself. It's been nearly two years since I've seen you."

Janet looked blank. "*Two years*? But it's been only a few minutes since. . . ."

Jerry laughed. "It's a long story, sweetheart."

"And it's going to have to wait," Om-Jak broke in, grasping Jerry's elbow, "the dwarf is about to emerge from the tunnel."   Jerry motioned urgently. "Over here, honey. Don't ask questions, just move!"

Om-Jak and Jerry urged Janet and the Hindu out of sight just as Brokk stepped from the tunnel under the rock.

It was just as fascinating to Jerry as it was to Janet, to watch the dwarf scuttle across to the stream and return with the potion that had relieved his pain.

To watch while Brokk constructed the travois, and carried man and dog underground. At last the big boulder rotated and lowered, sealing the mouth of the tunnel.

Jerry stood up.

"Father," he called, "Mother! She's here! Janet's here!"

He turned. "Hjalmar! Have the men make camp. Ulf. . . . No, wait. I'd better prepare her for you!"

The goblin's deep laughter sounded from a nearby gully.

Janet and the Hindu both goggled as scores of leather-and-steel clad men rose from cover and, grinning broadly, went about setting up camp.

Janet stared from the wild-looking, hard-bitten men to the husband who had just issued crisp orders which the men jumped to obey. Was this her Jerry?

This stalwart, self-assured. . . warrior. . . who commanded with such authority?

The Jerry she remembered, the Jerry of, in her time-frame, less than minutes ago, was confident enough, and certainly competent enough in his field.

But to be honest, her Jerry had never struck her as being a leader of men who could snap orders to a band of such obviously trained and experienced fighters as those surrounding her.

Janet took a longer look at this man of hers. Yes, it was Jerry, right enough.

He didn't exactly *look* like Jerry. There was a subtle difference, but he was her Jerry.

The love in his voice was her Jerry. The love in his eyes when he looked at her was her Jerry.

She took in the bronzed skin, his firm, assured expression. The barbaric dress, and weapons. This was a Jerry out of a romance novel!

She giggled.

Om-Jak had drawn the little Hindu aside, and the two were in deep conversation.

Bryn, with a puzzled look on her scarred face, seemed to be trying to figure out why her master's mate had no scent.

The war-dog whined her confusion, and Jerry patted her head. He grinned. "Don't let it throw you, old girl."

Brokk and Freya approached, smiling warmly.

"Father, Mother," Jerry said, "this is Janet.

"Sweetheart, I want you to meet my godfather, Brokk Hammermacher, and his wife, my godmother, Freya of the Black Forest Elves."

He smiled. "You just watched Brokk carry me down into Svartheim, the dwarfholm, and you saw how beat-up I was."

Jerry took Freya's hand and kissed it. "Freya is the one who sewed me back together and mothered me back to health."

Janet's hand flew to her mouth as she remembered the handless arm on the man Brokk had carried into the tunnel. Her eyes went to Jerry's steel fist. The red-beard raised it, and flexed the metal fingers.

"A gift from my godfather, the finest smith in all the Nine Worlds."

He looked at Brokk. "Odin, himself, said that even the gods couldn't have fashioned a better one."

The dwarf grinned at the praise.

Janet's expression was so bewildered that Jerry broke out laughing. "Poor baby. You must be having one hell of a time trying to take all this in. Men in armor popping out of nowhere, dwarfs, elves. . . two Jerrys. Talk about gods. . . ."

He chuckled.

"Honey, I've been here almost two years, and I still find it a little, shall we say. . . strange?"

Freya's face showed that she was almost as frustrated as Jerry that she couldn't take the girl in her arms. "You cannot know how happy it makes us to see the two of you together. Our Jerry talked of nothing but you while his spirit wandered in the Land of Weird."

The elf-woman laughed softly.

"To be sure, he has talked of little else since his senses returned."

Brokk grinned at Janet and put an arm around his wife.

"It was this one who badgered us into makin' this journey t' reunite th' two o' ye. An' a long, strange trek it's been."

The dwarf eyed Janet's insubstantial form and shook his head.

"'Twould seem th' journey's not yet o'er. But keep yer heart high, child, a way will be found."

The girl looked around at the bustle, as Hjalmar's men set up camp. She looked at the hillside above, littered with the horrifying aftermath of Jar Haz's epic struggle. She shuddered at the sprawled bodies of the fallen, and looked away.

The graphic results of mortal combat were much more terrifying when seen first hand, than when depicted on television.

Even news footage of actual combat casualties failed to prepare one for the sight of human bodies hacked and bleeding real blood.

The gentle girl looked at Jerry. The realization of the savagery of this world made her wonder how much it had changed her husband.

Freya's elfin awareness sensed the turmoil within the girl, and divined its origin. She touched Jerry's hand, and looked at Janet with understanding. "My dear," she said, "You are remembering the Jerry of, to you, only moments ago, and looking at the skilled fighting man two years of war have changed him into, and you are wondering if he is still the same gentle man you married.

"Janet dear, if Jerry had gone away to fight in one of the wars of your world, he would have returned to you changed by the experience. The only difference is that, if that had been the case, you would have had time to realize and accept that he would be changed.

"Look into his eyes, dear, and tell me what you see."

The girl peered intently into Jerry's eyes. A tender smile of happiness curved her lips. "I see my Jerry, Mother Freya. I see my Jerry."

It is well that none of Hjalmar's men were near. They would have been shocked to see tears trickling down the cheeks of their red-bearded leader.

Janet shook her head, her bewilderment showing in her face, and smiled a little lopsidedly.

"I don't suppose I have to tell you how confusing all this is to me."

Brokk chuckled. "Ye're not alone in yer confusion, child. 'Tis a bit mind-bogglin' t' me as well. I ha' t' tell ye, I'm not accustomed t' watchin' myself do things I did nigh two years ago!"

Janet smiled at the expression on the dwarf's face. It was comforting to know that she wasn't the only one whose mind seemed to be filled with mush.

The girl was drawn more and more to Freya and the dwarf. The same love that they had given Jerry reached out to her.

With camp set up, many of the Company drifted to a respectful distance, eager to see the Lord Jerry's Lady. Most hung back, aware that their kind were not generally acceptable socially.

Jerry eyed the hard, tough faces of the men who had borne so much on his behalf to bring him here.

He remembered their loyalty.

He remembered the battle of Ethelstane Keep where they all risked their lives to rescue Maryam and the goblin.

He remembered the murderous trek across Jotunhiem. He remembered a hundred and one times each of them had risked his life for him.

He waved them forward.

The men, embarrassed, grinned and came closer. Jerry overturned a large iron camp kettle.

"Sweetheart," he said to Janet, "will you step up on this?"

She looked at him questioningly. Jerry smiled. "Please?"

Janet nodded, and got up on the kettle. Jerry raised his steel fist.

The Company fell silent and Janet once more marveled at this husband of hers who commanded such respect.

"Comrades," Jerry roared, "this is my wife, the Lady Janet. You have all fought valorously, and suffered many hardships to bring me to her. For your sacrifices and your help, comrades, I thank you with all my heart, and so does my Lady."

He smiled at his wife. "Darling, without these stout hearts, I wouldn't be here."

Janet looked wonderingly at the crowd of, to her, alien creatures. Armed, armored, leather-clad, bearded, and fierce.

Nothing in her sheltered life had prepared her for the barbaric ferocity reflected in this band of tough, hard, professional soldiers.

Then she looked into their eyes and saw the admiration mirrored there. She had been homecoming queen her last year in high school, and had experienced in small measure the thrill of being the center of all eyes, but that was less than nothing compared to the adoration in the faces of these wild followers of this amazing husband of hers.

Admiration that she understood was for the Lady of their leader. Pride swelled in her breast. Pride in her husband's command of the respect of men like these. Men, she was sure, who did not give respect lightly.

Janet was surprised to find how easily she adapted to the weird circumstances in which she found herself.

She smiled at the Company, and raised one hand as she had seen Jerry do. She addressed them as Jerry had.

"Comrades," she said in a loud, clear voice vibrant with sincerity, "I thank you for bringing my husband to me. You have my everlasting gratitude."

The men-at-arms responded to the graciousness of their leader's lady. The mighty crash of weapons against shields startled the girl, causing her to give a little squeal of fright.

Jerry smiled encouragement. "It's a tribute, darling. They're expressing their admiration."

Janet faced the crowd, a tremulous smile on her lips.

The cheers of the men were loud and long. At length Hjalmar the Axeman raised his weapon for silence.

"Go ye back t' yer campfires. My lord an' his lady ha' much t' discuss."

The mercenaries raised one final shout and disbanded. The Axeman approached and bowed low to Janet. "'Twas a grand thing ye did fer th' men, My Lady. Our sort be unaccustomed t' kind words."

The mercenary Captain saluted Jerry, and turned back to the girl. "Yer husband an' th' Lord Brokk be th' first patrons ever t' treat common soldiers o' fortune as men, not dogs. We should ha' known that his Lady would do no less.

"Our swords, and our lives be pledged in yer service, My Lady."

The scarfaced Captain bowed again, raised his axe in respect, and went to join his men.

Janet's face was a mixture of humility, bewilderment, and a little awe. "Did he mean that? Their swords, and their lives. Isn't that a bit extreme?"

Jerry looked grim. "Not for Skandia, honey." He nodded toward the Company. "Many of them have already died to get me here."

Jerry's face showed pride. "The finest Free Company in all Skandia stands ready to do battle in your behalf."

Janet shivered.

"Jerry," she said in an awed voice, "What kind of world is this? Those men. Anyone can see that they're hardened men of war. Yet they look up to you as some sort of demi-god or something, and they treat me as though I were a princess or something. What's going on?

"*Jerry Haskins, who are you?*"

The red-beard lifted his clenched iron fist, and threw out his chest in a parody of a statue in the park. Janet giggled at the boyish exultation in her husband's laugh.

"Standing before you, woman," he said in ringing tones, "is Jerry Jar Haz called Thor's Fist, swordsman unparalleled, friend of giants, beloved of the Gods of Asgard, and the only tall dwarf in all the Nine Worlds."

Brokk choked with laughter.

"Swordsman? Thor's Fist. . .?"

Jerry blew on his fingernails and looked smug.

"Yep, that's me. Pretty impressive for an insurance salesman, ain't it?"

Janet giggled. "If Mr. Hemmingway could only see his star salesman now!"

Jerry grinned. "I've thought about that, too."

He beckoned to Lars, Olin and Maryam.

"I want to introduce you to the rest of my friends."

Janet watched the two men-at-arms and the pretty girl approach. She felt drawn to Maryam, as the only other girl, and smiled at the way the young mercenary lieutenant hovered over her.

Jerry hemmed and hawed a little.

"Uh, sweetheart, I've got one more friend I want you to meet, but I don't want to scare the hell out of you."

"I don't understand."

"You've never met a goblin. . . ."

Janet stared at him. "A *what*?"

Jerry grinned. "Ulf's a little hard to describe. He's brave as a dragon, as good a friend as any man ever had, and has a heart of marshmallow, but let's face it, he's ugly as hell."

"I am not," Ulf's mellow voice protested from behind the tent. "As I've said over and over, amongst my kind I'm considered quite handsome."

Jerry laughed. "Honey, please don't scream, it hurts his feelings. Ulf, come on out."

The tall goblin came around the tent.

Janet's eyes became big and round. She stared at the gangling spider-man, and held out her hand, a small smile trembling on her lips.

"Why, you're Tomkin," she exclaimed.

Ulf stopped and looked surprised. It was easy to see that he had been prepared for any reception but this.

"Eh? Tomkin?"

Janet laughed happily. "You're Tomkin. I made you up when I was a little girl."

Ulf eyed the smiling girl and his trunk lifted questioningly. "Did you, now?"

Janet looked into the goblin's eyes. "Yes. I was terribly afraid of the dark. It was full of scary things. So I invented a friend who was tall and brave and fearsome, who loved me, and could frighten off the bad things, and protect me from the dark. Tomkin. You."

The goblin laughed his warm, pleasant laugh. "Friend Jerry," he said, "I *like* this girl."

Janet felt comfortable among these strange beings whom her husband called friends.

She was thrilled by their devotion to Jerry, and felt honored that this devotion extended to her, that she was so readily accepted into their tightly knit brotherhood.

Maryam's obvious adoration of the young mercenary lieutenant so nearly paralleled her love for Jerry, that she felt a kinship with the girl.

Jerry had just finished demonstrating and explaining his iron hand, when Om-Jak and Mukkergee joined the circle.

The Vanir known to the Company as Thorwald Thorssen, the men-at-arms who had led them through the Land of Weird, drew Jerry to one side.

"The Hindu and I have been discussing your options."

He indicated Janet's lack of substance.

"Even in view of this unexpected turn of events, there are several alternatives open to you. I will lay them all out for you to make your choice.

"First, your Mystic friend was unintentionally misleading when he said that one could go only into the past. He overlooked mentioning that once one had gone into the past, he could return to his point of origin, since now that point would be in his past, not his future. Understand?"

Jerry looked blank. "No."

Om-Jak laughed.

"It doesn't matter. What I am saying is that the two of us could return to Asgard. There I could infuse you into a senescent Vanir. There would be no difficulty finding a female Vanir to return with us here and the Mystic, Mukkergee, is certain that he can transmigrate your wife's essence into a living person so long as the person consents.

"That is one solution, and we can all return to Asgard."

Jerry looked at the Vanir. "Questions."

"Fire away."

"Why couldn't Janet just go with us to Asgard?"

"We can go because we would be moving into our past, but *she* would be moving into her future, which doesn't exist for her yet, see?"

Jerry's eyes felt like they would like to cross. He shook his head.

"No. But say you pull this off, then Janet and I would be half Vanir and half us, right?"

"Yes. "

"And we'd have to stay in Asgard?"

"Yes."

"That's out. I can't desert my friends."

Om-Jak raised one eyebrow. "Has your wife no say-so in these decisions?"

Jerry started. Of *course* Janet had a say-so in what was to happen to her.

"He raised his voice. "Honey, would you step over here?"

Janet joined them, her face a question mark. "What's going on?"

"Sweetheart, this is Om-Jak. Believe me, there isn't time to go into who and what he is, but listen to him and make a decision."

Om-Jak smiled. "Janet, without going into all the mechanics involved, this is one of your options. . . ."

The girl's expression became more astonished and bewildered the longer Om-Jak talked.

She looked at her husband. "Jerry, is this for real?"

Jerry nodded, smiling. "This a pretty wild world here."

His face turned serious. "Janet, from what Om-Jak's told you, you do understand that you must never disclose the truth about the gods, don't you?"

Janet's eyes swiveled from her husband to the extraterrestrial.

"Beings from another planet! Yes, darling, I understand. I could never do anything to destroy a peoples' beliefs. The secret is safe."

She turned to Om-Jak.

"Let me get this straight. If we go along with this, we'll wind up practically immortal, but we'd be sharing life with two other guys?"

"Yes."

"And we'd have to live out our lives in your Asgard?"

"Yes."

"What did Jerry say?"

"He said no."

"So do I. Mister Om-Jak, you Vanir have your life-focus established by your thousands of years of custom and your longevity. We humans, at least we twentieth century humans, are an egotistical lot. Sharing identity would become unbearable to us."

The girl smiled at Jerry, then looked back at the other-worlder.

"When I make love to my husband, I don't want to be sharing him with another woman. It is wonderful of you to make the offer, but for us, I don't think it would work."

The Vanir smiled understandingly. "All right. I didn't really hold out much hope for that one, but I had to put it before you. You have two other choices, but I think we can rule one of them out right off the top."

"That being what?" asked Jerry.

"Returning to your original starting point, dying in a car crash."

Jerry grinned. "You're right. That one holds no appeal whatsoever. What's the other choice?"

Om-Jak looked from one to the other. "It will mean another separation."

Janet studied the Vanir's face. "How much of a separation? How long?"

Om-Jak's sympathy showed in his eyes. "I can't say. A year. Maybe two."

Janet looked at Jerry then back at the extraterrestrial. "It's either this or living as two other people?"

"I'm afraid so, my dear."

The girl drew in a deep breath. "All right. Let's hear it."

"While you were getting reacquainted, Mukkergee and I discussed your options.

"The little Mystic used his 'magic' to scout the planet on the off chance that he might find an avatar suitable for you. The chances were practically nonexistent, but the long shot paid off.

"Several years ago a Skandian sea-rover named Leif Ericssen led an expedition across the Salt Sea to a vast continent as yet unknown in this part of the world. . . ."

"America!" Jerry exclaimed.

The Vanir looked his question.

"In our time the continent is called America. It's where we come from."

"Ah! Then in a sense you'd be going home. For that is where she is.

"The Viking, Leif Ericssen, took along with them on the expedition, the wives of some of his men.

"One of the Skandians was recently slain in a battle with some of the natives of your America. His wife was sorely wounded fighting at his side.

"She is dying. Janet, the woman is a distant ancestor of yours, and the Hindu can perform the same transmigration for you as he did for Jerry."

Janet's eyes filled with tears. "How sad. How sad that this woman will die to give me a body. Om-Jak, I can't. . . ."

"Save your tears, Janet. Be happy for her. The man is already in Valhalla, and a goddess is standing by to rejoin her with the husband she loves as much as you love Jerry."

Jerry started to touch Janet's shoulder then remembered that she wasn't really there.

"It's all right, darling. What Om-Jak means is that they are being joined with the Vanir as he explained. They will be happy."

The Vanir once more caught the couple's attention. "So," he said, "What's your decision?"

Jerry and Janet looked long into each others' eyes.

"A year's not so long, honey," Jerry said. "With good winds and stout rowers maybe I can make it in less."

"You may," Om-Jak conceded. The sea voyage takes only weeks. But the Viking,

Leif Ericssen, has fought his way into the heartland of the continent.

You will have to find his trail, and trek many miles against hostiles."

Jerry laughed.

"The hike across Skandia from Svartheim to Asgard wasn't exactly a stroll down Market Street. We'll make it. At least there'll be no trolls to fight, or a Jotunheim to cross."

"No," said Om-Jak, "but this is not the America of your world, and it will have dangers just as unfamiliar as those you've faced in Skandia."

Jerry looked at Janet's face.

"Nothing is going to stand between me and you, sweetheart."

He grinned and struck a pose. "You have the word of Jerry Jar Haz called Thor's Fist on that!"

The red-beard fell silent as he tried to call up what he remembered about the geography of the northeastern part of the United States.

"It's roughly a thousand miles from the East Coast to Minnesota. Norse artifacts have been found there in our time, so I assume that's where Ericssen's Company is, or will be. . . ."

Jerry closed his eyes and sketched a map in the air with a finger. "We'll have to cross two or three of the Great Lakes."

He opened his eyes. "Piece of cake."

The girl looked dubious.

"Piece of cake," Jerry repeated. "Don't forget, sugar, you're looking at a genuine Viking Hero. Backed by the likes of Brokk, Ulf, and the Free Company of Hjalmar the Axeman? Honey, Mukkergee better get cracking with his magic carpet, or I might get there before you do."

Janet smiled. "What if they don't want to go?"

"Honey, they all signed up for the duration, and the quest's not over yet. They'll go."

Jerry grinned. "Besides, I'm irresistibly lovable."

Janet's tears spilled down over her smiling lips. "Idiot," she said, "My darling idiot. Be serious. I can't wait to be able to kiss you."

"Can't say I haven't been thinking along those lines myself. Hold that thought, sweetheart. See you in a couple of years. . . ."